THE SONGBIRD & THE HEART OF STONE

Crowns of Nyaxia Novels

Book 1: *The Serpent & the Wings of Night*

Book 2: *The Ashes & the Star-Cursed King*

Standalone Crowns of Nyaxia Novels

Six Scorched Roses

THE SONGBIRD & THE HEART OF STONE

A CROWNS OF NYAXIA NOVEL

The Shadowborn Duet
BOOK ONE

CARISSA BROADBENT

BRAMBLE

TOR PUBLISHING GROUP · NEW YORK

THE SONGBIRD & THE HEART OF STONE

Cover Art by K.D. Ritchie at Story Wrappers

Map illustration and chapter ornaments by Rhys Davies

A Bramble Book
Published by Tom Doherty Associates / Tor Publishing Group
120 Broadway
New York, NY 10271

www.torpublishinggroup.com

Bramble™ is a trademark of Macmillan Publishing Group, LLC.

The Library of Congress Cataloging-in-Publication Data is available upon request.

ISBN 978-1-250-36778-5 (hardcover)
ISBN 978-1-250-37914-6 (signed)

Our books may be purchased in bulk for promotional, educational, or business use. Please contact your local bookseller or the Macmillan Corporate and Premium Sales Department at 1-800-221-7945, extension 5442, or by email at MacmillanSpecialMarkets@macmillan.com.

Previously self-published by the author in 2024

First Tor Edition: 2024

Printed in the United States of America

0 9 8 7 6 5 4 3 2 1

For every lost soul who just needs someone to listen

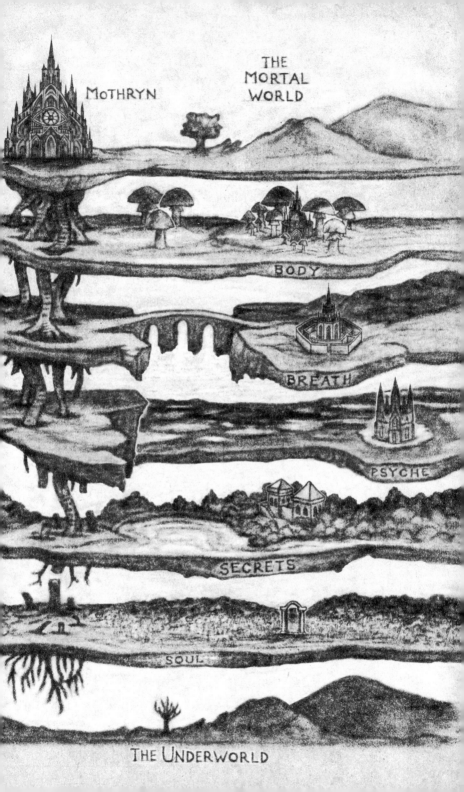

THE SONGBIRD & THE HEART OF STONE

PROLOGUE

This is the tale of how a chosen one falls.

Like most legends, it is unremarkable at its start. There was nothing special about the girl when the sun god chose her. He had his pick. He was among the most revered of the gods among his mortal followers. Every dawn and every sundown saw countless offerings upon his altars, food and silks and riches and soft bodies—every mortal pleasure a god could desire. He was particular with his favor. He chose for himself only the most flawless faces, the most powerful warriors, the most skilled sorcerers.

This girl was none of those things.

The two sisters arrived at the temple with nothing else in the world but each other. If they did not find shelter here, they would be cast back out to die, like countless other faceless innocents.

It always begins like this. In times of great darkness, humans crawl to light like flies to the gleaming silver of a spider's silk. These are the souls that gods feast upon. No one loves you more than someone who has no one else.

The older sister was almost beautiful, save for the stench of her difficult life and all she had done to survive it. She had scrounged together a silk dress designed to highlight her curves, carefully draped to hide the stains. She had thick, dark hair, lush lips, smooth skin—delicate in all the ways the gods typically enjoyed. She collapsed at the altar of her god, prayers spilling from her lips. She swore to him her faith, her life, her soul, all as the priests watched with curls of disgust over their lips. She was, in their eyes, not the type who was worthy of salvation.

Perhaps the young woman hoped that the candles arranged around the altar would burst to life as she offered her god her soul—a sign of the sun god taking a new chosen.

But the god accepted her fealty with only vague disinterest. He had been gifted thousands of other desperate souls just like this one today.

No, it was not the young woman who interested him.

It was the child with her.

She trailed behind her sister, eyes bigger, hair wilder, staring up at the sky no matter how many times the priests hissed at her to lower her lashes in supplication. She listened to her sister's tearful offerings and watched the priests' disapproving stares, and though she was only eight years old, she understood what would happen after this.

She had nothing to offer. And what would a god want from her, anyway?

Still, she reached into her pocket and closed her fingers around a fragile little reminder of her home. The shape of it was burned into her palm. She withdrew it and slid her own offering across the altar:

A feather.

Like the girl herself, the feather was not remarkable. It was small, a dull gold, bent and half-bare from weeks of the little girl's absent-minded grasp.

So why did this gift—this child—capture the god's attention so?

The god's other chosen had been glorious men and women, flowers plucked at the height of their splendor. This girl was pretty enough, but no great beauty. Smart enough, but no great wit. Perhaps he enjoyed the uniquely mortal slant of her smile or the way her freckles fell across her nose.

Or perhaps gods, like mortals, are simply mesmerized by their own damnation.

Because he paused then, peering through the veil between worlds, at this little girl.

The little girl, in turn, peered back.

In the background, the priests grew tired of her sister's weeping pleas. They took hold of her arms, dragging her away. Her sister's protests and the priests' harsh chiding faded into a hazy hum in the background. She lifted her chin to the sky.

And for many years later—decades, centuries—the child would not forget what her god's voice sounded like the first time she heard it:

I see you, little one. Reach out your hand.

The magic came to her so easily. As if it burned straight from her heart itself. The clouds thinned, the honeyed sunlight hot on her face. One by one, the candles around the altar blossomed to flame.

And at last, fire ignited in her splayed palm.

It took the others a moment to realize what was happening. But by the time she held the flame in her hands, the priests were gasping in awe. Her sister watched, wide-eyed, silent.

The little girl did not see any of them. She just stared up at the sky, cheeks aching with her grin and warm with the love of her god. She had finally found something that she had been chasing her entire short, fraught life. She would not know how to describe this for a very long time. But the word she was searching for was: *purpose.*

The sun god thought he had received another devoted acolyte that day. Even he could not describe what he found so charming about the child, but what did it matter? She would be another chosen one to add to his collection, happy to receive his attention when it suited him and easy to put aside when it didn't. She would follow him until the end of it all, just as all the others had.

He was right. For a time.

But such a boring story that would be.

This is the tale of how a chosen one falls. She does it screaming, clawing for her old life with broken fingernails. She does it slowly, over the course of decades.

And in the end, she takes the whole forsaken world with her.

PART ONE

LIFE

CHAPTER ONE

The dark went on forever. The candle would not light.

Sweat rolled down my brow. I sagged against the bars of my cell, eyes fixed on the unlit candle, which stood crooked and dusty within a cobweb-coated lantern that dangled from a hook on the opposite side of the room. It was precariously close to a heavy velvet curtain, once green but now dull with long-dried blood.

One spark.

One spark, and the candle would go up, and then the curtains, and then I would have a flame big enough to manipulate even now, with my diminished magic. Once, I wouldn't even have needed the candle at all. Once, I could've summoned the power of the sun in my palm. I could have burned my way out of here. Vampires were never quite prepared for it—the sun. They definitely never expected it to come from me, a vampire girl with big eyes and a bigger smile. I could always get so far on that.

My arm strained through the bars. A shaky breath escaped through gritted teeth as blood dripped a melody onto the floor. I reached for the magic that had once come as easily for me as breathing. Reached for the god who had once chosen me.

Please, my light, I begged him silently. *Please.*

But it had been more than a year now since Atroxus had answered my prayers. More than a year since I'd felt the warmth of his magic at my fingertips. Each attempt opened burns instead, as if to mock me: *What else does the sun have to offer a vampire?*

Tonight was no different.

I tried until my body gave out on me. Then I collapsed.

I pressed my forehead against the bars, shutting my eyes against the sting of tears and blood. I was covered in it. A lot of it was mine, but not all. The soldiers from the House of Shadow had killed a merchant, too, when they came for me. I relived the look on the merchant's face as the Shadowborn arrow had pierced his throat, the way the soldiers had casually tossed his body aside as they descended upon me. He'd been kinder to me than I deserved. Maybe he took pity on me, a dirty, broken-down traveler in the middle of nowhere.

How had they found me? I'd been on my own for months now, and I was so careful to leave as little a trail as possible. Of the three vampire kingdoms, the House of Shadow had the greatest mastery of spycraft. They dealt in secrets, emotions, knowledge. If anyone could root out a single criminal, I supposed the Shadowborn were best equipped for it.

But I'd still been miles away from the border of the House of Shadow. And I was just one girl. They came for me like they knew exactly where I'd be.

Then again, I wasn't "just" anything. I had murdered a prince of the House of Shadow.

I wasn't stupid. I knew it would catch up to me eventually. That was why I'd left the House of Night, wasn't it? To shield my friends from the consequences of my actions.

At least there was that.

My head swam. Maybe from the blood loss. Maybe not.

I choked back a sob and slipped my hand into my pocket. It was empty, as I knew it would be. The Shadowborn soldiers had taken all my possessions. I'd been half-conscious as they rummaged through them, their magic binding my thoughts, but I still had almost managed to reach out as they took Raihn's letters.

Raihn's unopened letters.

He had sent me so many of them. Oraya sent a few, too. They'd come to me if I was close enough to the capital of the House of Night,

sent by their magic. Every week or two, I'd take a detour to circle
back into range, and I'd cradle those wrinkled pieces of parchment
like precious riches. I could imagine what they said. Raihn's scrawled
handwriting: *Where the hell are you, Mish?* Oraya's looping script: *Don't
make me send Jesmine to go hunt you down.*

I could never make myself read them, though.

I couldn't make myself throw them away, either.

I fiercely regretted both decisions now. I could still see Raihn's
face in the moment I'd told him I was leaving. That puppy-dog look
of utter hurt. The memory made another near sob bubble up in my
throat.

Gods, I had made so many mistakes.

I jumped at the sudden sound of stone grinding against stone.

The door swung open, strings of cold light flooding over the
ground. I lifted my head and was punished with a powerful wave of
dizziness. More blood dripped onto the floor.

A woman and a man stood in the door. The woman was nobility. I
knew it the second I looked at her. She was tall and straight-backed,
her hands folded delicately in front of her. Long tendrils of deep chest-
nut hair tumbled down her shoulders. She wore a gown of emerald
velvet that wrapped tight around her body and brushed the floor. The
bodice was tight, pushing her breasts up against a low neckline. A
classic example of the Shadowborn style of dress—expensive stuff.
She stepped forward, surveying me with a cold, piercing gaze.

Something about her was familiar in a way that crawled under my
skin. It went beyond her appearance. I could *feel* it, even if I couldn't
place it.

Her companion closed the door behind her. Him, I recognized
right away. He was a hulking man, with slicked-back dark hair and
fine leather armor, a cloak that matched his mistress's dress falling
down his back. My gaze locked onto that cape. He hadn't changed
it since he'd dragged me in here. It was ruined. My blood was all
over it.

The woman stood silently as her guard returned and opened the
cell doors. She stepped into the cell.

"Get up," she said.

Her voice was flawless, melodic, and for those two syllables, it was the most entrancing thing I had ever heard. My body was broken. And yet, at her command, I *wanted* to stand. No other possibility existed, every alternate snipped away like branches from a vine.

I was on my feet before I made the decision to rise.

Shadowborn magic, I realized. The magic of minds and compulsion, illusion and shadow.

When little human children in a country half a world away told scary stories at night, the vampires of the House of Shadow were the monsters that came to them in their nightmares. Sure, the Nightborn were intimidating, with the wings and the swords and all that battle prowess. The Bloodborn were frightening the way rabid wolves were, vicious and unpredictable.

But the Shadowborn were like ghosts. They manipulated reality itself. They drank up the darkness like wine and relished the notes of fear within it.

The woman circled me slowly. I swayed. My mind had obeyed her command, but my body wasn't actually capable of standing right now. The floor felt like it was tilting.

Talk your way out of this, Mische, I told myself. But words, for maybe the first time in my life, felt so far away. And I couldn't find any before she stopped in front of me, surveying me feet to head, and gave me a cruel, unimpressed smile.

That was what did it. The smile.

The realization barreled into me. Who she was. Why she looked so familiar.

My eyes widened.

A little ripple of pleasure passed between us as she chuckled.

"So this is the one who killed my brother." Her smile soured, melting into a snarl. "What an embarrassment. A prince of the House of Shadow, murdered by some little bitch he Turned. He never could control his own impulses. That's what happens when you spend your whole life getting everything you want, I suppose."

She did look so much like . . . *him.*

And more than that, she *felt* like him—I could sense it, that little echo of our shared magic in her hold on my mind. He had Turned me, had given me the cursed gifts of vampirism that I tried so hard to shut away. Her magic made something stir behind that door, my own recognizing a hint of its maker.

Deny it, the final dregs of my rational thought urged in the back of my mind. *They have Raihn's letters. Your guilt implicates the House of Night. You have to deny it.*

It took every shred of my strength to force my charming smile.

"I think you have me confused for—"

She rolled her eyes. Her magic ripped into my memories like claws through paper. My skull felt as if it was exploding. Flashes of my past flew by as she rummaged through my mind: the Citadel of the Destined Dawn, my sister's face, the blue sky over the sea, the shores of the House of Shadow—

Then *him.*

She stopped. My breath was ragged. I was against the wall, her hand to my throat, even though I didn't remember her putting it there. The steady drip of my blood had gotten more rapid.

She smiled slowly.

"Ah. There it is. My brother's death day."

Her magic pushed through my mind like a blunt knife. She grabbed the memory and excised.

The prince of the House of Shadow was a devastatingly handsome man, and he was gazing at me like I was a pleasant surprise he looked forward to devouring. He stared at me from across the ballroom, and I dried the sweat on my palms against the gold fabric of my magnificent, ridiculous dress. Ten minutes ago, I'd felt beautiful in it. Now, I hated how much it made me stand out in this crowd. I couldn't tell Raihn or Oraya. Not when so much hinged on this party going well—

She pushed deeper. Pain split my head, seams between the present and the past popping.

"Careful, Egrette," the man warned. His voice sounded a world away. "You can't kill her yet."

Egrette. I'd heard that name before. Distantly, it clicked together.

The House of Shadow had a princess, too. A second heir, sister to the man I'd killed. But this knowledge flew by, lost beneath her assault on my mind. I barely heard her response.

"She'll die soon anyway. Before she does, I want to see how she did it."

She tore through my memories of that party—the coup, when Raihn had been kidnapped and Oraya disappeared. Pushed past the images of the Bloodborn guards dragging me away and locking me up, a gift for the Shadowborn prince's favor.

And then she stopped—right there, right at the moment it happened.

I had the prince against the wall. Oraya was behind me. His hands were on my throat. I was so, so angry.

This man had taken everything from me. He had Turned me into a beast undeserving of everything I'd devoted my entire life to. He was the reason I had lost my magic. He was the reason my god had abandoned me.

I thought about nothing but that hatred as I grabbed the sword Oraya had given me.

As I drove that blade straight through his chest and kept going, and going, and going, until I couldn't push anymore—until the prince's perfect face went slack—

Egrette stopped. Her magic clung to that image—her brother in his moment of death.

She smiled.

"Poor, poor Malach. How very sad."

But I could feel her emotions through the thread that connected us, too. She wasn't sad at all.

She released me, and I fell to the ground in a gasping heap.

"No use in lying," she said. "Besides, killing him was the most useful thing you'll ever do. Not a lot of time left to top it anyway."

I tried to roll over, tried to push myself to my hands and knees. But a delicately slippered foot emerged from beneath the princess's skirts, pushing me back to the stone, pointed toe burying into the worst of my wounds.

"Egrette," the man warned.

"Oh, pssh. The extra blood will add to the effect. My father will enjoy the suffering of a spy."

Spy?

"I'm not a—"

"Spare me. I just came to survey the quality of my gift before I hand it over."

"Gift?"

The word was slurred and gummy. Black blood gushed onto the cobblestones. Egrette watched it with a faint line of disgust over her nose.

I lifted my gaze past her, to the unlit candle hanging in that dusty lantern.

I could envision so perfectly what her face would look like engulfed by flames. Vampires burned differently than humans did. Humans melted, but vampires went up like dry paper, skin cracking and peeling and withering to white ash.

Mere months ago, I could have had her alight in seconds.

But instead, I just heaved helplessly as she rolled me over with her foot.

"I've seen what I need to," she said. Her voice faded. My lashes fluttered closed. I curled up around the open wound in my side. Death lingered in the shadows.

And still, my god was silent.

But why should I expect any different? Why should I *deserve* any different?

I was not a chosen one anymore.

The candle remained cold.

SAESCHA USED TO scare me with stories of vampires when I was a little girl.

"They're evil beasts," she would tell me. "They are more dead than alive, and they resent humans for having what they can't. And do you know what they like to eat the most?"

Sometimes, if I was feeling playful, I'd turn it into a game—*Toes!* I'd giggle. *Ears! Belly buttons!* But usually, I'd say proudly, "Blood!" I liked to be right.

And Saescha would shake her head slowly, lovely face drawn into dramatic seriousness. "No, Mische. That's a common misconception. What they really, really love, more than anything else, are souls. They'll eat your soul in one big gulp. And they *especially* love the souls of little six-year-old girls with curly hair!"

And then she'd lunge at me, tickling me as she pretended to *chomp chomp chomp* at my throat, and I'd laugh and laugh until I couldn't breathe anymore.

The memory of Saescha's voice drifted by like a lonely cloud in an empty sky, but I was not laughing now.

Maybe this was what she had been talking about, because I felt like my soul itself had been unraveled. Dreams rolled over me like the steady beat of waves on the shore, drawing me to reality only to cruelly drag me away again. Egrette's vicious rummaging through my mind left my thoughts ransacked, memories gushing together like blood from torn flesh, just as deadly as the wounds on my skin.

I lost track of who I was, where I was. Lost track of the boundaries between the past and the present.

You'll die here, I told myself.

Do something, I begged myself.

But I couldn't pull myself back to reality. I reached for a sun that rewarded me with burns. I reached for a god who wouldn't answer. I fell back into dreams.

At first, I thought the hands were a dream, too.

I wasn't sure how long I'd lain there when the figure leaned over me. I could barely open my eyes, and even when I could, they refused to focus. I couldn't make out anything but blurry shadow. A delicate scent wafted over me that I couldn't place—something cold and clean, and faintly floral, like poppies dusted with frost.

Someone was touching me. Someone was rolling me over. The strain it put on my injuries made me cry out. I couldn't see. I couldn't move. I thrashed weakly, but the figure hissed, "Shh! Enough."

They grabbed my wrists, pushing me back down to the floor.

Rip, as they tore open my already tattered shirt from the bottom. I slurred a groan of protest, but—

The hands pressed to my stomach, right over the worst of my wounds.

I gasped.

The touch reached past the surface of my flesh. It settled into my lungs like air; it slipped through my veins like blood. All of it was as natural as a forgotten song, a hymn that had been at the tip of my tongue suddenly restored.

"Stop—" I moaned.

"Let me help you." There was no comfort in the voice. The words were harsh and direct. The hands moved over my wounds, then to my arm, pushing up my sleeve. I moaned and thrashed, instinct more than anything, because I knew what my bare arms would reveal— years' worth of burn scars, the natural punishment of a vampire wielding the magic of the sun.

The marks of my failure.

"Stop," I tried to say. But unconsciousness had taken me again. I was falling beneath the waves. My visitor rolled my sleeve back down and pressed a hand to my brow.

And this time, the darkness didn't feel like a punishment. It felt like an embrace.

I HAD SO many strange dreams.

I dreamed that someone came to visit me, a slew of pretty people with ornate clothing and impeccable uniforms. I dreamed of a tight white dress and silver chains around my wrists. I dreamed of endless commands—*stand here, turn there, sit, stand, put out your hands, walk, Mother's sake, faster than that.* I dreamed of voices—*the king will be pleased, won't he?*—and eyes and hands, and though these touches were much softer than the ones I'd felt before, I knew, even in my dream, that they were much crueler. Still, it never even occurred to me to fight. My mind was limited to a single tunnel of options, none of which included disobedience.

I dreamed of stone and a starry night and a palace made of knives. I dreamed of a door and—

Wake her up, a lovely voice said.

Someone touched my face.

All at once, I wasn't dreaming anymore. Reality crashed down around me like an avalanche, frigid and catastrophic.

"Shit," I squeaked, before I could stop myself. My knees almost gave out, though someone grabbed me to hoist me upright again.

Several hundred sets of vampire eyes stared at me.

I was at the center of a magnificent ballroom, which seemed to be in the middle of a party befitting its grandness. Gods, the only other time I'd seen a place like this was in the House of Night's palace—and perhaps fittingly, the only other party I'd attended that was this grand was the one that had ended with me killing the prince of the House of Shadow, which seemed like a cruel joke.

The style of this room was very different, though, than the House of Night's castle. All hard edges instead of those rounded curves, sharp metal instead of smooth marble, velvet instead of silk. My eyes bounced between columns of intricate, glistening black steel, crafted to look like twisting vines, and then the real vines that covered them, dotted with roses of black and red. I could practically taste the blood from the fingers of the craftsmen who had worked on it. It was the kind of beauty that made you certain that surely, someone had to have suffered for it.

The people who surrounded me held that same painful allure, smooth faces of high cheekbones and full lips, hair tamed into severe updos or sleek waterfalls. They wore elaborate finery, bodies of men and women alike highlighted in impeccably tailored velvets and brocades. Women's blood-spattered bosoms heaved over tight corset bodices. Men's gold-laced jackets, likely once buttoned up to their throats, had been loosened, too, revealing smears of black and red.

The scent of blood—human blood, hot and sweet—nearly made my knees go out again, my stomach lurching and dry mouth watering. Gods, how long had it been since I'd *drank*? My eyes landed on a human man, a blood vendor, who sagged against a feast table. Blood ran down his throat and coated his upper thigh over torn fabric. I had to force myself to look away, ashamed of myself.

I was wearing a white gown in a similar style to the others—tight brocade, with a bodice so restrictive it made my ribs hurt. The fabric was thin. I looked down to see that my blood from my injuries had soaked through it—black spreading like rose petals on my waist, my right shoulder, my left forearm.

Intentional, I realized. Part of the presentation.

I could feel pressure on my mind encroaching from every direction, plucking at scraps of my fear like greedy fingers pulling the skin from a turkey carcass, but I straightened my back, lifted my chin, and hoisted my mental walls as high and firm as my feeble mind could handle.

And it took everything inside of me to keep them that way when my gaze landed on the man before me.

Oh, gods.

"Father," the Shadowborn princess said, voice smooth and yet booming through the massive room. "My gift for you on the auspicious night of your birth. I present to you, the murderer of your son."

The King of the House of Shadow leveled his gaze at me, a thousand-year-lifetime's worth of hatred in their depths.

CHAPTER TWO

Instantly, I was certain that he was everything they said he was.

Even the humans knew all about the kings of Obitraes, the land of vampires. After all, vampire rulers had centuries to build their palaces of grand myth, forged from the flames of their bloody acts.

In the human nations, they had been whispered of like monsters.

In Obitraes, they were talked about like gods.

I'd heard all the stories over the years. Vincent, Oraya's father and former King of the Nightborn, had been the drawn blade, a killer cold as the night itself. Dante, King of the Bloodborn, had been the beast larger than life, more teeth and claws than man. One day, the whispers would make legends of Raihn and Oraya, too, and I looked forward to hearing them.

Raoul, King of the House of Shadow, might have dwarfed them all.

He was the oldest of the vampire kings, and the one who had managed to cling to power the longest. Like most vampire rulers, he'd plucked his crown off the severed head of his predecessor, his mother, before even bothering to wipe his blade. Two centuries ago, he'd nearly destroyed the House of Blood without a single battle, relying on torture and spies instead of warriors. They said he could pick thoughts from your head like grapes from the vine and crush them just as easily. They said that he could enslave you without a single chain.

As a human, I'd loved the stories because I loved fantasies. And that's what they had been to me: fantasies. Myths and legends.

But in this moment, as the King of the Shadowborn looked at me and I felt his presence pressing down on my mind like the blanket of night falling upon the horizon, I realized I had been wrong. Surely it was all true after all.

I wondered if it was the human in me that had the visceral desire to turn around and run.

Or maybe it was the vampire, animal instinct recognizing its superior.

But I never ran away. Not even when I should.

Instead, I did what I always did: I gave that bastard the biggest, brightest smile.

Beside him, a fair-haired woman—his wife, surely—stared at me with rage more subtle but every bit as sharp as her husband's. She was so still, not breathing, her hand on Raoul's arm. She looked at me like her teeth were itching for my throat.

She was dangerous. The little razor blade no one saw coming because they were too busy looking at her husband's sword.

Someone gave me a rough push between my shoulder blades. It was intended to put me to my knees, but I caught myself, lifting my head as Egrette strode by me.

"I captured her myself, Father." Her voice, puffed up with pride, filled the ballroom. "It took time, but my spies eventually found her whereabouts. She was just a few miles north of our borders. Sent by the House of Night, no doubt. I considered killing her then, but I thought . . ." A vicious smile spread over her ruby-painted lips. "Perhaps you would want to take the first bite."

I pieced together what this was.

My gown. The party. Egrette's voice, too loud, too confident, too cruel. The way she kept looking at her father every few seconds, as if she couldn't wait until the end of her speech to gauge his reaction.

I had a knack for seeing people for what they were. And right now, I looked at Egrette and saw desperation.

I was a ploy to gain her father's favor. Something that, I guessed, she'd probably never been able to attain.

Gods take me. I'd die a pawn in someone else's family drama.

Raoul stared at me, those ageless eyes unblinking. "The House of

Night," he said slowly. Then he laughed, the sound slithering through the air. His cruel pleasure buried beneath my skull.

He rose in one sharp movement. "The kingdom of crows and bats sends spies to me? Neculai hasn't earned such nerve."

I blinked, brow furrowing.

Neculai? Neculai was the King of the House of Night before Raihn, before Vincent—he'd died hundreds of years ago.

The chuckles of pleasure in the partygoers withered. They exchanged awkward glances. Egrette took another step forward, her eyes darting between the crowd and her father.

"Neculai deserved to see his kingdom collapse as it did," she said. "Yes, the Nightborn have always been too bold, Father."

A weak attempt at covering for his mistake. It didn't work.

A line of confusion etched Raoul's brow. He rubbed his temple. "Vincent," he said, as if reminding himself. "Vincent has the gall to send me spies? I'll—I'll send them back to him in pieces, just as I did before—" He turned abruptly to his wife, a snarl at his lips. "This should not have been allowed to happen. Where is Malach? Get him for me."

Anger at another dead king. Asking for his dead son. Something wasn't right.

"Go get him," Raoul snarled, and the air itself just *shattered*.

I doubled over as pain split my skull. A low buzz vibrated in my ears. The room grew suddenly darker, shadows dripping down the wall like blood from a slit throat. I couldn't breathe. Couldn't think. I managed to lift my head just enough to see the other partygoers clutching their heads, too. The human blood vendors had slumped to the floor, eyes rolled back, foam bubbling at their lips.

The queen leaned against her husband's arm. She slipped a wine glass into his hand and helped him lift it to his mouth. He drank deep.

Just as abruptly, it was all gone. The sound. The pain. The darkness. Gone.

I straightened, still shaking with the aftereffects of Raoul's outburst. The guests collected themselves, rubbing their eyes and foreheads. I expected to see more of a reaction from the others, but no one acknowledged what had just happened.

It wasn't the first time.

Raoul was not well. And he was so ancient, so powerful, that losing control of his faculties meant losing control of his magic. That wasn't just an embarrassment to the House of Shadow. It was *deadly*.

The King of the House of Shadow was a massive liability.

Maybe my face showed the realization, because Egrette glanced at me and I heard her voice in my head:

Not a word, spy. Not a damned word.

But Raoul's face was smooth now, his eyes clear. He approached me. Vampires lost so many of their human affectations as they aged. Raoul, ancient as he was, no longer even had to blink.

"You killed my heir," he said.

He peeled my memories apart as carelessly as if he were disassembling the wedges of an orange. I could feel the sword in my hands all over again. Taste the prince's blood spattering across my face. I hadn't let Oraya see the way I'd licked it off my lips that night. How much I'd enjoyed the iron tang.

The king's magic repulsed me. And yet, it called to mine, and vice versa, sensing the hint of my maker in him.

"My gift to you is more than just retribution, Father," Egrette said. "Yes, she murdered Malach. But we all know she didn't act alone in that. Execute her for her crime. Send pieces of her back to the House of Night. Show the slave king and the half-breed queen what we think of their treachery."

At that, my heart stopped beating.

I imagined Raihn's and Oraya's faces when presented with my head in a box. They would start a war for me, even though their shaky newborn rule couldn't withstand it. They'd end the House of Night for me. No hesitation—no question. I'd left to protect them, and now I would still end up destroying them.

Raoul paused, interest piqued by his daughter's suggestion.

The momentary distraction bought me just enough time to stuff my emotions behind my mental walls. I forced a laugh. "Oh, gods. That's flattering. But if you think the king and queen would give a shit about me—"

"Silence," Raoul commanded, and my mouth closed. The dizzying desire to please fell over me.

Silence. Silence. Silence.

The king tilted my chin up. His touch was too smooth, too cold. It was repulsive, but I couldn't make myself pull away. He slipped into my mind, and I frantically slammed doors closed like a teenage daughter hiding her lover in the closet.

Still, he returned to that memory—the memory of his son's death. The memory of a face that looked so much like his, eyes going glassy and vacant as my sword plunged through his chest. He unraveled it over and over again.

And in this moment, I knew that there was no stopping what was about to happen.

Raoul released me. "Kneel," he commanded.

Kneel. Kneel. Kneel.

I hit the floor, my knees cracking against marble.

I was going to die.

"A gift indeed, my daughter," his voice echoed. "Let us show the House of Night what we do with murderers."

Tears stung my eyes. The tittering delight of the crowd faded to a grainy din in the background. Egrette gave her guard a command I didn't listen to. The partygoers laughed. The swords unsheathed. A sentence approached.

Raoul's command bound my muscles, forcing me to the ground. But would I have fought it even if I could? How long could one person escape death? I'd felt like I was supposed to die the first night my god finally abandoned me. I'd been chasing redemption for so long. I was never going to get it.

Maybe death was the best end.

But—gods—Raihn and Oraya. That was the only injustice. That my death would be used to destroy them.

I had failed them, too. Just like the others.

Someone grabbed my hair, twisting my head back to expose my throat.

A blade rose—

"Stop." A deep voice boomed through the party. "*Stop.* I need her."

CHAPTER THREE

A beat of silence.

One second passed, then two.

My eyes opened. It took a moment to recognize that I was, in fact, still alive.

The pressure of Raoul's command had released me. The guard behind me still gripped my hair, though, forcing my head to one angle. I watched Raoul as he stared past me, at the door. He had raised a single hand—the wordless command that had just spared my life.

For now.

His guests had gone silent, exchanging shocked glances. They stared, too, at whoever was at the door.

"A waste," the king said slowly, drawing out the word, thick with venom.

Behind me, Egrette laughed. "Avenging our brother, a *waste*?"

Our brother?

I searched my mind for what I knew of the House of Shadow's royal family. Raoul had two legitimate children—or he did, at least, before I'd killed one of them. But I'd heard stories of a third one, too. Old stories, centuries past. A bastard son who had once led Raoul's fleets of spies, before he . . .

What had happened to him? Hadn't he died?

"A dead prisoner is useless," the voice said. "Killing her now would be a stupid mistake."

Stupid.

He'd just called the King of the House of Shadow *stupid*.

Everyone in the room stopped breathing. Raoul's face went deadly still.

"It would be . . . shortsighted, Father," the voice said, softening his words, but the damage was already done. For a moment, it was clear to me that Raoul was holding himself back from commanding both of our deaths.

Why didn't he? Obitraen kings had taken lives for far less disrespect.

But instead, Raoul just said coldly, "Why are you here?"

"Maybe I've come because a son should attend his father's birthday celebration."

Egrette scoffed. "Better move that carpet, Elias," she said to her guard in a mock whisper. "It's been a couple of centuries since he's left his cage. I don't believe he's housebroken."

At this, the crowd chuckled.

But the king raised a hand again, this time directed not at the guards but at his daughter and his guests. Then he rubbed his temple, like he'd suddenly gotten a vicious headache.

"Enough. *Enough.*" He turned to glare at the newcomer. "Say your piece, Asar. I'm getting tired, and I'm getting thirsty, and neither is doing much for my patience."

Asar.

My blood went cold.

The name was the missing piece, snapping my foggy memories of the legends into place.

Asar Voldari. The Wraith Warden.

The stories seemed more befitting a myth than a man, even by the gruesome standards of vampire lore. They all ran together in my memory, grim tales of torture and spycraft, bloody tasks accomplished by bloodier means. Every king has someone to do their dirty work.

I hadn't heard him spoken of in a long, long time. Gods, I'd just assumed he was long dead by now, or else that he'd never really existed at all.

If this was my savior, maybe death was the real mercy.

I tried to lift my head, but the guard shoved it back down. My cheek pressed to the floor.

Footsteps broke the silence.

They were measured. Slow. Deliberate.

A pair of boots entered my field of vision—once fine, but now scuffed and worn, emerald green faded to near black. A cold, floral scent wafted over me, naggingly familiar but gone before I could place it.

Again, I tried to lift my head, only for the guard to push it to the floor, this time hard enough that my skull smacked against the marble. I saw stars.

"Shit," I hissed.

"Enough of that," the voice snapped. "Let her stand."

My vision blurred with both the impact and the aftereffects of Raoul's magic. I pushed myself up to my hands. The floor tilted sharply.

Gods. *Could* I stand?

You can, a voice whispered in my mind. I wasn't sure if I'd imagined it.

I raised my head just enough to see a hand outstretched before me—tan skin and long fingers.

But I didn't take it. I forced myself to my feet all on my own, barely swaying even as my stomach lurched with nausea, and—finally—lifted my eyes.

The gasp escaped me without permission.

He might have been handsome once—or perhaps beautiful would be a better word. His features had a powerful artistry to them. A finely angled jaw. Strong brows over intense near-black eyes. A chiseled nose with nostrils that flared slightly in interest as his gaze locked to mine. His hair, thick and dark, fell in waves over his forehead, a once-refined cut that had been long neglected. He was very tall, and broad-shouldered, the top button of his shirt undone to reveal muscles leading down to his chest. All of it free of wrinkles or marks of age, doused in that almost sickening vampire perfection.

But that was where the perfection ended.

In a lifetime of traveling, I'd never seen scars like these.

They crawled over the left side of his face like thorny vines. They dug deep into his flesh, black and luminescent blue, as if whatever had made them had clawed past muscle and bone all the way down to his soul. They ran from beneath his collar, twining up the muscles of his throat, over his jaw, his cheekbone, his ear. And his left eye—

No pupil. No iris. A sea of silvery clouds that rolled in constant movement, emanating tendrils of smoky light.

What had done that to him? It made the curious priestess in me, the girl who'd once devoted her life to studying the magical possibilities of the world, perk up. I couldn't take my eyes off it.

Asar held my stare for a long moment. I didn't realize quite how long until he broke it, clearing his throat. His gaze dropped down, to my wrists bound before me.

Those long fingers folded around my hand. The touch summoned goosebumps. A dizzying sensation stirred deep in my chest, rubbing against the bars of its cage.

Asar blinked, meeting my gaze for a split second before tearing it away. I felt the briefest ripple of his surprise pass between us, far better hidden than mine.

With one sharp movement, he pushed my left sleeve up.

I tried to yank it back, but he held my wrist firm. The rush of cool air against my arm was humiliating. I didn't want to look. But my eyes fell to my skin anyway.

I felt like such a hypocrite, being shocked by Asar's scars when my own had grown so horrifying. I avoided looking at them any more than I absolutely had to. Out here in the light, it appalled me all over again just how grotesque they'd become.

In the beginning, they'd been small, collecting at the crook of my elbow. After I'd been Turned, every time I used the magic of Atroxus—wielded flame or the power of the sun—I was rewarded with another burn. I had been so grateful that my god still allowed me my magic after my Turning that I didn't even care. Most humans who worshipped gods of the White Pantheone weren't nearly so lucky. Besides, didn't I deserve that punishment for being what I was? Vampires, after all, were a natural enemy to the light.

But over the years, the burns got worse. And this last year, now that Atroxus denied me my magic altogether, had been worst of all. The scars now ran all the way from my wrist to above my elbow. Some still wept pus and black blood, fresh from my attempts at calling the flame in my cell.

No skin was untouched.

Gingerly, avoiding the freshest wounds—a confusing mercy— Asar tucked my sleeve up past my elbow.

"There," he said.

Egrette and her guard had moved beside the king. Now all three of them followed his gaze down—at my tattoo, barely visible now beneath the scar tissue.

Gods, it had gotten so ugly.

Once, the ink had been bright as the dawn it symbolized, glowing with Atroxus's blessing. The golden bird perched at my forearm, feathers wrapping around my elbow, silhouetted against flames—a phoenix, the symbol of the Order of the Destined Dawn. Or at least, that was what it was supposed to be. Saescha had teased me after it was done because I'd brought the artist a design that looked more like a firefinch, an invasive, common songbird, than a phoenix. "Just like you," she'd said, shaking her head. "You make impulsive changes and then you end up with a pest on your arm."

"She's not a pest," I had replied, affectionately stroking my still-sore tattoo. "She's just *approachable*, Saescha."

Well, she didn't look approachable anymore. The tattoo was near-unrecognizable. The ink was dull and blurry, the glow long faded, shades of pink and gold and red smeared to brown soup.

Raoul, Egrette, and Elias looked unimpressed.

"And?" Egrette said, visibly annoyed that her grand gift had been so disrupted.

"This is a symbol of the Order of the Destined Dawn," Asar said. "There are far more useful things we can do with a Dawndrinker than butcher her up."

I was surprised—maybe even impressed—that he knew enough about the human nations to recognize a sect of Atroxus by that tattoo alone. But stronger than that was the primal reaction I had to what he called me. *Dawndrinker.* I hadn't heard anyone refer to me that way in a long, long time.

Egrette scoffed. "You'd waste this opportunity over an old tattoo?"

Asar gave her a disdainful stare. "Atroxus's magic is a rare resource in Obitraes. One that I need for my task." He said this like he were speaking to a child. Egrette looked as if it physically pained her not to roll her eyes.

His task?

"Countless Turned once worshipped members of the White Pantheon in their human lives," Egrette snapped. "All of them were abandoned by their gods once they became vampires. I'm sure she is no different. She has none of Atroxus's magic left in her."

Her words lodged between my ribs, shame bleeding from the wound.

She was right, of course.

But there was a little note of desperation in her voice, buried beneath that haughty superiority. She cast her father an uncertain, almost pleading, glance.

"You cannot delay retribution, Father—" she started.

"I have a task from the Dark Mother." Asar's voice was cold and hard. It cleaved through the air like a drawn blade. "You'd deny her for your petty taunts?"

I stopped breathing.

The Dark Mother?

Nyaxia?

Nyaxia was the goddess of vampires.

What mission could Nyaxia possibly have given him? What mission could she possibly have given him that *required the magic of Atroxus?* It couldn't be anything good.

"She's useless to you," Egrette said.

Asar's eyes shot to mine in a direct challenge. "Are you?"

I blinked, taken aback. Everyone had been talking about me like I wasn't here for so long that it was jarring to be addressed directly. "Am I—"

"Are you able to wield the magic of Atroxus?"

He spoke deliberately, each word pointed. I got the impression he knew—or thought he knew—the answer. I got the impression that he was not the type of man who asked questions he didn't already know the answer to.

My reply lingered at the tip of my tongue.

The truth would end in my death. I wasn't afraid of that anymore. But I thought of Raihn and Oraya, and my head in a box, and a war they couldn't survive.

The choice was easy.

"I have it." I forced a smile—brighter than I felt. "The tattoo's seen better days, I know. But I still have the magic."

Asar looked smug. Egrette looked annoyed. Raoul looked unconvinced.

Before any of them could speak—before I could second-guess myself—I thrust my hand out. "I'll show you."

Asar stepped back, giving me room. A barely there smirk twitched at the corner of his mouth.

If only he knew how premature that smile was. I didn't think this through.

I slowly unfurled my fingers. My heartbeat spiked. I knew they all could sense it, though I kept my mental walls firm around my dishonesty.

No one spoke. Hundreds of eyes fell to me, watching with hungry interest.

I felt like I was eight years old again, standing on the steps of the Citadel, my fate hinging upon one desperate call to a deity.

But I'd been so young then, so pure, so untouched. A perfect offering to a perfect god. Nothing but potential.

I was none of those things now. I was dirty and wretched and irreparably stained by my mistakes. I had nothing left to offer the god who had once offered me everything.

But however foolish some might call it, I still had my hope.

My light, I prayed. *I know I have failed you. I know I do not deserve you. But I call upon you now, one last time. Please.*

Silence.

Of course, silence. Silence like I'd heard every endless night for the last year.

My eyes burned. My palm was empty.

But then, the voice. It sounded exactly as it had that day on the Citadel steps.

I see you, a'mara. Open your hand.

I thought, at first, that maybe I'd imagined it. But then the warmth flooded me, unmistakable. It lit up my soul like the dawn had once warmed my face, euphoric, unmistakable.

Flame blossomed in my palm, stunning as a second chance.

I was that little girl all over again, saved by her god.

I choked out an almost laugh, cheeks stinging with my grin. It took every ounce of my self-control not to collapse into tears. I barely even felt the fresh burn open on my arm, another scar added to my collection. And hell, did it matter? What was a single scar compared to this?

My gaze lifted to Asar, who was looking at me with a tight smirk of approval. He turned to his sister as if to say, *I told you so.*

I beamed. "See? I still have it."

My voice was strangled, but they didn't seem to notice. Raoul clasped his hands behind his back, turning away.

"Very well," he said. "Take her. The underworld will be punishment enough."

My smile dimmed.

The underworld?

The underworld?

Asar bowed his head, accepting his victory, and took up my chains.

Egrette's berry-stained lips curled into a cruel smirk. Her voice slithered into my mind.

So foolish, she crooned. *You could have had a clean death.*

Instead, you've volunteered yourself for something far worse.

COOL, DAMP AIR surrounded me as we stepped from the party into the night. It was a small relief. I felt as if the flame I'd summoned was still burning in my stomach, my face hot, my steps shaky. Asar walked in front of me, holding the chain that bound my wrists. He didn't look back, but I didn't think I imagined the way his steps slowed as we left the castle, like he'd been stopping himself from rushing to escape it. At the threshold, he paused for half a step, shoulders lowering with a silent exhale, before we continued walking.

I kept summoning sparks to my fingertips. Off, on. Off, on. They hurt every time, but I couldn't stop myself. I wanted to skip. I wanted to jump up and down. I wanted to fall to my knees and weep. I wanted to pray to Atroxus so I could hear his voice again, prove to myself I hadn't hallucinated it.

Instead, I was so focused on putting one step in front of the other that when Asar slowed at the threshold of the door, I stumbled against him, my face planting right between his shoulder blades.

He jerked away, shooting a glare at me over his shoulder. It felt particularly foreboding with that eye, which glowed starker now against the night.

"Sorry," I muttered.

He ignored me and kept walking, giving my restraints an unceremonious yank.

Rude.

I stumbled to keep up with him, clumsily regaining my footing on narrow, uneven stone pathways. A chilly gust blew my hair from my face. It doused me in a brief, powerful scent—cold florals.

We rounded a corner, and a breathtaking panorama opened up before us. I stopped walking. "Gods, look at that," I whispered.

I'd spent the last few years in the House of Night, a nation of deserts and mountains. It had been a good long while since I'd gotten the chance to admire the ocean. The capital sat at the southeastern shores of the House of Shadow, and the Shadowborn castle perched upon its tallest cliffs. We were far above the sea, which stretched out in endless silver to the velvet-black horizon. Grand ridges of stone burst from the ocean in stubborn rebellion against the waves, obsidian-black covered in emerald-green moss. The lush blankets of the House of Shadow's famous foliage flourished to our left, consuming the stones, the buildings, the hills—grass and ivy and rosebushes.

It felt wrong to find it so stunning. After what this place had done to me.

As if to chase away that brief admiration, I summoned the sparks to my fingertips again, relishing the fleeting pain as Asar gave my chains another impatient tug.

"Where are we going?" I asked. Then, before I even realized I was still talking, "You have a mission from Nyaxia? To go to the underworld? To do what? Why do you need me? And—"

I bit down on my last question because I knew if I didn't, I'd never stop talking. I was too chatty at the best of times, but right now, I felt jittery, all my impulses too close to the surface.

Asar, again, ignored me. I watched his shoulders, stiff and square. Even from the back, his scars were visible in the sliver of bare skin between his collar and the thick waves of his hair. They seemed slightly purple out here in the moonlight, almost luminescent.

The Wraith Warden.

I'd met my fair share of legends. I was a chosen one of the sun god himself, after all. I knew better than to be intimidated by myth. They were just distortions of the truth, and we were all more similar than we'd like to admit beneath.

Still. It was impossible not to wonder if he really was everything they said he was.

But monster or not, he'd saved my life. So I said, "Thank you. By the way."

He peered at me over his shoulder again, that scarred eye moon-bright.

"I didn't do you a favor."

His voice was low, and a little rough, like he wasn't accustomed to using it. It sounded different than it had in the ballroom, as if the version of him I'd seen there had been a performance he'd since discarded.

I shrugged, my chains jangling. I gave him a smile—my greatest weapon. "I know, but still. Just seems like I should say it."

Asar turned away, unmoved.

I summoned another spark to my fingertips, an impulse I couldn't shake.

"Why do you keep doing that?" he said, without looking at me.

I folded my fingers together, self-conscious. I didn't have a good answer. "Where are we going?" I asked instead.

"Where do you think we're going?"

We rounded another corner. A gust of ocean wind doused us in cold, salty air.

I felt an uncomfortable pressure on my temple, like invisible fingers reaching for my thoughts. It was different from Egrette's or Raoul's rummaging. This was gentler, more delicate—and familiar in a way I couldn't place.

It made my skin crawl. It felt invasive. Intimate.

I shook my head, hard. "Don't do that," I snapped.

"Don't waste either of our time with questions you already know the answers to. Where do you think we're going, Dawndrinker?"

"I think we're going to Morthryn."

The name sat heavy on my tongue.

Morthryn.

A prison created by the gods themselves, long before Obitraes was Obitraes, long before vampires existed at all. Each of the three vampire Houses guarded a site of great divine power. The House of Night held the Moon Palace and the Kejari tournament hosted within it, held every one hundred years in Nyaxia's honor. The House of Blood had the barren fields where the god of death, Alarus, had been murdered and dismembered.

And the House of Shadow had Morthryn. A place said to be cursed, even by vampire standards.

"You know much about the House of Shadow for a Turned Dawndrinker," Asar said. "You must be very cultured."

The tinge of sarcasm gave me the distinct impression he was, in fact, insulting me.

"I read a lot," I said. "So that's why no one has heard from you in years? Because you've been in Morthryn?"

Locked up in it? Or caretaking it?

It's been a few centuries since he's been let out of his cage, Egrette had said. Maybe there wasn't much of a difference either way. Raoul's silence about his illegitimate son for a few hundred years certainly implied that regardless of the nature of his exile, it was a source of shame. Maybe a mocking joke, based on his nickname.

"Is that why Nyaxia came to you?" I guessed. "Because of your connection to—"

Asar spun around.

"What do you think is happening here?" he said. "Do you think I've given you some kind of mercy?"

He spoke quietly, but every word was sharp and deliberate, just like his movements. Darkness clung to the edges of his form as if finding comfort near an old friend. It gave him the appearance of being perpetually silhouetted, and it made him seem ominously large.

I could imagine someone being very intimidated by him. Not me, I told myself. But other people. Other reasonable people.

My fingertips throbbed with the remnants of my flames.

Why had Atroxus come back to me now, of all times? Was it to give me the tool I needed to free myself? The sun was a powerful weapon in the world of vampires—their natural enemy. If Atroxus wanted me to free myself, I had to do it now. If I let Asar take me within Morthryn's walls, I had the feeling I'd never get out.

I was a passable fighter. Good enough to get by. But I was a chosen one of Atroxus. That was greater than any blessed sword.

I took a half step backward, a door parting to my trap. "I'm just asking questions."

Asar let out an exasperated sigh and reached for me.

I seized my chance.

I reached down within myself, all that way to that tiny shred of my heart that was still human, and called to the sun.

The strain to bring it forth was unexpected, like attempting to drag a cart uphill in the mud. For one terrifying split second, I thought I'd been abandoned all over again.

But then the fire burst to life in my hands.

Asar's face shifted to shock, then anger, as mine split with a delighted grin.

I started to strike, but then—

Not yet, a'mara. This is not the time. Wait for me.

Atroxus's voice was distant, yet unmistakable. It distracted me, throwing my blow off-balance.

Asar diverted it easily, sending me toppling into a rosebush. When I opened my eyes to see him leaning over me, he looked merely annoyed.

"That was a foolish waste of time," he muttered under his breath.

"Wait—" I started.

But he just lowered his hand over my eyes, and with it came a wave of cool, black nothingness.

CHAPTER FOUR

Look, Mi."

My head lay in Saescha's lap. She let me sleep this way, I knew, because she wanted to watch over me. But I liked it because her skirt still smelled like home—damp soil and the salty ocean. When we got to the Citadel of the Destined Dawn, they would make her wash her clothes and the scent would be gone, along with everything else of our former life.

I was exhausted from weeks of travel. My lashes fluttered. But she shook my shoulder gently. "Look."

I blinked away the gritty remnants of sleep to see her, bathed in light, smile wide enough it seemed to wash away the dirt on her face.

She pointed, and I followed her gaze.

The sun was a splash of pure gold, smearing the horizon with brilliant pink and orange. It was nestled in the valley between two distant mountains, which framed the rays of brilliance as they spilled over the forest and the sky and the stone alike.

My sister surely hadn't slept for more than a few hours at a time in weeks. But despite the shadows beneath her eyes, she now looked downright giddy.

"The Lord of Light is on our side, Mi," she breathed. "Look at all that a sunrise can mean. We survived another night. And no matter what, the dawn will always come for us. Never forget that."

I knew this was true because my sister never lied to me. I watched that precious sunrise, and I nestled into those two embraces: my sister's and the sun's. Eternal. Warm.

So warm it was . . .

It was . . .

The heat intensified, smoldering, *burning*—

Pain ignited me. I gasped and leapt up. "Saescha, help me! Help me!"

My skin cracked. Flames burst through the open tears. But I looked to my sister and my cry of horror was louder than the cry of pain.

Her face was pale, her eyes empty, her throat an open mass of torn flesh.

"Saescha!" I screamed—or tried to, but the name drowned in my throat beneath a tide of blood. I tried to spit it out, but it filled my lungs. Distraught, I turned to the sun, calling for my god to save me—to save my sister, because she deserved it more than I did.

But I was too late. The blood poured from my mouth. The sun beat me down.

And it was the fire that took me, in the end.

I AWOKE WITH a start, my sister's name on my lips, the afterimage of her corpse burning behind my eyelids. My gaze settled on my hands—fingernails covered in black blood—and I let out a hiss of pain as I rolled over. I'd been scratching at my burns, the freshest ones now open and seeping. Any other wound and they would've been gone by now. But vampires did not mix well with the magic of the sun. They would take a long time to heal.

The dreams had followed me since I was Turned. For a while, during my years with Raihn, they weren't too bad—or maybe they just felt more manageable when I'd had someone else fighting his nightmares right alongside me. But they'd roared back with a vengeance ever since the Kejari—ever since the attack on the Moon Palace, when

Atroxus had finally taken away my magic for good. They were so vivid now. It took me a few long seconds to shake away the breath of a ghost on the back of my neck.

My joints groaned in protest as I sat up.

I was surrounded by . . . nothing.

Endless nothingness.

No walls. No bars. No guards. No windows. Not even a horizon line, a sky, a ceiling, a floor.

Just nothing.

"Hello?" I called out.

Hello? my voice answered in a distant echo.

The hair prickled at the back of my neck. That little shard of humanity at the center of my heart—that piece of my flesh that was still as vulnerable as ever—shivered in fear.

Morthryn was a god-touched place. Some said it stood at the edge of the mortal world. The House of Shadow, like all vampire kingdoms, guarded their secrets carefully. Little information existed about Morthryn other than whispers and legends. But I could feel the truth in those legends here, in a way that defied logic.

Raihn had often teased me for taking mythology so seriously. To him, the Moon Palace was a fancy house. Morthryn was a fancy prison. The Kejari was a tournament full of magic tricks. A prophecy was just a nice poem that seemed reasonable in hindsight. The gods were angry and fickle, and we couldn't attribute their actions to more than whim.

I understood why he felt that way.

But I also knew he was wrong.

Some things were fated. Some things were divine. The gods were playing a bigger game than any of us could see. And Morthryn, I knew—unmistakably in this moment—was far, far more than just an old castle.

I stood up. I was still wearing that white dress from the party. It was stained with my blood and singed a bit at the end of the left sleeve from my ill-fated attempt at escape.

I relived the echo of Atroxus's voice:

Wait for me.

Wait for what?

I turned slowly, eyes straining, and then stopped abruptly.

I wondered if I was imagining things when I saw the skull floating in the darkness.

It appeared to be that of a fox, maybe—two large, empty eye sockets, a delicate, long snout, and glistening teeth. I tentatively stepped closer, and then I could make out the rest of it: a body like a wolf's, but daintier, the legs long and slender like those of a deer, the movements smooth and silent like a panther's. The body didn't seem quite solid, at least not compared to the gleaming bronze of its skull face. The color seemed to change every time I looked at it, shades of black and blue and green, which shifted independent of light and shadow.

It was incredible. I'd never seen anything like it.

I sank down on my heels as it approached, as if not to threaten it—which, rationally, was probably a little silly. As if I could pose any threat to whatever this was. It was the biggest dog I'd ever seen—nearly as tall as me.

Still, I gave it a smile and held out a hand for it to sniff. As a child, I'd prided myself on my ability to make dogs love me immediately. Gods, I'd missed dogs. There weren't many domestic animals in Obitraes. Vampires didn't usually like to keep pets, unless they could provide some useful function like tearing the faces off their enemies.

Maybe it was a sign of dog-starved desperation that I thought this one still looked a bit cute, skull face and all.

"Hello there," I said softly. "What's your name?"

It stopped just short of me. Though its eyes were empty, I still got the impression it was offended by my cloying tone.

I didn't *hear* the word so much as I *felt* it, slithering straight into my mind:

Follow.

I blinked, unsure if I'd just imagined the voice.

My arms itched. I glanced down to see two tendrils of darkness wrapping around my wrists, and when I raised my gaze again, a doorway stood behind the wolf. It was made of simple gold, with one eye—the mark of Alarus, god of death—at the apex of the arch.

Follow, the wolf insisted, tilting its head in a way I understood was intended to show off its impressive fangs.

I should have been more afraid than I was. Phantom wolves. Mysterious doorways. God-touched prisons. But maybe I was still riding the euphoria of Atroxus's voice, because it fascinated me more than anything.

I stood, raising my palms. "All right. All right. I'm following."

The wolf let out a grunt of satisfaction, then turned to the door. But I let out a chuckle under my breath that earned another wary glance.

"Sorry," I said. "It's just, it's a bit funny that I'm the one jumping when the dog says 'come,' isn't it?"

Follow, the wolf deadpanned, its answer to that question obvious.

It was funny, I decided.

I hesitated at the door. It was only a freestanding frame, revealing no glimpse of what lay beyond, but—

Follow, the dog insisted. And with a firm push from its bony snout, I stumbled through the arch—straight into the halls of Morthryn.

It was one of the most beautiful things I had ever seen.

I stood in a long, winding hallway. The floor was mirrored, like the smooth surface of a still pond. If there was a ceiling, it was so high above us that it disappeared into ghostly mist. Balls of light hovered above us like little moons, casting silver and gold across ivory walls and golden columns, which curved and arched in a shape that was eerily reminiscent of ribs. Intricate carvings crawled up each one, quivering under the flickering light. Thorny vines cradling blood-tipped leaves encircled the columns, increasingly overgrown as they climbed and eventually disappeared into the mist. The walls were lined with arches like the one I'd just come through, though each was bricked over with stone. The door I'd just stepped through was now the same, framing a flat wall.

I took a few amazed steps, taking it all in. The black ink floor rippled beneath each one, though my feet remained dry.

"Holy gods," I whispered.

I'd spent most of my life traveling. And I'd seen some truly stunning things—the greatest works of mortal hands in art and architecture, the greatest works of the gods' hands in natural phenomena.

This trumped them all. The most stunning of both.

The wolf, which had walked several paces ahead, looked back.

"I know, I know," I said. "I'm following."

I TRIED TO keep track of our path at first, but that quickly proved pointless. The hallways twisted in ways that defied mortal logic, just as tangled as the vines that covered their walls—and somehow, I was certain, just as alive. The ivy wrapped around arch after arch, eyes of black stained glass sitting at each apex. Gentle waves of mist rolled over the floor and floated up the walls, making the prison feel as if it went on forever. Ahead, the wolf's silent footfalls left bloody prints in the mirrored ground, starting off bright and slowly fading. I peered over my shoulder and saw them falling behind us like a trail of discarded rose petals.

Eventually, we reached a doorway different from those we'd been passing—instead of an empty frame, this one held two heavy oak doors, an eye of Alarus carved upon each.

The wolf nudged them, and though it was barely a touch, they swung wide open. The wolf stepped aside, staring at me expectantly.

Foll—

"I know," I said. "I think I've got it by now."

I stepped through, my spectral guard at my heels. The doors slammed behind me, loud enough to make me jump. Then it was silent, save for the *tick tick tick* of a clock that seemed just a little fast.

I spun around slowly, taking in the room. My eyes grew wider and wider.

Everywhere I looked, there was more to see. It was unbelievable. It was *gorgeous*.

The roses were more plentiful here, trampling each other as they coiled up bookcases that stretched so high they disappeared into the silver fog above. A neglected fire languished near death in a grand fireplace to the left. Before it, a massive desk sat in foreboding watch, a faded, black velvet chair askew behind it. Open books and papers covered the mahogany surface, wet ink still gleaming on one sheet, as if someone had just stepped away mid-thought. Yet, even so, it was all meticulously neat—every piece of parchment aligned to the edge of the desk, every little trinket artfully arranged.

But the shelves—gods, the *artifacts*—

I just kept turning and turning. Every time I considered stopping, I found something more to see.

I'd spent decades in libraries across the human nations and beyond. But two minutes in here and I knew that this had to be one of the most impressive collections of magical relics that existed in the world.

The shelves were divided into sections.

Here, bones—a small horse skull with a twisted silver horn protruding from its forehead, a carefully reassembled skeletal hand with claws longer than its fingers, a lower jaw with jagged teeth that extended several razored inches.

There, a series of glass flasks holding what I recognized as various types of blood arranged by color. The red of human, the black of vampire—then several types I didn't recognize: gold, indigo, a strange silver that gave off waves of light.

Then, weapons. A broken sword pinned to the wall by an invisible force, shards painstakingly arranged to the shape of the blade with only a few pieces missing. A double-ended polearm, one blade curved and one straight, delicate carvings etched down the length of its golden handle. A black rapier that glowed purple, its handguard forming silver flower petals around the hilt.

At that, I gasped.

It couldn't be what I thought it was. There was *no way* it was what I thought it was.

I reached out before I could stop myself—

A growl rang out behind me. I peered over my shoulder to see the wolf glowering disapprovingly.

"Sorry." I tucked my hands behind my back. "I was just admiring. Your master has an impressive collection. Is this—was this *Nyaxia's*?"

The wolf growled again, though it settled tentatively back onto its haunches, satisfied with the space I'd put between myself and the shelves.

A *thump* came against the wall, making the glass vials rattle. The wolf's head snapped up. I spun around.

I hadn't noticed the door because there was so much else to look at. It was small and tragically unassuming. Now, it creaked as it swung open a crack. Red light seeped from beyond it.

I'd never been very good at controlling my curiosity. I stepped closer—

The wolf leapt to its feet. A bark split the air.

I raised my hands. "I wasn't going to—"

"I wasn't expecting you yet."

I turned to the door and stumbled backward.

Asar stood in the frame, blocking my view of the inside. He—unsurprisingly, from what I knew of him so far—looked irritated.

He was also half-naked and covered in blood.

He leaned against the door, one hand up against the top of it as if to keep it from opening any more than it had to. Drips of red rolled down his forearm, tracing over ropey cords of muscle. Human blood, I knew immediately—the smell hit me with ferocious force. He angled his body away from me, but my eyes still fell to his bare torso—to the black and purple scars gouging across the defined panes of his abdomen like the ivy over Morthryn's walls.

How much of him did they cover, I wondered? How had he gotten them? Definitely no typical wound—

"Excuse me. Up here."

I blinked and pulled my stare back to his face, where he scowled at me, eyes narrowed.

With a powerful wave of embarrassment, I cleared my throat. "I was just—"

"I've long ago stopped being sensitive about being stared at, Dawndrinker."

I was glad he cut me off because what was I going to say? *I wasn't looking at you in a lecherous way, I was looking at you in a curiosity-in-a-museum way.* Which was worse?

He ducked behind the doorframe, then reappeared wearing a plain, wrinkled black shirt, pushing past me and closing the door behind him. He shot the wolf a look of mild annoyance.

"You brought her early."

The wolf let out a low whine, and Asar sighed, rubbing his temple.

"It's fine, Luce," he muttered. "Just lost track of time."

"Luce?" I repeated. "It—" I glanced at the wolf, then corrected myself. "Her name is Luce?"

"Yes." He sat behind the desk and motioned for me to take the seat opposite.

"Huh." I perched on the chair and craned my neck to watch the wolf, instantly at ease now that we were in Asar's presence. She had settled into a graceful lounge, front paws crossed.

"Is that . . . surprising?" Asar sounded like he was already regretting asking this question.

Yes.

"No," I said. "It's a nice name."

It *was* a nice name. I decided it suited her.

Asar opened a drawer and withdrew a neatly folded handkerchief, which he used to wipe the blood from his hands. I watched, unblinking, as the cloth turned red.

My stomach twisted painfully.

Stop staring, I told myself. I pulled my eyes away, too late.

"You're hungry," Asar said.

"Me? No." I laughed brightly. "Don't have much of an appetite, all things considered."

He stared at me in a way that made me feel like he was peeling my clothes off. "You're lying."

Well, he was a mind reader, so that wasn't fair.

Instead of responding, I gave him a cheerful smile and gestured to the shelves. "Your collection is incredible. I've never seen so much—"

"That won't work."

He was now flipping through the papers on his desk, head bowed. I blinked. "What won't work?"

His gaze flicked up. That white left eye nailed me to the wall like a butterfly ready for hanging in the rest of his archives.

"I have been the warden of Morthryn for more than a century. I've dealt with better liars, more charming manipulators, and more beautiful women than you. So don't bother."

"More beautiful women?" I repeated.

I wasn't sure if that was an insult or a backward kind of compliment.

He set down the parchment, squaring it to the edge of the desk. "So. Mische Iliae."

He broke my name up into five pointed, deliberate syllables— *Meesh-uh Il-ee-ay*. Involuntarily, my body tensed at the sound of it. I hadn't heard my own surname spoken in decades. How had he learned that? Even Raihn didn't use it.

Mische Iliae was human. Mische Iliae was one of the most revered acolytes of the Order of the Destined Dawn. And Mische Iliae had a sister who shared that same surname.

That name didn't sit right on my shoulders anymore.

"How did you—" I started.

"You were born human in Slenka. You were eight years old when you traveled to Vostis and joined the Order of the Destined Dawn. You served as a crusader for a decade or so. You journeyed to Obitraes when you were nineteen, where you were Turned by my *beloved* late brother, Malach." His voice dripped with venom around the name as he flipped a page. "Then you befriended Raihn Ashraj. Competed in the Kejari. Helped him overthrow a kingdom. Murdered Malach—a great service to us all, so thank you for that. And now, you are here."

His eyes flicked up to me, impassive. "Did I miss anything?"

Hearing my own life read back to me with such stripped-down factuality made me nauseous. *Traveled* to sum up weeks barely evading death when I was just a child. *Served* to mean offering my entire life to Atroxus. *Journeyed* to describe a sacred mission.

And *Turned*—that horrific, gods-damned word—to sum up the night that a stranger had pinned me down and ripped away my humanity with his teeth buried in my throat. A violation so great I didn't even remember it.

I swallowed thickly.

"I wasn't a crusader," I said. "I was a priestess. A missionary."

Am a priestess, I corrected myself.

Asar let out a scoff. "See those?" He pointed his quill tip to a row of humanoid skulls upon one of the shelves. "Those are all that remain of one of the oldest Shadowborn bloodlines after some Dawndrinker *missionaries* were done *showing them the path of the light.*"

My gaze settled on the smallest of the skulls—so very, very tiny— before I yanked it away. "Not me. I was more of . . . a scholar."

I wasn't lying. But a long-neglected memory of chains spattered with black blood flitted through my mind, and I swallowed the sour tang of dishonesty.

He didn't believe me, and he didn't bother hiding it. "I don't particularly care, Iliae. Because you ended up here, in Morthryn, and everyone within these walls deserves to be here. I do better research than my sister, and I'm less impulsive than my father, which is why I understand that you're far more useful here than butchered up and shipped back to the House of Night. Everything else worth knowing about you, I've already figured out. Except for one thing."

He tapped his pen impatiently on the parchment, leaving a cluster of messy ink.

"The fire."

I resisted the urge to touch my burns, instead clasping my hands together.

"I am an acolyte of Atroxus," I said. "You knew that already."

"There," he said, pointing the tip of his pen at me like a blade poised at my throat. "*Am.* Not *was.* Countless acolytes of other gods have been Turned over the years, and the gods of the White Pantheon have abandoned them all for it. But not you." He eyed my arms—covered, but I still felt his stare on my scars. "Even if, it appears, you had to sacrifice to keep those gifts."

Sacrifice. I wanted to laugh at him. He had no idea the things I'd done to keep Atroxus's love. And was any of it enough? Sure, Atroxus let me keep the flame—for a while. But it was hard to put any other word but abandonment to that night in the Moon Palace, when the demons had closed in on me and I'd heard nothing but my god's silence as I begged him for help.

I smiled and shrugged. "I'm just special."

He cocked his head slightly. "Special," he repeated.

I stared back at him, peeling back his layers as he attempted to peel back mine. He looked different here than he had at the party.

He didn't fit in there. Everything from the clothing to the lighting to the smooth faces of the vampire nobles around him had served to highlight his differences, and I could tell that he'd felt every one of them.

But here? The lines of his face that had seemed too severe out there now verged on majestic, just hard enough and sharp enough to survive such a dangerous place. Even those scars seemed natural, like moss crawling over the trees.

He stood abruptly and walked around the desk. I pulled away as he approached me.

"What are you—"

He gripped my shoulder, gentle but firm, and placed his hand flat over my chest. I tensed at it—bare skin against bare skin, just above the neckline of my dress. I drew in a sharp breath. A shiver rolled over me, a visceral reaction to his touch. Like it was dragging something up from deep inside myself.

Wriggling clusters of shadow wrapped around his fingers. They collected at his palm, building where his skin met mine. And then, in a sudden burst, they fanned out like a star exploding, black lines etching into me. Darkness welled up in my heart, the sensation as terrifying as staring over the edge of a cliff into oblivion.

I clapped my own hand over my chest without thinking—covering Asar's. My eyes snapped up to meet his. The swirls of light in his left eye seemed restless, like a brewing storm. For a strange, disorienting moment, an innate connection bonded us—I could feel his emotions, just as tangled and nonsensical as mine, curiosity and anger and determination and fear.

Smoothly, he slid his palm away and released me.

My chest throbbed with the aftershock of his spell. It didn't hurt, though. The unpleasantness came from exactly how much *it did not hurt*.

Just like it had felt when—when—

"An anchor," he said. "It'll make sure you don't get lost on our journey."

I knew what an anchor was, gods' sake. I'd been the best magic user in the Citadel, and anchors were practically amateur spells by their standards. But I barely heard him anyway.

I blurted out, "It was you. The night before your father's party. You helped me."

Maybe I imagined the brief pause as he stacked his parchments up again, refusing to look at me.

"My sister likes to play with her food a little too roughly. You were going to die, and you're too useful to kill."

I opened my mouth, questions pooling on my tongue. But I wasn't sure how to put them into words.

What I wanted to ask was, *Why does it feel like that? So . . . intimate?*

But even acknowledging that question was too awkward, putting a name to things I'd rather ignore. So instead, I settled on, "I didn't know that Shadowborn magic could be used to heal."

"All forms of magic are just tools." Asar stood, slamming his drawer closed. "Anything that can be used to destroy can be used to create, too. I'm surprised that a *scholar* such as yourself doesn't know that."

I scowled, but he didn't give me a second glance, instead gesturing to the door. "Come. I need your help."

I was much more curious than I was offended. I jumped up and followed Asar to the door.

He swung it open, and I stopped short, hand going to my mouth.

"Holy fucking gods," I breathed.

It took me a moment to recognize exactly what I was looking at.

The room was small, circular, with no windows. It was plain compared to the rest of this place, free of decoration or glamour. But the mirrored floor had been painstakingly covered in spell-work—glyphs running in circles from the outer walls, spiraling to the center. I knew how to recognize skillful craft, and this was meticulous. So flawlessly done that those glyphs alone rivaled the grand elegance of the rest of Morthryn's halls.

And there, at the center of all of it, lay the corpse of a middle-aged woman, wrapped in white silk.

I knew what this was, even if I'd never witnessed it myself. I whirled to Asar, eyes wide.

"You're a necromancer."

CHAPTER FIVE

Asar gave me a slightly pitying look, the way one might look at a child who had just proudly declared that water was wet.

"Yes," he said, and strode into the room. I followed, a little dazed. Maybe the whirlwind of the last few days was starting to get to me, because choppy syllables poured out of my mouth instead of actual words that meant anything useful.

"But—it's—necromancy is—no one ever—I thought—"

Asar knelt at the circle, fixing a stray mark at the edge. "Are you horrified or excited?" he said drily. "I can't tell."

Shamefully, I couldn't quite tell, either.

"Horrified?" I meant for this to be a firm answer, but my voice rose at the end of the word, adding an unintended question mark.

To say that necromancy was taboo would be putting it lightly. It was such a universal subject of disgust and fear that it had transcended into the realm of myth. In the human lands, it had become an overused set piece in scary stories, often met with rolled eyes and scoffs. But the vampires took necromancy more seriously—maybe because they knew it was possible. I'd heard rumors that a few Shadowborn sorcerers had managed it over the years, though the Shadowborn denied it. It was considered, at best, unwise to tamper with the veil between the living and the dead. At worst, it was seen as an insult to Nyaxia—and no one wanted to risk that.

All this to say, necromancy was forbidden. Very, very forbidden. A rare point of agreement between both humans and vampires.

But a tiny part of myself was also fascinated by it.

As a child in the Citadel, I'd loved reading about rare magics. At least once a month, Saescha would drag me out of the . . . less-than-proper shelves of the archives in the small hours of the morning. But I'd been intrigued by them the way children were often intrigued by ghost stories. It wasn't *real* to me.

This was definitely real.

One look at the glyphs on the floor told me that this was powerful work, and conducted by someone who took it very seriously. There were symbols here that even I didn't recognize, and I'd spent the better part of a full human lifetime studying magic. Each stroke—every one of thousands—was meticulous, the work of a master craftsman. It was already advanced magic to create any kind of life, whether it be healing animals or promoting the growth of crops. The complexity that would go into bringing a soul back to life—a mortal soul, with all the countless factors within it—

I stopped myself.

This is necromancy, Mische. Necromancy. Dark magic. You shouldn't be impressed.

Every time I scolded myself, my inner voice sounded a little like my sister's.

I wasn't impressed, I justified to myself. I was just . . . interested. That was not the same thing.

"I just—I thought necromancy is forbidden," I said.

Asar continued painting over some of the strokes that didn't meet his standards. "And forbidden things *never* happen."

He was such a smug asshole.

"I know that," I said. "But it's your own father's rule, that's all."

"My father often needs to break his own rules. Every king does. And if they're smart, they all keep someone disposable on hand to do the rule breaking for them."

The bitterness in his voice was palpable.

I tore my gaze from the glyphs and watched Asar, his brow low in concentration.

The Wraith Warden. A title given to someone who had built their reputation on a mountain of dirty tasks. Asar was the second son. Illegitimate. The king probably never expected him to become an heir.

"So . . . is that why he exiled you?" I guessed.

I wasn't sure why I bothered asking Asar questions. He ignored me and stood. "Come here."

The tug on my mind had me taking a few steps before I could stop myself. But then I stopped short, pushing back against the pressure on my thoughts.

"Don't do that," I snapped.

Irritation flashed over Asar's face, but so did something much more satisfying—surprise.

"Just ask nicely," I muttered. "That's all!"

I joined him at the edge of the glyph circle. I could feel his gaze on me for a long moment, as if he was considering saying something.

"What?" I said.

He shook his head and turned to the body.

"I need your help with this."

He pointed to one part of the circle. Up close, I could see now that it was made of five interlocking parts arranged around the corpse. All but one had an object placed at its center.

It had been a long time since I'd read about necromancy, and I'd never seen what the ceremony looked like in practice, but I pieced together what I was seeing.

"It takes five elements to resurrect someone," I said.

I was very satisfied by Asar's momentary silence. I gave him a sly smile.

"What?" I said. "You think a Dawndrinker wouldn't know about necromancy?"

"Not very holy of you."

"Can't bring the light unless I know what the darkness looks like, Warden."

He let out a low sound that almost—almost—sounded like a chuckle.

"A mortal is comprised of five components that separate the living from the dead," he said. "And necromancy requires the spell to bring together all five again. So yes, it needs something to represent each of those elements."

He gestured to the first item in the circle—a long lock of silver hair bound with a red ribbon. It looked like it had once belonged to the corpse, a match to the silver-black tresses that fanned out around her shoulders.

"*Body*," he said. "In this case, I have the fresh corpse, so it's largely ceremonial."

Now he nodded to the next item—a little wooden flute. "*Breath*. This represents the passage of time."

Next, a gold necklace.

"*Psyche*. It represents memories. The past."

I squinted at the necklace, craning my neck for a better look at the emblem on it. It looked familiar—a circle bisected, with lines branching out from it. But before I could speak, Asar had already moved on.

He gestured to the next one—a tiny, bloodstained blanket. My stomach turned when I looked at it, though I couldn't quite identify why. It was small, and once had been white, but now it was covered with red-black blood. Whether it was vampire blood or old, dried human blood, I couldn't tell.

"*Secrets*," Asar said. "The things mortals hide from themselves. And finally . . ."

His gaze settled on the last piece of the circle, which was empty. "*Soul*. That's what I need you for."

"Why?"

"The representation of Soul can be anything, but pieces of their legacy are most effective. She was devout. A touch of Atroxus's light would work."

My gaze shot back to the necklace—the emblem that had looked so familiar.

"She's an acolyte of Atroxus, too."

That was it. The emblem wasn't that of the Order of the Destined Dawn. It belonged to one of the smaller sects that worshipped Atroxus—the Helianen.

My eyes narrowed at Asar. "Who is she?"

"She was a prisoner."

A human locked up in Morthryn?

"Why?" There were too many *whys*. "Why was she imprisoned? Why do you need her back? Why is she dead? Does this have something to do with your mission, too?"

Asar sighed wearily. "I need your magic. Not your questions."

"Why do you need two followers of Atroxus?"

"Because it's always important to have redundancies in case one of you dies."

I stared at the corpse. "One of us already died."

"This hardly counts," Asar said, exasperated. "She's been dead for a few hours. If you die out there, I can't help you."

Out there.

The underworld.

A shiver ran up my spine that had nothing to do with the cold.

"What if I refuse?" I said.

"That would be unwise."

"I can't participate in necromancy. Atroxus might take away my magic for associating with a forbidden art, and then I'd be useless to you."

I crossed my arms. I felt a bit less smug than I looked because, as the words left my lips, I realized it was a perfectly valid concern.

I didn't know why Atroxus had given me my magic back. But I was determined to keep it, and associating with necromancy, of all things, seemed like an excellent way to prove to him that I was just the dirty, tainted vampire after all.

Asar—begrudgingly—considered this. Then he grabbed a lantern from the wall, opened it up, and withdrew the warped stump of wax within, dousing the blue flames of nightfire with his palm. He held it out to me.

"You bless the candle. I do the rest. Your eternal soul remains untainted."

I stared at the candle—misshapen, dusty. It looked nothing like the ones I'd lit all those years ago upon the steps of the Citadel. Still, it seemed like yet another mocking reminder of the day I'd been blessed and just how far I'd fallen since.

My gaze slipped to the corpse. It was, indeed, fresh. I could still smell the blood, not yet rancid in her veins, and my stomach didn't let me forget it. The woman could have been sleeping, eyes closed, mouth relaxed, brow smooth. She looked just like countless priestesses I'd shared my childhood with. Serene, elegant, and so very human.

"What's her name?" I asked.

I really did think Asar would refuse to answer. But he said, "Chandra."

It was a religious name. It meant *one who spreads the light unto dark places* in the old tongues.

Someone who had been born into the world of Atroxus. Unlike me, who had clawed my way into it.

I sighed and lifted my hand over the candle. I reached down, down, down into my heart, where that little piece of humanity still remained.

For a few terrible seconds, I thought the light had abandoned me again. But then a golden spark jumped at the wick, a flame flickering to life.

I winced as a fresh burn opened somewhere on my forearm, safely covered beneath my sleeve. I touched my arm before I could stop myself, then glanced up. I meant to look at the flame, but my eyes traveled beyond it, to Asar.

I didn't like how he looked at me. Like he could see it all.

I'd meant to give him a bright smile and a flippant *you're welcome,* but something in his stare made me pause. It spoke to all the vampire impulses inside me, instincts nudging me toward a dangerous conclusion.

Here I was wondering why Atroxus had picked me—picked me all those years ago, and picked me now. I couldn't answer that question without prayer. But maybe a question just as important was why Nyaxia had picked Asar for this mysterious mission of his. My human instincts and my vampire ones clashed, both screaming at me that we were headed somewhere dangerous.

Asar broke our stare, taking the candle from me with a faint wince at the proximity to Atroxus's magic. He placed it in the circle, filling the final missing piece of the spell.

"That'll be all," he said. "You should rest. And drink. I can sense your hunger from—"

"What has Nyaxia asked you to do?" I cut in.

There was no charming lightness to my voice anymore. No playful curiosity. I had a bad, bad feeling in my stomach, and it wasn't from the stench of the corpse.

Asar didn't look up. "I'm surprised you haven't figured it out yet, Iliae. Seeing as you consider yourself so attuned with the gods."

Stop calling me that, I wanted to say. But my thoughts were going too fast, stringing pieces of knowledge together.

"Nyaxia is sending you to the underworld," I said. "And you're a necromancer. So she likely needs you to bring someone back."

Asar said nothing. He also didn't correct me, which I took as agreement.

But one didn't typically need to literally go to the underworld to perform necromancy—as evidenced by the ceremony before me.

That is, unless it was an especially difficult task. One that required an even closer connection to death.

But why wouldn't Nyaxia do it herself?

Why would it require the magic of other gods?

"But who would Nyaxia need—"

I stopped mid-sentence.

"*Oh.* Oh, gods."

I hoped I was wrong.

I prayed I was wrong.

But the twitch at the corner of Asar's mouth made my stomach sink.

There was only one dead soul that Nyaxia could want back whom she wouldn't be able to resurrect herself. Someone who had been executed by the god of the sun. Someone who had held a closer connection to the underworld than any other.

I had to be wrong. It was impossible.

Asar's gaze, piercing and indecipherable, flicked up to mine. "You are finally speechless," he remarked.

"Alarus," I choked out. "It's Alarus. You're going to resurrect the god of death."

Nyaxia's deceased husband, who had been murdered by the White Pantheon—an execution led by Atroxus himself.

Asar's mouth curled into a grim smile, his scars warping with the expression.

"No, Dawndrinker," he said. "*We* are going to resurrect the god of death."

CHAPTER SIX

I sat in my cell, staring into darkness.

I was in shock.

I knew I was in shock because I was actually at a loss for words after Asar confirmed my suspicions—a state so rare that most people who knew me had never witnessed it. I'd gaped at him, words bubbling up in my chest but never making it to my lips, as he turned me around, led me from the room, declared that he had *work to do,* and deposited me with Luce to be brought back to my cell. He said something about *resting* and *waiting* and *drinking something for Mother's sake* and *we leave soon, so be ready.*

I didn't quite remember.

The last few days had been a haze. Days—had it been days? I couldn't tell if it felt like longer or shorter. How long ago was it that I trudged through the forest on my way to gods knew where? How long ago was it that those Shadowborn soldiers had dragged me away?

It felt like minutes. It felt like years.

The gravity of everything that had happened left me shaken. But that was nothing, I was sure, compared to what was still to come.

For the first time since I'd heard Atroxus's voice in that party, I was alone with my thoughts.

I pulled up my sleeve—still the dirty, bloodstained white dress Egrette had dressed me in—and looked at my arm. The new burn I'd gotten in exchange for the flame I'd given Asar seeped yellow pus a few inches shy of my wrist. Farther up, my phoenix tattoo stared back at me, its face warped and bright feathers dull beneath scar tissue.

I'd been so proud the day I'd gotten that mark. I could still remember just how lovely it had looked over smooth, untouched skin. When I'd prayed at sundown that day, Atroxus had come to me easily, and he'd smiled with such amusement when I'd shown him my new gift in his honor.

It was easy back then. Prayer.

Though Atroxus had allowed me to keep my magic for a while after I had Turned, he had immediately stopped appearing to me. Still, I sent him my hymns every day. I performed my rituals and made my offerings. But as the years passed, it grew harder and harder to hear his silence. And lately . . .

Lately . . .

I'd found myself avoiding it entirely.

Now, everything I had longed for for decades was in reach. He'd spoken to me. If I called out to him now, he would answer. I was certain of it. Yet, I hesitated, and I didn't know why.

Was I afraid of what he would say to me? Was I afraid to see his face as he witnessed everything that I'd become?

I pulled my sleeve down, pushing away my insecurities. I extended my hands, one palm layered over the other to receive the gift of the sun. And just as I had countless times before, in my best and my worst moments, in my greatest joys and greatest devastations, I prayed. The syllables came easy as breath.

And the words were still on my tongue, seared there like scar tissue, when my eyes closed.

HELLO, A'MARA.

I'd lost track of how many times I'd startled awake to the sound of that voice, those words, only to find that they were just a figment of my desperate subconscious. But faith meant that you never stopped letting yourself hope, even if it hurt.

I opened my eyes.

Atroxus stood before me, so brilliant my eyes stung to look at him.

I scrambled to my feet only to fall to my knees, pressing my forehead to the mirrored glass floor.

"My light," I choked out.

I was shaking. I wanted to weep; I wanted to laugh. There was so much I wanted to say to him. I had thanks and blessings and apologies built up over decades, painstakingly cultivated during sleepless days full of unanswered prayers. Now, all of them were lost to me.

I didn't lift my head, but I felt the scalding heat of the sun bearing down upon me with each step he approached. I drew in a gasp as his fingers brushed my chin. His touch felt like relief at the end of an endless night.

And . . . gods, it *burned*.

He tipped my head up, guiding me to meet his gaze.

He was the embodiment of perfection. Eyes as brilliant as dawn over the desert and tan skin dusted with embers. His crown, a glowing orb of the sun, hovered behind his head, framing cascading waves of gold that swayed in an invisible breeze, burning off into infinity like rays of dawn. He smelled of tomorrow and yesterday and eternity.

"Rise, a'mara." His voice was the wind and the sky and the earth. It reverberated through my every muscle. Deeper still, into my soul.

A'mara.

The tongue of the gods, for *my bride of the sun.* My title as one of Atroxus's rare chosen ones. A word I hadn't heard in so long.

I obeyed, swaying slightly on my feet. I had imagined so many times what I would do, what I would say, in this moment. Yet, the swell of emotions still shocked me. I expected the joy, the relief, the amazement. What I didn't quite expect was the little ball of complicated anger beneath all of it—the petulant child inside me crying out, *Why weren't you there when I needed you?*

I couldn't stop crying—I'd never been good at holding back tears. I hated that about myself right now. A long time ago, Atroxus had found all my silly mortal vices amusing. I found it hard to imagine he still thought so after all these years. Vices were only charming when you were young and innocent, and I wasn't anymore.

"I never—I never—"

I never doubted you, I was trying to say. And I told myself it was true—that even on my loneliest days, when I could only see the dawn through cracks in the curtains, when the hole in my heart that had once held the sun felt so empty that my chest ached for a stake, I knew he would come back.

I told myself it was true, even though I wasn't sure if it was.

"I was always faithful, my light," I managed. "Always."

His warmth wavered, the distant caress of a cool breeze over my face. His gaze lowered, fingertips tracing my jaw and running down to my throat. Vampires didn't scar the way humans did. The bite that had Turned me left no mark—not on my flesh, or even on my mind, the memories eaten away by the sickness that killed my human self and remade me vampire.

But at Atroxus's caress, fragments of those lost moments flashed through my mind—full lips, cool as night, pressing against my flesh, and a soft, sensuous voice. I had the powerful urge to cover my throat, knowing that he was looking right at that fifty-year-old wound.

Instead, I touched the burns on my arms. Normally, I was ashamed of them because they were marks of everything I'd lost. Now, I wanted to bear them as badges of honor, physical marks of decades of commitment.

A silent satisfaction settled over him, as if those marks—proof I was willing to bleed for my faith—were enough to satisfy him.

He straightened, drawing himself up to his full majestic height.

"I come to you with a matter of great importance."

I wiped my tears away with the back of my hand. I tore my gaze away from him long enough to take in my surroundings. I stood surrounded by hazy nothingness, which I recognized as the nebulous space between consciousness and unconsciousness. Atroxus's presence had overwhelmed me, but I could see now that he appeared to me at just a fraction of his true greatness—his form faded, his light dimmed.

"I cannot venture into Nyaxia's territory," he said, as if hearing my unspoken realization. "At least, not without inconvenient consequences. Even here, my time is short, and we have much to discuss. We stand on the precipice of a great darkness."

A great darkness.

The House of Shadow. Nyaxia's mission. Necromancy.

Asar's mission: to resurrect the god of death.

"They plan to—" I started.

"I am aware." Atroxus's voice grew grim. "I have heard whispers of it. I long suspected Nyaxia would make another attempt at rebellion. But I did not have confirmation of it, until I saw that truth through you."

My tattoo pulsed, as if reacting to his voice. The realization dawned on me—that this was why he had finally answered my call. Not to save my life, but because I'd been acting as his spy without even knowing it.

I pushed away a brief stab of disappointment.

"But that can't be possible," I said. "To resurrect a *god*?"

"It is an abomination." He spat the word, the light around him flaring like a freshly fed flame. "But Nyaxia has no limit to her depravity. A major deity cannot kill another of our own. These are the rules set out upon our making an eternity ago, a bid to prevent us from falling into wars against ourselves." A sneer flitted over his nose. "What little good such rules have done."

The hairs prickled at the back of my neck. No, no divine rules had managed to keep the gods from their infighting. The twelve major deities of the White Pantheon had, at least, managed to stay unified for the most part, though they certainly still had their drama.

But what they had done to Alarus was far more than a petty argument. Alarus and Nyaxia had defied the White Pantheon with their marriage. Atroxus, joined by five other gods, had lured Alarus to a private meeting with promises of a pardon for Nyaxia.

Instead, they had killed him.

The betrayal had shaken the immortal and mortal worlds down to their bones.

"So does that mean that Alarus is . . . alive?" I whispered.

"No. He is far from alive. But my siblings and I could not snuff out his soul forever, either. So, that night, we did what we could. We sliced open my brother's heart. We cut his body into pieces and scattered him, believing that whatever small shards of his soul might remain somewhere could never be restored to him. It was all we could do to prevent a war that would consume the mortal worlds."

Atroxus's eyes darkened, clouds passing over the dawn, and for a moment I felt like I had been there—that night two thousand years ago, watching six gods hack apart Alarus's body. And still, despite my commitment to the god that had chosen me, the brutality of it made my chest ache. Nyaxia had gone mad with grief when she was given Alarus's head—a grief that had made her powerful enough to defeat the rest of the White Pantheon and stake out her own kingdom in her husband's abandoned territory. A grief that had driven her to create a following of her own—vampires.

"The death we gave Alarus was the death of mortals," Atroxus said. "It is not a true death. Necromancy, given the right tools, does not require an intact body."

So if a mortal soul could be resurrected, Alarus's could, too.

"But why now? Nyaxia has grieved her husband for two millennia. Why didn't she try before?"

"In the battles in the House of Night, Nyaxia has now witnessed her own husband's remains defiled and used as weapons among her own followers. At the culmination of that same battle, she, too, witnessed a goddess of the White Pantheon act against her. She is staking her claim among human nations. She is hungry for power." His lip curled in disgust. "Nyaxia's madness has been growing since the moment she left the White Pantheon. Alas, now, she shatters. Just as I could not kill Alarus myself, she cannot resurrect him herself, either. So instead, she turns to her children to do this work for her. An irrational decision, but who can say why Nyaxia acts as she does?"

Who can say? I resisted the impulse to laugh at him for that question—because for all that a god understood of the universe, how could something so painfully simple be beyond him?

Nyaxia had always struck me as the most human, the most fallible, of the gods. Her story was one of all those imperfect mortal emotions—love, lust, grief, rage. She had been a young lesser goddess confined to a life of servitude. She'd broken out and found her freedom—found love—only to have it ripped away from her as punishment.

She had built a kingdom on top of her loss, but that didn't do a thing to heal the wound.

Still, that didn't mean she wasn't dangerous. Nothing was more deadly than a hurting person pushed to a breaking point.

Atroxus leveled a piercing gaze to mine. "Whatever version of Alarus that Nyaxia succeeds in bringing back, whether she is successful or not, will be a source of great power. You understand this."

Gods, I did. I had helped Raihn and Oraya fight for their rule of the House of Night, where fragments of Alarus's *teeth* had been used to horrific ends. It was power that no mortal should wield. Power that very nearly toppled an empire. All from a few shards of bone.

A resurrection could rip apart the world.

"She will destroy," Atroxus said. "Indiscriminately. She will wage war on the White Pantheon. She will scorch the human nations. She will never stop."

With every word, he showed me a glimpse of that future—the Citadel of the Destined Dawn soaked in blood and scattered with broken bodies, the seas boiling, the skies alight. It was everything that had once haunted my nightmares before my time at the Citadel, but many times over. I knew what war did to innocents. And I knew that a war between gods would be unimaginable.

The visions drowned me. When I became aware of myself again, I was on my knees, retching against an empty stomach.

Atroxus stood before me, tilting my head up again, his touch so comforting that I didn't even care about the burns on my cheeks.

"You came to me with this because—because you want me to sabotage it," I said. "You need me to make sure his mission fails."

But Atroxus shook his head. "No. You must ensure he succeeds."

My brows leapt. "Succeeds?"

"One cannot kill what is not alive. Alarus's resurrection provides a path to his true death. Indeed, it may be the only opportunity the White Pantheon will ever get to kill him permanently."

"But—but how will you do that?"

Atroxus caressed my cheek, his touch the kiss of a thousand suns.

"I will not, a'mara," he said. "You will."

CHAPTER SEVEN

For the second time in a single day, I found myself speechless. My lips parted and no words came out.

I will kill a god.

I could imagine that Raihn or Oraya might be capable of killing a god. They were the kind of people who would look very good immortalized in tapestries and paintings, wielding their fancy magical blades.

Not me. I was a priestess. A scholar. A bringer of the light.

For some reason, Asar's sneer danced through my head: *crusader.*

I managed to get out, "No mortal has *ever* killed a god."

"Alarus's state will be greatly weakened in the aftermath of his resurrection." Atroxus spoke like he was offering reassurance to a nervous child. "His flesh will be tender as a mortal's. His heart soft as a human's."

I will kill a god.

"Nyaxia's necromancer will need to travel through the five Sanctums of the Descent between the mortal world and the underworld. He will need to recover a relic from each, placed there by Alarus before his death. I could not tamper with my brother's magics, but I did what I could to lock them away in anticipation of these very events. The necromancer will need the magic of the sun to claim them."

Hence why Asar was collecting followers of Atroxus. Because he knew that the relics he'd need for the resurrection ceremony had been barred by the magic of the sun.

But my head spun around these logistics. I couldn't think about the *how*. I was still stuck on the *what*.

I will kill a god.

"You will find a weapon within the Descent that will have the power to pierce a god's flesh," Atroxus went on. "You will know it when it presents itself to you. But the less I tell you now, the better. You must guard your thoughts against the necromancer. You must ensure that he sees as little of your truth as possible."

Because thought was a vulnerability in the presence of a Shadow-born.

I imagined myself standing before Alarus. I imagined myself plunging a sword through his chest.

I will kill a god.

Oh, gods. I was going to vomit.

"I—I—"

The words *I can't* danced on the tip of my tongue. They were dirty words, never to be spoken. They could *especially* never be spoken to Atroxus.

I forced myself to my feet. Forced myself to meet Atroxus's gaze once more. He was fading more now, the brilliance of his light wavering, his body slightly translucent. But still, he was so painfully beautiful.

I thought of my offering day—my wedding day, in all the ways that mattered. I'd been wearing such a gorgeous dress, so heavy with beading and embellishment that it physically dragged me down before the altar. When Atroxus had appeared to me to accept my vows, I'd thought that at sixteen, I was already the luckiest woman in the world.

I had promised myself to him that morning. I'd promised him my body, my love, my loyalty. I had promised him both my life and my death. And I had promised him that I would devote my eternal soul to bringing the light to the edges of the horizon, no matter what it took.

Because I was special. Not because I was *born* special—I wasn't, I was nobody—but because he had *made* me special by choosing me that day. Choosing me over my sister, even though she'd deserved it more.

And what had I done with that gift?

It was impossible not to think about the last time he'd stood before me like this, entrusting me with a task. So much had changed.

He watched me, solemn. "You are afraid."

A painful lump rose in my throat, a knot of all the questions I was so afraid to ask.

"Why are you trusting me with this?" I said. "After . . ."

"After you failed."

I flinched.

He said it so simply. And yes, *failed* was such an ugly word. But it was also far too light for the truth of what had happened. *Failure* wasn't powerful enough to describe the images that haunted me in the darkness—darkness I could no longer escape at all.

I blinked away the unwelcome memories. A pretty boy's face with a missing jaw. My sister's body lying in the dusty dirt, throat open, blood crusted on torn flesh.

Failure.

"Yes," I said softly. "After I failed you."

Because he had sent me to Obitraes to spread the light. And I'd been so gods-damned arrogant.

He stepped closer, his light burning my cheeks. He looked at me with a shade of pity.

"Tell me, a'mara, why did I choose you all those years ago?"

I asked myself that question so many times.

A tear slithered down my cheek.

"I don't know, my light," I admitted.

I almost said, *Maybe I did a long time ago.*

But that would've been a lie, too, and I couldn't lie to a god. Even when I'd shone brightest, at the height of everything I'd once been, I'd never known—really *known*—why Atroxus had chosen me that morning. Every time I thought I did, I'd look at Saescha and doubt it all over again.

He touched my face, as if surveying a piece of fruit. "I found you amusing, yes. But there was more, too. Gods can smell fate upon a soul. And yours . . ." He lowered his lashes, drawing in the inhale of a summer breeze. "Yours smelled of revelation. I can still sense it there, beneath the stench of rot. One day, it will be gone, but that day has not yet come."

He pulled back, his eyes meeting mine. I wanted to look away. I wanted to hide myself.

"I sent you to Obitraes to be the force of that revelation I sensed upon you," he said. "You brought your fellow acolytes with you to help you fulfill it. Your mission is not yet over. Your entire life has led to this. The lives of your parents and grandparents. The lives of your ancestors. Do you not want your redemption?"

My parents had been poor farmers in a country half a world away from the Order of the Destined Dawn. They'd been casual worshippers of Vitarus, god of the harvest, as most farmers were—or at least, that's what Saescha told me of them, because I didn't remember them myself. When I thought of the home I'd had before the Citadel, I thought only of Saescha. Saescha had her makeshift altars for a god that no one else in our town worshipped, Saescha and her commitment to a cause that everyone else rolled their eyes at. When things had gotten bad, Saescha had said that the light would save us, and she had been right.

Atroxus spoke to me of fate and prophecy; he spoke of the things priests bellowed in church services every dawn. He spoke of *purpose*. The kind of purpose that any acolyte of any god would lay down their lives for.

And yet, I wasn't thinking of my parents and grandparents and ancestors, or prophecy, or my name upon the scriptures of the Citadel.

I thought of my friends, who would be ripped apart in the jaws of a war between gods.

I thought of the people who had trusted me, who had followed me on this cursed mission to begin with, and who deserved to die for a greater purpose than the one I'd given them.

Do you not want your redemption? he asked me.

I didn't care about my redemption. But gods, I would give anything for theirs. To make it all worth something in the end. To finish the holy mission that I'd started with them.

"Yes," I whispered. "I do."

His approval fell over me like the final warm rays of waning dusk.

"You have always amused me so," he said. And for just a moment, the way he looked at me seemed almost like the way a mortal husband might look at a mortal wife. I fought the sudden urge to embrace him, let him wrap me up in his arms like the sun against the bleached white sands.

But of course, we didn't have that kind of marriage, and that wasn't the kind of comfort he offered me. Our binding ceremony was more about faith than love, the night after it more of a physical offering than a lovemaking session.

Still, a piece of me longed for that—for what Oraya and Raihn shared when I watched them laughing together in the halls of the Nightborn Palace, or the way they held each other after their nearest brush with death.

But one couldn't expect a god to love you like a mortal did. A greater gift, still, to have that love at all. And Atroxus's, I knew, was very much conditional.

The dream had begun to disintegrate around him, the rays of light around his form dyed red like the blood of a future that hadn't yet come to pass.

A future that, I vowed, wouldn't come to pass.

"This task is the most crucial of your life, a'mara," he said. "Speak of this to no one. I cannot follow where you go. But know that my light is with you."

There was no question, no *Do you accept?* But why would there be? It wasn't a choice.

Atroxus reached for me as he faded, and I fell to my knees before him.

"I won't fail," I whispered. "I promise."

And I pressed my mouth against his outstretched hand, the kiss scorched upon my lips.

PART TWO

BODY

INTERLUDE

*T*he blessed girl lived a blessed life in her new home. Sometimes she missed things about her old life, but she had been so young when she lost it—it was easy to replace those memories with new ones, little stone homes with grand monasteries, empty kitchen cupboards with banquet tables overflowing with fruit. "She's such an adaptable child," she would hear her sister saying to the other adults, and the little girl did not know what adaptable meant, but she certainly recognized her sister's tone of pride when she said it. It was easy to patch up any little pangs of homesickness with that pride, especially when her sister was just so happy here.

What was there to miss of their life before anyway? Only brief weeks or months of comfort carved out of farmer's shacks and covered wagons before they were inevitably chased off again. Here, everyone was nice to them. They were not pests to be driven away. No one came in the middle of the night to tell them they had to leave. They even let the little girl eat all the apricots she wanted. And the girl's sister smiled as she had never seen her smile before. She'd always been an attractive woman, but here, she was as effervescent as the dawn that had led them to the Citadel steps.

This, the little girl decided quickly, was a good place. She was so grateful to Atroxus for letting them stay.

The priests got very excited when Atroxus came to visit the girl, spending a long time fixing her dress or her hair and handing her bouquets of fresh flowers to hold when she met him. The little girl thought this was all a bit silly. When she used to see the stained glass portrayals of gods, she thought they looked terribly frightening. But Atroxus was not frightening at all. He was always kind to her. He laughed with her at her silly games and did not even mind at all if it messed up her hair or her dress. But the little girl let her sister fuss over her appearance anyway because she could tell it made her feel better.

Anyway, Atroxus didn't come to visit that often, only on several sacred holy days per year. The rest of the time, the little girl slipped easily into life in the monastery. She squirmed and struggled her way through the dull lectures in the libraries, but thrived under the priests' magic instruction. Nothing made her feel more alive than wielding the power of the sun. It was carefree and joyful and fun. She studied all magics under Atroxus's domain—magics that manipulated the light woven into the fabric of the world itself. She and her sister practiced endlessly, even after dark, when their lessons were long over.

On her free days, she would run in the forests with her best friend, a young boy around her age. She loved to watch the golden birds flit around in the trees. The first time she saw one, she'd breathlessly proclaimed it to be the most beautiful creature she'd ever seen.

The groundskeeper had scoffed at that.

"Invasive buggers," he'd grumbled. "Some priest five generations ago brought them over here as pets for his concubine. Set them out in the forest when she left him and they've been multiplying ever since. Won't stop nesting in the rafters. I'll have to cull them soon."

It wasn't the birds' fault that their great-great-great-grandparents had been dragged here, the little girl wanted to say, but her sister told her to never argue with the priests, so she let it go. Besides, as much as the groundskeeper complained about the birds, he never harmed them, and she was content to watch them dance around the treetops to their dulcet songs.

The months slipped by like that—a blur of light and prayer and adoration.

The little girl had been at the Citadel for one full year the first time she saw one of the accursed—the first time she saw a vampire.

The girl knew that some priests of the Citadel were warriors. She saw the weapons hanging in the armory. She saw the scars on their faces. She was no stranger to violence, but she was content to let that ugliness exist out there, somewhere where the light did not touch.

The day it arrived at her doorstep, she was playing with her friend in the gardens near the front gate when a great calamity rose from the steps below. She and her friend ran to the doors just in time to see a gaggle of men dragging a figure inside. They watched around the doorframe as the crowd parted. They *fought a man to the ground before Atroxus's altar. The little girl recognized him; he was one of the younger warriors, and he always had a soft word and a sweet smile for her sister. He had been handsome and kind.*

Not now.

Now, his face was distorted in vicious snarls, his teeth bared and dripping red, skin pale and sweat-slicked. When the stream of sun through the stained glass fell across his face, he howled, the scent of burning flesh filling the air.

Shouts blurred together as more acolytes rushed into the chapel. The girl's sister was among them. They had forced the man to his knees. Days ago, these men had been brothers. Now, they held him down as he screamed.

The girl's sister spotted her across the room. She rushed to her.

"You shouldn't see this," she whispered, ready to usher the children away. But the head priest called out, "No. Let them stay. A future bride of the sun should witness the truth of the darkness."

Her sister hesitated, but she was not one to disobey a command. And so the two children watched, unblinking, horrified, as the priests rolled the man over and pinned him down upon the mosaic floor. They splayed his limbs, aligning him to the perfect golden circle of the sun through the window. And then the girl's sister had been handed the blade, and she had been the one to drive it through the center of his chest, black blood spewing over her face.

Afterward, the little girl ran to the gardens, hoping the fresh air might ease the nausea. She looked up into the trees at the firefinches playing in the leaves. She watched one land on a branch before her, tweeting a greeting. She let out an unsteady breath. Her heartbeat slowed a little. But then—

THUNK. The bird toppled to her feet, black eyes wide open and gold feathers smeared red. An arrow jutted from its chest.

"Good distraction, little priestess!" came the distant cry of the groundskeeper. "One down, just a few hundred to go!"

The girl stared at the dead bird.

Then she fell to her knees and vomited in the rosebushes.

CHAPTER EIGHT

et up.

At first, it was Atroxus saying it, the echo of his voice haunting me like a ghost.

Get up.

GET UP.

Something hard and cold nudged my shoulder, right over one of my remaining wounds from Egrette's beating.

"Ow!" I yelped.

My eyes snapped open.

Luce glowered down at me.

My head was pounding. The memory of Atroxus's visit haunted me. My gaze flicked down to my arm—where my tattoo sat beneath my sleeve—but I knew without looking at it that it wouldn't be glowing anymore. Still, I had no doubts that the meeting had been real, not a dream, and the consequences of it made my head spin.

I will kill a god.

I let out a long, shaky breath, steadying myself beneath the weight of my task, which struck me all over again.

I just had to travel to the underworld with my Shadowborn captor, resurrect the god of death, and then kill him—ideally without starting another war of either the mortal or immortal varieties.

I tried to tell myself that it sounded no less outlandish than any of my other reckless missions.

Tried.

And anyway, a cruel voice whispered in the back of my mind, *how did those end?*

Another blunt shove, somehow in just the right place to be as painful as possible, had me yelping again.

"Fine, fine." I raised my hands. "I'm getting up, Luce."

She thrust her snout to the ground beside her. A pile of clothes sat, neatly folded, next to her. They appeared to be practical leathers, not quite armor but only a few steps from it.

The message was clear: *change.*

I picked up the clothing, unfolding the shirt—a white blouse in the House of Shadow style, loose with a leather vest designed to go over it, and tight-fitting black pants with boots that reached their knees. Not my style, but I'd take it in a heartbeat over my stained, dirty dress, which now reeked of my blood and gods knew what else.

"Privacy?" I asked. "Please?"

I wasn't especially modest, but getting ogled by a skull wolf was a little much even for me. I was a priestess, after all.

Luce didn't dignify that with a response.

Figured.

I sighed and began to strip.

THE CLOTHES WERE restrictive, but at least they were clean, so I instantly felt more prepared for what I was about to do. Marginally. I'd take what I could get.

Luce led me through another conjured door, then down Morthryn's winding hallways. This time, instead of going up, we went down—down stairways that coiled like dueling snakes. The vegetation on the walls grew thicker with every turn. Ivy and roses crunched beneath my feet. It got darker, and darker, and darker. When I was Turned, I'd been forced to embrace the darkness, but I had never stopped mourning the sun. And here, in shadows so deep that they strained even vampire eyes, it felt so painfully far away.

Eventually, we came to a door—a single circle of stone nestled among overgrown roses. At a nudge of Luce's nose, it creaked open, and I peered inside.

The hairs stood at the back of my neck. This was an old, old place—my bones reacted to it, like the pressure of a body crushed under the ocean. I felt time—thousands of years, pressing down on my shoulders, their weight oppressive. There was no decoration here, just plain, smooth stone. An archway revealed a set of stairs that spiraled down.

The room was empty, save for one woman who sat on the floor, back to the wall. The smell hit me before the sight of her did—the thick, sweet scent of human blood.

The woman's eyes fell to me. They were pale blue, bracketed by faint lines. She twirled a long strand of wavy black-and-silver hair in one wrinkled hand. She wore an outfit that was a near exact match to mine—white shirt, black leather vest, plain trousers. A small gold emblem dangled around her throat.

It took me a moment to recognize her. After all, she looked so different when she wasn't dead.

And—gods—she really, really wasn't dead. She was so alive that it briefly made me question my sanity—had I really seen her corpse? Had I really helped bring it back to life?

Chandra lifted one hand. "Hello." She had a lovely voice, youthful and melodic, even though the word was uncertain.

It was one thing to know, logically, that necromancy was possible. It was a whole other thing to see the results of it right in front of you.

I heard the echo of Asar's voice—*Are you excited or horrified?*

I smiled at Chandra and waved back. "Hello."

She shied away as I stepped closer. I stopped short, pinching my lips closed as my tongue pressed to the tip of my pointed teeth.

"It's all right. You don't have to worry about me like that." I settled on the ground next to her, keeping a healthy space between us. "I'm . . ."

I almost said, *Like you*. But of course, I wasn't, was I?

Instead, I opened my palm and summoned a wisp of flame.

Chandra's fear fell away. Her eyes lit up.

"A vampire who wields the power of Atroxus," she gasped. "I've never seen such a thing."

Her accent sounded painfully familiar. It had been so long since I'd been to the human nations that the memory of the many languages I'd once known now blended together. Still, the affectation was slight. She'd been in Obitraes a long time.

How old was she? She was maybe a hard sixty years or an easy seventy. I guessed closer to the former.

Her face broke into a smile. I found myself appreciating the lines that framed her eyes and mouth. Wrinkles had grown so much more lovely to me once I'd realized I would never bear them myself. I liked being around humans. They reminded me of home.

She looked nothing like Saescha—her skin was freckled, eyes fair—but when she made the sign of the sun over her chest just like my sister used to, a raw familiarity twisted in my chest. Maybe Saescha's hands would look like these if she'd gotten the chance to grow old.

"How are—" I stopped myself. How much did Chandra remember of what had happened to her, I wondered? Did she remember her death? Did she even know she'd died?

Finally, I settled on, "Are you feeling all right?"

Her smile wavered. "Sweet girl," she murmured. "You're trying so hard to spare my feelings, and for that, Light bless you. He told me what happened to me. Though I admit, I don't know if it's sunk in." She rubbed her temple. "I feel . . . odd. Like I drank too much wine last night. I felt like I was sleeping. I don't remember . . . how it happened. It's a shadow out of the corner of my eye. I was there. Now I am here." She smiled weakly. "Perhaps that's for the best."

Every word of it was uncomfortably familiar—from her description to the forced smile. My Turning was a mangled blur in my head, the memories directionless paint smears that didn't form a complete picture. I remembered my arrival in Obitraes. I remembered waking up in an inn with Raihn leaning over me. Everything in between . . .

Well, perhaps that was for the best, too.

She leaned closer, a line of worry between her brows. "Did he tell you what he plans to—"

Behind me, the door opened. Chandra's eyes lifted over my shoulder, her mouth closing instantly. Strange, how I felt him before I saw him—the cold sensation of shadow falling over my back.

I turned to see Asar in the doorway. Luce trotted over to him to wind around his legs. Though he'd given Chandra and me clothing akin to armor, he apparently didn't think he needed any such protection. He wore the same black pants and black shirt and a long leather jacket. A pack was slung over one shoulder, and a sword hung at his hip in an ornate copper sheath that glinted, barely visible, beneath his coat.

He barely glanced at us.

"You both look rested," he said, striding across the room. "Good. We have a long journey ahead. Get up. Let's go."

I got to my feet, confused.

"Go where?" I said.

Asar gave me a pitying look, like I was very stupid. He really never missed an opportunity to do that.

I sighed. "Yes, the underworld, I know. I got that part. But it's just—aren't we in a basement right now?"

I couldn't make any more sense of the layout of Morthryn than before, when Luce led me down here. But I knew we'd only gone one direction: down. I'd heard lots of stories about journeys to the underworld, most of them ancient, most of them fictional, and most of them vague on the *how* part. I imagined that opening such a passage would take an immense amount of magic.

"We have a long walk ahead, Dawndrinker," Asar said wearily. He dumped the pack on the ground and knelt down to rummage through it. "I assume your legs and mouth can work at the same time."

He was such an ass.

"Well," I muttered, "you're in a hurry—"

The door flew open hard enough to slam against the wall, the *BOOM* of metal against stone clapping through the room. Chandra jumped. I spun around.

A tall, broad-shouldered man stood in the door, wearing Shadowborn military leathers and a long green cloak. His hair was wet and messy. He held a blade in one hand, which dripped red blood onto the floor.

He looked *pissed*.

His face was so contorted in his obvious fury that it took me a moment to recognize him: the princess's guard. The one who had been with her in my cell.

"Did you think that would fucking work?" he snarled.

Asar did not bother to turn. But from my angle, I could see the wince flit across his face. I *felt* it, too—a fleeting pang of frustration.

"You're late," he said coolly. "Weren't you supposed to be here at nightfall?"

"You sent me on a Mother-damned goose chase."

Asar straightened slowly. He peered over his shoulder and flicked a cold, nonchalant glance at the door.

"Did the moat get you? Easy mistake. No shame in getting lost, Elias. Morthryn is a complicated place."

I pressed my lips together tight, trying very hard not to have any expression. Suddenly, I understood why Asar had been in such a rush to depart.

Elias's rage collected in the room like smoke.

"You were leaving," he said.

"We couldn't wait for you." Asar turned back to his pack. "Besides, perhaps you're more useful here. There might be important guarding work that needs doing. Peasants that need slaughtering. Women that need beating. Royal rings that need kissing. That sort of thing."

Women that need beating. He cast just the quickest glance my way at that, tossing me a leather pack. I caught it. It took me a moment to realize that line had been referring to *me*. The entire string of insults, in fact, had been delivered so smoothly that it took a few seconds for them to sink in.

It was impressive. If he was anywhere near as good at physical assassination as he was at verbal assassination, no wonder he'd earned himself an intimidating nickname.

Elias stepped into the room, letting the door slam behind him. Chandra jumped again at the sound, falling back into the shadows.

"That's terribly hypocritical of you, isn't it, Asar?"

"That's not my title." Asar handed the second pack to Chandra, who took it like a mouse snatching a piece of cheese from a trap.

A vein pulsed erratically at Elias's temple.

"My prince," he ground out between his teeth.

Asar still didn't deign to even glance at Elias, but a smirk flickered across his lips.

So, *so* petty.

"I'm not here by the command of the princess," Elias said. "I am here by the command of the king. And surely you know, *my prince,* that despite your newfound position of heir, you're still bound by your oaths to him, as I am. So—and please, correct me if I'm mistaken—I don't think you're in a position to turn me away."

Asar's smile disappeared. A muscle now twitched at his jaw.

Oaths. I got the feeling that we were speaking of something much deeper than typical vows of loyalty. The most powerful of the Shadowborn were known to use their powers of compulsion to create bonds of absolute blood loyalty among their key followers. It was difficult and rare, but Raoul was certainly capable of it.

Asar's resentment wafted from him like smoke. He was silent for a long moment as he closed up his pack, then stood and slung it over his shoulder.

"Fine," he said. "Good timing. We were just going."

A breeze rustled my curls into my eyes. I adjusted my bag over my shoulder and wrangled them back into submission with my free hand.

"So—going where, exactly?" I chanced. "We're still in—"

"Morthryn," Asar said. "Yes."

He stood at the other door, that cavernous arch where stairs disappeared into nothingness. The wind picked up when he ventured closer, and another gentle gust had me swallowing the cold scent of flower petals.

The darkness called to me. I found myself stepping closer, closer—

A hand caught my arm.

"Careful," Asar said.

I couldn't tear my eyes away from the staircase. Nothing about it looked unusual. Indeed, it was downright plain compared to everything else I'd seen of Morthryn—narrow stone spiral stairs with walls devoid of any decoration, not even lanterns to light the way.

It reminded me of an open mouth swallowing a great inhale.

"Don't you know what this place is, child?" Chandra said softly.

More than a prison.

Morthryn was a relic from another time, when this land was still the territory of Alarus, before vampires existed at all. Of course it was more than a place to let criminals rot, and of course its true nature would be kept from the other vampire Houses.

I could smell it. Taste it. Death.

No wonder.

I looked at Asar, wide-eyed.

"It's a door," I said.

"Bridge would probably be a more accurate comparison." He gazed down into the darkness with the affection of one greeting an old friend. "A bridge to the underworld."

ASAR WAS WRONG. It wasn't a bridge. Bridges were flat. Nice and flat and straight.

This was a staircase. A staircase comprised of, surely, at least one million stairs. Stairs that were *just* narrow enough and *just* steep enough that you couldn't quite get a good rhythm with the pace of your steps.

My thighs burned. Chandra was already swaying, and we hadn't even made it to the actual Descent yet. It seemed a little cruel to put her through this when she'd died a few days ago, especially given that she was a sixty-odd-year-old human.

I was grateful, at least, that Asar decided to offer up some real information as we dragged ourselves down staircase after staircase.

"We'll need to travel through the five Sanctums of the Descent," Asar told us while we walked. He was not out of breath, and I hated him for it. "Body, Breath, Psyche, Secrets, and Soul. To resurrect anyone else, it's enough to merely bring together representations of each of the five elements of a mortal being. But we aren't talking about a mortal."

My brow knitted. "So the five elements of Alarus's essence are . . . in the path to the underworld? Why?"

I couldn't keep the note of eager curiosity from my voice. I wished I could pretend that my interest was solely in service of my task. Even the oldest scriptures didn't talk about Alarus much. He'd been dead for two thousand years, and after his death, Nyaxia had turned his territories into the vampire kingdoms. Every other god had acolytes to spread the word of their scriptures and practice their magic. But no one had worshipped Alarus for a long time, and that meant most of his mythos had been lost to time.

"The mortal world and the underworld are both far older than the Descent," Asar said. "Alarus understood that death was a journey, not a stark end. He wanted to ease the transition from life to death."

"Right. Hence the Sanctums." I knew this part, at least. "So mortals can shed life piece by piece."

"Yes. But even by god standards, constructing a new realm was an intimidating project. He would have had to offer a part of himself to each Sanctum. And those relics are the only things we know of that are powerful enough to fuel his resurrection." A pause, and then, pointedly, he said, "Your sun god, apparently, knew that, too. He put measures in place to prevent anyone from attempting exactly what we're about to do."

"He did?" I tried to sound surprised, but not too surprised. Just the right amount of surprised. "So that's why you need us?"

"Yes. That, Dawndrinker, is why I need you."

"Gods help us," Chandra murmured to herself.

Asar was several steps ahead of me, and he didn't look back as he spoke. Even with vampire eyesight, I could only just make out his silhouette—square shoulders, a mess of dark hair, the flowing shape of his jacket. Fittingly impenetrable.

"Did Nyaxia tell you all this?" I asked.

A beat. "Yes."

That was a partial truth if I'd ever heard one.

I wondered what that meeting had looked like. Did Nyaxia come to Asar in his cluttered office back at the surface? Did he fall to his knees in prostration before her, just like I'd done for Atroxus?

I found it hard to imagine Asar prostrating in general. He didn't seem like the type who went to his knees easily, goddess or no. Even his deference to the king had been so palpably resentful.

I wondered what Nyaxia had told him. The unwanted images of Atroxus's vision flashed through my mind—the Citadel in flames, the blood-red sky, the ocean shores littered with maimed bodies.

Did Asar know what would happen if he succeeded? Had Nyaxia spun a different future for him? Or had she simply offered him something he wanted so much that he didn't care?

"What if Alarus should stay dead?"

I blurted out the question before I meant to and instantly regretted it. Gods damn my mouth.

Asar stopped short. I nearly tumbled into him, catching myself just in time to avoid colliding with his back, but I still found myself only inches away when he turned. I was two steps behind, which put us nearly nose to nose. His left eye was bright silver, like a cloud-shrouded moon.

"What if Alarus should stay dead?" He put great emphasis on every word, like he was speaking to a small child, and a stupid one at that.

This sparked a little flame of aggravation. He was acting like it was a foolish question, but it wasn't.

"If you're so well-read, you must know that messing with the affairs of gods can be catastrophic," I said. "What makes you think that it would be a *good* thing to bring Alarus back?"

Asar's face was still as marble. "Was it *a good thing*"—he drew out the phrase with sharp stabs of sarcasm—"that Alarus was killed to begin with?"

"Well, it wasn't *good*, but it was—" *Necessary* felt like a cruel term. I bit it back. "The White Pantheon thought they were protecting the peace."

"And did they protect the peace?"

"They avoided war."

"You say that because hellfire didn't rain down from the skies. But there are many ways to wage a war, Iliae. I know that better than most. I suspect the vampires your kind dismembered for their holy offerings knew it, too."

My face was hot. He started to turn away, but—stupidly, recklessly—I grabbed his shoulder and pulled him back.

"I've been caught up in other people's wars my entire life," I said. "I *do* know what that means. And that's why I know that it's not a decision to—"

A wave of cold passed over me. A shiver ran up my left arm, the one holding Asar's shoulder, and then the next thing I knew, it was at my side again. I looked down to see wriggling black waves rolling across my skin like sand blowing over the dunes, encircling my hand before melting back into the stone.

"I don't make this decision lightly," Asar snapped. "If you have objections you'd like to take up with the Dark Mother, you are welcome to. Or, I can hand you back over to my sister and let her send your head to the House of Night, if that's a war you'd find more acceptable."

I shut my mouth, though it took considerable effort.

Words had always been my most valuable weapon—more powerful than the magic, even. They were the lantern I used to peer inside people and then lead them wherever they needed to go.

But that wasn't the task I'd been given. And besides, Asar was not going to be led anywhere. That was abundantly clear.

"Not to interrupt this riveting discussion." Elias's voice came from several steps back, where he'd been standing behind Chandra. "But what is that?"

He pointed. I followed it to the turn in the stairs ahead.

It looked like . . . water. Like the edge of the ocean against the shore. But the boundary of it, where the liquid lapped up against the stone steps, glowed an unsettling crimson red. The movement of the ripples didn't seem quite right, too fast for the stillness of the air.

Asar's annoyance fell away.

"That," he said, "is the edge of the veil."

The membrane that separated the world of the living from the journey toward death. It was said to be lorded over by three guardians—the viper, the songbird, and the lioness.

"We'll have to pass through the veil?" Chandra whispered. "Wouldn't that mean dying?"

She was shaking more now. I wondered if her body was reacting to being so close to death yet again, so soon after she'd come back from it. Even if her mind didn't remember, her flesh would. I knew that firsthand.

"In a sense," Asar said. "Morthryn will offer us a path through, which will avoid the guardians. But it's . . . more treacherous than it used to be. Be very careful not to call attention to yourselves. And under absolutely no circumstances should you leave the path. You *must* stay on the path."

He turned and began walking, waving us to follow. The stairs narrowed, forcing us into a single line—Asar, me, Chandra, Elias, and Luce at the rear.

"Give us some credit," Elias scoffed. "I think we can manage to walk in a straight line."

Asar said, "It can be . . ."

We turned the corner. The red-rimmed not-water lapped up to my calves. It felt like warm nothingness.

The walls fell away. An endless expanse of velvet black spread out around us.

"Holy shit," I whispered.

"Gods help us," Chandra murmured, voice wavering.

"Ah," Elias said, in a tone that reluctantly conceded to Asar's concerns.

Shimmering, translucent hills extended in all directions, undulating like the sea to the horizon. Clusters of moving dots moved over them, and it took me too long to realize what I was looking at: people. Countless people, reduced to silver-lined silhouettes, dragging themselves over the doorstep of death.

The guardians loomed over all of it. A snake coiled around the dead, so massive I couldn't make sense of where her body ended or began, scales glinting like stars. Beside her, the lioness perched on her haunches, waves of light rippling over the sleek gleam of her fur. Both wore the faces of golden skulls, cavernous eyes seeing all.

The path rolled out before us in a single narrow, crumbling line of stones suspended in eternal oblivion. It passed right through the center of all of it—through the clusters of the dead, and between the two guardians.

"Intimidating," Asar finished.

I COULD'VE SWORN that the path wobbled beneath my feet. Was it possible for a bridge suspended by ancient, god-touched magic to collapse? It certainly seemed possible as I gingerly shifted my weight onto another unsteady rock. If this had been a proper bridge at one point, it was now little more than a collection of stones. Most of it was only the width of a single slab. It reminded me of the games I used to play with Eomin when we were children—trying to see who could get across the creeks with the fewest steps. Whoever got wet lost.

The stakes felt a little higher here.

The not-water was now up to my chest. Everything beneath it was cloudy and obscured. I stared down into the darkness below. I could see only a thick blanket of mist, but my body could sense that much more lingered beneath those depths.

Still, as terrifying as looking down was, it was downright comforting compared to the alternatives. The dead were just far away enough that I couldn't make out their features, and they were partially transparent, as if I saw them through sheets of gauze. But their movements were unnerving enough—lurching, graceless, silently screaming their pain and confusion. Some kept trying to turn around. Others threw their hands up to the blackened sky, reaching for life. The guardians corralled them—the viper with her serpentine body, the lioness with gentle nudges of her great paw. But despite their efforts, the dead devolved into chaos. The lines disintegrated. The souls collected into tangled masses.

"Where is the third guardian?" Elias asked in a near whisper, before I could. "The bird?" He had to turn his head to speak over his shoulder. Asar had rearranged us before we'd stepped onto the bridge—Luce taking up the lead, then Elias, Chandra, me, and Asar.

"The bird fell many years ago," Asar said. "Keep your eyes forward."

The not-water was high enough now that Luce was fully submerged. She didn't hesitate as she passed beneath it—actually, she seemed to relish it, like a mortal dog happily trotting into the sea. Elias seemed far more uncertain. He was so tall that though he was at the front of the group, it was only to his chest, while it neared Chandra's chin. I could smell her blood, hot and rushing. Hear her heartbeat quickening. She was terrified.

"Gods help us," she kept whispering.

I caught her hand, squeezing it tight.

"The water is harmless," Asar said. "Just a representation of the transition from one world to another."

"Very comforting," Elias said.

Maybe the water was harmless. But something out there wasn't. I'd watched warily out of the corner of my eye as Asar had drawn his sword behind us. It was a stunning weapon—a saber with a red blade and a copper grip, the guard forming intricate whorls of ivy around his hand. But the blade was broken, the delicate curve disrupted by a jagged edge several inches before its natural end.

Now, Asar kept it at the ready, vigilantly watching. I wasn't sure if I wanted to know for what.

I touched my own weapon, a simple sword that Asar had given me before we left. At the time, I'd been surprised he had trusted Chandra and me with weapons. Now, it felt like a toy he'd handed to a child to make them feel useful.

The not-water brushed my chin. Chandra now was beneath the surface, cringing as she ducked her head under. Even though Asar had told us it was harmless, I still found myself bracing as it swallowed me.

I felt breath on my throat. A hand on my thigh. A lush pair of lips curling into a smile. *Tell me all the ways that I have sinned.*

I shivered, forcing my eyes back open. I recognized those moments from my dreams—moments of the Turning that I couldn't remember. Fitting, I supposed, that I'd relive fragments from the last time I'd come so close to death.

Beyond the transition, the guardians seemed a little more solid, the dead a little closer. Gods, those beasts were huge. We were so close to them now. I had to crane my neck all the way back to see the underside of the lioness's golden jawbone. Still, they ignored us, preoccupied with their unruly souls.

"More than halfway," Asar said quietly.

My eyes fixed on the end of the path—where the stones disappeared into a thick cluster of fog that seemed to suggest the arched shape of what had once, maybe, been a door. But the condition of the road had worsened. There were large gaps between the stones. Chandra, the shortest of us, had to stretch her stride to reach across them. Our pace slowed. But at least the end was in sight.

Then, something struck us.

I couldn't make out what it was. It was a brief, fluttering impact, as if I'd startled a bird too close to my face. Movement blurred at the corner of my eye, but when I turned my head, nothing was there.

Ahead, Chandra startled. Elias stopped short. Even Luce halted, the hair at the back of her neck rising.

"What in the fucking Mother's name was that?" Elias said. He drew his weapon—a broadsword that was bigger than I was—and spun around, just looking for the right direction to swing it.

"Move," Asar commanded. I didn't like the tiny, tiny note of fear beneath his words. "Don't fight. Just *go*. Now."

Chandra's heartbeat was fast as a baby rabbit's. "I can't," she whispered. "I can't move—"

I clutched her hand hard.

"Tell me the hymn of the second sun," I told her. "You know that one, right? I am the line upon which dawn is drawn—"

She took a few tentative steps. "I am the movement of the sun to the horizon," she finished shakily.

Another step.

"No darkness can unmake me."

Another.

"No walls can contain—"

All at once, pitch-black swallowed me.

All senses dulled, like someone had thrown a heavy blanket over my head. For a terrifying moment I was certain I was falling, plunging into the depths of the Descent. There was nothing, no stone under my feet, no sound, no sight, and—

And then a *scream*.

A scream like a death cry. A promise of vengeance. A torn-open heart.

I'd barely clung to my balance, awkwardly lurching to right myself. My hand still clutched Chandra's. Luce's barks fell beneath the roaring drone of the blood in my ears. My fear was that of a prey animal's, illogical and uncontrollable.

Something was out there.

Something was *hunting* us.

Above, the lioness slowly lowered her chin.

I lifted my own just in time to see Elias, eyes wide, raise his weapon.

"Elias, *no*—" Asar roared.

But instinct had taken over. Elias was the kind of man who saw a threat and swung something sharp at it until it was dead.

The blur—the *thing*—swept over us again, and he lunged.

This time, that terrible death howl sounded almost like a laugh.

The path quaked beneath me, as if a giant, invisible hand had grabbed it and given it a good shake.

"Oh, gods," I gasped as my footing slipped beneath me. Someone grabbed my arm—I knew, just by the feel of it, that it was Asar. The darkness lifted just in time for me to see Elias's hulking form toppling from the stone, hand outstretched. Chandra lunged for it, but she was half his size—of course she couldn't catch him. The two of them went over together, swallowed by gray mist before I could reach for them.

Luce barked after them, turning back to look for Asar's command.

Asar muttered a string of curses and pushed me forward. "Go with her. Now."

Luce nipped at my sleeve, dragging me along.

But I hesitated. Asar's blade was raised, eyes lifting to the lioness and the viper, who now stared down at us.

But my gaze fixed on a point beyond him.

To the shadows over his shoulder that moved just oddly enough to catch my attention.

Before I could react, they rushed at him, clustering in a way that almost resembled a figure—almost resembled a cruel, smiling mouth and an outstretched arm—

I didn't think.

I dove down, down within myself, hauled the flame up to the surface with every shred of strength I had, and I threw myself in front of Asar.

We collided in a tangle of limbs. The searing light of my flames burst through the bodiless figure. An enraged shriek split the air. Somewhere in the distance, Luce barked a frantic warning.

The bottom of my stomach dropped out.

Asar gripped my shoulders. I opened my eyes. The horrible beauty of the veil framed his face. Time seemed to slow. We both understood that we were about to fall, and there was nothing we could do about it.

He looked so, so pissed.

"I told you all," he growled, "to *stay on the damned path*."

And then we plunged into oblivion.

CHAPTER NINE

I felt the burns first—fresh ones on my hands, my penance for the flame I'd used to save Asar. They throbbed fiercely.

Throbbed, and then—

"*Ow—!*" I let out half of a strangled yelp before a hand clapped over my mouth.

"Hush, Iliae," Asar said. "The dead crave the living. Let's not rush the inevitable."

I opened my eyes. We were in—some kind of cave, maybe? My back was propped up against something hard and uncomfortable. Fair, smooth stone encircled us, the empty sky visible through an opening behind Asar. He removed his hand from my face and returned to his work—on my hands, which he leaned over with a singular focus that reminded me of priests at morning prayer. I bit my lip as he finished removing a piece of burned skin and flicked it aside.

"Your god doesn't love you half as much as you think he does," he muttered. "You burned yourself to the bone. It's beyond me why Atroxus still allows you to use his magic, but be careful of the price you pay for it."

"It's not—*ffff.*" I swallowed my curse as he smoothed cool liquid over my palms.

"Almost done."

He covered my hands with his, his touch so gentle that it sent an uncomfortable shiver from the base of my spine up through my shoulder blades. Pulsing waves crawled toward us from every shadowy crevice—from beneath his arms, from between the cracks of stone, from the place where we touched. Something else inside me reacted to the call, too, reaching for the surface. It made my skin prickle, like a caress of the crest of my ear or breath against my throat. Almost ticklish, if it hadn't been so damned *pleasant*.

I couldn't stand it.

He released me just as I was about to pull away. I looked down at the red, angry burns. They usually healed slowly and scarred badly. But the wounds were already closed, and before my eyes, flesh stitched to flesh.

"It'll take some time before they're completely gone," he said. "But at least you can use your hands in the meantime."

"How do you do that?" I asked.

"The potion did most of the work."

"No, it didn't." I'd tried them all, from the cheap tonics peddled by street vendors to the expensive ointments crafted by royal healers in the House of Night. None worked this well. Injuries by the vampires' natural enemy posed a unique challenge. "How do you do that with Shadowborn magic?"

The vampires of the House of Shadow could manipulate the darkness, obscure the truth, look into minds. They could spin illusions and bend you to their will. It was the magic of deceit and secrets. Not healing.

"Shadowborn magic can bring the dead back to life," Asar said. "It's more than *deceit and secrets*."

I slammed my mind shut, hard. I'd sensed Asar's presence lingering, but I'd misattributed it to the aftereffects of his magic. Stupid mistake. "Don't do that," I grumbled.

He remained a moment longer, pushing against my mental boundaries—an intrigued hand testing a door—before withdrawing.

He stood, dusting off his jacket. "You respond better to it than most." He spoke without looking at me. "As if your body wants to return to its natural state."

He tried to sound casual, but I could feel his interest clinging to me. He was curious and trying not to be. And maybe I should've used that curiosity to fulfill more of my own, but—and this was uncharacteristic of me—I just didn't want to. I didn't want to think about why my skin was still tingling. I didn't want to listen to Asar talk about *what my body wanted*.

I'd rather ignore it all, and thankfully, he didn't press it. "We should be going to find the others," he said. "Goddess knows what kind of mess they've gotten up to already." He shot me a cold glance. "I told you to stay on the path."

The tingling was now gone.

"I didn't *mean* to fall. And the reason I did was because I was saving your life. You're welcome!"

"I've made this trip countless times. The guardians wouldn't have been an issue."

"I'm not talking about the guardians, and I think you know that."

Whatever had attacked us wasn't one of the dead, and it definitely wasn't a guardian, either. And even though I wasn't quite sure *how* I knew it, I was certain it had been targeting Asar.

Asar didn't say anything, which I took as confirmation. He slid his hands into his pockets and went to the cave entrance. I followed him.

"Anyway, where are—"

I stopped short at the mouth of the cave.

"Oh," I breathed.

Before us, a river coiled lazily through the velvet night like a snake writhing through the grass. But instead of water, it held blood. Ruby deep crimson spilled over dehydrated white dust. Tributaries split off from its main body like veins splitting into capillaries. In the distance, mountains of ivory rose into the sky, jagged as broken bones. Ruins dotted the landscape, so eroded that they were only the faintest suggestion of what they'd once been. Glistening ivory stalks topped with ridged caps of white, blue, black—every color, reduced to paint strokes in the distance—crawled over them, intertwining with the stone in an unnerving collision of man and nature.

Something warm hit the top of my head, and I looked up to see that the rivers coiled above us, too, wild as vines swaying under a brisk breeze. Some broke mid-air, blood pouring down into a water-fall before resuming their path again far below. All of it continued up into the sky, streams splitting and tangling until they disappeared beyond the mists.

"Welcome to the Descent," Asar said.

I jabbed my finger to the distance, eyes round despite myself. "Are those *mushrooms*?"

I wasn't sure why, out of everything, the giant mushrooms were the most shocking. At least the bone mountains and blood rivers seemed appropriate for a path to the underworld.

"The Sanctum of Body is the level of decay. It's where the dead shed their physical forms. So, yes."

"They're actually—"

Beautiful, I was going to say. But a breeze rustled my hair, and with it came a smell so putrid I had to cover my mouth to keep my blood breakfast from ending up in the dirt.

"Holy fucking gods. What *is* that?"

"Neglect," Asar replied bitterly. "It'll pass."

Thankfully, he was right, and I forced bile back down into my stomach as he surveyed the landscape.

"There will be a temple that acts as the epicenter of the Sanctum," he said. "Probably in there."

He pointed to the distance, where the massive mushrooms grew particularly thick around a cluster of ivory cliffs in a dense jungle of decay.

He didn't wait for my confirmation. He just started walking, and I had no choice but to follow.

"Probably?" I said. "I thought you've been here before."

"There are parts of the Sanctums that are difficult for me to go now."

Now. As if it hadn't always been that way.

"Difficult?" I said.

"Dangerous."

That was encouraging.

"What about the others?" I said. "Where are they?"

He touched his chest—the anchor. I did the same, and I could feel an ever so faint tug somewhere off in the distance.

"They made it here," he said. "Luce will have found them quickly. She'll lead them toward the temple, too. We'll come across them soon, I'm sure."

I thought about Chandra's hands, frail and human, trembling in mine.

"I hope Chandra is all right," I murmured. "She was terrified."

Asar scoffed beneath his breath. "If she'd moved faster—"

"She wasn't going to *move faster*. She was afraid. Of course she was! She died a few days ago."

"I made sure she didn't remember it."

"That doesn't make a difference. You still feel it. It's—" I shut my mouth. I felt like I'd just cut something inside me too close to the quick. "She's just a scared human."

Humans showed their emotions differently than vampires did. Even Oraya, who had trained herself all her life to hide hers. I could still smell them on her like smoke—the byproduct of burning your own vulnerability for survival.

I wondered if my fear had smelled like that once, fifty years ago, when I'd met a handsome vampire prince and realized he would kill me.

"She's not *just* anything, Iliae," Asar said. "I told you that every-one in Morthryn deserves to be here. Her affinity to Atroxus gave her forty years of life she didn't deserve in the hopes that she might be useful one day. Lucky for her, she was."

Forty years? Chandra looked to be in her sixties. So she had committed her crimes when she was in her twenties?

"What did she do that was so horrible?" I asked. It was hard to imagine frail, quiet Chandra as a true threat to any vampire.

But before Asar could answer, a jolt yanked through my chest, right over my sternum—the anchor.

At the exact same moment, a scream rang out in the distance.

This one was different from what we had heard on the path above. That had been ethereal, going beyond the physical. This was all mortal, a sound of pure physical agony. It was hoarse and gurgling, as if ripped from a broken throat.

I froze mid-step. Asar's gaze snapped to the horizon. He let out a hiss of frustration between his teeth.

The sound was soon joined by others—more and more shrieks until they fused to a formless cacophony.

"That'll be them," Asar muttered.

I followed his stare.

The figures in the distance were so tightly packed that, at first, they looked like a single writhing mass. But no, they were people . . . or at least, they had been once. Now, even this far away, I could see that something was very wrong with them. They moved in fits and starts, bodies lurching, limbs bending in discordant directions. And at their front, running toward the temple, were three familiar forms: one bearing a sword, one bearing light, and a wolf made of shadow.

"Holy gods," I whispered, but Asar was already off, strides long and quick. I had to awkwardly run to keep up with him.

"What are those?"

I almost didn't want to ask.

"Death is hungry," he said. "Starving for what they once knew. Like you and I crave blood. That's what we are to them. Get your sword out—don't give me that *look*, Dawndrinker, *yes*, the sword. I'll need you functional at the temple. No burning yourself alive before we make it there."

His steps quickened to a run. Of course, he still unsheathed his sword with all the grace of a raven taking off into the night, not so much as missing a step. I stumbled behind him, fumbling with my own, which was awkward and heavy and a little too long to draw comfortably while I ran. Still, as much as I hated to admit it, I couldn't argue with him too much. I winced as my palms—still tender—closed around the hilt. I couldn't risk incapacitating myself early.

The screams were now a constant, rolling roar, drowning my thoughts. The waves of the dead grew closer. I could see the others now, hacking and fighting their way through—gods, there were so many—

I felt the eyes of the dead turn to us.

"Don't let them touch you," Asar said. The last thing I heard before his words were swallowed by the howls of their hunger.

I raised my sword and braced myself.

The wave crashed down upon us.

DON'T LET THEM *touch you,* he said, like it was that fucking easy. I was starting to realize that Asar often gave advice that wasn't very useful.

I wasn't sure what I expected to find on the path to the underworld. Dead, of course. But I was expecting, perhaps, disembodied souls, mournful ghosts. These were living corpses, still encased in the rotting remnants of their mortality. The stench of decay surrounded us as they descended, all open mouths and outstretched hands. Their hunger buried into my bones—deeper than flesh, like they'd slide inside our skin just to remember what it was like to be alive.

I swung my sword clumsily to bat them back, but it occurred to me that perhaps a sharp piece of metal wouldn't exactly do much to deter opponents who were already dead.

Elias, Chandra, and Luce collided with us, the five of us circling into a tight pack. Elias hacked admirably away, fending off corpse after corpse. Chandra shook like a leaf, but blinding light spilled from her palms as her lips moved in constant prayer—her chosen weapon over the sword. The Helianen specialized in the art of distilling the magic of the sun. It wasn't as deadly as flame, but was still very powerful. The dead lunged for it only to shrink away when its rays fell over their faces. They were so desperate for the warmth that they let it burn them over and over again, and I wasn't prepared for the sharp twist of sympathy I felt for that.

I watched Chandra out of the corner of my eye, a tight ball of jealousy forming in my stomach. She was no fighter—she'd probably been a healer once, if I had to guess—but her mastery of the light was obvious. It came to her so easily. Simple as breathing.

"The passage!" Asar was yelling, pushing back the dead with one arm and pointing to the narrow opening in the cliffs with the other. "Move!"

I started to run.

But then I heard the voice:

Mische . . . Mische!

My steps faltered. My head swiveled around. My eyes searched the morass of dead. Their pleas blended together into a wordless hum.

I'd imagined it. Surely. But I couldn't stop myself from looking—

Pain tore through my arm, punishment for that distraction. I yelped and spun around, managing a direct hit across the face of a pale woman with purple beneath her eyes and blood dripping from her mouth. I didn't have time to examine whatever she'd done to me, but as I tried to regain my footing, I stumbled against a sudden wave of dizziness.

She, on the other hand, recovered quickly. She let out a moan, hands outstretched.

A wave of darkness rolled over us. It passed right through me, momentarily numbing sound and sensation, then left my opponent gasping against the ground. Someone grabbed my wrist and pushed me toward the temple.

"I told you not to let them touch you," Asar growled in my ear. "Go!"

I started to obey, but he had planted his feet, squaring off against the sea of the dead. I skidded to a stop.

"What are you—"

But Luce, who dove by me, bit down hard on my hand, forcing me to follow. *He knows what he's doing,* she seemed to say. *Run.*

I fixed my sights on the gap in the stone. Chandra and Elias were several strides ahead, bolting like their lives depended on it. The cries of the dead rose behind me.

I couldn't see what Asar did, but I certainly felt it.

It was as if someone had gathered up all the shadows in the air and wrung them out like a wet towel. Everything twisted. The sensation sank into muscle and bones and then left through the soles of my feet. Ahead, Chandra stumbled in shock, nearly tripping Elias as he let out a string of curses. We were within a few feet of the temple now. Smooth trunks of white rose up all around us in a dreamlike, fungal forest. Fluffy silver spores drifted slowly to the ground from the rainbow ridges of the mushroom caps above. I hadn't been able to see it from a distance, but the temple was constructed of sheets of glass that had been stained blue, nearly black. A few panes had split under the crowding of the overgrown mushrooms, sending lightning cracks over the walls.

The air went eerily silent.

I chanced a glance over my shoulder to see Asar running to catch up with us, and behind him, motionless heaps of bodies. They looked like driftwood piled up at the ocean's edge.

"Temporary." He was out of breath, sweat beading on his brow. "Step back."

He pushed past us and threw himself against the temple doors, one hand upon each. Black-red blood spilled from his palms. It pooled in the ancient carvings, spiraling around his hands before tracing the outline of the eyes of Alarus—lashes, lids, irises, and then, at last, bloody, piercing pupils.

The doors swung open, and Asar ushered us inside, shutting them behind us.

The scent of damp decay filled my nostrils. Dim light from the misty skies filtered through warped expanses of glass. Once, they'd formed intricate designs—probably some kind of religious tableau— but now, the fungi had overtaken them, piercing panes of blues and purples and greens with blooming ruffles of translucent white. It pushed up from the cracks in the floor, breaking the marble tile to reveal black earth beneath. It was so dense that I could barely see anything else, a rainbow of fungi, just as alive as the Citadel forests.

"This is . . . something," panted Elias, the way one might say, *I hate everything about this.*

My eyes were wide. "It's amazing," I whispered.

Chandra shook her head, shooting me a pitying glance. "It's death, child."

Something about the way she said it—the way she looked at me— reminded me of a morning I'd spent in the gardens with Saescha, hands buried in the dirt. Hidden beneath a rosebush, I'd found a dead firefinch. It had been gone for some time. Its wings had been splayed like a dancer's skirt. Its eye sockets were black and sunken with decay. Maggots writhed in the wound that had likely killed it. A single bright stalk of green had sprouted up right in the center of its body, right in the middle of what remained of long-unmoving organs.

I'd stared at it for too long.

When Saescha had seen it, she'd let out a sound of revulsion.

"Poor thing," she had said. "Don't touch that, Mische. It's disgusting."

"It's not disgusting," I'd replied. "We'll all look like that one day."

She had given me an odd look, then batted my arm. "Not anytime soon."

But now, I thought back to that look—a twin to the one Chandra gave me now. Saescha was the wisest person I'd ever known. Maybe she saw a hint of what I'd become that day.

I broke Chandra's gaze and turned to the temple. A single broken path led through the mushrooms. Perhaps once it had been an aisle? A hallway?

Asar nudged past me, Luce at his heels.

"We don't have much time before the dead are all over us again."

I followed him, Chandra and Elias behind me.

"What are we looking for?" I said.

Our voices echoed in the silence. Gods, this place was enormous— much bigger than it looked from the outside. What I'd expected to be a short path just went on and on. Speckles of moving light played over the floor, and I looked up to see that the ceiling was even higher now, the mushrooms reaching far, far above us.

A numb buzzing sensation built behind my skull. I lifted my hand in front of my face to see the tiny hairs on the back of it standing upright.

I'd spent enough time studying places of great spiritual importance to know when I was standing in one. A god had given up a part of himself here. It was an inflection point, and I could sense the power of it pulling at me beneath the surface.

"We're close," Asar murmured under his breath.

He felt it, too.

We stepped through the crumbling remains of a doorway and into a massive, circular room. A sheet of glass rose from the far wall, silhouetting the vegetation beyond. A massive stained glass eye, circles nested within circles, stared back at us. Before it, perfectly framed, stood a silver altar.

"It has to be there," Elias said, starting forward.

A soft *whoosh* rustled the silence.

He halted mid-step.

Again—louder this time. The strands of hair around my face quivered. A shadow blotted out the watercolor light over the ground.

I started to lift my chin.

I recognized the sound of flames roaring to life before I even finished the movement. My arm flew up to shield my face from a sudden wall of heat.

I nearly fell back to the floor. I barely managed a wavering, "Shit!"

A monumental bird wearing a golden skull face soared above us, wings extended, talons bared. Flames engulfed its massive body. It framed itself against the ceiling, wingspan so great that I couldn't capture the width of it at once. Its skeletal face, half-broken, stared down at us with deathly promise.

The third guardian.

The *supposedly dead* guardian.

The bird let out a terrible, wretched cry, and dove for us.

CHAPTER TEN

I thought you said that it was dead!"

I barely managed to get the words out between panting breaths. No one had to tell us to run. We wove through the narrow gaps between the mushroom stalks, the guardian's screams echoing behind us.

"It was dead." Asar sounded frustrated by the very possibility that he'd been wrong about something. "It *is* dead."

"It doesn't look dead to me," Elias huffed.

A screech raked down my spine. The mushroom I'd been squeezing through shifted, sending me tumbling backward into Asar's chest.

Light blinded me. The guardian ripped the mushroom out of the ground and tossed it aside as if it were a twig. I found myself staring directly into its skull face. One eye socket was cracked open, giving the appearance of flaming tears as fire surged from within it.

Elias seized that moment to run at the bird with his sword drawn.

No one could say he didn't have balls.

But, predictably, this didn't go well. Another screech and a column of inferno burst from the skull's beak. Elias narrowly dodged, protecting his face with his arm and diving behind a half-crumbled stone wall. Luce leapt at the guardian, too, hissing and growling, but the bird howled and flung itself back toward the ceiling.

I fell to my knees next to Elias. He let out a hiss of pain, cradling his arm. I didn't need to look to know what I would see—I knew those wounds by smell alone at this point. No ordinary burn.

"This is Atroxus's work," Chandra said, echoing my thoughts.

The bird circled above us. Asar peered over the stone to the altar on the opposite side of the room.

"We certainly aren't going to stab it to death," he muttered. Then he turned to me and Chandra and stared at us expectantly.

I threw my hands up. *"Me?* What do you expect me to do?"

"I don't know, Dawndrinker. It's your god, not mine."

Again, I peered over the wall, up at the guardian circling above. Its wingspan covered the entire ceiling. It was just . . . so, *so* big.

"I was only a priestess," I whined.

"I have faith in your abilities," Asar said, and unceremoniously pushed me out from behind the wall.

I stumbled out into the open. The bird's empty, flame-filled gaze fell on me. Gods fucking above, what had I gotten myself into? For a moment, I genuinely considered turning around and running until I got back to the cave. At least if the dead got me, it would be less humiliating than succumbing to the magic of the god I was supposed to serve.

Instead, I turned to Chandra, who quaked beside me. "We do it together," I said. "We'll strike it at the same time. All right?"

She nodded.

Across the room, Asar and Elias had abandoned their hiding place, making a run to the altar—an attempt at distraction. When the bird dove for them, Chandra and I struck—me with what I could summon of the flame, her with the blinding light of the sunrise. Dragging the magic to the surface of my skin was slow and painful, and as I squinted against the fire, the agonizing reward of the fresh burns on my arms had tears collecting in my eyes.

The guardian screeched, lurching from one side of the room to the other. I hadn't noticed this at first—I'd been too overwhelmed— but its movements were awkward and choppy, like it didn't have full control of itself. It careened into walls and nicked its wings on mushroom stalks, veering out of the way a little too late.

Still, whatever was wrong with it had nothing to do with us. Our plan was comically ineffective. I was willing to keep trying, but eventually, Asar yanked me back behind a pile of ruins.

"Let's not waste our time," he grumbled.

"We're being persistent," I protested. But his gaze flicked pointedly down to my arms, where I could sense him staring through my sleeves, right down to the fresh burns that I was trying to pretend I didn't feel.

"Asar." Elias jerked his chin to the wall behind us. It took me a moment to realize what he was gesturing to. And then I saw it—the shadows beyond the glass.

Not rocks. Not mushrooms.

"Are those—" Chandra whispered.

Asar winced. "I told you they'd be up again. They sense the living in here."

I tried not to think about exactly how many corpses were on the other side of that wall.

That *glass* wall.

Gods above. We were fucked.

I spun around, watching the guardian circle above us—watching those erratic movements.

Think, Mische.

"What did you mean when you said the guardian was dead?" I said to Asar.

He followed my gaze.

"It fell," he said. "Long ago. Atroxus must have commandeered the body."

"So the fire isn't natural."

He scoffed. "No. No, it is not."

I stared hard at the bird. At its movements.

No, the more I watched, the more *none* of it looked natural. It seemed addled. Worse, in pain.

I touched my arm without thinking.

Of course it was in pain. It was a creature of the underworld, meant to be a vessel for Alarus's magic. Instead, it had been forced to hold the flames of the sun. The light pooled in its chest, leaking out through every translucent quill of its feathers. If I looked closely, I could even see the darkness warring against it, a cloud of tangling shadow and light at the underside of the beast's stomach.

It almost looked like—

I sat upright and grabbed Asar's arm in a burst of realization.

"The bird isn't a guard. It's a vessel. Look at its stomach. He put the relic inside of it."

Asar didn't seem convinced. But he also didn't immediately contradict me, which counted for something.

"Do you feel anything coming off that altar?" I pressed. "Wouldn't you sense something, if a piece of a god was in there?"

He blinked. A wrinkle flitted across the bridge of his nose, like he was annoyed he hadn't made this observation himself.

I was right. I knew I was.

"Chandra and I can pull the fire out of it," I said. "And you can retrieve the relic."

"If we can get the damned thing down first," Elias said. He had one eye on the wall still, where the silhouetted shadows of the dead beyond were growing concerningly close.

I could see the thoughts turning, turning, turning in Asar's head. "How close do you need to get?" he said. "To pull the flame out?"

I stared up at the bird. "Closer than this."

"You need it on the ground?"

I chewed my lip. There was just *so* much fire. "Almost."

Asar stood. "You had better be right, Iliae."

And then he lifted his hand and flung a spear of magic across the room—straight through the glass wall, unleashing a wave of dead into the temple.

Elias cursed. Chandra leapt back, eyes round. I swallowed the immediate impulse to shout, *What the hell are you doing?*

But Asar didn't hesitate.

"Hold off the worst of them," he said to Elias. "Let a few through."

Then, to Chandra and me, "Come. Quick."

His plan became clear right away. The guardian's attention snapped to the trail of dead dragging themselves into the temple, as if the sight was a thread jerking it back to its former life. It swooped down, the beat of its wings dousing my face in scorching heat, ready to herd the wayward souls back into place.

My face broke into a smile.

Smart. I had to admit it.

Asar pressed his hands together, then drew them apart, threads stretching between them like thick ropes of black honey. He kept stretching and stretching them, more darkness seeping from the crevices of the room to thicken it. And then, with a grunt of exertion, he cast them toward the bird's skull and *pulled*.

"Go!" he commanded.

The guardian let out a screech, veering off to the left, one wing flailing out and drawing a sweep of fire across the room that narrowly missed our heads. Chandra and I ran to the fallen bird. The light burned my cheeks, my eyes. I could barely look at it. There was so much flame—far more than I'd ever manipulated at once, even at the height of my prowess.

But no time to doubt ourselves. I pushed down my uncertainty and grabbed instead for the last dregs of my humanity, calling to Atroxus's power.

I reached for the magic trapped inside the guardian's body. I could feel the pressure of it pushing against the creature's ribs in an endless attack against its host, warring with the cool dark within it—an unrelenting struggle waged for nearly two thousand torturous years. The guardian's pain erupted through my skull as I established the connection between us, so unexpected that I nearly released my grip.

Chandra, though, saved me. Her jaw was set, eyes unblinking. She grabbed hold of the light alongside me and gave it the first powerful heave when I was too unsteady to do it.

I felt it shift.

The bird let out a scream, thrashing against Asar's restraints as the fire began to slip. It swirled and lurched within its ribs as Chandra and I pulled at it, inch by inch. Sweat rolled down my temples. My breaths were ragged and shaky. My arms screamed in pain beneath a fresh set of scars.

"Better fucking hurry!" I barely heard Elias's strained voice in the distance, just as I barely heard the rising groans of the corpses' cries.

Snap, as one of Asar's shadowy ropes disintegrated under the force of the bird's thrashing—

I let out an ugly roar of exertion as Chandra and I gave one final yank.

Atroxus's magic snapped free. I opened my eyes just in time to see the wave of fire rolling toward us, at last unleashed from the guardian's body.

I gasped and dove out of the way. Chandra simply let it roll over her, arms outstretched, like she was embracing the refreshing tide of the sea. A pang of hurt in my stomach reminded me that I could have done the same, once, but I didn't have time to dwell on my own self-pity. Glass cracked as the wave of dead widened the hole in the wall. The flood was now far more than Elias could hold off on his own, pouring into the temple.

The guardian had collapsed to the floor, body now dim and flickering. It no longer screamed or fought. Up close, I could see that its body was comprised of countless delicate tendrils of silver, which shuddered with its final remnants of life.

Asar climbed on top of it. "Get up here," he barked.

I obeyed, crawling over a twitching wing to join Asar on its back. When I knelt next to him, my palms pressing to the bird's flesh, I jolted. The creature's woe pulsed through me, wretched and furious.

I thought I heard a voice in my head whisper, *It was not always this way.*

Asar gave me an odd look—an unspoken, *What?*—but we didn't have time to talk. He drove his blade through the bird's back, cutting through spiderweb-fine feathers and silver ribs and flesh that seemed to be both solid and smoke at once.

The guardian let out a final wail that vibrated through my bones. But it wasn't a cry of pain. It was a cry of grief for the past and relief for the present. It reached for the cool solace of the shadows. I splayed my hands against its back as Asar made another cut.

"It's all right," I whispered. "You did your job. You can rest."

Asar forced the wound open, smoke erupting free, and the guardian at last went still.

"Asar!" Elias barked, frantically. Chandra was helping him now, but the dead were countless.

"I know!" Asar snapped. Then, to me, "Help me."

The guardian's body was so large that Asar and I needed to

climb inside the wound, into a swirling mass of black and purple and blue and gray. It was delicate, like the foam that formed at the ocean's edge.

"What are we looking for?" I asked. But the words had barely left my lips when I *knew*. My fingers brushed a solid object, and that one touch zapped through my entire body.

Asar halted—he felt it, too. We both reached down at the same time. My hand wrapped around something smooth and hard.

Suddenly, I was no longer here.

I stand at the edge of my territory, where the underworld begins to encroach on the mortal realm. A sensation that is almost pain radiates from the center of my chest. The goddess is coiled like a wolf ready to strike, and her teeth are bared like one, too. She has long dark hair that slides over her shoulders in a waterfall. It glints purple and black, every shade of night, stars twinkling within it. The only sign of divinity on such a waiflike little thing, and yet, I can sense that it is a sign of so much more potential.

I look down at my chest, and the obsidian branch jutting from it.

"Do you not know who I am?" I say. "You thought that this would kill me?"

"No," she replies. "But I thought it might even the ground if we are both bleeding."

I am amused. No wonder this creature has caused such a stir among my brethren.

I grab the branch and pull it free. The jagged tip drips my blood.

"I assume that you are the wayward goddess that everyone is searching for."

She stiffens. "Perhaps."

"What is your name?"

"I will tell you if you swear you will not send me back."

I smile despite myself. "I will not send you back."

She relaxes slightly. She sweeps a strand of night-hewn hair over her shoulder. "Nyaxia," she says.

I lurched back to awareness. I was standing now, and so was Asar. Between us, we held a smooth black branch of an obsidian tree, tough as marble. Its twisted point was coated in shimmering, luminescent blood—the blood of a god, as vibrant now as it was more than two millennia ago.

Asar and I looked at each other, dazed over what we'd just

witnessed—a memory? But Luce let out a frantic bark, reminding us we had no time to waste.

The dead now had overtaken the room. Elias and Chandra had climbed up onto piles of rubble to keep from getting dragged away. Lifeless hands clawed at the guardian's now-still body.

Asar thrust the branch into his pack and pointed to the opposite side of the room—to the altar, and the pool of blood around it. "Over there."

I didn't know how that was going to help us, but I didn't have time to question it. The altar was so close, and yet making it that far seemed impossible. The temple had been totally overtaken. We fought our way through the onslaught. I clumsily batted my sword around, wincing as each strike tugged on my fresh burns, and only narrowly managed to avoid the hungry, reaching hands of the dead. Asar made it to the altar first and dropped to his knees at the edge of the pool. Blood lapped angrily at the edge, splashing over his knees. Chandra and Elias were at his side. I struggled to fight my way through, the dead closing in. Luce attempted to forge a path for me, dragging corpses aside with her teeth.

Asar thrust his palms into the liquid. A grand arch, a twin to those that lined Morthryn's halls, rose from the pool of blood, crimson pouring over its frame.

"Chandra," Asar barked, thrusting his chin to the door.

Chandra didn't have to be told twice. She bounded into the pool, nearly tripping at its sudden depth, and disappeared through the arch. Shortly after, Elias followed.

I was only a few strides away. Luce had managed to clear a path for me, and I made a mental note to remember to give her some thorough head scratches later. I didn't care if she was a magical skull wolf. All dogs liked head scratches.

Asar looked over his shoulder at me, waiting.

I stepped into the pool—

A figure burst from the blood and threw itself at me.

Reaching arms wound around my neck. A voice moaned into my ear, *Mische, please, I've been waiting so long, I've missed you—*

I whirled around clumsily and found myself staring into a face

I hadn't seen anywhere but nightmares in fifty years. He'd been so handsome once, with those soft boyish features and shiny golden hair. He used to have a dimple on the right side of his mouth, but he didn't anymore because half of his jaw was missing.

My mouth opened, but I couldn't scream. I couldn't fight. I couldn't move.

Eomin wound himself around me like a flower clinging to light.

Mische, let's go home—

Someone ripped him off me. I gasped for breath and raised my head just in time to see Asar lifting his sword—

"No!" I screamed.

Asar hesitated, confused, and was rewarded with the grasping hands of three more corpses. I swung my sword wildly, barely fighting them off him.

Not bothering to hide his annoyance, Asar grabbed my arm and hauled me through the arch in what was more of a controlled fall than a purposeful leap.

And we sank down.

And down.

And down.

Until there was nothing.

CHAPTER ELEVEN

The first thing I became aware of was the sound of some-one vomiting their guts out.

I opened my eyes to see familiar silver rafters, arching overhead like a ribcage. Stone walls. Stretches of ivy.

Morthryn?

I sat up and was rewarded with a spinning head, so violent that it made me want to follow Chandra's lead. She was on all fours, dry heaving, even though there was apparently nothing left to come up. Elias was already on his feet, though he swayed as he wrung out his cape of rotten blood. I was covered in it, too.

"Gods, what is that *smell*?" I muttered, and then realized it was me.

Asar lay beside me, not moving.

Elias eyed him. "Is he . . . ?"

I probably didn't imagine that he sounded a little hopeful. Luce growled low in her throat, like she was offended by the mere implication of the question.

Asar was alive—I could see his chest rising and falling, albeit weakly. Still, a knot of concern formed in my stomach as I thought of the four dead who had grabbed onto him after I'd distracted him.

I leaned over him.

"Asar?" I shook his shoulder. "Asar!"

Then I raised my palm.

"Oh, for fuck's sake," Elias muttered. "What are you going to do, slap him awake?"

Spoken like someone who didn't know how good I was at slapping people awake. Couldn't even count the number of times I'd done it on Raihn. Blessed hands.

Asar's eyes snapped open.

Immediately, his face pinched into a scowl. He sat bolt upright.

"What were you about to do?"

I lowered my hand. "Nothing."

Asar looked unconvinced, but he didn't push it. His hand shot to his pack, and a wave of relief fell over his face as he touched its contents—the relic.

A very brief wave of relief.

Asar, I was quickly learning, didn't seem to experience any pleasant emotion for longer than two seconds.

"That," he grumbled, "did not go as it should have." He shot Elias a glare. "I ordered you to hold your strike."

A vein throbbed in Elias's temple. He pushed his hair out of his face, the blood in it now flowing down his cheek. A well-timed breeze made me acutely aware that he smelled just as bad as I did.

"I wasn't going to just stand there," he said. "We got the relic. It ended fine."

"The next time you disobey an order, you've just given me the excuse I need to let the dead have you," Asar snapped.

Elias's mouth opened. Then closed, a tiny movement that looked like it took herculean effort.

"Wise," Asar said—though I sensed that his long, combative stare was a bit of a goad.

Men. They were the same everywhere.

I let out an exasperated sigh, and then, at the dagger glares Asar and Elias shot me, somewhat regretted it.

We were at the end of a hallway, a sheer stone wall behind us. The other direction extended off into mist. Ivy and roses crawled up the walls, encircling the rafters. Shallow water collected around our feet, mirroring the darkness above.

"Are we . . . back where we started?" I asked.

This was Morthryn. I was certain of it. My bones shivered with that same mournful song, the same call, that I'd sensed in those halls.

Yet, there were differences, too. Deep cracks ran down the walls, smoky gloom pouring through them. The ivy sparkled—upon closer inspection, I realized that it was covered with frost, the leaves coming to silver-sharp points. The air was colder, and the light dimmer, flickering as if bestowed by candles on the verge of death. The mirrored floor quaked with barely there ripples, distorting the reflection.

Asar stood, adjusting his jacket. "In a sense."

"You like giving nonanswers."

"It's not a nonanswer. It's true. We're in the Descent now. We left Morthryn behind, and we didn't go backward. But Morthryn isn't a building."

"It's a passageway," I said.

"And to bridge the gap between worlds, it needs to run deep into the Descent, not just perch on top of it."

I closed my eyes, envisioning it.

"Like a tree," I said. "The building in the mortal world is the trunk. And now, we're in the roots."

"Yes. The paths can take us some of the way down. Though they'll get . . . difficult to access as we go deeper."

"Difficult?" Chandra repeated.

Asar cast us a humorless smirk. "We've barely gotten started."

Gods. It hit me all over again that this had just been the *first* Sanctum. The first of *five*.

I wasn't one to shy away from intimidating tasks, especially not when I had a god at my back, but I felt a little sick at that thought.

Maybe it was the smell. I told myself it was the smell.

"But for now, we have an easy journey. For a while, at least." Asar picked a thread of—was that *sinew?*—off his coat, unmoved. "It will be a week or two before we reach the doorstep of Breath. Get some rest. Clean up. We'll be off again shortly."

He began to stride away, as if that was all the explanation any of us needed—and I was too tired to argue. But Elias called after him, "What about the relic?"

Asar stopped. Turned. "What about it?"

Elias's gaze was fixed upon Asar's pack, held tight in his grasp. "What was it?"

I was wondering the same thing, though Elias knew even less than I did. He'd been so busy holding off the dead that he likely hadn't seen the branch at all.

Asar lifted one shoulder in an almost-shrug and turned away. "Does it matter?"

"Yes," Elias said. "Yes, it does."

But Asar didn't turn back, disappearing down the hall without another word.

MORTHRYN, IT SEEMED, had been ready for us. There were only a couple of rooms accessible to us—the rest were empty arches, bricked over—but they held clean clothes tucked away in dusty dressers, and carafes of blood, and even large tubs of water that we were able to use to wash away the worst of death.

I was especially grateful for the blood, though I tried not to show it. The smell of Chandra's wounds was getting distracting. Acolytes thrived on self-deprivation, so in a twisted way, my time as a priestess had prepared me well for my vampire life. Still, I gulped down that cracked goblet of blood with shameful pleasure.

That night—or was it day? I couldn't tell anymore—we commandeered the bigger of the two rooms for rest. Luce curled up near the door, though Asar was nowhere to be found. The rest of us gathered dusty blankets to create something that could pass for beds. Elias cleaned his sword in the corner, intently focused on his work. Chandra attempted to patch her wounds with torn scraps of fabric.

With my hunger sated, I allowed myself to approach her. She whispered beneath her breath, and up close, I recognized her words right away. Prayers, in a language so familiar it made my heart clench.

"You speak Atrean?" I said in my mother tongue.

It had been so long since I'd spoken it that the sounds were clunky on my lips. Did I have an accent now, I wondered?

Her brows rose. "I'm more surprised that you do."

She shielded her wounded arm as I approached. I didn't get too close, and gave her an easy smile. "I was born in Slenka."

She winced. Everyone knew what it was like in Slenka.

"It wasn't so bad," I said—a half lie. "Then I went to Vostis. Spent most of my life there. Those forests! Those beaches! So beautiful." I shook my head, smile bittersweet. "I miss it."

"I'm from Aerenne. We had the forests there, too. Not like here. So . . ." Her eyes swept around the room—across the frost, the stone, the frozen ivy. ". . . dead."

I couldn't quite bring myself to agree with her. Raihn and I had traveled all over Obitraes. At first, I'd thought I would have to force myself to love it. But there really was so much beauty in this world. And even Morthryn seemed so far from dead. It already felt like one of the most alive places I'd ever been.

"Can I see your arm?" I held up a bottle of medicine. "I'll patch it up for you."

She seemed wary, which was understandable. But then she smiled. It was a kind, grandmotherly expression, shifting our power dynamic. Now I was the frightened child and she was the reassuring elder.

We were probably almost the same age. In another life, my face might look just like hers.

"I'm a healer, child," she said. "I can do it."

"Easier if someone else does."

After a moment, she acquiesced. She watched me carefully as she extended her arm, the wound still dripping blood through her make-shift bandage. A test, I knew.

Even though I'd just eaten, the scent was agonizing. But I shoved my thirst down and tended to Chandra's cut as if it were nothing remarkable at all.

"I met some members of the Helianen, back then," I said as I worked. "Sometimes we would meet with a local sect, not too far away. A long journey, but always worth it. Gods, they had the *best* food."

"Ah, yes. Perhaps you came to one of our parties. The food was the least of the pleasures, but I'm sure a pretty girl like you knew that."

I laughed. Yes, the Helianen were known for being . . . free. They were often healers, and secondarily worshipped Ix, the goddess of sex and fertility. The parties put even vampire debauchery to shame, which was saying something.

Not that I ever indulged. No one wanted to make a cuckhold of the King of the White Pantheon.

She sighed. "Gods, what I would give to be at one of those parties again."

"Why did you come to Obitraes?"

The warmth disappeared from her expression.

"I didn't choose to," she said. "They needed a midwife."

She didn't need to say more. Vampires were unique creatures biologically. Reproduction was difficult, and their own magic—the magic of Nyaxia—was not well suited to healing. Thus, they often relied on human healers. Sometimes, they would force humans in their own districts to take up the practice. Other times, they would simply kidnap those who had the skillset they needed from nearby nations. One of our own was taken once. A middle-aged woman who never came back from one of her mission journeys.

"I'm sorry," I said softly.

Chandra shook her head. "There is no light without darkness. There is no life without suffering."

She said it in Atrean, and it sounded so painfully familiar that my heart hurt. "My sister used to say that."

Chandra smiled. "She must have been very wise." She drew a bisected circle over her chest—the sign of the sunrise, a common gesture among followers of the Helianen. "I can't bemoan my circumstances. I still feel the sun. And you must be very devout, to still have your magic after . . . your change."

I started winding the bandages around her arm, watching the red bleed through the fabric. Watching too intently.

"It's just a part of me," I said lightly. "I can't abandon it."

I still feel the sun, she had said.

It was rare that Atroxus spoke directly to his followers, outside of those who were chosen, like me. But again, I found myself wondering if Atroxus had visited her, too, before this journey.

Redundancies, Asar had called us. Had Atroxus felt the same way?

I couldn't ask her—I'd been explicitly forbidden to—but the question hung heavy in the silence.

"At least once this is done," she said, "we'll have our freedom. We can return home."

We, she said. As if the Citadel would take me back now, even if I could return. But I appreciated how easily she said it, like it was a simple truth. I wished I lived in that world.

"You'll have more than that," Elias said from across the room. "Nyaxia will reward you for this. Whatever you desire."

Chandra's face hardened. "That is the only thing I want. Home."

I thought of a forest and a great stone Citadel. I thought of Saescha. *Home.*

I tied off Chandra's bandage and presented it with a smile. "See? Good as new."

It was satisfying to fix a straightforward problem.

She gave me a kind smile, but it quickly faded.

"If only this would all be as easy as this," she said.

I LAY CURLED up in dusty blankets, exhausted but unable to sleep. I'd listened to Chandra's whispered prayers until she finally dozed off. Now it was silent.

I needed to sleep.

But in the darkness, I saw the bloody face of the boy who had grabbed me in the Sanctum. I'd pushed that memory away while I could cover it with distractions. Now, there was nowhere for my thoughts to go but in.

I imagined it, I told myself. I'd projected a face from my memories onto one of the dead. That was all.

Still. It shook me. I curled up, pulling the scratchy wool tight around myself. It had been a long time since those memories had been so vivid.

I missed Raihn.

In the beginning, when it was all at its worst, he used to catch me crying in my sleep and wake me up by sweeping me into one of those great bear hugs. I'd go straight from the cold claws of my nightmares to the warm safety of his protection—no in-between. I had always told myself that I had to be there for Raihn because I knew how much he needed someone to protect, especially in those early days. But it was selfish, too. We both knew it.

No one in the world was better at hugs than Raihn. The last time I'd seen him, it was that hug goodbye that almost broke my resolve.

They wanted me to stay, I knew. Oraya even *said* it—multiple times!—which felt like a great triumph. They'd make me a part of their family forever. They'd give me a room in the Nightborn Palace, a space at their dinner table, an overstuffed chair near the hearth. Never for a moment did I doubt how much they loved me.

And I loved them, too. So hard it hurt.

But I could feel the stains on my soul growing every day. I had disgraced a god. I had broken vows. I had killed a prince of the House of Shadow within their walls. When I would kneel to pray at sundown, the silence wasn't just dismissive, it was ominous. I didn't know how I knew something was coming for me, but I knew it in my bones. And I wasn't about to let it hurt them. Not when I had seen, firsthand, how much they had suffered for what they built and just how fragile it was.

Besides, I was a missionary. This was my purpose. I found a broken soul. I helped them. And then I left. I had done it countless times before. Why would I stop now?

Still, the night I had set out, I'd paused at the end of the road, just before the palace gates, and I'd looked over my shoulder. Oraya and Raihn were on the balcony, but they weren't looking at me anymore. They were standing nose to nose, laughing softly at words meant only for each other. She looked at him like he was a question answered. He looked at her like she was the only one worth asking.

I knew, in that moment, I was making the right decision. And even now, as much as I missed them—and gods, I missed them—that I had done the right thing.

Two souls saved didn't make up for the ones I had damned. The mission I was on now just might.

Still. I wished I'd responded to their letters.

My lashes fluttered. I was so exhausted that I didn't even feel it when sleep took me.

I dreamed of my wedding night.

I'd never felt so beautiful. I stared at myself in the mirror. I wore a gown of gold, the perfect shade to complement the rich brown of my complexion, the gold of my freckles. My hair had been tamed into elaborate braids, a few rogue curls escaping around my face.

Still, I felt uncomfortable. The dress was heavy, like my sixteen-year-old shoulders were too small to bear its weight.

"Such a beauty. A phoenix incarnate."

I watched him in the mirror. He lounged on the bed, flawless lips curled against an apricot.

"What do you wish to ask, a'mara?" He stood and approached me, voice against my throat—right near the mark that someone else would leave years from this moment.

I turned around to face him. It hurt, genuinely hurt, to look at him sometimes—he was the perfection of a sunrise over the mountains, sunset over the sea, warmth after a long winter.

"You'll never abandon us, will you?" I asked.

The words sounded so pathetically mortal. The kind of thing that I imagined human lovers whispered to each other in the dark—*promise me you'll always love me, promise me you'll always stay.*

My vows had included no such things. A god does not have to promise to love you forever. He doesn't have to give you fidelity or affection. Instead, he takes your soul and offers it something so much greater: purpose.

I was so certain that he'd be angry at me for asking. But Atroxus—kind Atroxus—instead laughed.

"Of course not," he said. "You are mine forever."

He put down the apricot and lowered his mouth to mine, his lips still damp with another mortal pleasure.

CHAPTER TWELVE

I jerked awake with a gasp.

The cavernous halls of Morthryn moaned a greeting as I sat up. I could've sworn that someone had grabbed my arm and shaken me, but when my eyes opened, there was no one before me but the shadows. No sound but my heartbeat.

Chandra and Elias were asleep. No Asar, but that wasn't surprising—he had stalked off to gods knew where after he unceremoniously declared we'd be stopping to rest, and hadn't returned.

But . . . Luce wasn't here, either. That seemed odd. She often stood guard when he didn't.

A thick breeze rustled my hair, insistent, like the prison was grabbing my hand and pulling me to my feet.

I rose unsteadily and went to the door, careful not to wake the others. I peered out into the hall.

Strange. I didn't remember the hallway branching out like this. But now, an open arch stood before me like a gaping maw, revealing stairs that led down into darkness.

Another breeze—this time, almost a gust.

Come, the prison seemed to whisper. *Hurry.*

Raihn would've called it reckless to just wander off into a shadowy hallway in the underworld.

But contrary to common belief, I wasn't reckless. I just followed my gut. Some might even call that faith.

Right now, my gut said to follow.

And so, I did.

THE STEPS BLENDED together. The halls pulled me forward. The wind blew faster—as if Morthryn was whispering, *Hurry, hurry!*

I found myself running, even though I didn't know why. I half slid down the stairs. When I hit flat ground, I had so much momentum that I almost sent myself flying face down to the floor.

I caught myself, skidding to a stop.

When I lifted my head, I had only seconds to make sense of the scene before me.

A gate of twisted wrought iron stood before me. A stained glass eye stared down with a half-shattered gaze from the apex of its arch. The gate was open; one look at what lay beyond it told me it was not of this world—undulating mist of purple, black, blue, green, stars and sunrises and fire and ice.

Smoke poured through, filling the small room—and with it came the dead.

I couldn't count how many, but at least half a dozen broken forms lurched through the fog. Asar stood before them, silhouetted against the infinity of death, a one-man shield. His long jacket flew out behind him, swept up in the force of his spellcasting. He called to the shadows from every corner of the room, and they surrounded him like outstretched wings. His sword burned through the darkness, the broken blade glowing white.

He was magnificent.

He was also losing.

One of the wraiths clung to his left arm, while another lunged for his exposed right side. I couldn't see his blood—it was too dark for that—but I sure as hell could smell it. And more dead poured through the open door, threatening to overwhelm him. Luce ran back and forth across the door, trying to stave them off, but the two of them were sorely outnumbered.

I acted before I allowed myself to hesitate.

I dove into the morass, lunging for the dead that clung to Asar's sword arm. I stretched out my hand and reached inside myself for the light of the sun.

The dead turned to me, black eyes dragging me in.

The flame did not come.

Shit.

Asar shot me a look of shock that I only saw for a split second before a wraith collided with me. I staggered back, barely protecting my face. I, stupidly, had not brought my sword—I had no weapon now but the sun that had abandoned me. The wraith clawed at me. One of my sleeves slid down to my elbow and I let out a gasp of pain as her death-black fingers wrapped around bare skin.

Asar's warning echoed in my head: *Don't let them touch you.*

I tried the flame again. I had to push deeper this time to grab hold of that little piece of humanity and *pull.*

Light flared to my hands, and the corpse lurched back into the gloom.

But there were so many more. I fought another back, drawing it away from Asar before Luce pushed it back through the gate. Another grabbed my shoulder, and I whirled around, ready to strike again—

He looked at me with pleading eyes, half his face sloughing off.

Mische, help me, he begged.

He looked even less human than he had out in the Sanctum. His one visible eye was a pit of darkness. And the voice—it didn't come from his throat. It slipped straight into my mind, like an echo of a memory.

Mische, let's go home. He'll forgive you.

I couldn't move. My flames had withered away. The dead boy pulled me closer.

Help me, he moaned.

I was reviled by him. I was entranced by him. I wanted to push him away. I wanted to let him drag me to my long-overdue death.

"Get him off!" someone was shouting at me.

I couldn't. This was a friend—a friend who was begging me for help. He pushed me, my head cracking against the ground as he crawled over me—

But then, just as quickly, someone hauled him away, leaving me gasping for breath. I sat up to see Asar and Luce dragging him to the door. He reached for me as they cast him into the dark.

Take me home—

I lurched after him on instinct, before I stopped myself.

After the final wraith was through, Asar collapsed to his hands and knees. I approached him, uncertain, and when I drew closer I could see black blood plastering his shirt to his body. But save for one confused glance, he barely acknowledged me. He dragged himself to the right side of the door and pressed his hand to the bent silver frame. His lips moved with silent words. A bead of sweat rolled down his temple, pasting down a perfect swirl of deep brown hair.

He needed help. I knew he did, but I didn't know how, or why, or with what. The ghost of the wraith's grasp still burned on my skin, making me dizzy.

"What are you—"

"Concentrating," he barked.

With a rough shove, Luce pushed me to the opposite side of the arch. I stumbled against the frame, knees hitting the ground hard. Darkness sloshed within the arch like water raging against cliffs. A wordless scream was building, building, in my ears, and I couldn't tell if it was from beyond the door or within my own head—both?

I ran my hands over the metal frame. Carvings had been etched into it, which now erratically pulsed with faint, flagging light. I pressed my fingers against them, trying to discern the shapes. Glyphs. Not any kind I recognized, but—

Luce jabbed my back. She frantically darted between me and Asar, who now sagged, barely conscious, against his side of the door.

Tell me what to do, I started to say. But then the ether within the door surged, and I pressed my hand to the glyphs in just the right way, and awareness flooded me.

I could *feel* it all.

Could feel the door, metal and magic and a thousand invisible forces more, straining to hold back what thrashed beyond. Could feel the sharp edges of broken glyphs and tired spells, uselessly twisted like scraps of rusted iron. And most of all, I could feel the hunger of what lay beyond that gate—ravenousness that could crush the world in its starvation pains.

The threads of Asar's magic flapped free like a frayed net. He was trying to restore those broken glyphs and pull the gate closed again. He poured everything he had into it—I so acutely sensed his exhaustion, just as I sensed, beyond any doubt, that his remaining strength would not be enough.

The answer was so close, so easy, so natural. Like gulping down a breath of air when your head broke the surface of the water. I didn't even consciously choose it.

Asar's open invitation was right there, a sentence waiting to be finished, and I took it. Power flooded me, from his unfinished spell, to the shadows in the corners of the room, to the pool inside myself that I'd been ignoring for the last fifty years.

The gate snapped closed.

The force sent me flying back. My head smacked against the ground. I tasted blood at the back of my throat. I thought perhaps I saw Atroxus's disapproving face, but he was gone before I could reach for him.

Luce stared down at me, dancing urgently in place.

Get up get up get up—

I sat up.

The gate was now just an empty arch, silver bars crossed over it like arms across the chest of a resting corpse. Visually unassuming. But power still pulsed at its edges—want howling beyond it.

Asar was crumpled in a heap next to the gate.

Luce trotted over to him, nudging him, circling him, before returning to me.

"I'm coming." I stood and almost fell back to my knees. When I made it over to Asar and knelt next to him, it was tempting to just lie down with him and go to sleep.

Luce let out a small whine as I rolled Asar over, gently prodding him with her nose.

My heart warmed. She really loved him.

"He's all right," I told her. "I promise."

Was he, though?

Asar's eyes were closed, his lashes dark against his cheeks, even in contrast to the shadows that perpetually ringed his eyes. He was breathing, but shallowly. Did I imagine that his scars looked more severe?

I shook him. "Asar. *Asar.*"

Luce whined impatiently.

I raised my open palm just as Luce jabbed him hard with her nose.

Asar's eyes opened just before my hand made contact with his face. It was too late to stop.

"Shit," I squeaked. "Sorry!"

"Fuck," he groaned.

It was a bit satisfying to hear Asar curse.

But even that was short-lived. His lashes fluttered. A sweet, heady scent hit my nostrils. He was bleeding so much that my knees were soaked through with it.

Gods, why did his blood *smell* like that? Better than human.

"Up," he ground out.

"Up?"

His arm twitched, like he was trying to point but couldn't make his body cooperate.

"Where?" I said. "Asar, help me here. *Where?*"

Luce darted to the staircase. She ran up a few steps, then back down. Up. Down.

Follow. Follow.

I looked down at Asar, who teetered on the edge of consciousness. Then back to the stairs.

My first instinct was to laugh. Asar was lean, but he was still much larger than me. But Luce's distraught whines twisted a knife in my heart. They left little to argue with.

I grabbed Asar's limp arm and slung it over my shoulders. I could barely keep myself upright. I didn't know how I was going to manage this.

"You've got to give me a little help here," I said. "Please?"

He moaned a sludge of almost-words. I chose to believe it was meant to be, *Whatever you need, Mische, because I am so, so grateful that you're saving my life. Again.*

I started climbing.

LUCE WAS PRACTICALLY dragging us both along by the time we made it to the top of the steps. I had been expecting that we'd end up back where I started, in the hallway near the others. But instead, when Luce summoned me to the landing with an urgent *yip,* only a single wooden door stood before me.

Maybe I'd gotten my directions mixed up. Or maybe Morthryn just didn't follow the rules of the physical world. I couldn't bring myself to care in the moment. The edges of my vision blurred, and my muscles screamed. It took all my focus just to keep myself standing.

I shifted Asar's weight to free up a hand to open the door, but it swung open in an unprompted invitation.

I wasn't about to question that gift, either.

"Thank you," I said, because it seemed like it was probably best to be very, very polite to the sentient, god-touched prison.

With Luce's help, I dragged Asar inside, and the door shut behind us.

It was a bedchamber. Light spilled from dying candles over neat bookcases, a desk, an armchair, a cramped upright piano. A slightly ajar door in the corner revealed a glimpse of a washroom. A large bed stood in the middle of the room, velvet blankets smoothed over the mattress but still bearing the imprint of whoever had last sat there.

It was all so . . . lived-in. Fine, clearly belonging to someone of means, but not nearly the level of cold opulence that I'd seen at the palace. It was inviting.

That bed looked incredible. Hell, I'd take the carpet. I wanted to curl up in those furs and sleep.

I wanted it so, so, *so* much. Gods, I was exhausted—

A bark made my eyelids snap open.

Luce stood beside the washroom door, dancing from one foot to the other.

"Not the bed?" I asked.

Why were my words slurring?

She growled her disapproval.

I sighed. "If you say so."

The ten steps across the room were more painful than the flights of stairs before it. Asar was now useless, his head hanging back, feet dragging. The scent of his blood was unbearably distracting.

A copper claw-footed tub sat at the center of the washroom. It was already filled with . . . water? No, not water. My eyes couldn't focus on it. The surface was blurry, ripples blending into ripples. Depending on how the light shifted, it looked clear, or white, or black, or red.

Luce took Asar's now-limp hand in her jaws, dragging him toward it.

"You're not making . . . this easy, Luce . . ."

My voice sounded very far away.

And then I was slumped against the rim of the tub, Asar's body leaning on mine. Luce was trying to hoist him in, tentacles of shadow pulling at him. His clothing was disheveled. We'd lost the jacket somewhere in the stairwell and now his torn shirt had slipped down his shoulder to reveal tan skin and black scars.

My blurring vision settled on the lines of black-blue spreading over the muscles of his chest. *It's very pretty, actually,* I thought. *Like flower roots.*

Luce jabbed at me. My eyes snapped open. My cheek was pressed to the copper.

Help me, she commanded.

She positioned herself under Asar. With her help and a dizzying wave of pain, I managed to hoist him into the tub—barely. His forehead smacked against the metal, one arm dangling free, blood dripping from his head to the tile floor. The liquid within splashed a waterfall over the edge, drenching my trousers.

I sagged, breathing heavily.

Something hard sharply pushed at my backside. I swatted at it in annoyance. I was so tired. I could sleep right here on the tile floor.

A rough bark.

Luce wound herself under my stomach, tendrils wrapping around my wrists. She barked, firmly.

Get in.

In the tub?

"Silly girl," I slurred. "He's already in there."

Asar, I was certain, wouldn't like it if I climbed into the bath with him.

But Luce just kept barking.

Get in, she insisted. *Get in, get in.*

"Fine, fine!" I mumbled.

I managed to throw myself into the water. I landed against Asar, his arms cocooning around me, my head tucking beneath his chin.

He'll be very unhappy when he wakes up, I thought, but I couldn't make myself move. His body was warm. The water was gentle. He smelled like ivy. I was so, so tired, and being here made it easier to stop thinking about the disfigured face of a boy I used to know.

The last thing I saw was Asar's blood running down hammered copper—or was it mine?

Luce licked my dangling fingers, as if to say, *It's all right. Let go.*

But I didn't have a choice. I was already gone.

CHAPTER THIRTEEN

The breath was soft against my cheek.

I felt that first, before anything else came back to me. That steady, soothing rhythm, raising goosebumps at the back of my neck.

Nice, I thought, dreamily. *It's nice.*

The water was still warm. I'd sunk down as I slept, so it came up past my shoulders. I had settled deep against Asar's body—his long arm folded around me, his chin lowered against the crook between my throat and shoulder, his torso molded to the curvature of my back.

My exhausted mind pieced these circumstances together far too slowly.

I opened my eyes.

What really made the situation sink in was the sight before me: my toes pressed to the lip of the copper tub, with Asar's long, elegant feet emerging from the water on either side of them. I wasn't sure why we were barefoot. Maybe Luce had dragged our boots off.

It felt indecent to be staring at the Wraith Warden's feet.

I was in a *bathtub* with *the Wraith Warden.*

Gods fucking help me.

Slowly—so, so slowly—I shifted my head to look at him. I was close enough to count the drops of liquid shimmering in his eyelashes. Moisture dotted his skin, painting a sheen over his tan cheeks that emphasized the angle of his cheekbones. His scars glistened beneath the lantern light. I hadn't noticed before, but there were hints of green and blue in the deepest ridges, shifting as if an aurora were hiding under his skin. Awake, his face was always hard with concentration or disapproval, but now, his expression was soft, mouth still, brow smooth. I felt like I was witnessing a rare natural phenomena.

He was, I had to admit, very pretty, even by vampire standards. No, more than pretty. His features begged to be immortalized in stone or paint. Before the scars, he must have caught plenty of attention.

Or maybe not, since he was apparently off doing whatever one had to do to earn a title like "the Wraith Warden" at that time. Probably didn't leave a lot of room for parties and flirtation.

Still, the thought of Asar—grumpy, eternally put-out Asar—swanning around ballrooms with a legion of admirers was so funny that a snort escaped my lips.

His eyes opened.

The awkward giggle died.

He didn't move. His brown eye seemed darker than ever here, endless black, like the oldest vampire blood. His scarred one shone like a stone freshly polished, galaxies of silver and green and gold in its depths. Every time I'd looked at Asar, that eye had always held a tempest. Now, it was the mists on a winter dawn. Quiet.

He didn't blink. Just stared at me, so intently that he might have been counting the freckles on my face or the threads of gold in my irises. It was the kind of stare that made you stop breathing. The kind of stare that made you feel like your clothes were being peeled off.

Then a wrinkle slowly etched itself between his eyebrows.

"Iliae," he said slowly, "why are you on top of me?"

There were probably many people who would be happy to be asking that question, but Asar was not one of them.

A wave of long-overdue self-consciousness crashed over me. He tried to push himself upright, and I stood too fast, sending a waterfall of silver over the edge of the tub.

"I saved your life," I said. *"Again.* You should be more appreciative."

Fine, the truth was, I wasn't sure what I'd saved Asar from or how I'd done it. But I didn't need to know those things to wield it over him.

Asar stepped out of the tub and turned away. He pushed wet hair away from his face like he was trying to forcibly clear the remaining fog from his head. His shirt, once white and now mauve from the blood and whatever had been in the tub, clung to his body, practically transparent. I could see the shape of his scars underneath the fabric, extending all the way down the left half of his body over lean swells of muscle.

He returned, two towels in hand. He paused awkwardly, eyes flicking down for a moment too long. A sudden awareness of the cold air had me looking down at myself and realizing that my own clothes did little more to hide my body than his did.

Sun take me.

I snatched a towel from him and wrapped it around myself.

"Where are we? What is this? What happened at the door? Why were the—"

He rubbed the bridge of his nose. "Iliae, please. If you want me to answer, you'll have to let me."

I shut my mouth. Fine. One question at a time.

"We're in one of my rooms," he said.

I took in our surroundings again—the oddly lived-in, comfortable bedchamber beyond the half-ajar door.

"Your rooms?"

"I've lived in Morthryn for a long time. I've carved out little sanctuaries for myself here and there."

Sanctuaries. What an odd word to apply to Morthryn. Yet, I had to admit, this room felt like a sanctuary—like someone had lovingly curated it. This alone brought to mind so many other questions. Had he traveled these paths before, then? Why?

But instead, I looked down at the liquid around my knees—all those metallic colors. "And this?"

"It's designed to wash away the influence of the dead. They're starving for life. When they touch you, they leach it from you bit by bit. The death can cling to you even after they let go."

I was, despite myself, fascinated. "This bathtub washes away death?"

"The potion washes away death," Asar corrected. "The bathtub is just a bathtub."

I wanted to be offended by how condescending that answer was, but the fog in my head had cleared enough for the memories to come rushing back. I closed my eyes against the too-vivid image of Eomin's face.

I let out a shaky breath.

"What happened out there? At the door?"

Asar's face went grim. The tempest in that left eye returned. He turned around and stepped behind a folding screen in the corner, the sounds of rustling wet fabric punctuating his words.

"I knew that we'd earn some . . . followers once we started our journey. The dead are attracted to the living, and they don't get to see them often. But they never should have been able to broach that." The words were sharp, a scolding that seemed to be directed more toward himself than me.

"Your wards are breaking," I said.

Asar's head poked out from around the screen, eyes narrowed, like a teacher expecting to catch a cheating student.

I smiled brightly. I enjoyed when I knew more than he expected me to. "Priestess, remember?"

He stepped out from behind the screen, though he kept his body angled away from me as he buttoned up a dry shirt.

"They aren't *my* wards. They're Alarus's wards. And everything decays after two thousand years. Even death itself. The Sanctums have gotten unstable. Some souls make it through the Descent into the underworld, as they should. But some aren't able to pass and remain trapped in the Sanctums. They put pressure on the gates that never used to exist."

I hoped I misunderstood Asar, because if I hadn't, it meant that my friend had languished that way for decades, stuck only a fraction of the way through his journey to true death. I heard his voice in the back of my head with renewed horror: *Help me, Mische. Take me home.*

Saliva pooled over my tongue, and for a horrible moment, I thought I might actually vomit. But I was grateful that Asar didn't seem to notice my reaction.

"They simply require more maintenance," he said. "Still, I never let the gates fall. Never."

I didn't need Asar to explain to me what broken gates would mean. Veils like those separated many different realms in our world, and they had been designed by the gods to remain in careful balance. If there was no boundary between life and death, the paths to the underworld would collapse entirely.

"You almost did tonight," I said.

Asar let out a breath through his teeth. "It was too close," he muttered. "It's getting harder. All of it, it's . . ."

His voice trailed off as he turned back to me. I was certain he was about to thank me for my help, and I looked forward to hearing it. But instead, his eyes lowered—to the several inches of my wrist visible under my wet shirt. To the fresh burns over it.

His face hardened. "I told you to stop being so careless with that."

Gods above. Here I was thinking I'd get an actual *thank you*.

"You'd rather I just let the dead take you?" I said. "Magic has a cost. You of all people must know that."

An odd expression flickered over his face, clouds churning in his scarred eye.

"You're right. I do know." He crossed the room in three long strides, and seized my hand before I could move, twisting it to reveal the seeping wounds. "And that's how I know that this is a ridiculous risk. You're a Shadowborn. Use the gifts you're made for instead of flaying yourself for the ones you're not."

You're a Shadowborn.

Those three words struck me across the face. I lurched back with the force of them, but his grip on my wrist was strong.

No one had ever called me that before.

"No, I'm not," I said. "I'm a Dawndrinker. I'm—"

"You are a *vampire*, Iliae. Not just a vampire, but one created by one of the most powerful bloodlines in Obitraes. Call yourself whatever you want, but your stubbornness isn't worth your life."

"Stubbornness?"

My hurt curdled to anger.

"I didn't *choose* this," I spat. "I didn't want this. I was nineteen years old when your brother Turned me and then left me to die in the dirt. Don't try to tell me that it's some kind of *gift* that I'm supposed to embrace. I lost *everything* that night. I lost—"

I squeezed my eyes shut. I saw a young man with half his face ripped up. I saw a woman with her throat torn out and just how thirsty the dust was for her blood.

I drew in a long breath and let it out. "Whatever magic I have from—from *him*, prince or not, I don't want it," I said. "I wield the magic of Atroxus. Not Nyaxia. I have my faith, and I have the love of my god. That's all I need."

Asar was silent for a long moment, gaze lowering. His thumb traced the scar on the swell of my palm. I hated that they now extended to my hands, where my sleeves could no longer cover them.

"Right. Looks like love," he muttered bitterly.

The shadows between our skin quivered. The necrotic power I tried to pretend wasn't within me rose beneath his touch, pushing up against the surface. I wished he would let me go. I wished I would pull away. Neither happened.

"Malach had no respect for the world around him," he said. "He was selfish, and he was entitled, and he didn't know how to find pleasure in anything but exerting power over weaker beings. I'm glad he's dead, and I'm glad that you were the one who killed him. Perhaps it makes my cynical heart believe that there's some justice in the world."

Justice. That was one word to describe his body sliding down the wall, my sword staked in his chest. Secretly, I treasured that final, shocked look on his face. Like he was seeing me for the first time.

"I believe you when you say that you didn't want this power," he said. "But it's not my brother's anymore. It's yours. And you can't tell me that you don't feel how strong it is. Because . . ." A wrinkle etched between his brows—curiosity, confusion, or both. "Because I feel it."

He slid his hand around so his palm hovered over mine. The darkness between our hands pulled like spider's silk. Unwelcome pleasure skittered up my spine.

I wanted to pull away, shut it down, pretend it didn't exist. But my curiosity was too powerful to hold back now that he had acknowledged it, too.

"Why does it feel . . . like that?" I asked.

He hesitated before he answered. "My brother Turned you. You and I would share some of the connection you would have with him because of it."

He presented this as fact, but I could hear his uncertainty.

"But he was only your half brother," I said. "And I felt it with your sister and your father, but not so strongly. Even with Malach . . ."

I remembered Lilith and Vale's wedding in the House of Night. I had seen Malach across the room, and I had just *known*. Before then, I didn't even know who my maker was. I didn't remember his face. But one look at him, and I felt it. A connection that bolted straight through my black-blooded heart.

Raihn used to talk about how much he hated that—how no matter how much you despised the one who Turned you, you still had an intimate bond with them. It deepened the violation, extending it from a moment to a lifetime. The ghost of their lips would always remain on your throat.

That was exactly how it had felt.

But this, with Asar, was different. It felt more like my blood was answering a mutual call rather than bowing in subservience. Still, it reminded me far too much of things I preferred not to think about.

I settled on, "It's just . . . different."

Asar's frown of thought deepened.

"A connection, no matter how biological, is only worth the attention one gives it," he said. "Many factors could contribute. But regardless of the cause, what you did at the gate tonight . . . I've been studying magic for a very long time. I know how to recognize someone who has worked hard to perfect their craft. The magic may be different, but the techniques still apply."

He spoke awkwardly, like he was unaccustomed to giving compliments.

I couldn't help it. I smiled.

"That's actually nice of you, Warden."

He scowled. "I'm stating a fact, not stroking your ego, Dawndrinker."

Still nice.

"Learn how to utilize what was given to you," he said. "You could become just as powerful as Malach was. More, maybe, because you're probably willing to work harder at it than he was. The Descent will be dangerous. You can't afford not to use the tools you have. And—"

He hesitated.

"And the gates are growing harder for me to close by myself. I could use . . . assistance."

My brows lifted. "You're asking for help."

This was much more comfortable territory for me. It was a little embarrassing, actually, just how much my heart jumped at it, like a Pythoraseed addict reaching for their next smoke. I knew how to help people. It was my most comfortable role.

Asar scowled, but he didn't correct me.

"What about Elias?" I asked. "He's Shadowborn."

Asar's lip curled, as if he'd just been forced to eat something rancid. It was an excellent expression, and I appreciated it.

"Elias is the type who's better off swinging swords around," he said, leaving no doubt it was a grave insult. But I had a feeling there were plenty of other reasons why Asar did not want to show Elias those broken gates.

The sensation of Asar's skin near mine, his magic calling to me, grew too distracting. I pulled my hand away and tucked it into the towel.

He was right about so much. We'd barely made it through the first Sanctum alive. It would be stupid to deny myself a weapon. My mission was important—the fate of the world, and my soul, depended on it.

But I had clung to Atroxus for so long. A few burns were such a small price to pay to drag myself that much closer to my humanity. Maybe the pain made it easier to ignore that I had to reach deeper and deeper over the years to find those remaining pieces of faith. Easier to ignore the spread of the vampire in me, a necrotic infection in a slow march to the surface.

I had promised Atroxus that I had always been faithful. But this didn't feel like faith. It felt like temptation—like crying out the wrong name in bed.

"I can't." My voice was weaker than I wished it was. "It's not who I am."

Asar pulled another towel from a crooked copper rack. "Here. You're still shivering."

I wrapped it around my shoulders, grateful to put an extra layer between myself and the rest of the world.

"When I was exiled to Morthryn, I thought that I had nothing left worth living for," he said. "I was the bastard second son who was always lucky to be allowed to live. But I did what I had to, to earn something like respect. To build something out of nothing." He let out a bitter laugh. "And believe me, I *bled* for it, Iliae. Carved out my own heart for it. And I destroyed it all. I couldn't even hate my father for sending me here, because I deserved it. I was happy to let this place be my end."

His gaze flicked up to mine. The light of his left eye pulsed faintly with his heartbeat. "But it wasn't. It was a beginning."

"How?" I asked.

I could only manage the one word. But what I meant was: how could something so terrible be anything but an end? How could a wound that deep be anything but fatal?

Asar took a long time to answer. He pressed his hand to the cracked wall.

"I began to hear things that no one else did," he said quietly. "Cries that needed answering. The world is built atop the invisible, abandoned souls. They needed someone."

They needed someone.

There was no mystical Turned connection that could make me feel Asar's soul more deeply than I did in this moment.

I thought of him silhouetted against that broken door, one man standing between the collision of worlds.

Asar, I now understood, was like me. Not because he was related to my maker, or because he wielded a magic that spoke so innately to mine. But because he, too, was a healer. He had devoted himself to fixing the broken things that no one else saw.

How could I deny him help with that?

It was still in service to my mission, I told myself. It was the rational thing to do.

But I still felt like a traitor when I said, "Fine. I'll help you."

PART THREE

BREATH

INTERLUDE

he years went by easy. The little girl grew slowly toward woman-hood. The glimpses of darkness in her life at the Citadel blended into the background, innocuous strokes in a grand mural of pur-pose. Her visits from Atroxus continued, and she continued to be as awed by him as he was delighted by her. She swallowed up her studies with verve and enthusiasm. She began to go on missions with her sister and her fellow acolytes, presenting her god with the trappings of her victories—souls converted to the light. But while the girl loved the approval of her god, she did not do this for glory or praise. The light had saved her when she'd had nothing to offer it at all, and now, she found genuine joy in every sunrise. She and her sister traveled far and wide. Everywhere they went, the girl found more people just like her—hurting people who needed someone to help them home.

"It was all for this," her sister would tell her. "So that we can be their torch."

Her sister, indeed, was perhaps even better at this than she was. While the girl thrived upon working with lost souls, she often struggled to sit still in lessons. And though she loved magic, she hated combat training. She was too young to be sent off to fight in the name of the light—battles with rival sects of other gods, or to protect persecuted followers of the light, or, most terrifying of all, vampire hunting—but she dreaded the day she would be called upon for that purpose. Her sister went, sometimes, and the girl never liked how she looked when she returned—exhausted and blood-smeared, with eyes that looked right through her for a few days after.

Her best friend—now a young man, tall and gangly—was called away be-fore she was. They sat together in her room the night before he left. He was a handsome boy, with large eyes and fine features. They had sat next to each other like this countless times, but tonight, the girl could not stop thinking about the spot where their elbows touched. She watched his mouth as he talked and wondered what it would feel like against hers, and as the hours wore on and his pauses grew longer, she knew he was wondering, too.

But before it could go any further, her sister threw the door open. The girl pulled away from her friend, who leapt to his feet and mumbled an excuse to leave. Her sister watched him go silently, and then she closed the door and unleashed the greatest verbal firestorm that the girl had ever witnessed from her eternally calm, sweet, wonderful sibling.

"Do you have any idea what you almost did?" she said. "Do you not understand what you are? Do you not understand why we have this life at all? You are a chosen one of the sun. He chose you."

She put great stress upon the word he. It was clear who he was. He was not the sweet fifteen-year-old boy with the big eyes.

"You have been bestowed with the greatest honor anyone could ever dream of," she went on. "The punishment for disrespecting gods is unimaginable. You cannot betray him. Not ever."

"Betray him?" the girl gasped. "I would never do that. Why would you think I—"

But even as she said the words, her own stupidity dawned on her.

The acolytes of her sect did not take chastity vows. And for all the years that Atroxus had visited her, he never laid a hand upon her. No one had explicitly told the girl what it meant to be "chosen." She knew she had given her god her soul; it wasn't until now that she realized she one day would be expected to give him her body, too. That from the moment he'd plucked her from nothing, it had already belonged to him.

The girl felt foolish and naive. Her sister let out a long sigh and sat beside her.

"I'm sorry," she said. "You've been given such a great responsibility for your age. But you are extraordinary. He saw that in you. You don't get the opportunity to make mistakes the way other young people do."

The girl nodded, mouth dry. She watched her sister as she adjusted her hair, the firelight tracing the outline of her cheek. She was, by any measure, the prettier sibling. Surely, if she had been the sister chosen, she would have understood right away what was expected of her—just as the long hours of prayer and the combat the girl found so distasteful came easily to her, too. She would have made a perfect bride of the sun.

And yet, the girl was the one who received the first pick of food at dinner, who avoided the most dangerous chores, who was treated well by even the strictest priests. Meanwhile, her sister still fought for her respect, and never once complained.

The contrast in their treatment, gone unnoticed for years, now lurched into ugly focus. The full responsibility of her role settled over her, heavy on her shoulders. But she quickly chased that feeling away. This was no sacrifice. Atroxus had given her and her sister a home, he had given her the magic that brought joy into every facet of her life, and, most valuable of all, he had given her purpose. She loved her life. She loved her god. It was an honor to be chosen.

Still, the next morning, the girl waved her friend off from afar, careful not to notice the dimple in his cheek. She walked the long way back to the Citadel. The lush greenery was wild and untamed out here, but she glimpsed a flash of light among the emerald green. The bars of the gate were lovely polished gold. She wrapped her hands around the warm metal.

She didn't mean to push against them, but she found herself doing it anyway.

CHAPTER FOURTEEN

Our journey to the next Sanctum dragged on. Time muddied the farther we got from the surface of the mortal world—there was no sunrise or sunset to mark the end of a day, after all, and we soon traveled so far that I couldn't even feel the sun in my veins at all.

Asar led us through a twisting maze of hallways and staircases. The path was convoluted. Sometimes, we had to leave the halls of Morthryn and venture briefly into the Descent. It was barren out there, the ground dusty and sky empty. I could hear cries in the distance, but Asar always quickly shepherded us back to another mysterious branch of Morthryn's roots before we had any encounters with whatever made them.

Asar reminded us often that this was nothing compared to what we'd experience in the lowest Sanctums—where Morthryn's roots didn't extend at all, and we would have no reprieve from the Descent itself. Still, the journey was tiring. Our bodies knew we were venturing into territory where mortals didn't belong and reacted appropriately. Our fingernails blackened. Our eyes were tired. Chandra, as a human, had the lowest tolerance for it. Her face grew wan. The prayers at her lips were constant. When we all lay down to rest, I'd hear them whispered long into the night. It reminded me of the hushed hymns I'd hear at the Citadel, the distant echoes audible even from my room.

It should have been comforting, and I wasn't quite sure why it wasn't. Maybe because I increasingly felt as if I were hiding something from my god.

While the others rested, Asar would come and get me from my makeshift bed. He led me to various arched doorways that looked like the one I'd saved him from. Some were much calmer, intact, if straining. Others crumbled, clearly at the precipice of collapse. Together, we would restore the glyphs.

It was easier than I wished it was.

Asar had been right—the same techniques applied, even if the magic was different. It wasn't complicated stuff. Asar basically fed it to me, doing all the hard work of the setup and leaving me to extend the reach of his magic. But it reminded me of my early days in the Citadel, when I'd gleefully discovered magic for the first time, and had thought that nothing could be so easy or fun or *simple* like this.

Meanwhile, every time I would huddle alone at night and try to call the power of the sun, I had to haul it to the surface like a boulder that just kept getting heavier.

The contrast scared me. I walked the line of my faith carefully. I'd agreed to help Asar with the gates, but I refused to go further than that. Maintaining the veil, I figured, was beneficial to Atroxus, too. And besides, if the Descent collapsed, we'd never make it to Alarus's resurrection at all. I couldn't justify anything more than that. Not when the temptation was so great.

This aggravated Asar, who, I quickly learned, was borderline gleeful at the prospect of pushing my magical abilities. Maybe he saw me as another interesting artifact to add to his extensive collection. Or maybe he was just confused by me, and it offended him to leave questions unanswered.

Either way, I had to constantly slip from his attempts to dissect my abilities. It started out as me turning down training exercises. Then he started to get sneaky about it. He went through a stretch where I would constantly sense him pressing on my mind, and I'd be forced to steel my mental walls against him.

Eventually, I pushed him violently away and snapped, "I told you to stop doing that!"

He just smirked in victory.

"You're unusually good at that," he said, too casually. "You should practice more."

The bastard had been *testing* me.

That one had almost worked, because the last thing I wanted was to incentivize Asar to rummage around in my head, knowing how important it was that I kept my secrets intact. But I held my ground. I reinforced the gates. I helped Asar when he needed it. No more than that.

Only one other time did the dead breach a gate, like they had the night I rescued him.

It wasn't nearly as bad this time. Only a few of them got through. Asar and Luce barely needed my help fighting them off. And I was grateful for that because *he* was one of them.

I tried to hide the way I shied away from him and the sigh of relief I let out when Luce herded him back through the door. He'd reached for me, and only me, as he fell through again. I could hear his pleas echoing in my head as Asar and I repaired the gate.

Afterward, I lingered with Asar longer than I usually did. I wasn't in any rush to go lie down and see the ghost of that half-rotted face as I listened to Chandra's prayers to the god that had failed him. We sat in a dusty old sitting room, gnawing on a piece of bread—after I'd complained enough, he'd started offering me real food, too, not just blood. I appreciated it, even though it also gave me the distinct impression that I was probably being trained like a dog. The food didn't taste like much these days, but it reminded me of what it felt like to be human.

Asar was talking about something that I wasn't paying attention to. "Iliae!"

I flinched. "I don't like it when you call me that."

He gave me an odd look over his shoulder. He was sorting books on a crooked bookshelf. Apparently, he didn't approve of Morthryn's organizational systems.

"It's your name," he said.

I didn't feel like explaining it.

"Why are you still here?" he asked. "You're usually long gone by now."

I didn't have an answer for him. So I asked the question that had been nagging at me instead. "Are any of them here for you?"

He turned around and set the book down. "Who?"

"Them. At the door."

"You mean the wraiths."

I nodded. Something flickered in his face. I liked trying to read Asar. I found most people easy to decipher, but he was a nice little challenge, like the wooden puzzles Saescha used to give me when I was a child.

"I don't have many who would follow me anywhere, dead or alive."

Luce whined at this, as if offended by her erasure, and Asar scratched her head absentmindedly.

"That's not a no," I said.

He paused before answering. "We all have things that haunt us. I've damned many souls to the Descent. I wouldn't fault those scorned souls if they were looking for their vengeance."

Vengeance. My heart lurched at that. I hadn't thought of it that way. Was that what Eomin wanted? Could I blame him, if it was?

I was quiet, gnawing on my crusty bread. I could feel Asar's stare, though I dutifully ignored it. It was a mistake to stay here. I should've just gone to bed, where he wouldn't be looking at me like that.

"Who's the boy?" he asked.

I stopped chewing.

Of course he'd noticed. I hated that he had, and I hated that I wasn't surprised.

I held up the bread. "Do you have anything better than this hiding somewhere?"

"A lover?" he guessed.

I thought of an elbow touching mine.

My heart clenched, but I laughed lightly and gestured to myself. "Priestess."

"The Order of the Destined Dawn doesn't require chastity vows."

Gods fucking help me. Leave it to Asar to know every inane detail of a religious group half a world away.

"My sect did," I lied. "We should get back and get some rest before the others wake up." I started to stand.

But behind me, Asar said, "What was his name?"

I stopped mid-stride.

I tried not to say it, even to myself. It was too painful. I hadn't spoken his name—any of their names—in so long. Not even to Raihn, in his many fruitless attempts to learn more about my past. I didn't get to say their funeral prayers or write upon their gravestones.

"What happens to them?" I asked quietly. "The ones who are stuck out there in the Descent? Can they pass through on their own?"

A pause. "Sometimes," Asar said.

He was trying to spare my feelings, which was actually sweet.

"The truth," I said.

"The ones who get trapped occasionally can slip through to the underworld, as they were supposed to. But most of the time, they just wander, frozen in whatever phase of the transition they got caught in, trying to get to life or to death."

"Forever?"

I thought of how many souls I'd seen in the Sanctum of Body alone. Hundreds. Thousands. And surely, there were countless more that never crossed my path.

All those people, stuck between life and death, forever?

My friend, stuck there, *forever*?

Asar's nonanswer said all it needed to.

"What was his name, Iliae?" he asked instead. "Just his name."

I hadn't said it in so long. But he deserved to be acknowledged aloud. "Eomin," I said, and I turned away before Asar could see the tears stinging my eyes.

CHAPTER FIFTEEN

"That looks welcoming," Elias said.

Chandra made the sign of the sun over her chest.

We stood at the end of Morthryn's hall. An arched doorway towered over us—much grander than the gates Asar and I had been maintaining these last weeks. White smoke swirled within it, and mist clustered around its base, rolling across the floor.

But it, too, was damaged. Long lightning-strike cracks ran through the frame. Red liquid dripped from them, pooling in the intricate filigree and spilling over the tile. The smoke rose and fell with a steady cadence that looked just like a frozen winter's exhale.

The Sanctum of Breath. The second level of the Descent.

I eyed the blood on the floor. "Is it supposed to do that?"

"It's part of the Descent," Asar replied.

"Does that mean . . . yes?"

"It means that many things here don't follow rules."

He said this like it greatly pained him to admit it. I'd gathered by now that Asar enjoyed rules.

I leaned closer to the arch. A shimmering silver veil, like a translucent silk curtain, fell over the open doorway. It was so delicate that the shadows beyond nearly consumed it, only visible when it caught the light just so.

Asar pulled me back sharply when I ventured too close.

"We step through together. There will be a sheer fall on the other side, and I don't want anyone getting lost this time."

"No path?" Elias asked.

He didn't do a particularly good job of hiding how unnerved he was. He liked threats that he could stab into submission. The ones we were about to face weren't so simple, as Asar had warned us many times. "The dead we saw before were nothing compared to what we're about to face," he had said. "Those still had a body, or at least, parts of it. It's harder to kill something that doesn't have one at all."

Now, Asar simply shook his head. "No. No path this time."

He offered no elaboration, but I'd seen enough these last few weeks to know the truth behind it. Maybe there had once been a path. But it, like so many things about the Descent, had collapsed.

Then he added, like he couldn't help himself, "Not that the path helped you last time anyway."

I resisted the urge to jab him in the ribs.

Chandra summoned a golden glow in her hand—a habit she'd developed these last few weeks—and pressed it to her chest, letting out a shaky breath of resolve.

Asar affixed a thread of shadows to our anchors, binding all five of us together. At his instruction, we formed a chain. Luce was in the front, extending a wriggling tentacle of shadow to Elias, who looked somewhat disgusted before taking it. Then he took Chandra's hand, who offered me her other one. It was still warm with the remnants of Atroxus's light. I gave her a bright, encouraging smile.

I offered my other hand to Asar, who was last. His long fingers wound around mine.

To Chandra, I played the role I was born for: bright, reassuring optimist, immune to all doubt. But Asar, I knew, felt my nagging unease. He squeezed once, so quick I questioned if I'd imagined it.

"Ready?" he said.

No one answered. None of us were ready—not really. But Luce stepped forward anyway, sending us toppling through the door. The mists welcomed us with open arms.

And then we were falling, and falling, and falling.

My mouth was full of dust. It was so fine that even after I spit it out, a layer still coated my tongue.

Blegh.

I shook my hair and coughed when it sent up a cloud of gray. Beside me, Elias patted the dirt from his cloak as he rolled onto his hands and knees. Chandra rubbed her temples, as if she was battling a nasty headache. Asar, of course, was already on his feet. Beside him, Luce licked her paw as if she couldn't imagine what was taking us all so long.

I blinked the sand out of my eyes and looked around.

The first Sanctum, Body, had been the closest to the mortal realm, and the one that most resembled it. Now, we'd ventured deep enough to see the labyrinth of the underworld start to take shape. Above, there was no more sky, only endless layers of red rivers that layered over each other to a sea of ominous dark crimson. Smooth stone walls of bright white towered around us. Dots of red and black beaded on the porous surface. The blood pooled into countless ancient carvings that looked as organic as the veins in leaves.

I touched the nearest wall. Bone.

Luce looked out to the gap between the walls, a long pillar of darkness, and whined.

"Let's go," Asar said. "It's only a matter of time before they notice us. The quicker we get to the temple, the better."

They. Wraiths.

There would be many of them here—definitely more than Asar and I encountered at the gates. Who else would find me? The dread that I might see Eomin's face again—or worse, what if I saw—

Weathered hands wrapped around mine. I'd been shaking. Chandra gave me a comforting smile. Gods, she really did remind me so much of the priestesses when she looked at me like that. I weakly returned her smile and followed the others.

We started toward the gap in the cliffs.

"What exactly are we looking for?" I asked as we walked, grateful to fill the silence. "What does Breath . . . *look* like?"

It had been easy to wrap my mind around Alarus's sacrifice for the Sanctum of Body—a branch bearing his blood. But Breath was so abstract. It could be interpreted in countless different ways.

Asar took a long time to answer, which by now I knew meant he was trying to avoid saying *I don't know.*

"It could be anything that represents . . . vivacity."

My brow furrowed. "Vivacity?"

"A perfect corpse is still not living until it breathes, or its heart beats, or it changes with time. That's Breath. The nature of being alive. It may be something intangible, but it would represent the essence of connection to life."

"Makes perfect sense," Elias grumbled.

"It does, in a way," I said. "It's the things that make your heart skip or your breath quicken."

I thought, involuntarily, of Asar's hand over mine, and the flush of my skin as darkness writhed between them.

We passed through the narrow opening in the cliffs, and I stopped short.

The world opened up around us. We were on a narrow bridge, hundreds of feet above the dusty ground below. The landscape encapsulated every shade of the mortal world. Undulating waves of a distant sea. Platinum sands like those of the House of Night. Rolling fields of lush green. Blankets of overgrown forests.

Any static picture of it would have been beautiful on its own. But what made it breathtaking was its constant evolution. It changed moment by moment. Mountains towered and leveled. The desert dunes swept away and back again. Forests rose, withered, regrew. All of it constant, like the steady rhythm of a heartbeat.

The wraiths were everywhere—gray spots wandering across the distance and cluttering the ground below. I leaned over the rail to peer down at them. Their bodies were whole, just translucent, a shadow of what they'd once been. A few looked up, as if they smelled my presence. Their mouths opened in a soundless moan as they reached for me.

The dead in the first Sanctum were still angry, raging against their fate. These had moved past anger. They were grieving.

The others had moved ahead, but Asar stopped behind me. "You don't want them looking at you too long," he said.

I nodded, but I still stared out at the horizon, at the ever-shifting landscape, and the wraiths, frozen in time, within it.

"Entranced, Dawndrinker?" he said, when I didn't move.

"I was trying to decide why this felt so familiar," I said. "And then I realized, this is what it feels like to be Turned. You're stuck between layers as the entire world changes. And you're in the middle of it all, watching it happen, and yet none of it can touch you."

Not living. Not dying. Starving for both.

At Asar's silence, a wave of self-consciousness passed over me. I chanced a glance at him and was startled by the way he was looking at me. So intently, like he was unraveling a tapestry.

I looked away quickly and shrugged. "I know. That doesn't make sense."

But he simply said, "Yes. It does."

He nudged me along, and we kept walking.

WE WOUND THROUGH bridges and pathways, navigating the maze of cliffs. As we walked, the wraiths grew more numerous. Soon, they surrounded us. Up close, they were even more unnerving—faces hollow, eyes white and milky.

"Ignore them," Asar had told us, keeping his gaze fixed ahead. "They're attracted to us because they can smell the life on us. But the less attention you give them, the less they have to grab on to. They want to be acknowledged."

It went against my every instinct to walk past starving souls who wanted to be seen so desperately. I felt their pain every step of the way.

They were particularly attracted to Chandra. Maybe it was because she was human, the stench of her mortality so much stronger. They surrounded her, watching her like a caged animal.

"Asar . . ." Elias said uneasily as he narrowly avoided the curious reaching hand of what looked to be a dead priestess, blindfold over her eyes.

"Keep walking," Asar hissed. "Don't look at them."

We passed through another hall, which, fortunately, was so narrow that it forced back some of the wraiths. When we emerged, we were at the end of a long, straight path.

"There," Asar said.

I followed his gaze, and my heart sank.

The building ahead rose straight out of the earth like an organic growth, the bone forming three spires that pierced the rivers of blood in the sky. Deep ridges spiraled around each one, which then interwove around great arched windows and an imposing door. Above the entrance, a massive, circular stained glass window stared down at us—a crimson eye, another mark of Alarus.

Elias let out a curse, and Chandra whispered a shaky prayer.

Beasts surrounded the temple.

They weren't quite as big as the guardians at the veil, but they were damned close. Their long, reptilian bodies clung to the walls and curled around the spires. The light reflected off sleek black fur, and their eyes glowed with ethereal white. One opened a cavernous mouth and rolled out a long black tongue to lick the glistening red from the bone.

I counted at least ten, and that was just what we could see from this angle.

"Souleaters." Asar spoke in a near whisper, careful not to draw more attention from the wraiths. "They have a taste for—"

As we watched, a wraith wandered a little too close to the temple. One minute he was shuffling along, and the next, he was gone; the beast was settling back around the spire and licking its chops.

The name made sense.

"Why are there so many?" Chandra whispered.

"There used to be measures to keep them out of the Descent, but they've learned how to slip past," Asar said. "They've multiplied the last few centuries."

"But why are there so many *here*?"

"They're attracted to the wraiths."

I pieced together what that meant and swallowed a curse.

"So the temple is full of wraiths?" I said.

Asar didn't answer, which I took to mean, *Yes, but I don't want to say it and make everyone panic again.*

"If we're quiet and calm, they shouldn't bother us." He shot us each a pointed look, one by one. "Quiet. And. Calm."

The temple seemed at once steps away and painfully far. Most of the distance between us and the door was a wide-open stretch, which meant there were no cliffs or rocks to shield us from the wraiths. We had already assembled quite a following, and as we crossed into open space, more drifted toward us like flies to a rotten carcass.

Up close, the souleaters were terrifyingly large. Their eyes released trails of glowing smoke. Their stares were a thousand miles deep, even as they gave us disinterested, impassive glances. Asar was right. They didn't seem interested in us so long as we didn't give them a reason to be.

And to our credit, we did manage *quiet and calm*. At first.

The pack had tightened around us. It was getting harder and harder to keep ignoring them. The woman moved so swiftly in the crowd, we didn't even notice her until she had broken through. She wore the ethereal remains of a long white nightgown, though everything from the hips down was covered in black bloodstains. Loose braids hung about her angular face in the remains of a once-elaborate hairstyle, now frizzy and half-undone.

She stretched toward Chandra.

"I *kno-o-ow* yo-u-u," she moaned, fanged mouth twisting around the words like they were foreign objects. "I know y-you!"

The wraith lurched closer, long fingers clawing at Chandra's arm.

In a matter of seconds, *quiet and calm* unraveled.

Chandra let out a panicked cry as the wraith grabbed her. I pulled Chandra's other arm, yanking her from the wraith's grip. Elias swung his sword, which passed harmlessly through the woman's translucent body. But the strike at least bought me enough time to call the flame, which took too long to come to me.

The wraith threw her hands up with an enraged cry. Asar jumped in, muttering spells under his breath as he swung his sword. One strike, and she dissipated like smoke.

But I raised my head to see the beasts upon the temple walls raising their heads, those eternal eyes spearing through us with renewed, hungry interest.

"The door," Asar bit out. "Go!"

Quiet and calm was officially abandoned in favor of *run as fast as you fucking can.*

We'd made it more than halfway to the temple doors. Only about a hundred paces remained. And yet, that distance seemed infinite as we broke into a frantic sprint. Chaos erupted. The wraiths descended upon us, pleas rising to a crescendo, awakened to fresh desperation now that one of their own had touched us.

Luce bounded ahead, clearing the path as best she could. The souleaters stirred, more and more white eyes turning to us. As they began to move, she snarled and snapped up at them, like she was ready to take them all down herself.

Thirty paces.

The door loomed. We were an inelegant tangle of running limbs and swords and light and magic, all barely holding off the onslaught.

Two souleaters slithered down from their perches, black tongues sliding free in preparation.

Fifteen paces.

The doors groaned open in an ominous invitation.

I should have been relieved. Instead, dread prickled at the back of my neck. Not that I was in any position to question shelter when both the dead and the beasts that consumed them were bearing down upon us.

Cold, dead fingers closed around my arm, and I stumbled, fighting off the wraith with a sputtering blast of light—the best I could manage.

The ground shook as the first souleater leapt from its perch.

Ten paces.

So close. Luce bounded through the door, quickly followed by Elias, then Chandra.

I pushed myself through one final sprint—

Something hard caught the toe of my boot. The ground flew up to hit me before I even knew I was falling. My face cracked against the sand, limbs tangling as my momentum threw me into a grotesque somersault. I recovered quickly, but as I pushed myself back up, I found myself staring into a massive open mouth.

I expected teeth, a tongue, all the typical trappings of the jaws of a deadly beast. Instead, within the souleater's mouth was simply . . . nothing. Torturous, starving emptiness, stretching beyond the bounds of this world.

The jaws opened, and opened, and opened.

"Iliae!"

Asar's shout echoed distantly. I didn't even have time to turn my head. But then, I didn't need to look at him—I felt him, just as I did at every gate we repaired. His magic reached up inside of me, an open hand ready to be seized.

I didn't have to think. I just did it.

A blast of darkness erupted around me, consuming my vision. The souleater let out a high-pitched wail. My body went flying with the force of it, but someone took hold of my arm before I could hit the ground, and together, we *ran*.

The sand turned to tile beneath my feet. A deafening BOOM rang out just behind me. The next thing I knew, I was on all fours upon a smooth floor. Asar's hand was still on my arm.

"Holy gods," I gasped. "I thought—"

"Too close, Dawndrinker." Asar sounded more shaken than I might have expected.

I rose shakily. "Thank you. For the help."

He shook his head. "It was you."

It wasn't *all* me, but it was nice of him to share the credit.

Elias's voice pulled my attention away. "Didn't you say that there would be many wraiths in here?"

I looked around at the temple. *Beautiful* wasn't the right word. This was complex and dark and interesting. The ceiling rose above us in majestic peaks, white, blood-slicked stone dyed red with the filtered light through stained glass windows. Massive carvings stretched over the walls, depicting the sun, the moon, the earth and sky—countless works of excruciatingly stunning art, so much of it that my eye couldn't even find a place to rest. Six doors stood before us, each bearing the eye of Alarus at their peak.

My hair rustled with a distant breeze, even though the door was closed. A hollow wheeze echoed through the hallways. Breathing, I realized with a chill. Breathing from the walls.

Elias's words sank in.

Yes, it felt alive in here, in a strange way. But it was empty. No wraiths. No dead.

Asar's brow furrowed. He stepped to the center of the room, turning slowly. His scarred eye glowed, silver unfurling from it like funeral incense.

Something was wrong. The dead should be here, drawn to the remaining scrap of Alarus's power.

They *should* be, but they weren't.

Did that mean that Alarus's power wasn't here at all?

Or did it mean that something more terrifying was here instead? Something that frightened even the dead away?

Luce let out a low growl. Dread fell over Asar's face.

"We need to—" he started.

The breathing of the temple stopped.

Everything went dark.

A plume of smoke devoured the light that seeped through the windows. I felt the magic in here sour, like fruit going rotten. My mouth tasted rancid. My skin puckered to gooseflesh.

I could barely make out Asar's silhouette at the center of the room. The air around him writhed—misty ebony snakes coiling, coiling, coiling around his body.

And then I saw her.

The woman emerged from the darkness like she was rising from beneath the depths of an endless sea.

"I knew you'd come back," she crooned. "That's what I always loved about you. You were always so very, very loyal."

CHAPTER SIXTEEN

Don't look at her," Asar commanded. But it was too late. I couldn't take my eyes off her. How could I? She was repulsively stunning.

She melted into the shadows, her body comprised of countless tattered shreds of darkness wavering in and out of solid form. She was clearest out of the corner of my eye, and difficult to pin down in a direct stare. Her face was striking—high cheekbones, full lips, deep hair the color of vampire blood, which fanned out around her as if underwater. Her limbs were long and delicate, and at certain angles, I glimpsed the bone within. She wore a scarf around her neck, eye-searing red, floating in an invisible breeze.

But of all of it, I couldn't look away from those eyes. Empty as the mouth of the souleater had been, belonging to neither life nor death.

She was not a wraith.

I knew that immediately. Her want, so keen-sharp I could feel it beneath my fingernails, was so much more painful than the mindless hunger of the dead.

With every blink, she melted to a new location. First she was at the corner of the room, then behind Asar, then coiling around him—ribbons of dark sliding over his shoulders, around his throat, caressing his face. An embrace. A noose. Luce circled her, barking, hissing.

"I've missed you so much," she breathed. "It has been a long time."

Asar was not looking at her. He was still, his jaw tight, body rigid, like it took every shred of focus to keep his composure intact. But his gaze met mine over her shoulder, and that one look drove a stake through my heart. Because despite his stoicism, there was no denying what I saw in his eyes:

Terror.

"Run," he whispered.

The word made the world stop.

Blink, and the woman spun around, her death-stare spearing me.

RUN.

I started to move—not away from Asar, but toward him, a gut instinct that even I didn't understand in the moment. But Elias grabbed my arm and hauled me back through one of the arches. Asar's stare held mine until Elias dragged me around a corner.

"We can't leave him there." My legs tangled under me. Elias was now at a full-on sprint. Chandra was long gone ahead. Ivory carvings smeared past me. The halls twisted and forked, and Elias chose his route seemingly at random.

"Sure as shit we can," Elias said. "He wants us to follow orders? We'll follow orders."

"She'll—she'll *kill* him." I barely got the words out. But even as I said them, I knew *kill* wasn't the word for what she would do. I'd felt her starvation. I somehow knew it would be worse than that.

Elias scoffed. "If only."

The silence of the temple had shattered, those steady breaths now warping to grotesque gasps. A throbbing beat thumped under the walls, the floors, like the temple itself couldn't quell its quickening heart. Dread nipped at our heels. At some point, Elias stumbled, and my hand slipped from his grasp. When I reached out for him again, he was gone. Chandra was, too, and I was alone in the winding halls.

Fear screamed in my ears. Far in the distance, I thought I heard Luce's frantic barks—but was I imagining them?

I slipped in a slick puddle and collided with a turn in the hall, forehead smacking against ivory. I spat a curse, but as I pushed myself up again, the shock of pain actually cleared my head. My palm pressed to the wall as I tried to make sense of my surroundings. How far had I run? I wasn't sure—I'd been lost in such a blind panic.

Think, Mische. Don't just bolt. Think.

I forced in a breath, slower than the ones that shook the temple walls.

It was easy to run. It was what this place wanted us to do. It was manipulating our fear until it made us panicked animals.

I squinted down the two paths that split before me. Both fell into shadow, identical.

This was a maze, I realized. That was the test. Like the second Trial of the Kejari. But I'd already gotten myself hopelessly lost. I didn't remember how I'd come, or even when I got separated from Elias. It felt as if someone had reached into my mind and scrambled those memories—hell, maybe that's exactly what this magic had done to me.

There had to be a way out. A key Atroxus had left.

I flattened my hands against the wall. They were covered in carvings, glyphs that reminded me of the ancient ones on the gates Asar and I repaired. I tried testing my magic against them, but it was like trying to speak a language I only understood in fractured syllables—one that had been dead for thousands of years now.

Then my fingertips passed over something familiar.

I stopped. Dragged my hand back, then repeated the movement.

The wall *looked* like smooth ivory here, unmarked. But when I touched it, I felt the indentations beneath my fingertips. And these were so familiar that I didn't even need to see them to recognize them.

Glyphs of Atroxus.

They were small, running in a straight line that extended, as far as I could feel, all the way down the hall.

The sun felt so, so far away now. It took me too long to find a scrap of it inside myself, and even then, the spark of magic was so tiny that I struggled to make it catch. The burn would earn a disapproving stare later from Asar—or I hoped it would, if we made it out of this alive. But with a hiss of pain and a spark of light, fire at last leapt to my fingertips. It flowed into the glyphs immediately, burning a streak of ancient prayers along the wall of ivory.

Lighting a path.

One path.

A smile broke over my face, but then I hesitated. I looked over my shoulder to see that the trail of light extended behind me, too—potentially, I guessed, all the way back to the doors. It wasn't exactly subtle. Asar would see it, surely. And I had a feeling that it would draw *her* attention.

Maybe that was a good thing. If this brought us to the center of the temple, where the relic was, it could distract her. It would, at least, get Asar to the same location as the rest of us.

The breathing of the walls quickened, as if to say, *Hurry, hurry.*

I didn't have time to doubt it.

I *ran*.

I FOLLOWED THAT streak of light around countless turns. I whispered constant *thank-yous* under my breath because with each one, it became increasingly clear that I would have died in those hallways without Atroxus's help. I prayed Elias and Chandra had spotted it, too.

Eventually, the path ended in a great circular room. It was dark and windowless, plain compared to the entrance's unsettling ornamentation. The thread of fire continued its path all the way around its perimeter, tracing the outline of a single closed door on the opposite side. My eyes snapped to that door immediately. Surely, the relic was behind it—I could practically feel it inside me, tugging and scratching.

But then, as I began to start toward it, something nudged my foot. I looked down.

"Oh, gods," I gasped.

Asar had been right that there had been lots of wraiths here.

Had been.

They covered the floor like withered leaves in winter. Their bodies, or what remained of them, bled into the air like the smoldering remains of a fire. Most were motionless. A few still twitched, as if trying to drag themselves back to whatever scraps of life they'd once had. The fire etched into the walls seemed to awaken a renewed desperation.

They twitched as the light rolled over them, half-formed pleas at their lips. One wraith, an elderly man, weakly grabbed at my ankle.

"Warm," he whispered.

His emotions were a raw, open wound. Fear and grief and pain.

I knelt beside him. "What happened to you?"

But even as I asked, I knew.

They'd been eaten. Something had been preying on them.

Something that was not the souleaters.

Sudden cold fell over me. Smoke gathered in the corners of the room, drawing inward. The wraiths on the floor, or what remained of them, pushed themselves away, as if trying to retreat into the ground.

Her.

Run, Asar's command echoed in my head.

But the terror paralyzed me.

The shadows wove around my throat in a searching embrace. It reminded me of the way Atroxus's hands had slid under my dress on my offering night. Like peeling back the skin of a rare fruit.

"It has been so long since I have been warm, too," she whispered in my ear.

On shaky legs, I forced myself to stand. Her want wrapped around me. She was so hungry—for warmth, for food, for love, for light, for the moon, for the stars.

She pulled back just enough so I could see her face. More solid than those of the wraiths. But more dead, too. Gods, those eyes—

"I used to be as pretty as you," she said wistfully. But I could still see that she had been much more so than I ever was. She still wore the ghost of captivating vampire perfection.

A shiver racked my body as she drew me closer.

"Wh-what is your name?" I asked.

My voice shook, but I tried to sound gentle. Pleasant. She craved life just as the wraiths did. Maybe the key to survival was granting her some of its dignity.

She paused, like this surprised her. But she didn't answer. Instead, her touch lingered over the fresh burns at my wrist.

"You pay a great cost for your light," she crooned. "Don't you, pretty bird?"

And then she smiled, revealing sharp teeth and a rotten pleasure in a rotten truth.

"Leave her."

Asar's voice echoed through the room.

The woman drew back, tightening around me as she shifted behind me. She caressed the underside of my jaw. Back and forth. Back and forth.

Asar's eyes met mine. Only for a moment, before he dragged them away again. But that split-second glance was enough. The woman's wounded chuckle rippled through me.

"Ah." Her lips brushed the crest of my ear. "He likes you. Even if he doesn't know it yet. But don't be fooled. He will ruin you one day, too."

Then, to Asar, "She is very interesting. I see why you enjoy her. Another attractive curiosity. But she only knows how to love things she can fix, and there is no fixing you, is there?"

The laugh that rippled through the air was ugly, rasping, closer to a sob. "Or perhaps that's why you would be so perfect for each other. A girl who can only love broken things, and a boy so broken he can only love what he cannot have. A perfect match."

Asar said, "You're not here for her."

"And who am I here for? You?" A hitch in her voice. "Are you here for me, Asar? Did you come back for me?"

Asar's left eye glowed bright, trails of light streaking from it like tears underwater. His hand fell to his chest, and I felt a corresponding tug on the anchor on my own. He was calling all of us, I realized. Dragging the others back, while feigning a gesture of overwhelmed emotionality.

She can't pass through the door, he said into my mind. *As soon as I tell you to, run.*

But how would I get it open? I didn't know how to answer him, how to ask the question. But I wouldn't have time to form the words anyway. I could already hear footsteps rushing down the hall.

"I've come back for you so many times," he murmured. "You know that. Let me try one more time."

She wrapped tighter around me, balancing on the edge of fury and despair. There was such a fine line between them, and anger was so much easier to bear. "You never say my name anymore," she whispered.

But Asar just said softly, "Please."

Gods, the way he said it. Like he put his entire soul into it.

Asar kept masterful control of his walls, but that didn't mean he was a good actor. I knew, beyond a single doubt, that his desperation was real—deliberately unleashed, yes, but *real*. It was uncomfortable to witness. It reminded me of when I'd seen him in that soaked shirt. Like I was leering at something I was never meant to witness.

He held out his hand.

She wanted to resist him, I could tell. Wanted to toy with him a little longer, make him suffer, to make him beg. Somehow, I got the impression that all those things had happened before.

But above all, I felt her loneliness. And as it so often did, that won in the end.

She slithered away, leaving me swaying in her wake. Asar opened his arms to her. The light that poured from his left eye intertwined with her shadows like a stream reunited with the sea.

His gaze locked to mine. He didn't have time to speak into my mind—but he didn't need to. He'd timed it all perfectly. I was already halfway to the door. Chandra and Elias broached the last turn of the hall, mouths opening in horror at what they saw.

Now.

I wasn't sure if Asar said it, or if I did.

I threw myself against the door, fingers digging into the ridge around it. Firmly closed. Atroxus's glyphs burned into my hands. The door bore a carving of the eye of Alarus, but the sun had been carved over it, magic nested over magic.

I called flame.

Again.

Too slow—

Chandra threw herself against the door beside me, pressing her hands to the door. The light surged from her immediately, searing my eyes as it illuminated the symbol of the sun.

And in the same moment, shadow snaked around me. At first, I thought it was her—but no, this was refined and gentle. Asar. Handing me the last key.

I pressed my palms to the stone, and I breathed Asar's magic deep into my lungs and exhaled.

Dark light flooded from my splayed fingers, radiating out, pouring through the carvings of the door. It illuminated whorls around my hands, then countless words in some lost, ancient language, and then, at the apex of the arch, two eyes of Alarus—lids, iris, pupil.

The door disappeared, revealing spiral stairs.

A roar shook the stone, the frantic gasps of the temple coming to a brutal crescendo. Something wet hit my head, and I looked up to see blood pouring down from the ceiling.

Chandra bolted through, Elias not far behind, and then Luce. But I turned back at the threshold. Asar was surrounded by a collision of darkness and light, his left eye so brilliant that it reduced the rest of his face to silhouette. He cradled the woman close, and for a moment, I thought maybe he was about to kiss her.

But then she screamed. It shook the walls. It shook the earth. It shook the veil between worlds of the mortal and the dead.

He was holding her back to buy us precious seconds for our escape.

And she just kept screaming, a promise of vengeance, as he at last released her and dove for me.

I pulled him through just as she threw herself after him. He collided with me, the two of us falling down the stairs together. Stone clapped against stone as the door slammed shut.

Silence consumed me as the darkness did.

CHAPTER SEVENTEEN

Asar's hand was wrapped around mine. It was the first thing I became aware of as I collected my senses again. Quickly followed, of course, by the delightful assortment of aches and pains.

We were crumpled up together at the bottom of the stairs upon a floor of reflective, polished ivory. It was silent—so much so that I thought at first, *Maybe we died.*

We weren't dead. Everything hurt too much for that.

Asar opened his eyes and held mine for a second that seemed to last an eternity. Luce danced around him, nudging him with her snout. Chandra was next to me, helping me up.

Asar's grasp slid from mine, and he avoided my gaze.

I sat up, and the unbelievable weight of everything I'd just seen crashed down upon me at once.

"Oh, gods—what was—and with the—" The words poured out of me too quickly to form a proper sentence. "What *was* she?"

Who was she?

But before anyone could even attempt to answer, a voice rang out:

You reek of the living.

It went beyond the mortal bounds of sound. I wasn't sure if I was hearing it aloud, or if the words embedded directly into my mind. I knew instantly that it was not human, nor vampire, nor mortal at all.

Slowly, so slowly, I turned my head.

There were no walls, only endless black in all directions. A circular pool of crimson sat, mirror smooth, before us. Within it was a single ivory altar lit by a streak of warm light.

Beside it, a panther emerged from the shadows.

It was golden, translucent, like its form was crafted from the bright streaks of sunbeams in a waning afternoon. Its spots were inkblots of midnight, rippling over lean muscle. Its face was bone. A skull, like Luce's, though gold to her bronze.

Elias coiled, readying his weapon. Chandra made the sign of the sun. Luce curled around Asar's legs, a low, gravelly hiss rising from her throat.

I froze mid-movement, mid-breath. The panther's empty eyes fell to me.

You are a very long way from home. It settled on its haunches. Its body was thin, the jut of bones visible beneath the sheen of its fur. It lifted its head, revealing chipped, glistening fangs.

Many years, many years, since we last scented the sun upon these hallowed halls. Many years since we have allowed it through. Many have fallen to the hands of the traitor. The decay spreads. The guardians wither. He tried to banish us, too. But still we stand. Thousands of years, and we protect our charge. That will not end tonight.

Something moved beyond the panther. At first, I couldn't make sense of the squirming masses. But slowly, more lithe bodies of smoke and bone faces of gold took shape. First two, then four, then too many to count. Some of the panthers were whole, like the one that stood before us. Others bore the wear of their endless watch—their teeth chipped or masks broken, faces slashed in two.

"Gods help us," Chandra whispered, but the irony of that plea was not lost on me.

The gods wouldn't help us. Our gods that damned us. These beasts had been here a long, long time. Long enough to remember Atroxus's betrayal of his brother. Hell did not forget. And as they encroached, I couldn't help but wonder what other betrayals they might smell on me, too.

Above, we could still hear the dim echoes of a tempest raging.

Elias stepped backward, glancing up the stairs. His hands closed around the hilt of his sword, his calculation clear: Which horror was worse? The one in here, or the one out there?

The truth, of course, was that we wouldn't survive either. It was just a matter of deciding whether we were food for ghosts or food for gods.

The panther prowled closer, teeth bared. Before I could give myself time to think, I blurted out, "We come only to right an ancient wrong, g-great guardian. We mean no harm to you."

I mostly kept my voice from shaking. Mostly.

The panther cocked his head in a way that gave me the distinct impression it was laughing at me.

A truth that is not a truth. A lie that is not a lie, it crooned. *Oh, the curse of mortal tongues. Do you think we do not see your soul, fallen one?*

My heart lurched. Its stare pinned open my ribcage, revealing all the ugly complications within. For a moment, I was frozen in fear, terrified my truth was about to be revealed.

But Asar nudged past me. He approached the altar, then set down his sword and lowered to his knees. The beasts circled him. No matter how powerful he was, I knew they could tear him apart. But if Asar was frightened, he didn't show it.

"I serve your master," he said. "I have stood watch over his realm for one hundred and fifty-four years. This, I know, is a blink compared to your eternal vigil. I know, too, that I am but a fallible mortal. I have little to offer but my intentions. But I see the way this realm hurts. I see your sacrifice." He bowed his head. "I ask you, guardians, to trust me with the relic Alarus left behind. Trust me to restore this realm to what it once was."

Asar could not lie to a guardian. This was a being that saw truth.

And yet, though he made no mention of Nyaxia and the task he had been given, I could sense that this *was* truth. Asar was a vampire, a child of Nyaxia. But his heart belonged to the dead.

The leader regarded him. Then lifted its head. It had no eyes, and yet I thought it looked straight at me.

We are no soothsayers. Yet we are close to the threads of fate. We can feel how they vibrate with your intentions. Indeed, a noble mission for such fragile souls. But no mortal can complete such a task. You will not survive the journey you attempt.

"Death is not the same as failure," Asar said.

A sibilant hiss of amusement.

Perhaps, the guardian replied. *But what I say is true all the same.*

It examined us, as if rifling through our souls.

For millennia, we have stood, it said. *We grow weak. The inevitable bears down upon us. Soon, our bones will collapse beneath it, to be buried beneath the million other damned innocents whose fates balance upon your shoulders. Tell us, do you still wish to cure the incurable?*

Asar's answer was immediate.

"Yes," he whispered.

The panther lowered its chin. *Very well.*

It stood and curled around his body. Another panther joined it, and another, and another, until the mass of spotted bodies enveloped him in a sleek ocean of gold and black. The mists hissed from the corners of the room, thickening until there was nothing left to see.

And then, the memory came:

Nyaxia is surrounded by flowers. The poppies paint red around her as she lies back in the grass. The galaxies in her hair have grown more vivid these recent weeks.

Above us, rivers of blood weave through the sky. The breeze shivers through the field. Fate stirs. It has been restless since she arrived, and I should care, but I do not.

She plucks a poppy from the earth and slips it into her mouth. I watch how the petals caress her lips, and I want.

"I like it here," she said. "But you should have made more of it."

"Why?" I ask, and she laughs.

"Why not? Because you can."

Nyaxia is eternally hungry. I see now that this is why my siblings resent her. Because they fear her.

They are right to. She is terrifying.

But I have grown fond of her, and now, when she speaks of great plans of bigger worlds, I see them reflected in the eternity of her eyes.

I touch her cheek and tilt her face toward me. Red, the stain of a poppy petal, smears her lower lip.

It is a mistake. I know this. My heart is heavy in my chest, my breath close to the surface of my ribs. Mortality looms over me. It is intoxicating to feel so fallible. Even gods crave danger.

It is a mistake.

Still, I kiss her.

The images faded. The fog cleared. I was left swaying on my feet. The remnants of fear and desire rushed in my heartbeat—the remnants of Alarus's, his gift to the Sanctum of Breath.

The panthers now sat silently at the edges of the room. The darkness had parted, revealing a stone wall beyond the altar, and a familiar arched, golden door.

Asar was left kneeling alone, his hands cupped around blots of red. Poppy petals.

The guardian bowed its head as its brethren settled at the edges of the pool. Perhaps I imagined that beneath that mask of gold, it actually looked sad.

We were not created to understand such things, it said. *He could have had any woman. And yet his heart was so hungry for her that he let it devour the world for a fleeting taste.*

It lifted its head. Staring at Asar?

Or staring at me?

Asar bowed in thanks, then slowly rose. One by one, we followed him in a silent procession to the waiting door. The guardians did not stop us. Only that one still stood, watching us go.

Be wary, mortals, of such deadly cravings, it said.

I tore my gaze away. Still, its gaze skewered my back as I passed, the arrow of its accusation lodged deep in my heart.

I smell fate upon you, its voice echoed.

But I also smell hunger.

CHAPTER EIGHTEEN

I t's odd that Morthryn had started to feel like safety. We stepped
back into its familiar halls, and immediately, I let out a shaky
breath of relief. Elias let his sword clatter to the stone floor. Chandra sank down on her heels, hands clasped. Even Asar leaned against
the wall, head bowed, like the stone was the only thing keeping him
from collapsing.

Maybe we were all on the brink of collapse, Morthryn included.

The decay was so much worse here. Shattered windows framed
night-black oblivion within twisted metal panes and tattered curtains. Deep gouges ran through the floors, splitting mosaics like gut-
ted carcasses. The distant rumble of settling stone moaned down the
hallways, as if warning of impending defeat.

The guardian's words echoed:

No mortal can complete such a task.

A million damned innocents rest upon your shoulders.

It was not the first time I'd been given an impossible mission.
And the guardians were beings created by a god—not mortal, no,
but certainly not deities, either. They were fallible, just as we were. I
couldn't say whether they spoke belief or prophecy. Just as I couldn't
say whether those words were directed at Asar, or at me.

I couldn't decide which was worse.

Elias was the first to speak. He turned to Asar, lip curled into a
sneer.

"What. The *fuck*. Was *that*?"

His voice rose with each word, until it boomed from the ceilings in a thunderclap. He stalked toward Asar like a starving wolf.

"You were expecting her," he snarled. "You *knew* she was there."

Her.

Immediately, I knew who we were talking about.

A blanket of cold fell over Asar's face.

"I warned you that we would see the dead—"

"Don't shove that bullshit down my throat. Did you think I wouldn't recognize her?"

Asar's eyes slid away, pointedly impassive in a way I knew would drive Elias insane.

"We don't have time for this," he said.

"Is that what you're dragging us to fucking hell for? For *her*? I should have known. There was never any quest from Nyaxia, was there? There was just you, the bastard spare prince that no one wanted, and the dead woman you can't just let—"

I acted before I thought. It was in my nature to be a peacekeeper, and I could see these two hurtling to catastrophic collision.

I touched Elias's shoulder. "Let's just—"

The impact was so swift that I didn't even know I'd been hit until I saw stars. When Elias whirled around, he struck me square across the face. His arm was a mass of muscle that he swung with all the unyielding force of a hammer.

Luce snarled. Asar's left eye flashed with a violent burst of light.

I didn't even see him move.

One minute, darkness enveloped him. The next, Elias went flying against the wall.

"Do. Not. *Touch*. Her." Unlike Elias, Asar didn't growl, didn't yell. His words were clear. Four precise swipes of the blade. "It isn't her fault," he hissed, "that you can't handle witnessing the results of your own actions."

Elias spat blood onto the floor as he pushed himself up. "*My* actions? Don't pretend that you haven't followed your fair fucking share of unpleasant orders, *Warden*. And don't pretend that I was the one who turned her into whatever the fuck that was."

Asar's body was a drawn bowstring, ready for another strike. "Get out," he said quietly. "I don't care where you go."

Elias pulled himself up to his full, imposing height, wiping a trickle of black from his lip. "I wish I could," he scoffed, "instead of following you to the grave. But we can still end this. We don't have to die because you're still chasing after her. You're looking for power, bastard prince? You're looking to redeem yourself after your exile?" He thrust his palm to Asar's pack—to the relics within it. "We have two artifacts of Alarus. *Two.* Did you hear of what the House of Night managed to do with a few of Alarus's fucking teeth? Imagine what could be done with—"

"No."

I put myself between Elias and Asar. I was there during those battles. I saw what had happened when those god teeth, offered by Septimus, Prince of the House of Blood, were used as a weapon. A challenger for the throne had leveraged them to great power, but it had come with catastrophic costs.

"No," I said again. "You can't do that. No mortal should have that kind of power."

I felt like such a fool. I had been so focused on the end goal of this mission that I hadn't even stopped to think about the sheer power that Asar was casually collecting on the way. The thought of what the wrong hands could do with these items—Alarus's purest essence—made bile rise in my stomach.

"Is that what your friends in the House of Night think?" Elias said. "That it's dangerous? Makes them terrible hypocrites, since they've been cultivating it, too."

"That isn't true," I said, without hesitation.

The corner of Elias's mouth quirked, the pleasure of a cat with a bird between its teeth.

"I run the spies, little girl, and we have good ones. Don't know what your Nightborn friends have, but they have something. And I don't blame them for it. They pissed off Nyaxia, killed a Shadowborn prince, and made an enemy of the Bloodborn. I'd be hoarding every weapon I could find, too." The smirk withered as he turned to

Asar. "Can't you taste it in the air? All the Houses are fighting for survival. The House of Blood has conquered a human nation, for fuck's sake—"

"They *what*?" Chandra gasped. "Where?"

My stomach dropped. If that was true, it crossed a line that had never been challenged since vampires first came to be.

The visions Atroxus had showed me of beaches soaked in blood now seemed terrifyingly imminent.

"Some inconsequential island," Elias said. "Glana. Glaea. Something like that. Do the details matter? Even the gods are getting restless. We must be ready to fight. Your sister knows that. Your father—"

"My sister and my father are *ignorant*." Asar spat the word with a sneer. "They see nothing but what's right in front of their faces, and sometimes, not even that. Be lucky that we both still are bound by our oaths, Elias, because otherwise, I'd throw you back out there to rot. And if I listened to your advice, it wouldn't matter anyway because Nyaxia would smite us all for our disobedience."

Elias started to speak, but Asar roared, *"Silence."*

Silence. Silence. Silence.

The command—the compulsion—reverberated against stone. Elias's mouth closed as he stared Asar down with a dagger glare.

Asar surveyed us, shadows clinging to his silhouette. He started to cross to the hallway, then paused at me, eyes lingering at my cheek. Lingering, I realized, at the point of impact where Elias's arm had met my face.

His lips thinned, and he turned away.

"Rest while you can," he said to us. "We'll be moving again soon."

And with that, he disappeared down the hall, Luce at his heels.

CHAPTER NINETEEN

We trudged on for several long, gray days. Asar was quiet and sullen, even by his standards. Elias barely spoke, save to mutter angrily under his breath. Chandra continued with her whispered prayers. Morthryn grew darker and colder.

Asar did not come to get me to help with gates or to push me into training, and I was surprised to find myself oddly disappointed by it. He said nothing at all, actually, even to me. At least I got to rest. But resting just meant being alone with the nightmares, which were painfully vivid since returning from Breath.

The worst one came three nights in. I dreamed I was back in the temple. Wraiths surrounded me, broken bodies on a broken floor, the delicate silvery mist of spirits trailing weakly into the air.

I looked down at the souls scattered at my feet like dead leaves, half-eaten, barely alive enough to fear their own oblivion.

They would die here.

"I'm so cold," a familiar voice said. "I just need to get warm."

Eomin.

I dropped to my knees. Eomin looked up at me through a translucent eye. His body wasn't solid anymore. Chunks of flesh had been bitten away. I tried to touch him, but my hands passed straight through.

"It's all right," I said. "I can help you."

I can help you. Magic words. I tried so hard to always make them true. But now, they tasted like a lie.

A silver tear fell through his body, splashing on the tile floor.

Another voice, a woman's, came from behind me.

"All we need is light, Mi," she said. "That's all. Please."

That voice. It had been so long. I'd started to forget what it sounded like—a little like mine.

"Look at me," she said.

But I squeezed my eyes shut. I was such a coward.

"I can help you," I whispered.

I tried to offer light. But though the burns gnawed my skin, my god was silent.

"Please," Eomin begged. "Please."

"Please, Mische," the voice pleaded. "I followed you. I trusted you."

"I can still save you," I wept. I forced my eyes open and turned around, but all that was there was a dead firefinch, its guts crawling with maggots.

I FLEW UPRIGHT before I was really awake. My dream, thick and sticky, still clung to me. Morthryn was calling to me. I wasn't sure when I started to feel like it was speaking to me, too, all those creaks and moans beginning to take on the cadence of sentences. The others slept, exhausted by our journey and already dreading the next leg of it.

Eomin.

It wasn't just a dream. I knew nightmares, and this wasn't one. This was a vision. I leapt up, running down the halls. I didn't need to think about where I was going. Morthryn guided each step, all the way to the gate.

This one was in poor shape. The top of the arch had broken off completely, leaving just two lonely bronze pillars standing in a slightly crooked monument to death. The veil shifted anxiously, a little faster than it should be in the breeze that shouldn't be there.

Eomin's voice still echoed in my ears, tangling with those of the wraiths in the temple: *I'm cold, I'm hungry, help me, Mische.*

I trusted you.

He was here. I was certain, he was here. I expected to see him, that half-eaten wraith, clawing through the gate.

I ran to it—

A firm grip stopped me.

Mische! the voices called, the veil rippling with the imprints of their fingertips.

"They're coming for me." I barely recognized my own voice. "The gate, they're—"

"You can't touch it."

Asar's voice. I didn't look back at him, railing against his hold.

"They're right there. I can see them, I can hear them—"

"Wake up, Iliae. *Wake up.*"

Bitter cold pierced my cheek, piercing the veil of my dream.

My back was to the wall. Asar held me there, his brow furrowed, forehead bent toward me. His hands cupped my face, holding my gaze to his.

"Look at me," he said. "Remember where you are. Breathe."

I tried to, but my chest hurt. The inhale was a ragged mess. I was crying. Not just crying but sobbing.

"I—I—"

"One more," he commanded.

I obeyed, forcing in and out another shaky, painful breath.

He nodded, as if I'd passed evaluation. But he didn't let go of my face, and even though it was probably because he wasn't sure what I'd do if he released me, I was shamefully grateful for the touch.

"They're here," I forced out. But this time it was weaker, wavering with uncertainty.

"No one is here. The gate is standing." He let out a breath, and then said it again, lower, as if to himself. "No one is here."

I blinked, looking over Asar's shoulder into the room. Nothing but dust and broken stone. No dead. No wraiths. No voices. The shattered door stood, silent and empty, in the gloom.

"It wasn't a dream," I said.

I was sure of that. I knew nightmares well enough to know by now.

Asar's hands fell. Their warmth, and that press of cold, lingered on my cheeks, which now felt oddly exposed to the word. I glimpsed something green in his hand. Ivy, I realized—that was the chill against my cheek. He'd grabbed the nearest freezing thing and tried to shock me out of my vision. Now it thawed in his hand, his palm wet with the glistening remains of melted ice. He glanced at it briefly, but didn't drop it, curling his hand and tucking it into his pocket as he turned to the desolate gate.

"We're getting deep into the Descent now. The boundaries between worlds are weaker. And the rules of the mortal world are getting farther away. So far, the dead have been our biggest threat. But the next Sanctum is Psyche. Soon, our own minds will start preying on us, and that's . . . just as dangerous."

His throat bobbed as he looked to that broken door. It occurred to me that it had been no coincidence he found me. Something had driven him here, too.

Who had he seen?

Her?

I closed my eyes, but just saw Eomin's half-eaten face among those dead wraiths. *Help me, Mische.*

A fresh wave of nausea rolled over me. I leaned against the wall, my head spinning.

"Goddess's sake, Iliae." Asar steadied me immediately. "I just told you, it's all right. Nothing is here."

He didn't understand.

"That's the—that's the—"

Gods fucking dammit. I was crying again.

"It's not about the gate," I managed.

"Then what is it about?"

I sank to my knees, and Asar came right down with me. When I managed to get my eyes open, he was looking at me like I was an ancient tome that didn't make any sense.

"What?" he pressed.

I finally managed, "We haven't seen him. Eomin. Not at the recent gates, or in Breath. He's gone. He was killed by a souleater or—"

"Oh."

I could've sworn Asar let out a breath of relief, though he hid it well, and I found his dismissiveness infuriating.

"He doesn't deserve that," I bit out. "Just *nothing*, like that? *Forever?*"

Not even the suffering of his half death. Just . . . nothingness. I couldn't imagine anything more unjust.

I'd led him here, and that was the end he got?

Asar was silent for a moment.

Then he said, "Your friend was not eaten by a souleater."

"How do you—"

"I know."

"But how—"

"I just know."

I sniffed. My sobs had subsided. Now I scrutinized Asar, whose face was a mask, save for the faintest, faintest twitch at the corner of his mouth.

"How?" I demanded.

He didn't answer.

I leaned closer to him, slowly, inch by inch, until my nose was nearly touching his.

"Asar Voltari, Wraith Warden, Prince of the Shadowborn, caretaker of Morthryn, I can read you like a gods-damned book," I said. "And you *want* to tell me, because if you didn't, you would have wandered off to go loom menacingly in the shadows by now."

His brow furrowed. "Is that what you think I do?"

"How do you know? How do you know he wasn't . . ."

The dream came back to me, powerful and unwelcome. Suddenly, teasing Asar seemed much less fun. It must have shown on my face because his smirk disappeared.

And maybe, just maybe, the notorious Wraith Warden of the House of Shadow actually felt sorry for me.

He sighed wearily, stood, and extended his hand.

"Come with me."

CHAPTER TWENTY

Asar led me deep into the belly of Morthryn, through paths so convoluted I didn't even bother trying to keep track of where we went. With every step, Morthryn broke down further. By the end, it couldn't even be called a hallway anymore. The stone was misshapen and uncut, like cave walls, with remnants of Morthryn's structure buried into it—a patch of broken tile here, a lingering metal rafter there. The air, moist and cool, smelled like iron.

Eventually, we came to a creek of blood that ran through a crack gouged into the slab floor. It looked like it might once have been a much grander river, something like the ones we saw in the Sanctums. Now it was barely a trickle, nestled deep in glistening stone banks far too large for its current state.

Asar surveyed it with his hands on his hips, looking unimpressed. "It'll have to work," he muttered at last. "Best we have."

He helped me down the slick rocks leading to its edge, and then motioned for me to kneel next to him. He pushed his sleeves up to his elbows, revealing the ropey muscle of his forearms, one smooth and tan and the other a spiderweb of bumpy black, delicate as lace. I stared longer than I should have—not at the scars, but at the flesh beneath them.

Asar caught my eye and his mouth flattened. He pushed his hands quickly into the blood, hiding his bare skin.

I wanted to correct him—*I wasn't looking at the scars, I was looking at you*—but the words died awkwardly in my throat.

He said, "Touch the bottom."

I did as he said, pressing my palms down against stone.

Puffs of darkness slowly congealed over the surface of the blood, first around his wrists, then spreading, until dark swirls now engulfed the entire surface of the creek.

"Say his name," Asar said softly.

The black surface of the water was now perfectly smooth, nearly a mirror. I stared at my reflection. My hair had grown past my shoulders, messy curls framing my face. Eomin had always liked it long. Had he found me so quickly down here because I looked just like I had back then? No lines of age, no features weathered by time. Both of us frozen on that night.

I whispered, "Eomin?"

The blood trembled. My reflection disintegrated. And when the ripples smoothed again, I was no longer looking at myself.

It was him.

Eomin.

He was perfect. No wounds. No death-black eyes. He looked just as I remembered him—youthful face, golden hair, dimple on his right cheek. There was no more pain in his expression, no more fear, no more hunger. He gazed peacefully off into the distance, a hint of a smile twisting his mouth.

I let out a shaky exhale. Tears burned my eyes.

"He's healed."

"No," Asar said. "He's dead."

"But he's—"

But he's already dead, I was going to say.

But no. That wasn't true. Eomin hadn't been alive, but he also hadn't been dead. He had been stuck halfway between.

Not anymore.

A tear rippled his face, right over that dimple.

"He made it," I whispered. I didn't even want to blink. He looked as if, at any moment, he might turn to me and smile and say something mundane meant for another version of myself—the girl who was still the brightest star of the Order of the Destined Dawn, beloved by her god, with nothing but goodness ahead of her.

I wanted to stare at him and cradle this little precious shard of my past like a baby kitten. I wanted to hold on to him forever. I wanted to—

"That's enough."

Eomin's face disappeared, leaving me staring at my own reflection again.

His sudden absence was a devastating blow. I choked out, "No!"

"It's dangerous to look too long," Asar said gently. "Best not to give death too much time to call to you."

Too late. It already had. For a moment, every shred of my soul longed to throw myself after my lost friend.

Instead, I sat up and stared at Asar.

"How did you do it?" I asked.

His gaze slid away. "Sometimes they're able to make it through."

I let out a cracked laugh. "You're such a bad liar. You did this. I know you did."

I fully expected him to keep denying it. But after a long moment, he said, "I help them. When I can."

"Help them?"

"Sometimes, I'm able to lead them through the Sanctum back to their intended path. Help them on to the underworld." He staunchly refused to look at me—gods, he almost seemed embarrassed. "It doesn't always work. And it's harder than it used to be. I can't do it often."

A note of shame imbued his voice.

Shame.

As if it weren't the most compassionate thing someone could do for another being. As if even *attempting* to help those who were so helpless to all others weren't such an act of bravery.

It was easy for me to heal the hurts of others. I helped them strip back the bandages on the emotional scars they didn't want anyone to see. It was harder when those wounds were my own. I didn't know what to do with the weight of this kindness. It swelled up inside me, too big, too powerful, to distill into words.

I was still trying to find the right ones when Asar said, very quietly, "He doesn't blame you. You should know that."

The words pierced my chest.

"You—you talked to him?"

"Sometimes they just need someone to listen." I could hear the amused smile in his voice. "He damned near worshipped you, Iliae."

Eomin had seemed so much older, so much wiser, back then. Now, he looked like such a child. He had been so young. Of course he had worshipped me. I had been the chosen one. He'd loved me with all the innocent infatuation of a teenage crush, and I'd led him right to his death.

I drew my knees up to my chest, wrapping my arms around them as if they could protect my exposed heart.

"He was a good friend," I said. "A good person. He didn't deserve it. And I should have . . ."

My voice trailed off. There were so many *should haves*.

A good person, Chandra had called me. It felt like such a hollow compliment. Maybe it had been true a long time ago. Now I had a deficit, a debt taken out against my morality one too many times. All the wrong people had paid for it.

I had been barely conscious when I found what was left of them— him and Saescha. My body was still raging with fever. I remembered wondering if it was a nightmare, a hallucination. Praying it was.

It had been the first of many prayers that would go unanswered.

"What did he tell you?" I asked, even though I didn't quite want to know.

"The dead aren't the best at maintaining a logical conversation. He told me bits and pieces about his life in the Order. And . . . a truly perplexing amount of information about boating."

I choked a laugh. Yes, that sounded like Eomin.

"And he told me about your journey here." Asar's voice softened. "It takes a brave soul to travel to the land of vampires to preach the light, Dawndrinker. I will give you that."

There was not even a hint of mockery in the words. He said it as if he truly meant it.

Once, I would have told him that it wasn't bravery—it was faith. Now, the word that came to mind was *stupidity*, and I hated myself for even thinking it.

I gave him a weak, forced smile. "I told you I wasn't a crusader. It took a conversation with a corpse to make you believe me."

He let out a snort beneath his breath. "Five more minutes with you, Iliae, and I knew you weren't a crusader."

And then, when I frowned, he added, "That is a good thing."

Was it?

I believed that all souls held the potential of light. I believed it even in my darkest regrets, even now. But if Saescha had taken that mission, she would have offered Atroxus a vampire heart with a sword and a stake, not with my sweet, soft, vulnerable words.

If Saescha had been Atroxus's chosen, she never would have needed to buy back his love at all.

As if he could hear my doubts, Asar said, "We all have ghosts in our pasts, Iliae. We can't give them the power to define our futures, too."

It was an uncomfortable reversal, for someone else to offer me the comforts I was so accustomed to doling out. My eyes slid to Asar's face. He stared down into the calm red waters below, deep in thought.

"Was she one of yours?" I asked. "The woman in Breath?"

He flinched, as if he'd been both anticipating and dreading this question.

"Not all the dead are so easily put to rest." He said it with an air of finality, a firmly shut door to any further conversation.

Still, I thought of the way he'd looked when he held out his arms to her. An expression I knew so intimately, I could feel the knife of his regret between my own ribs. I didn't need to know the details to know that the story, at its bleeding heart, was always the same.

"It doesn't make the love worth less," I said quietly, "just because you can't help her the way you wish you could."

Because I knew he needed to hear it. Because I believed it, in the end—or tried to, even if I couldn't always make it true for myself.

His gaze slipped up to meet mine, revealing a fleeting, indecipherable tempest of emotions.

Then he turned away, clearing his throat. "We've lingered too long. You won't see your friend in the Sanctums again. But there will still be other—"

He started to rise, then let out a surprised *oof* as I threw myself against him.

The hug was awkward in every way, the angle making our bodies an uncomfortable mishmash of limbs, my arms around his neck, his knee jabbing my hip. Asar stiffened like a cat unexpectedly captured, debating if he should wriggle away. But I just tightened my arms around him. My face buried against his shoulder. The delicate scent of ice and flowers filled my lungs.

"Thank you," I whispered.

He started to protest, but I said again, more firmly, *"Thank you."*

I didn't mean to hold on so long. But it had been a long time since I'd hugged someone. I didn't realize how much I'd needed it. I couldn't bring myself to pull away because the tears just kept coming, rolling down my cheeks and sinking into the fabric of his shirt.

"Just accept it," I murmured.

"Never."

But his hand fell to the small of my back, and he didn't pull away.

WHEN I FINALLY extracted myself from him, we made the long walk back in near silence. My body and soul were exhausted. I was eager for rest.

Still, right before the turn that would lead back to the others, we paused. Something had been weighing on me these last few days, and I couldn't not bring it up.

"What Elias said when we got back," I said. "About the relics. You can't let anyone use them as weapons, Asar. Not ever. It would be—"

I couldn't even find words to describe something worse than what I'd witnessed in the House of Night.

"Bad," I blurted out. "Very bad. So, *so*—"

"Bad?" Asar provided flatly.

"It's not a joke. I saw what that magic is capable of. It's the kind of power that would be paid for by thousands of innocents."

Some might say it was pointless to warn a vampire prince away from power. Vampire nobles were raised to be vicious—they had to be, to survive in a world where they were born an inherent threat to creatures much stronger than them. Their lives only held as much value as the flesh they managed to carve out of the line of succession, and that meant being deadlier than their competition at all costs. The only thought they gave to the blood of innocents was to consider how much of it they could drink.

Asar was a disgraced second son, an unexpected bastard heir, with everything to prove. Maybe it was naive of me to think he wouldn't want to—*need* to—seize whatever scraps of power he possibly could.

But his smirk had disappeared. "I'm no fool, Iliae. I have enough marks against my soul as it is before tampering with forces that destructive. I'm not here to grab whatever petty power I can and run."

And yet, here he was, attempting to bring a murdered god back to life. Suddenly, I felt silly for even worrying about a tree branch and flower petals, when divine war loomed on the brink of fate.

What if we already are? I wanted to ask. But instead, I chose my words more carefully.

"So this is all about pleasing Nyaxia. This mission."

"You doubt it, too?" A humorless quirk at the left side of his mouth warped his scars. "Egrette found it terribly convenient. Can't say I blame her. A mission from a goddess with no witnesses, just when my father was deciding whether to allow his accidental bastard heir to keep his newfound title, and his life."

Well, when he put it that way, it didn't sound good.

But I shook my head. "No. I believe you."

I knew, of course, that Asar's mission was real. But even if Atroxus hadn't told me so, I would have seen it. This wasn't a cheap grab for glory. There was real weight to his voice when he had told those guardians of his intentions.

"Then what?" he said. "I don't seem the religious type? I will admit, I'm not much for prayer."

"She just must have offered you something incredible."

Asar chuckled under his breath. The halls of Morthryn moaned with it, as if laughing along with him.

"All the typical rewards," he said. "The greatest Shadowborn king in a millennia, history shall know thy name. Et cetera, et cetera."

"You make it sound so compelling."

He lifted one shoulder in a half shrug. His hand pressed to the wall as he swept his gaze down Morthryn's halls. I had never once seen Asar pray. And yet, I recognized the look on his face immediately—reverence.

"It's a powerful gift," he said softly. "To right a wrong."

I heard the echo of Atroxus's offering to me: *Do you not want your redemption?*

I twisted a curl around my fingers, pushing away a sudden awkward discomfort. I yawned.

"I need some sleep," I said. "Before I need to get up and start listening to Elias complain again."

Asar snorted. "Wise." He straightened and tucked his hands into his pockets, looking me up and down. "I haven't been able to travel this deep into the Descent in a long time. The gates will be poorly maintained. We'll need to get back to work." He paused, then added, somewhat awkwardly, "If you feel ready for it."

I stared at him. A smile tugged at my cheeks, and I tried to fight it. Unsuccessfully.

His eyes narrowed. "What?"

"What?"

"Why are you looking at me like that, Dawndrinker?"

It even surprised myself that the real answer was, *I missed fixing things with you.*

But I just shook my head. "Nothing, Warden. Nothing."

CHAPTER TWENTY-ONE

It was getting so, so cold.

We carried onward toward the Sanctum of Psyche. The path became increasingly convoluted, our stretches of easy travel within the bounds of Morthryn's crumbling halls growing shorter. Frost now coated the walls, and the ivy that crawled over every surface was ice white. I could not feel the sun at all.

As we encroached upon the Sanctum of Psyche, the nightmares grew unbearable. I no longer dreamed of Eomin—maybe even my subconscious sensed that he was now at rest. But my other ghosts followed me relentlessly. I dreamed of Saescha and a thousand different terrible versions of her terrible death. I dreamed of Malach and his breath on my throat. I dreamed of Atroxus and his divine rage. I dreamed of Raihn and Oraya, crushed beneath the armies of the House of Shadow or by the wrath of Nyaxia. And I dreamed of the future Atroxus had showed me—not of the grand disasters, but the mortal costs that lived within them. All those invisible souls, just like I had once been.

Naturally, I tried to sleep as little as possible.

Instead, Asar and I tended to the gates. We went out every day now. There was so much that needed repair. We ventured through collapsed rooms and crumbling tunnels. The desolate landscape of the Descent beyond leached into them, frigid snow or dusty sand or tepid, trickling blood rivers seeping through the cracks in the walls and floors. Most of the gates had partially collapsed, the wards so long abandoned that they were thin and fragile as cobwebs. Sometimes, we would arrive at a gate to find that it was totally non-functional, ghostly wraiths wandering around the hall like they'd forgotten where they put their glasses.

Even the wraiths were directionless out here—sad and confused rather than angry. Asar said that any who made it out this far between the Sanctums had been lost for a long time. "They're tired, and they've been gone too long to even remember what they're looking for anymore," he said. "They'll be more of a threat once we reach Psyche."

It struck me as such a devastating end—no end at all. Eomin's fifty years of suffering were agonizing to think about. These souls had languished for many times longer.

"Can't we help them?" I asked. "Like you helped Eomin?"

A pained look flickered over Asar's face, though he turned away quickly.

"I can't release them all. We're too far out. It would expose us too much. And besides, their path through to the underworld might not even exist anymore."

This, I quickly learned, genuinely troubled Asar. I could feel it every night we worked together—every time he linked his magic to mine to close another gate. Each night, he would kneel beside each broken hold, inspecting for damage with all the gentle care of a stablemaster assessing a lame leg on a prized, beloved horse.

Sometimes, I would watch him and marvel at the fact that this man tutting like a mother hen over a cracked wall was, in fact, *the Wraith Warden*.

One time, he caught me staring at him and scowled at me. "You could be helping, Iliae, instead of sitting there gaping at me."

I'd never been good at controlling my mouth. I couldn't help but ask.

"Are the things they say about you true?" I asked.

He scoffed. Asar had, I'd learned, a delightful variety of sounds of displeasure. The man could express the deep woes of being surrounded by idiots without any words at all. It was really impressive.

"*They* say all kinds of things. You'll have to be more specific."

I bit my lip. I knelt beside him, helping etch some fresh glyphs into the doorframe. The silence stretched out between us.

Maybe I didn't want to know. But I'd never been good at restraint.

"They say you could kill a thousand men without lifting a sword," I said. "They say that you collapsed entire rebellions without anyone ever seeing your face."

He remained intently fixated on his work. Maybe I imagined the hesitation before his answer.

"It isn't hard to kill lots of people. If you find just the right hearts to stake or leaders to compel, just the right weak point to exploit, you can kill ten thousand with a single stroke. It's a terrible measure of greatness."

"But is it true?"

"I've killed many, many people, Iliae. Yes."

I was quiet. We worked at the glyphs.

Then he asked, "Does that disappoint you?"

"I knew who you were."

It was true. Still, as I watched Asar's delicate fingers work at the metal with such obvious, thorough care, it amazed me that that same deliberateness had been used for destruction. The very same skill, wielded to the opposite end.

"I was young," he said. "I had nothing else to offer to make myself worth keeping. My father killed all his other bastards. I was eight years old when he met me, and apparently he saw some potential to be honed. I committed myself to being very, very good at my role."

I thought of myself, eight years old, standing upon the altar of Atroxus.

"You don't have to justify yourself to me," I said. "A past doesn't define a future. I'd be a terrible missionary if I didn't believe that."

"It isn't a justification. It's an explanation."

An odd thought struck me. I sat back on my heels, frowning, brow furrowed.

He caught my eye. "What?"

"Asar, do you actually *care* what I think of you?"

He turned back to his work and didn't answer.

A slow grin spread over my face. "You *do*."

This felt like a triumph.

"Absolutely not," he muttered. "Arrogant of you. Get over here, Dawndrinker. Help me with this."

I dropped the subject, though I intensely wanted to tease him about it. Somehow, it didn't seem right to. The victory felt fragile and precious, and, at the same time, deadly sharp.

Later that night, when I was alone, I thought of the wraith's words:

He likes you. Even if he doesn't know it yet.

But he will ruin you all the same.

They followed me when sleep finally took me. I dreamed of Asar's hands, skillful, artful, thorough. I dreamed of how they might feel on my breasts and throat and inner thighs. I dreamed of his breath on my mouth and a kiss that tasted like damnation.

But in the distance, I heard the call of Atroxus. I reached out, and the sun pulled me away. He was dim, far away, calling to me from far beyond the veil between the mortal and immortal worlds.

We are running out of time, a'mara, he told me. *Darkness looms on the horizon. You must complete your task.*

I thought about telling him that it was beautiful down here, in a haunted kind of way. That so much could still be saved. But to say it seemed like it would expose a black mark on my soul, a weakness I was desperate to hide.

I will, I promised.

He kissed me, a scalding promise, and I prayed he couldn't taste the blood on my lips.

PART FOUR

PSYCHE

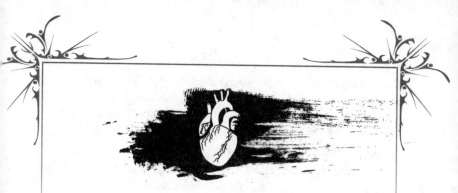

INTERLUDE

*T*he years passed, and the bounds of the girl's existence grew more defined. Her ceremony of commitment came and went upon her sixteenth birthday, a grand affair of treasure and gold and feasts. At the end of it all, the girl was formally a bride of the sun.

Despite her young age, her role advanced her to the upper ranks of the Citadel. She took it seriously. She pushed herself in her magic studies. She traveled farther for missions, found more lost souls, stitched together more broken hearts.

Atroxus still doted upon her. He visited every few months, much to the delight of the priesthood. He was always kind to her, pleased when she completed the tasks he gave her with ease. He was gentle enough in bed. She was grateful for that, even though she found herself wondering what all the fuss was about—

"That's it?" she'd whispered to her friend once, after her wedding night. "That's the thing that has people running around betraying vows and starting wars?"

He had turned bright red. "Shh!" he'd hissed, pointing up to the cloudless sky. "He, uh, probably wouldn't like you talking like that."

Still, for all Atroxus's kindness to her, the girl never forgot the nature of what he was and what she was to him. No one else forgot it, either. Sometimes, the girl thought she could smell something shifting in the air, see a darkness out of the corner of her eye. She would sit up at night and stare out over the courtyard, lining up seeds on her balcony railing for the firefinches, and she'd whisper to them, "What do you think, little friends? What's coming?"

The answer to her question came when the vampire arrived.

It had been the subject of much celebration. The uproar at the gates was just as loud as the day the girl had seen the Turned warrior killed at the center of the church. But these shouts were far more celebratory. That man all those years ago had been one of their brethren. This one was just a monster. The girl rushed down to the church to see the acolytes—her sister among them—wrestling the vampire to the ground, shouting praises to the sun. He was bound in silver chains blessed by Atroxus's light and strengthened by the work of Srana, goddess of machinery. They burned into his flesh, smoke rising to the stained glass ceiling. He hissed and spat words that the girl didn't understand but was certain were curses.

"An offering to Atroxus!" her sister shouted, falling to her knees before the altar, the words bringing forth a wave of cheers.

The vampire, her sister told her later, had been found miles to the south. They'd received word of sightings. Acolytes often went vampire hunting, but never before had they brought a living one back to the Citadel.

The girl had never been good at denying her curiosity. She stole away when she could. The vampire was kept in an open-air cell with barely enough shade to keep the sun from killing him, though he had to hug the wall during the high daylight hours. The girl was surprised by just how human he looked. He had the appearance of a man in his twenties, though he had streaks of silver in his ashy brown hair. They had bound his throat, wrists, and ankles with the blessed chains, which continued to smoke against his skin. The girl winced at the sight of them. It looked unimaginably painful.

She sat next to his cage, watching him. He watched her, too, in silence. He was doing something with his hands. At first, she couldn't see what—then, she realized that he had a small, crumpled-up flower pinched between his fingers. It was wilted, like he'd been carrying it for a long time.

The girl thought of a day she now barely remembered. When she had come to this very place and she'd pulled something out of her pocket, too—that dirty golden feather.

The next day, she went to visit him again. This time, she brought him a tiny yellow flower from the courtyard, which she dropped through the bars above him before climbing down. She sat beside him for a few hours until her duties called her away. And then she did it again, and again, and again. She talked to him often, and sometimes, he tried to say a few words to her, but she didn't understand his language. It didn't matter, though—words, she'd learned, were only one small part of a connection. And she sensed something in this man that was much more complicated than what she'd been told vampires were.

She had given her life to spreading the light. She had reached out to countless broken souls. She'd seen time and time again that no matter how dark a person's past, a little flicker of light still shone in every single heart.

Could that not be true, too, for vampires?

She chanced asking this question of Atroxus, upon his next visit.

Atroxus had scoffed cruelly, fire in his eyes. "Vampires are tainted. They are the product of their goddess's betrayal."

"But that isn't their fault."

"No, a'mara. It is not. But their goddess is to blame for that. She is the one who damned them to such a fate. There is nothing left in them to save."

The girl thought of the flowers lined up on the floor of the vampire's cell.

She knew she should stop talking. But the words came anyway.

"There has to be a way to redeem them," she said. "No living creature is soulless. And no living creature deserves to be killed for fun."

She knew right away that she had spoken too bluntly. Once, Atroxus had found her mortal imperfections amusing. His tolerance for such things was growing thinner as the years passed. She was not as young and harmless as she used to be.

"Fun," he growled. "This is how you refer to the mission of the dawn—"

"No," she said quickly. "Of course not, my light." She swallowed the rest of her protests, slipping instead into bright, agreeable chatter for the rest of the day.

Atroxus remained with her for a long time. She was gone for many hours. She did not discover what had happened until near dusk.

The priests had decided to finish their sacrifice. The vampire hung by his chains, upside down, in the courtyard. His shirt had been stripped off, leaving most of his skin exposed to the sun. The burns, purple and bubbling, extended across his entire body. A gold arrow was buried in his chest, black dripping down his chin. The blood was much fresher than the burns. Befitting of their offering, the priests had let the sun do most of the work.

The girl walked into the courtyard. She knelt beneath the body and picked up five wilted flower petals, which had fallen from the vampire's pockets.

The girl was rarely angry. But this—this enraged her. It made her think of dead firefinches scattering the forest floor for no reason at all. She turned around and ascended the Citadel stairs until she reached the top balcony of the courtyard. Then, she climbed from the rail onto the trellises.

A crowd had gathered below, her sister at its forefront, watching in horror.

"What are you doing?" she cried. "Come down! It's dangerous!"

It's dangerous.

She knew her sister was not talking about the height or the unsteady climb or even the infected corpse. She was talking about something far deadlier.

She was right. It definitely was dangerous.

But the girl had always been too reckless. She sawed away at the restraints at the top of the arch anyway, and when that vampire corpse fell, her blessed life went crashing down with it.

CHAPTER TWENTY-TWO

W e are now closer to death than life."

Asar's words floated softly into the frigid night.

We stood at the precipice of the Sanctum of Psyche. Glass-smooth red spread out before us. Islands of bone white dotted the surface like lily pads. The sky, endless black, shifted with storm clouds that moved a little too fast, cracking with silent slivers of lightning that somehow did nothing to illuminate the darkness. Cotton puffs of fog slithered over the horizon, blending the boundary between the sky and sea.

Our proximity to the underworld was unmistakable now. Death surrounded us. I could feel it clinging to my clothes, my hair, my tongue. It tasted like smoke and flower petals.

The others were affected by it, too. Elias had been growing tenser and tenser with every passing day, a drawn bow string getting ready to snap. And Chandra, as a human, was most affected by the presence of death. She muttered prayers constantly, the shadows under her eyes dark and her cheeks hollow.

Elias stared out over the landscape before us. "And, pray tell, what do we have to look forward to here?"

A question I'd been asking myself for days. My eyes found the wraiths dotting the landscape, too far away to see their features and dreaded the thought of what familiar faces might be among them.

"Psyche is the Sanctum of memory and thought," Asar said. "There will still be wraiths and souleaters to worry about, but our greatest threat will be the Sanctum itself. Here, your thoughts can be manipulated against you. Used as bait."

"Bait?" Chandra repeated.

"Everything about the Descent is designed to draw in life," Asar said. "You cannot trust anything you see down there. Psyche will manipulate your own thoughts to make you stay. The souleaters will use them, too, so be careful. And stay out of the blood."

Chandra let out a shaky sigh and drew the sign of the sun over her chest. "Gods above, I cannot *wait* to go home," she muttered.

I didn't have the heart to remind her that we still had a long, long way to go before that happened. Instead, I gave her hand a reassuring squeeze, which she returned with a weak smile.

Asar started toward the rocky steps that led down to the Sanctum below, Luce bounding after him.

"Watch your footing," he said. "This is steep."

I bit back a laugh as I followed.

He shot me a flat glare that I knew very well by now to mean, *What inane thing are you giggling at now?*

"You're just so matter-of-fact about it." I scrunched my eyebrows together, lowering my voice in a mimicry of his deep, perpetually cool tone. *"Now we shall go face the nightmares of our worst memories. Watch your step."*

Asar's lips grew thin. "I sound nothing like that."

He sounded exactly like that. Luce let out an amused whine, and he shot her a disapproving glare.

"I am surrounded by traitors," he muttered. But I still saw that little twitch at the corner of his mouth.

Victory.

I glanced over my shoulder just in time to see Elias and Chandra shooting each other a lingering glance.

Asar started leading us to the cliff's edge, but Elias said, "We've been walking for Mother knows how long. Maybe we should rest before we throw ourselves into another near-certain death."

Asar did not hide that he thought this was a ridiculous idea. "The sooner we go in, the sooner we come out."

"It would be foolish to go in unprepared."

"It would be foolish to waste time we don't have." Asar turned away, the decision made. "Let's go."

Elias's jaw ground, but he followed when Asar set off. We started making our way down the cliffs. The stairs quickly lost their shape, devolving into slippery piles of stone. It was hard, slow-going work to navigate. I found myself extremely jealous of Nightborn wings.

By the time we finally reached the bottom, my muscles were screaming. The stench of death was overpowering down here, making my eyes water.

Still, up close, the landscape, like so much of the Descent, was unnervingly bewitching. The blood lakes were so still and flat that they looked like dyed glass. The fog rose in waves, twisting into shapes that almost resembled silhouettes before they dissipated into the night sky. I looked up and noticed that the cracks of lightning revealed brief glimpses of long, twisted bodies hidden in the clouds, carried on wide, bat-like wings.

"Are those souleaters?" I gasped. "They can fly?"

"There are all sorts of souleaters," Asar said. "They evolve to hunt, and they're better fed the deeper we go." He pointed down to the lakes. It took me a moment to see it—a silhouette beneath the surface, a long, twisted body that circled the islands. It passed right under us, then delved deep into the red. "It seems they've started to smell us."

He said it so casually.

Still, though he sounded unconcerned, I noticed his eyes trace the horizon—as if looking for something. Not wraiths, I knew. Not souleaters, either.

He turned back to us, pushing his hair out of his face. "We'll just have to stay out of their way. If I'm right, the temple will be over—"

He stopped mid-sentence.

At first, I thought that maybe he'd seen something horrible in the blood or the mists—that maybe Psyche had already started to take him in its clutches, the past preparing to drag him under.

But Asar wasn't looking out at the landscape, and his gaze wasn't hazy with the past. Instead, he was looking down—down at his hands.

A particularly bright bolt of lightning ripped the sky in two. A sudden roar that sounded too alive to be thunder shook the slick stone. I staggered backward, catching myself on a rock before my heel hit the water. I looked over my shoulder to see the blood rippling as if with the movements of thousands of invisible fish. The souleaters circled beneath us, ever tighter, the blood darkening with their silhouettes.

Something was wrong.

"What happened?" I said, taking a step closer. Elias did, too, watching him like a wolf.

Asar's eyes lifted to mine, and I felt a bolt of his panic slice through me.

Then, wordlessly, he loosened the laces on his leather arm guards. He pulled off his gloves and pushed the sleeves of his black shirt up to his elbows.

He stared down at his arms, like he couldn't quite believe what he was seeing.

I couldn't quite believe it, either.

His right arm, his unscarred one, was now entirely black up past the wrist. There, the ink then disintegrated into tendrils that twisted up the muscles of his forearm. On the back of his hand, an open eye stared back at him, the iris ringed with swirls of shadow. It reminded me of his scarred eye—clouds and stars and galaxies within. On his left arm, the ink was deep red, interlocking with his scars like tangled roots. The eye on the back of that hand was closed, lightning bolts of ink bursting from it. Red wisps of smoke pulsed from both tattoos, like steam from a freshly forged blade.

That was a Mark.

An Heir Mark, denoting the rightful ruler of one of the three vampire kingdoms.

Asar just stared at his hands, not blinking, not speaking—hell, he looked like he wasn't even breathing. His brow was furrowed in that particular hard line of thought, like he was trying to decipher whether it was real or a trick played on him by the underworld.

I didn't have to wonder. It was real.

It was real.

And that meant that his father, Raoul, King of the House of Shadow, was dead.

When Asar finally managed to tear his gaze from his Mark, it found mine immediately, as if he was clinging to a safe harbor.

Elias stepped forward once, then twice. He was silent. His expression was indecipherable. For a moment, I thought perhaps he was about to fall to his knees. He was a knight, after all.

But when he finally opened his mouth, it wasn't to offer words of allegiance to his new king or words of mourning for his old one.

He just said, "Fucking finally."

And drove his dagger into Asar's side.

CHAPTER TWENTY-THREE

I t was a lazy strike. Asar never would have allowed it to land under any other circumstance. Elias twisted the knife, yanked it from Asar's flesh. Luce released a roar worthy of a guardian and lunged for Elias. I let out a strangled cry and jumped forward, but Chandra yanked me back.

"No! Don't get in his way—"

Asar recovered quickly, drawing his sword as Elias batted Luce away with a mighty blow. His magic flared, but it was erratic, lacking his typical skill. He was injured and disoriented.

I ripped free of Chandra's grip, calling for fire that was too slow to answer.

Elias pulled Asar close, their weapons locked between them.

"You'd make a shit king," Elias said, and gave Asar a forceful push, right toward the cliff's edge.

I didn't think. I just ran.

Luce dove after us. Chandra screamed my name. Asar's eyes widened as he flew back, and I could've sworn he started to shake his head. *No.*

My body slammed against the stone, my hand grabbed Asar's, and we were falling together. I tasted my own blood. Smelled Asar's, thick and sweet as honey.

I grabbed hold of a ledge of stone at the edge of the steps, fingernails digging in. With my other hand, I held on to Asar—

And then there was nothing.

No weight. No hand in mine.

I looked down and saw only a sea of endless, rippling red.

Asar was gone.

Luce—gods bless her—didn't even hesitate. Her stride didn't break as she dove over the cliff's edge.

Elias knelt before me.

"I'd like your help getting back through Morthryn to the surface, since it seems to have taken a liking to you." He offered me his hand. "The queen would be appreciative. Perhaps grant your freedom."

Chandra was already getting ready to help pull me up. But I looked down at the blood below, still rippling where Asar had plunged into it.

If I fell, I'd be at the mercy of Psyche. Likely get gobbled up by a Souleater or torn apart by wraiths.

But if I let Elias take me, Asar would be lost.

It wasn't even a choice, was it?

You always do the most reckless things, Raihn would always say to me. His voice crossed my mind now, and I had to admit, he was right.

I let go.

"Mische!" Chandra cried after me.

In those final seconds before I hit the ground, I pressed my hand to my chest—threw all my awareness into the anchor, into tightening the thread of connection between Asar and me.

And then the Sanctum of Psyche swallowed me up.

THE YEARS FELL over me like rain.

I was two years old, five years old, six years old. A clay house in a bustling city, the deep green leaves of the forest I'd once loved, the endless roads of endless travel, and the hands of a sister who led me through all of them.

I was eight years old, kneeling at the Citadel of Destined Dawn before Atroxus's light. I was so young. I didn't know to be afraid. And why should I be? The sun had saved me, and a god was smiling at me. He cupped my young face in his hands, examining me.

You will be mine, he said, and I had never felt so happy in my entire life. When my body glowed with the sign of Atroxus's divinity, everyone was smiling at me.

But the only face I looked at was Saescha's, beaming, tears in her eyes. She knelt before me, her hands on my shoulders. "Everything will be different now," she said. "He has saved us because of you. A god has chosen you. Do you know what that means?"

I did—it meant we would be safe. I grinned at her, too overjoyed to speak. But then, my smile faded. I noticed something odd in the background, buried in the leaves of the forest behind her shoulder. A silhouette—a familiar silhouette. It was barely visible, just the faintest outline. It looked so familiar. Why?

A firefinch let out a shrill chirp, startling me. It perched on the statue of Atroxus's visage. Its feathers were more brilliant than the sunrise, its song lighter than the breeze. But something was wrong. Its brilliance was too bright, too sharp. Its song was an octave too low, like a funeral hymn.

I reached for it—

"It is not as beautiful as you are."

I lowered my hand. The firefinch now sat in a magnificent cage of gold.

I was no longer upon the altar. I was in the highest room of the Citadel, a place of such incredible finery that I was afraid to touch anything. Dawn poured over the bed, the room, through the glass ceiling, creating a glittering symphony of all the gold treasure within. All offerings to Atroxus.

I was sixteen years old. I was wearing the most magnificent dress I'd ever seen. At every fitting, I had stroked the silk with such tentative fingers, in disbelief it was real. My friends, artisans at the monastery, had pored over its creation—painstakingly stitching beads and embroidery, designing flawless drapery to sweep around my body. It was more revealing than anything I'd ever worn, the bodice framing my cleavage, my shoulders and back exposed, two long slits revealing my thighs when I moved.

The first time I'd worn it, I'd tried to hide my self-consciousness. It felt like a costume, too heavy for my sixteen-year-old shoulders.

But it was a wedding dress, or at least, the closest thing to one I'd ever wear. Shouldn't it be grand?

Now, as I looked at myself in the mirror, gold makeup dusted on my eyelids and cheeks and cleavage, I realized just how well I fit within a room of offerings to a god.

The offering was not the dress. The offering was me.

Atroxus lounged on the bed, an apricot to his lips, watching me.

The ceremony had been completed, but he hadn't yet laid me down on that bed. I was nervous and excited, my head spinning slightly from the wine I was now allowed to drink.

In this moment, I was happy.

I'd had a wonderful day surrounded by people who loved me. The god I adored was now looking at me as if I were a delicacy. The possibility of my physical offering still lay before me, ripe with hope.

"Come here, a'mara," Atroxus said. His command was dawn— inevitable. He finished the apricot and left the pit discarded on the sheets.

But a strange sensation prickled at the back of my neck. I looked at the firefinch. There was a shadow beside it. An odd trick of the light.

I started to move toward the bird.

"Stay here," Atroxus said.

I paused, a brief glimmer of clarity falling over me.

That wasn't how it had gone. He hadn't said that, just as I had not reached for the bird. But there was such pity, such compassion, in his voice. More than I had ever gotten from him in life.

Stay here. Stay in this moment, when you're happy and you have purpose, when everyone loves you, and you're wearing a gorgeous dress that your friends worked so hard to create for you, and you truly believe that what he feels for you is love.

Stay in this moment, before he opens you up and takes you like another meaningless offering, before he leaves you alone in a room of gold, staring at the dress he ripped off you and discarded.

Stay in this moment, before you have that little crack of doubt.

Because the doubt would lead to the desperation, and the desperation would lead to the mistakes, and the mistakes would lead to my downfall.

But I was never very good at listening.

I reached for the bird anyway.

I stood on a ship at the edge of the world, a candle in eternal darkness. My friends were with me, people who trusted me more than anyone. Saescha's mouth was drawn into a thin line.

"This is a mistake," she said.

"It will be wonderful," I countered. And the worst part was, I believed it—believed that our god would protect us, that we would find a vampire soul to save in his name, that we would return home heroes. I believed it because I had to. I had to earn his love, and the price to keep it just went higher and higher.

None of us were naïve. We had endured horrors that would make most pale—starvation, war, abuse. But it's a strange cocktail, suffering and faith. A dangerous one that makes you think you can survive anything.

I looked up at the firefinch, perched on a leafless tree upon the shore. It hurt to look at it, its feathers too bright against the darkness of the Obitraen sky. Someone stood next to it, but I couldn't pull them into focus.

Mische, someone called.

"Wait," I started to say, the word sticky on my tongue. But I couldn't get it out. After all, one cannot change the past.

The world shifted again.

I sat in a memory that had long since abandoned me.

I was sitting in a garden beside my soul to save. His beauty rivaled even that of Atroxus—full lips, high cheekbones, smooth skin. I knew he was old, likely centuries so, but he barely looked older than me. All except for his eyes—his eyes were black and ancient. I kept staring into them. They reminded me of the dark brown of someone I knew—someone—

The vampire leaned close to me. He slid his arm around my shoulder. Gods, he was so stunning. I kept slipping back into that allure like a shore that wouldn't relinquish me.

"Come with me," he whispered. "And you can show me all the ways I have sinned."

An open door loomed beyond us, a promise of a future that hadn't happened yet—one that, in this moment, still could be everything I wanted it to be. *Stay*, the memory begged.

But my gaze rose over his shoulder, to a little golden bird.

A little golden bird, perched on the shoulder of a man.

I could not see his face, which was shrouded in shadow. But one eye glowed silver, light trailing from it.

Something nagged at me.

The vampire's mouth was on my throat now, tongue pressing against the most sensitive parts of my flesh. A kiss, or a taste.

My breath hitched, but my eyes still locked on that bird—that shadow.

"Stubborn girl," the vampire murmured. "What would it take to make you stay?"

He pulled back to look into my face, and I startled.

It was no longer the face from my memory. A different vampire prince—vampire king—stared at me now. I hadn't realized that I'd memorized Asar's face so clearly. Every harsh angle and soft curve. Even the intricate arrangement of his scars.

"Is this more your taste, Iliae?" he said. The hand moved farther up my skirt, a shock running through me as fingers stroked the slick there—even that one touch more attention to my pleasure than Atroxus had ever offered.

My lashes fluttered as he kissed my throat.

"You've seen how I've studied you," he whispered. "I wouldn't stop until you were so exhausted from pleasure that you begged me for rest."

One finger slipped into me, and I gasped, his groan vibrating against my throat.

His tongue darted out against the angle of my jaw, pressing to the pulse of my jugular vein. His other hand moved up my body, thumb rolling over my hardened nipple.

It was so easy. My body opened for him like a blooming flower. His cock, hard and straining, ground against my core. His mouth moved to mine.

"Let me defile you, Dawndrinker," he murmured. "Please."

I tensed.

What was it that dragged me back to reality? Was it the odd, sad tinge to the way he said that word? *Please.*

I struggled to force myself to awareness. Where was I? What was this?

It hadn't happened this way.

I opened my eyes. The firefinch perched right above us now, screaming a cacophony of warnings.

"Asar," I whispered.

I drew back from him. He stopped, too, as if he were waking up from a dream. He blinked the desire from his eyes.

He had said that Psyche would try to draw us in. It would offer us bait.

Bait. We were each other's bait.

His eyes widened. "Iliae," he breathed. And as the realization crashed over us, he was already starting to fade, fingers tightening around me—

But a violent force yanked me away, and our strange, tangled memory unraveled.

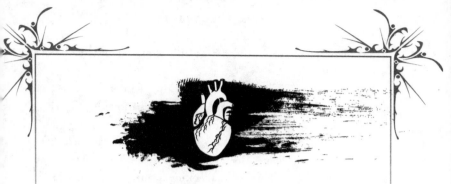

CHAPTER TWENTY-FOUR

Someone hauled me onto the shore. Blood ran down my face in rivulets. I coughed it up onto smooth ivory. My head spun. The world smeared. My hand went to my chest, which throbbed in twin rhythmic beats. The anchor.

Asar.

He was near. That had been him, in my memory, even if he hadn't meant to be there—I was so certain of that, even if I didn't entirely know why. All it had taken was that single second of locked eyes.

I had to go back—I had to—

"Mische!" Delicate hands grabbed my sleeve, stopping me before I could throw myself back into the sea. "Stop, for gods' sake! *Stop!*"

Chandra.

The shock of seeing her forced me to catch my breath. She leaned over me, brows furrowed, silver hair whipping around her. The cliffs stood behind us. Ahead, the temple loomed, a jagged collection of ivory spires dipped in black red. It sat at the apex of multiple rivers, the streaks of blood all flowing into arched passageways beneath it, as if to provide a constant source of food for an eternally ravenous host.

It was windy and cold. The skies roiled, darkening in waves as spatters of red rain painted blood on the ivory patches of solid ground. The cliffs and earth trembled. And gods, the wraiths—so many of them. They crawled over each other deliriously. They dragged themselves from the blood, over the rocks, through the distant abandoned ruins, and it was only a matter of time before they descended upon us.

"We have to go," Chandra said urgently. "Hurry, child, before they get here! Elias can help us get back to the surface."

She thought I had fallen. She didn't know I let go.

I was briefly offended on Asar's behalf that anyone would ever think Elias could navigate Morthryn on his own. Then I noticed the hungry, hopeful way Chandra was looking at me, and I wondered if maybe there was a reason beyond benevolence that she came for me.

Still. I appreciated that she did. It was kind of her.

"I—thank you, but—"

The anchor throbbed at my chest, and I got to my feet too fast, swaying. It was harder to see anything with the wraiths panicking and the waters churning.

Something about a mission and Atroxus and a holy task jumbled in my mind, but the truth was, none of it loomed nearly as large as my imminent fear for Asar.

"I have to go," I said, but Chandra caught my elbow.

"Where are you going? This is our chance for freedom. Atroxus has given us this blessing. We need to take it!"

She forced me to look back at her, and for a moment, I was struck by just how much of a toll this journey had taken on her. She looked little better than the dead—gaunt and hollowed.

I didn't have the heart to tell her that Atroxus had nothing to do with this. Nor the time.

"You go," I said. "I'll be fine."

But she didn't release me. "Don't die for one of *them*," she spat. "He's a fallen soul. Leave him. You're different from them. You're a child of the light. Let it save you!"

A gust of wind whipped past me, and with it came a familiar bark. My heart leapt. I turned to see Luce at the edge of the shoreline near the temple, pacing frantically.

"Go without me," I said, and ripped my arm from her grasp.

But then, when I'd only made it a few steps, another tremor shook the earth. Chandra's frantic scream split the air. A sweet, unmistakable scent hit me—human blood.

I spun around to see Chandra thrashing on the ground beneath a wraith woman. The wraith had dragged herself out of the water and now snarled as she crawled over Chandra, red dripping from her fanged teeth. A second was clawing up the shore to join her, too, her blackened fingers wrapping around Chandra's ankle.

You took them, the first hissed. *I remember you. I remember it all.*

Chandra wailed and thrust her hand out for me. "Help me! Gods, help me! Don't let them take me!"

Of course I wasn't going to leave her there. I didn't think before I dove back for her and grabbed her outstretched hand.

At her touch, I saw it. *Felt* it.

Her past crashed through me, keening with the pain of its ghosts.

I saw Chandra, a young woman, brought to the House of Shadows' shores in chains. I saw her kneeling before labor bed after labor bed, guiding screaming vampire women through their difficult deliveries.

And I saw her hold those tiny vampire babies, so much more fragile than what they would one day become, and snuff them out.

Bile rose in my throat. I tried to yank my hand away, but she clung to me. She saw the horror on my face—she knew what this place had shown me.

"Don't let them take me!" she begged. "I don't deserve it. I did what I had to. You understand."

I did understand. She had offered every one of those tainted vampire lives to our shared god. She had culled the population of the creatures that had kidnapped and abused her.

She believed it was right.

An acrid sensation curled in my stomach—something I tried to deny I was capable of at all.

Hatred.

Behind me, Luce's barks grew more distraut. I couldn't save them both.

Chandra fought the wraiths' hold as they dragged her into the river. Her eyes were wide with betrayal as I wrenched my hand free.

"Please, Mische. You can't leave me!"

Under the laws of Atroxus, there were few greater sins than killing a fellow acolyte. My soul was already tainted. I could tell myself that I was not killing Chandra at all. I could tell myself that my inaction was not the same as murder.

I knew it wasn't true. Not in my heart.

No, I couldn't save them both, but I wouldn't have tried even if I could.

Chandra let out a final, agonized cry as I turned away and bolted for Luce.

The wraiths were everywhere now. The entire Sanctum seemed to have awakened to our presence—or maybe even the Descent felt the power shift that had just happened. I wove through them, avoiding their reaching hands, until I met Luce at the shore.

There, there! she seemed to say, thrusting her snout to roiling red. If I looked closely, I could maybe make out a silhouette that could have been him, rapidly falling.

"You're coming with me, right?" I said to Luce, and she yipped in agreement.

Dogs. We didn't deserve them.

Third time I'm saving his life, I thought. *Lucky man.*

And jumped.

THE LITTLE BOY knew he shouldn't be crying. Still, tiny dots of silver fell into the dead dog's fur, dampening patches of congealed blood.

I recognized him right away, even though he looked so different now. I stood over him. It didn't occur to me to speak. How could I? I had no throat, no mouth. I was floating, bodiless, watching a memory that wasn't mine.

Asar had a lovely face, big dark eyes that peered from beneath a mop of messy dark brown hair. But the rest of him was disheveled, his clothes once fine but now patched and slightly too small. He knelt before what had once been his dog. Her long, slender legs tangled, two of them broken. Her sleek black fur was matted with red, but the wounds no longer bled. No, there wasn't much blood left in her at all.

Malach stood over him and laughed.

"No tears, little brother," he said. "What will our father say if he hears you're weeping over food?"

Malach was cruel, arrogant, and vicious. Everything the heir of a vampire kingdom was groomed to be. Asar understood this, even at his young age. *You are a king,* his mother would slur between glasses of wine. *Let them hate you. It will taste better when you eat their hearts.*

It had been a mistake to tame the dog. A bigger one to love her.

Asar scrunched his eyes closed, hoping he could will the tears back inside of him. His arms wrapped tight around Luce's mangled body, as if maybe she might offer him this one final gift of this one final comfort, when he needed it most.

But still, the tears came.

Malach knelt before him and smiled a perfect, vicious smile, fangs still wet with the blood of a beloved pet.

"Cheer up," he said. "Just think, it could have been you."

And then he sauntered away, leaving Asar alone, crying over his dead pet.

He didn't understand, Asar thought.

Malach thought that the tears were sadness. And indeed, Asar was sad. But the tears that rolled down his cheeks weren't of mourning. They were of *rage*—rage that boiled over inside of him, that made his small body shake as he drew his former best friend close.

In this moment, the boy made a vow:

They could beat him, they could break him, they could hurl fists and ugly words at him, and he would endure it.

But they would never take another precious thing away from this world ever again.

"Never," he whispered, voice trembling with fury. "Never, never, never."

I looked down at myself, lifting my hand. It was a shadowy outline, too faint to even be called a silhouette. I tried to reach for the child, but the memory faded away.

Reality reformed around young Asar in a dark room filled with bookcases. Luce's corpse lay before him as a tall man enshrouded in dark stood over him. "Your father would like to see if you are capable of it," he said. "Think of it as a test."

I saw young Asar painting the glyphs under his instructor's careful watch. I saw him collecting five little trinkets that represented the sum of his beloved pet's soul.

The creature that Asar's first attempt at necromancy created did not look like Luce, but he knew it was her. His instructor was impressed. Even his father was satisfied. None of that praise was worth nearly as much as Luce's lithe body settling beside his, her snout nuzzling his cheek in a way that said, *Thank you.*

Memories blurred past me, years condensed into moments.

Asar, still a boy, before his father, who told him, "We shall make the most of your talents."

Asar, training over magic, over glyphs, over swords, over knives, over countless different instruments of violence, as the years passed.

Asar, now a young man, putting that training to use. He wielded death like an artist. Delivering it quickly or drawing it out slowly. Promising it to those who feared it or denying it to those who begged for it. Driving a body to its brink only to pull it back again at the precise moment he desired. He could distill death to a single breath, a single heartbeat. He could haul back a soul who had met it prematurely. He delivered it in mercy, in revenge, in punishment, in reward.

He was committed to his craft, and he mastered it.

The memories withered again.

I stood in the center of a grand party. Shadowborn—I knew it instantly by the bronze, deadly pointed architecture, the tapestries of emerald and black, the ivy and roses that covered the walls. I felt strangely heavy, and I looked down to see that I did, indeed, have a body now. I wore an elaborate golden dress, smooth, unmarked skin exposed in a plunging neckline and slitted skirt.

My offering dress.

But no one seemed to take any notice of me. The party overflowed with vampire debauchery. Buffet tables had been picked over, the tablecloths now a collage of blood and discarded food. The air swelled with music, magically enhanced, shaking every corner of the ballroom at once. Vampires draped themselves over human blood vendors, suckling lazily at wrists or necks or inner thighs.

A man stood at the edge of the dance floor. My eyes found him immediately, though he seemed to be trying to disappear into the shadows. He held an untouched drink in his hand. The fine clothes fit him now, though he still looked like he was wearing a costume, as if everything was just slightly ill-suited.

He had no scars. His face was perfect. Made for paintings and sculpture.

"Asar," I whispered. The shape of the name on my tongue cut through the haze. I started closer to him, sliding deeper into his memory.

Asar hated these parties. He knew he didn't have much of a choice in attending—his father was not the kind of man one said no to, and besides, he was grateful that he was finally invited to them. Or at least he was supposed to be grateful. The Shadowborn king had decided to cultivate his spare heir, which, of course, Malach did not like. Fuck him.

It was almost worth it to suffer through it for the look of joy on his mother's face when she saw the invitation. *See?* she told him. *You are a king. I told you.*

Asar knew that his mother saw him as a pawn, a stepping stone to power and acceptance in the court. And he knew just as well that her hopes were futile. One day, the Shadowborn king would decide that she had outlived her usefulness, and Asar would come home to find her dead in her bed, just as he had found Luce all those years ago. And he knew when that happened, he would mourn her, even though he spent his whole life trying not to love someone who did nothing but abuse him. But then again, so had his father, and here he was, kissing his ass at a party he didn't want to be at.

He looked into the untouched blood wine—

I forced my thoughts to untangle from Asar's memory. I pushed through the crowd. My shoulders jostled against some other party-goers, but no one reacted to me.

"Asar!" I called. Gods, he seemed so far away.

Asar paused. His eyes, black as the night over the ocean, landed directly on me. That signature line between his brows deepened. He cocked his head, and I could've sworn, just for a split second, I saw the ghost of scars over the left side of his face.

His mouth opened—

But just as he was about to speak, someone touched his arm.

The memory pulled him back.

Asar turned, barely tilting his drink away in time to avoid dumping it all over the woman's dress.

"Oops," she said, looking down at the flecks of blood on her hand. She was the perfect image of vampire nobility—dark auburn hair that ran over her shoulders in a silky waterfall, an immaculate black velvet gown, and fair eyes that assessed him with something between hunger and curiosity. A bright red scarf wrapped around her throat, striking against the pale of her skin.

Her gaze flicked to his glass. "That's your fault for having a full drink this far into the night."

Her lush lips curled. Asar watched them. She was nobility. He was a bastard, and no one let him forget it. He needed to focus on his work, not pretty smiles from pretty women.

Still. He watched.

"Ophelia," she said. "If you were going to ask."

Asar told himself that he had not been going to ask.

But when she extended her hand, for some reason—even though he knew he shouldn't—he took it.

"Asar!" I called, but the world fell apart again, the party shredding like paper. I threw my hands up in front of my face as a loose scrap sliced my cheek, leaving a trail of blood. The memories moved faster now, coming apart before they even had time to form.

I felt Asar's happiness.

No, not quite happiness—satisfaction. But for someone who had been striving his entire life, what was the difference? Ophelia was everything he was not. She manipulated hearts the way he manipulated death. Her weapon was shrewd charm, and her battlefield was Shadowborn high society. She was every bit as good at her art as he was. And he knew that he was another tool in her arsenal, a strategic decision. It didn't matter. He had forgotten what a soft touch felt like, and he could not imagine giving it up again. They loved each other in all the ways that counted. It was already more than he could ever ask for.

Until it all came crashing—

I held my hands up, pushing through an onslaught of the past. A little house in the city. Party after party, this time navigated with Ophelia's astute skill, contrasted by rotting bodies and open hearts and bloody last words. A gathering at the palace. A sword gifted to him by his father, the swell of pride in his chest at the recognition. The hateful gaze of a jealous older brother.

It all rushed by, faster and faster, until I lost my footing and tumbled along through nothingness.

I landed on a hard wood floor, body cracking with the impact. The edges of my vision pulsed, as if someone was tearing at the edges of this reality, trying to rip through it.

But the memory was so vivid.

Asar knelt on the floor of that little house in the city. He was wearing the cape of the House of Shadow's royal guard. The sword he had been so honored to receive, a weapon he'd once felt could do anything, had clattered uselessly to the floor when he came in.

I pushed myself up to my hands and knees. I had to fight for it. Everything about this memory was repressed, driving me down.

Asar was crying.

And in his lap was Ophelia, her body torn apart, blue eyes staring unseeing to the ceiling. Just like Luce all those years ago, they didn't leave much blood in her, either.

Asar's agony flooded me. Pain and grief and rage, rage, *rage*. He held Ophelia's lifeless corpse close. No one was here to jeer at him this time, but he could hear the taunts nonetheless. He knew what had happened. He knew that Ophelia was punishment for rising too fast. A beautiful life with so much potential, ended for nothing but his brother's petty jealousy, his need for dominance, his desire to destroy something just because he could not have it.

Dread rose in my chest, choking me, drowning me. I crawled toward Asar, reaching for him. His pain ached in my heart. I wanted to soothe the wound before it festered and became something so much worse.

But it was too late. Asar shut the door against the tender parts of his grief and opened the door to his violent fury. He had made a vow once, a long time ago, and he would fulfill it.

No, I tried to say, and I thought that maybe I heard it echo somewhere else, too, deep in the shadows.

But Asar was already rising, his damnation sealed.

Darkness fell over me. The floorboards under my hands splintered, then reformed. It was so, so cold. I was in the same house, but so much of it had changed—clutter everywhere, rancid carcasses in the corner from feeds, the air thick with the scent of death. Asar had painted every inch of the walls and the rafters with glyphs in white and red paint. The furniture had been pushed to the walls. Ophelia's corpse lay in the center of the room, a circle painted around her.

He knew that it was not wise. Selfish, even. Ophelia had been dead for days by the time he found her. Wherever her soul had wandered, it would be gone now.

His necromancy had always been conducted in service to his father's crown. To do it unsanctioned—let alone upon a noble-blooded vampire—would be punishable by death. Asar had sacrificed to earn the position he held. He'd scraped together those flimsy morsels of respect with blood and spit and guts, by doing the things that no one else wanted to do, things that kept him awake in long daylight hours, things he could never unsee. He would lose it all for this.

It wasn't that Asar was not aware of the consequences of what he was about to do. It was that he simply did not care.

He had made a vow. He was a man of his word.

So he drew the circles, placed the items of Ophelia's soul around her with the same care with which he smoothed the matted hair from her face, and he began his work.

The magic was so forceful that it stretched the seams of the universe itself. The corners of the room darkened. Red poppies bloomed through the floorboards, slinking over Ophelia's lifeless limbs. I watched, unable to move, unable to speak, as Asar guided the mortal and the immortal worlds to collision. And for a few precious seconds, it was all so stunning—I had to admire it, the way a lifetime student of painting admires the work of a master.

But so quickly, it went so wrong.

The darkness kept coming and coming. The poppies multiplied too many times, pulling Ophelia's body to the earth, the petals withering and rotting. Ophelia began to stir. A smile twitched over Asar's gaunt face, the hope in it clear as a summer's night. But my heart clenched. No. It was wrong.

Dread.

Maybe the first flutter of Ophelia's eyelashes was her, the way she used to be. But the magic spun out of control. A tear of darkness ripped through the center of the room, catching her body in its grips. She let out a terrible wail, rolling over and clawing at the floor as her flesh and her soul were pulled in two different directions.

Asar's little smile of hope so quickly soured to fear. He tried to dive to the center of the circle, but the forces of the dead surged through the tear he'd opened with more force than he could match. Countless hands stretched through the spell, cleaving straight through Ophelia.

He managed to get to his feet, grab his sword. He sliced the hands of the dead off Ophelia, or tried to, but he had been sloppy. The magic was powerful, but unstable. He had offered the dead what they wanted more than anything: a path back to life, and they would tear Ophelia apart to get it.

Ophelia lifted her head. Her eyes were pits of darkness, her mouth open in agony.

"What have you done to me?" she cried. She held on to him as the ceremony finally collapsed, the hole to death itself in the center of the room at last splitting open. Asar's left arm fell into the shadow as he tried to hold on to her. The hands reached up his arm, clawing at his shoulder, his chest, his face, tearing at his left eye.

Ophelia screamed and screamed, the most inhuman, terrible sound.

"What have you done to me?"

I tried to crawl forward as Asar sank into the depths of death. Tried to get myself to my feet. But the floor shook violently, shards of burned paper falling from the ceiling. Was the house shaking, or was the memory collapsing? Did it make a difference? Either would eat him alive, savoring his agony with every moment.

Ophelia drew him closer. Tentacles of darkness now surrounded her, wrapping around him like chains.

"Asar!" I managed to choke out. "Come back!"

And I could have sworn that he hesitated—just for a moment.

But Ophelia's death eyes snapped open.

They landed on me. A slow smile spread over her lips.

Run, I told myself. *Run, run.*

But my body wouldn't move.

"Nosy, nosy bird," Ophelia purred.

Asar looked up. His eyes met mine. Realization crashed over him. He leapt up and dove for me, my outstretched hand brushing his.

Someone grabbed the back of my shirt and pulled us up, just as Ophelia lunged.

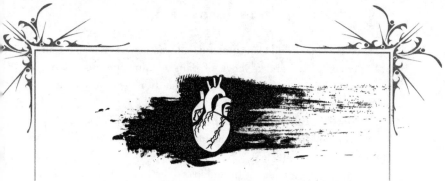

CHAPTER TWENTY-FIVE

Luce dragged us out into the open air. Asar and I fell upon the bone shore together in a heap.

The world assaulted me, light and sound and texture overwhelming. My chest burned as I coughed up lungfuls of rancid blood. It seemed thicker now, as if tainted by the memories it held. Ophelia's eyes burned into me.

She was here. She was coming. We had to go.

Still, when I lifted my head and looked into Asar's face, I pressed my hand against his chest just to make sure he was real. His hair was plastered to his forehead in whorls. Red pooled in the grooves of his scars. His left eye shone bright, the storm clouds within thrashing. They calmed slightly as his hand pressed to my cheek—making sure I was real, too.

My hand slipped over his, tracing elegant bones and muscles. Then I pulled it away and looked at it. The Mark on his hand, the eye of death, stared back at me, smoke pulsing from it with his quickening heartbeat.

"Shit," I whispered, because what else was there to say?

A muscle feathered in Asar's jaw in a way that said he agreed. But he looked up to the temple looming over us.

"No time," he said. He stood, arm braced over his midsection, where black bloomed over his shirt. The scent of it made my stomach twist with hunger.

"Chandra?" he asked.

I thought of her reaching hand. *Don't leave me.*

I shook my head, and I was grateful that was answer enough for him.

I started to rise and a shock of pain cut through me. I looked down to see my leg twisted at an angle that didn't seem quite right.

Asar's face went stone still.

"It's fine," I said brightly. "I'm fine. We have to go."

Ophelia would be here any moment. The wraiths were restless. The souleaters roiled.

But Asar gave me one of those looks—the kind I hated, the kind that cut right through me.

"You don't deserve this."

He said it so earnestly, so softly. It reminded me of that little boy clutching a dead dog. Maybe a part of that boy had still been inside him all along. A little boy who still believed in justice. A little boy who still thought people got what they deserved, and that I still deserved anything.

I couldn't let myself acknowledge that. Not now.

I shook my head, and we staggered for the temple as fast as our pathetic, mangled bodies could carry us.

"We're almost there," I said. "Gods, Alarus had a hell of a taste in architecture, didn't he?" I talked a lot when I was nervous. I couldn't help it, and the sound of my own voice was preferable to the low murmurings of the dead, growing louder. "Such an affinity for drama. I have to admire it. Really never passed up the opportunity for—"

We crossed the threshold and my words died. The damage wasn't visible from the outside, but the temple had started to crumble—the roof was partially caved in here, and rubble blocked half of the double doors. The building moaned as we entered, as if lamenting its sorry state.

We dragged ourselves through, into the belly of the temple.

The front half of the large, open room still remained standing, high ceilings cradling rib-like rafters. But the entire back half had deteriorated into little more than rubble. The rivers ran straight through it, and twisting staircases and arched bridges crossed over them. A twinkling melody played as a few chips of broken glass fell from the ceiling into the bloody pond below.

At the center, perched upon an island atop those winding rivers of scarlet, sat a small marble building. "Building," actually, was too grand a word for it. It reminded me of a tomb in a graveyard, or the confessional rooms in the monastery—a simple stone box to contain the dead, or sins, or oftentimes both.

Neither Asar nor I had to acknowledge aloud that we felt it. The air bent toward it, vibrating with a silent hum of power. The altar would be in there, surely, and so would the relic.

Shadows of the souleaters circling above us swirled over the floor. The hair rose on the back of my neck. I could sense the countless wraiths encroaching upon the temple, no doubt acutely aware of the presence of mortality by now.

Worse, I could sense *her*.

Fifty paces to that altar, a clear shot, and it still felt like a trap.

Asar's blood dripped onto the floor, a rhythm increasing with my heart rate. "Let's not linger," he muttered.

The box was smooth save for a single wrought-iron door. It had no handle, and not even any visible hinges. But when Asar reached for it, it swung wide open like parting jaws.

A streak of light burst through the open door.

Asar hissed a curse and leapt out of the way, dragging me with him. The scent of burning flesh filled my lungs. The two of us pressed to the wall just to the right of the entrance. Asar's right hand, which held me tight to the stone, was smoking, the flesh purple-black where the light had touched him.

The light from within the door was so bright that it slashed a brutal streak of white all the way down the pathway, across the blood rivers, and up the wall.

Atroxus's trap.

The ground groaned, red liquid trembling, as if the entire Descent was moaning in protest.

They were coming. Ophelia. The wraiths. The souleaters. The thousand blades poised at our hearts.

Hurry, hurry, the wind whispered.

Asar peered at the open door, the light within so blinding it was reducing to a searing square of white. He could barely even look at it, and I could smell the mere proximity eating at his skin.

"Can you manipulate it from here?" he said.

I pressed my palm to the stone. I could sense the power of Atroxus throbbing behind the thick layer of marble—once it might have been invigorating, but now it stung, dissonant like an off-key chord. Still, it was distant. The wall was too thick, and no doubt reinforced by measures that went far beyond the physical. My magic, weak as it was now, couldn't reach through it.

I shook my head, and Asar's teeth gritted.

"We can't go in there," he said. "We'll have to find another way."

But I knew without even looking that there wasn't any other way. The light was the guard, exactly as Atroxus had planned. Whoever intended to make it to the relic would have to enter the crypt and confront whatever was inside. It was almost funny that the door alone had driven us back when that wasn't even the test.

I thought of Chandra's face in her final moments, eyes wide with terror, reaching for me.

I hadn't even tried to save her. Hadn't wanted to.

Maybe it served me right. If Chandra was here, she could have walked right through that door without hesitation. The light was nothing to her but warmth.

I looked down at my hand. Only a sliver of the light had touched me before Asar had pushed me out of its path, and he'd been in front of me, taking the brunt of it. My little finger and a slice of my hand throbbed, the skin reddened. But my burn was much less severe than Asar's.

"I'll go," I said.

Asar looked at me like I was an idiot.

"You certainly will not."

"It's magic, not sunlight. It won't kill me."

"Because Atroxus's magic has never hurt you before."

His sarcasm cut deeper than I wished it did. But I forced a smile.

"I said it won't *kill*. Not that it won't hurt."

Asar did not look convinced. And truthfully, I wasn't sure if I was, either. A tight ball of fear sat in my stomach. Was I *really* certain that Atroxus's magic wouldn't burn me up, too? Was I *really* certain that I was different than any other vampire? That I still held enough of his love to earn his protection?

But neither of us had time for doubt.

Asar's arm locked, pinning me to the wall as if to hold me back by force if necessary.

"If you think I'm about to let you run into—"

Before he could finish telling me what he *wouldn't let me* do— useless, anyway—our time ran out.

The darkness came slowly at first—so slowly I didn't notice it happening until the entire temple was coated in a thick, grainy fog. I felt her at the back of my neck, the underside of my chin. I felt her breath against my cheek.

"This is my favorite Sanctum, you know."

Ophelia unfurled from the air like a blooming flower.

"So interesting to see what lives inside those fragile mortal minds. So much of it is the same. The same regrets. The same fears."

She rose above us, shadow surrounding her like great, powerful wings. And as she raised her arms, the dead surfaced from the bloody water at her call.

Perhaps it was because we were stuck here in such a confined space with them, but when they rose, their pain was momentarily staggering. They were caught exactly halfway between death and life, feeling the deep gouges of both losses on their souls. Stuck here, in the chamber devoted to the memories of what they had once been and the scars of their greatest regret, forever unable to move on. They crawled toward the light, drawn to the rare glimpse of the sun and starving for the life it promised.

There were so, so many of them.

Dozens. Hundreds. They blended together in formless, writhing want.

Asar cursed and drew his sword. I felt his weakness through the bond we shared, though he buried it deep inside himself.

"We run," he said.

But I could tell that even he knew that wasn't feasible. There was nowhere to go. The only place that the dead couldn't follow would be the passage the relic would afford us.

"Go," he said. "I'll cover you."

He was telling me to flee to safety. To Morthryn's halls.

Behind him, I thrust my hand out into the streak of light and winced at the sting. Smoke rose from my skin, but the burns, while painful, wouldn't be fatal. The light sang a melody I knew a long time ago, and though my body no longer was as attuned to it as it once had been, I could manipulate the notes enough.

Enough.

I hoped.

I looked back over my shoulder to the rising onslaught, and Asar bracing himself before it all without hesitation, just as he did before those broken gates. Beyond him, and past the wave of dead, Ophelia rose, her smile spreading across her lips. She looked past him—straight to me, her interest digging into my soul.

"I know what it feels like." Her voice slithered around me, cruel and pained. "To call for a great love and hear no answer. I called for him seventy-two times when they murdered me. I counted every one."

Her fingers rifled through my mind. Found the memory of the attack of the Moon Palace in the Kejari—when I had lain helpless among the demons and the Nightfire, calling and calling in exchange for only a god's silence.

"I wonder," she whispered, "if yours will answer you now?"

Me and her both.

But I didn't have time to doubt it.

Perhaps Asar sensed what I was about to do, because he started to turn, eyes locking to mine.

"Hold them off," I told him. "Be back soon."

And as he grabbed for me, I dove into the light.

I HAD BEEN right. The light didn't kill me.

But gods, it hurt like a bitch.

It ate at my flesh, acidic and stinging, as I hurled myself through the door. I sang hymns under my breath, as if to remind the magic here that I belonged to it, beneath my vampire flesh. Perhaps to remind myself, too.

I leapt forward blindly, eyes squeezed shut, hands flailing out until my feet tripped over a step and I stumbled against a wall. The burning sensation ebbed, fading to a constant sting instead of a breathtaking agony, and I chanced opening one eye.

I could see, barely, though I had to keep my hand up to shield against the brightness. It all emanated from a smooth marble box at the center of the room. Scattered around it were three broken golden skulls—horse skulls, maybe? Perhaps they had once been guardians, like the panthers in Breath, but they had long ago fallen. It was bigger in here than it appeared from the outside, though I couldn't tell if it was the work of magic or optical illusion—because the walls were mirrored. My own form stared back at me, silhouetted against the light, duplicated countless times in all directions. A dull roar shook the ground, the walls, set the mirrors trembling. Outside, the sounds of the dead grew louder and louder, and I could feel the echo of Asar's weakness in the anchor that connected us.

Using my arm to shield myself against the light, I approached the box. It was smooth white marble, like the crypt itself, though concentric circles had been carved into the top of it. Glyphs, or something like them, though more ancient. I ran my hand over it. A bisected circle, a simplified version of the mark of Atroxus, had been carved from the stone—a change clearly made after the fact, because the missing piece cut straight through the older, delicate lines beneath.

It needed to be completed, surely. There had to be a key, or—

Movement out of the corner of my eye startled me. I lifted my eyes, and leapt backward.

My reflection stood at the other side of the box. My reflection, but . . . not. Her large, empty eyes glowed. Her freckles emanated streaks of white, like pinholes against a noon sky. It was difficult to make out what she wore, or much about her body, because a hole in her chest throbbed with searing radiance—so brilliant it hurt to look at her.

I stepped back, but she didn't. She approached me and stretched out her hand, palm up, over the box.

Beckoned.

I didn't move.

The sound of the battles beyond the walls had grown louder. Asar's fear—not on his own behalf, I knew, but on mine—pulsed faster and faster in my chest.

I chanced a tentative step closer.

The reflection smiled, light pouring from her lips.

The moment I moved, she grabbed my wrist with one hand, yanking me closer, as she plunged the other into my chest.

My own scream filled my ears in a world that felt a thousand miles away.

Pain exploded through me, fire in my stomach, in my chest, in my veins. But I couldn't move. I couldn't pull away. Memories flashed across my vision.

No—not just memories. Sins.

An elbow against mine in my teenage bedroom.

A corpse hitting the ground in the Citadel courtyard.

Lush lips upon my throat.

Chandra's reaching hand in her final moments.

Countless sips of blood filled with countless shameful pleasures.

A thousand burns, and a thousand unanswered prayers.

And something else—something lost in the cloud of all I couldn't remember, a faraway memory that twisted like a knife in my gut.

The reflection released me abruptly.

My throat hurt from the screams. My knees were jelly. I nearly collapsed, slumping against the marble box. I touched my chest—whole and unwounded, despite the pain. But the reflection frowned down at the hand she just withdrew from me, which was covered in black sludge, blotting out the brilliance of her glowing form.

In the back of my mind, Asar's distant voice called to me, his magic banging at the doors to the walls I so carefully maintained: *What happened? Where are you?*

The reflection shook her head sadly. The word rang out, though her lips did not move:

Tainted.

A clear judgment. My soul had been weighed and found lacking.

But this wasn't real. This was the Sanctum of Psyche, picking apart my mind and using it against me.

It wasn't real. *It wasn't real.*

But it felt real when she leveled her empty stare at me again, eyes gleaming, and rushed at me.

Maybe she was Atroxus's version of the guardians that had lorded over the relic of Breath. Or maybe she *was* the key. Maybe this was a combination of Atroxus's magic and the Sanctum's, twisted to create a horrifying mutation.

It didn't matter.

My back hit the ground. She leapt over me and I only just managed to stop her before she tore at my face. She was solid, but barely. I swung my sword, but she batted it from my hands easily, sending it skidding across the floor. The skin of my hands, my cheeks, the tip of my nose bubbled as the light within her flared. The hole in her chest sparked flame.

It was in there—the key. I was sure of it. I could *feel* it, a knot of the sun's power ready to be unraveled. I just had to pull it apart, like a bow on a gift box.

It would've been so painfully easy once.

But now, I couldn't even find my grip on that magic. I reached down into my heart for humanity, for the sun, and all I found was that black sludge. *Tainted, tainted, tainted.*

She pressed her hands to my face. Her light flared, igniting me.

My scream ripped me in two.

Iliae!

I wasn't sure if I was hearing Asar's voice in my mind or in my ears. All I knew was that it was frantic, and I desperately wanted to answer him.

The reflection frowned thoughtfully. She pushed her hand into my head and plucked out another sin.

The memory of Asar's body under his wet clothes. His hands against the broken gates of Morthryn, elegant and deft. The muscles of his forearms. The curve of his lower lip. The smell of his skin, of his blood. The sound of his voice around those words: *Let me defile you.*

The way I felt when I thought of these things. Hungry.

I managed to push her off of me. Managed to roll away, though I could barely drag myself to my feet. Everything hurt. The light had grown brighter, the mirrors reflecting it over and over again. I couldn't find a door. Had there ever been a door? Or had I been here forever?

My mental walls were in shambles. Asar's magic pushed through them.

You have thirty seconds to answer me, Iliae!

But I couldn't grab hold of that magic, either. Couldn't even make sense of my own thoughts. Every spare breath went to evading her. But she moved as I did—she anticipated every move before I made it. I kept reaching for the sun, and it kept slipping from my grasp. Burns opened over burns.

I was in the Moon Palace all over again, lying on the floor, waiting to die as my god was silent.

The reflection pinned me against a mirrored wall, the glass searing my back. Her brow furrowed in pity.

You should have died there, she said.

I let out a choppy sob.

She was right. I should have.

I attempted once again to reach for her magic, and once again—again, again, again—I failed.

But then, a great, terrible roar shook the floor. The reflection flickered in distraction. I tore my eyes from her face as glass rained over us. The walls trembled. The ground quaked. A pillar of stone crashed through the far corner of the room, ripping open the crypt.

The reflection's mouth opened in a silent scream, her body flickering with the impact. My eyes struggled to adjust to the stark contrast between the darkness outside the crypt and the blinding brightness within it. I could see movement in the hole opened by the pillar, but couldn't make sense of what it was at first. I realized it was because the wraiths were so numerous that they had become a living sea.

Yet I felt Asar's presence more vividly than that of the dead.

My eyes found him in the darkness for just that split second. He was on the other side of the pillar with Luce at his side, his sword drawn and glowing, his magic surrounding him as he fought back wraith after wraith. Long fingers of darkness fanned from his back, wrapping around the pillar. He'd been the one to make the ruin fall. He'd smashed through the stone of hell itself to get to me.

My heart stirred.

He'd had to dive out of the way when the wall shattered and streaks of light spilled over the temple ruins, and he'd done it without breaking his stride in his own battles. But through it all, his eyes met mine over his shoulder, just for a split second, and he looked at me as if the sight of me alive was a prayer answered.

He opened his mouth, like he wanted to say something, but neither of us had time for that.

The reflection solidified again. Two of the mirrors had been destroyed, but the rest remained intact, light bouncing between them. Still, the influx of darkness cleared my head, breaking the disorienting sea of white. When the reflection came for me again, this time, I managed to stave her off at first.

At first.

But still, that sun inside her evaded me. The magic was too complex—it refused to respond to me. I was wounded. The wraiths were overwhelming Asar. They began to crawl through the opening created by the fallen pillar, licking the sunlight off the stone. Luce snarled and snapped at the reflection, attempting to drag her off of me only to be sent sprawling across the room with a single strike.

In the distance, I could have sworn I heard Ophelia's amused laugh.

We had no more time.

It was almost over.

I gasped for breath and dragged myself to my sword. But the reflection yanked me back by my ankle. She crawled over me, each touch finding another sin.

Every sip of blood I enjoyed too much. Every brush between my legs at night. Every unanswered prayer.

I reached for the sun.

But my eyes slipped past my own sun-drenched face. To Asar, who stole one more glance over his shoulder at me once again. I felt a tug on the anchor—on the thread of magic that connected us.

I realized what he was trying to say to me:

You are a Shadowborn.

You are a Shadowborn vampire. You are surrounded by your greatest weapon. Use it!

Now I understood.

He hadn't torn down that wall so he could save me. He had done it to hand me the weapon I could use to save myself.

I couldn't seize enough control of Atroxus's magic to snuff out the reflection on my own. But I could manipulate it in the crudest sense. I could pour everything I had into stoking those flames, driving them to uncontrolled madness. And the brighter it burned, the darker the shadows would grow. Even now, I could feel them, rich as the finest alcohol, begging me to let them in—waiting for me, right there in Asar's open invitation.

But fear clenched in my heart. I couldn't pretend I didn't hear it calling to me over the years. But I'd kept that door inside myself tightly closed. I'd nailed it shut with prayer and sunlight.

What would I unleash if I opened it?

What if I couldn't close it again?

I fought my way to my feet, trying once again to call the flame—

But Asar's voice rang clear in my mind now, the final vestiges of my defenses against him gone.

You are too good to be this afraid of yourself, Iliae, he snapped. *You are better than this.*

And though his words were harsh, his touch on my mind was soft. I knew that he understood. That he, too, feared the power he had been given by people he hated, and regretted the pain he had caused by using it.

I felt as if I were staring into a different mirror, now, at a more monstrous reflection than the one that pinned me to the temple floor.

I took Asar's power, and I threw open that dark door in my heart.

I didn't have time to second-guess.

I grabbed the reflection's face as she grabbed mine, both of us cradling each other.

Instead of calling to the sun with my joy, I called to it with my anger.

Instead of attempting to control the light, I set it ablaze with my fury.

The reflection's face shifted to shock, then pain. Her mouth opened, eyes widened. Blazing white poured from them, the light of her freckles spreading like scorched paper catching fire. I was burning, too, but I didn't feel it anymore. I didn't feel any of it.

The light grew brighter, and brighter, and brighter, and with it, the shadows became inky black and rich as velvet.

I seized upon them.

They flooded me like a breath of fresh air above the water.

Gods, I hadn't realized how much energy it had taken to hold it back until this moment. How had I forgotten that magic could feel like this? So right? Using the power of the sun had become so painful. But this was anything but. The shadows enveloped me, protected me, flared around me like wings. I could feel the thoughts and emotions of the dead, waiting for me like strings of an orchestra to be played. I could feel the silent song of the Descent hitting its perfect notes.

And I could feel Asar, walking with me into the dark.

This is what magic should be, a voice whispered. *Easy. Like breathing.*

Then my own face stared back at me, cracks spreading between brilliant features. The fire spilled from her eyes, her mouth, her nostrils. I felt the magic within her crack, pushed to the limits of its ability, just as the flood of shadow rushed through her. Cracks spiderwebbed across her horrified face. Liquid black bubbled under her skin, growing, consuming, until the flames screamed their death cries against the stifling shadows. And the darkness just kept going, until it smothered the light. Our positions were reversed, though I didn't remember moving. I pinned her beneath me.

The cracks burst open, darkness spilling from her. For the first time, I stared myself in the face.

Not Mische, chosen of the sun, teenage prodigy of light.

Mische, vampire, Shadowborn, who had already let the dark devour her a long time ago, and had simply refused to see it.

My hand plunged into the hole in her chest. Closed around the core of her power, now drenched in inky shadow.

Tainted, I thought, and I even smiled when she burst apart into blackened shreds.

I didn't remember standing. My senses blurred, my awareness drowning in sensation and impulse. The wraiths were everywhere. But Asar was pushing them back, drawing from the well of power that we shared together. I understood now that the shadows were simply a part of them—I could feel their souls, reduced to shades of what they once were, all pain and hunger and fear. It was so easy to let this blanket of darkness fall over them, too, ushering them away. I didn't remember taking Asar's hand, only that when his fingers intertwined around mine, it felt like a key sliding into a lock.

I wanted to drown in it.

I wanted more—I wanted everything. It all blurred around me. A distant laugh echoed in the layers between worlds—Ophelia. *How exciting*, she said. *The songbird has talons. But what a price she will pay for them.*

But even she was inconsequential.

Nothing felt real.

Not until elegant fingers brushed my cheek, cool and smooth, the only real thing in life or death.

I blinked, clearing my eyes.

Wisps of light trailed from his left eye into the sky, intertwining with the magic that still poured from my hands. His thumb swept over the curve of my cheek, and I heard his unspoken comfort: *It's all right. Come back.*

The blind fury of my magic faded. I saw another version of myself in his gaze:

Mische, the woman he looked at like that.

We stood before the altar. I didn't quite remember how we got here. I lifted my hand and looked down at the disc of stone I held within it. The key.

Asar cradled my hand in his. Together, we slid it into place. And when the box fell open, gold surging through the carvings, we reached inside together. Alarus's memory encirlced us.

Nyaxia and I stand at the veil between worlds. Here, we are at the inflection point between all things—the underworld, the mortal world, the Descent, and the land of gods. An obsidian tree towers above us, black leaves gently floating to the ground. In the distance, my kingdom looms.

It is fitting that we do this here, at the collision point of worlds. We are about to shatter the paths of fate.

She wears a poppy in her hair, blood-bright against the galaxies within. Her eyes contain endless shades of night, infinite possibilities.

I hold her hands in mine. I swear myself to her, and her to me. We bind our fates together.

We speak our wedding vows in the old language—a language not spoken now even by the gods. These were the same syllables once used to forge the bedrock of our world. It seems appropriate that they, too, should be the ones we use to destroy it.

When it is done, I slide my ring off my finger. It is a mark that binds me to the White Pantheon, and I have forsaken them now.

My wife kisses me, and I cannot imagine there was ever any other choice.

The past faded. Asar and I withdrew our hands. Sitting in my palm was a simple silver ring, glowing faintly with long-abandoned divinity.

I lifted my gaze to Asar's. The want still curled low in my stomach, a new, disconcerting wave of it unleashed at the sight of him.

Then his eyes flicked down, and his fear made the world snap back into focus. I began to feel pain.

So much pain.

I looked down.

I was covered in blood.

"Whose is that?" I started to ask, but I only made it halfway through the words before the injuries crashed back into my body, my tether to my magic snapping.

And then I was on the ground, and Asar was holding me.

"I've got you, Mische," he murmured. "I've got you."

I smiled.

"You said my name," I said, and this time, it didn't feel like power when the darkness took me.

CHAPTER TWENTY-SIX

Atroxus lay on the bed, meeting my gaze through the mirror. His eyes were not the sparkling gems of pleasure that they had been before. They watched me the way one watches a snake slither through tall grass.

"You told me you had never been disloyal," he said.

I turned around, panic driving a spike through my chest. "I haven't, my light."

His eyes traveled down to my dress—my ceremony dress. I looked down and gasped, balling the fabric in my fists. Once it had been brilliant gold. Now, the silk was ink black.

He rose, unblinking.

"You told me you are committed to your calling."

"I am, my light. Always."

He lifted my chin, staring into my face. His brow furrowed, like he was seeing something new in me, and he didn't like it.

He said, "Show me."

I WOKE UP with a start. A bolt of pain speared my inner arm, and I instinctively yanked it away, or tried to.

"Thirty seconds," Asar said gruffly, holding tight to my wrist as he wrapped bandages around my forearm. He looked like he was in prayer—head bowed, messy dark hair falling over his brow, mouth serious in concentration.

He leaned down and tore the fabric with his teeth. I was so disoriented that I almost didn't feel it when his lips brushed my skin with the movement. Almost.

"Thanks," I said. My voice was hoarse.

Asar affixed the bandage and straightened. Both of my forearms had been patched up, though it seemed that the worst of the burns this time clustered on my right arm, near the inner elbow—right around my phoenix tattoo.

Asar had mended the worst of his own wounds, too, though some of the dressings were messy where I assumed he'd struggled to reach by himself. We were in a small chamber—maybe a living room once, though it was hard to tell now. There was a single couch in the center, which I occupied, sprawled out over beaten-up green velvet. Asar knelt before me on a threadbare rug. The walls— curved, the trim uneven bone—were lined with books and dusty paintings.

"We're back in Morthryn," I said.

"One of the last safeholds. It will be a more difficult journey from here on out."

"You really do say that constantly."

The corner of his mouth tightened. "Am I ever wrong? We were lucky the temple gave me a quick path here. If it hadn't . . ."

He didn't need to finish. How many wraiths had been in that temple? Hundreds?

The full weight of what I had done crashed over me as the memories pieced together.

The worst part wasn't that I had done it. It was that I had loved it. The magic. The darkness. Even my damning judgment of Chandra in her final moments.

And there was nothing more dangerous than a sin that felt right. Nothing.

My hands felt so filthy. I wanted to scrub them until the skin peeled off.

Maybe my face changed, because Asar said quietly, "You were magnificent, Iliae. Never doubt that."

Magnificent. The word fluttered up my spine. My hand still rested in his, and that brush of skin against skin captured all my awareness.

Another sin crashed over me:

Asar's touch sliding between my thighs in our shared dream. The trembling want in his breath against my throat, in the way my legs opened for him. Hunger beyond anything I'd ever experienced. And he had felt it in me, just as I had in him.

Perhaps it was a dream. Perhaps he didn't remember it. Who knew how the Descent worked?

But my gaze fell to his hand, perfectly still, thumb pressed against my wrist.

To the ripple of goosebumps on his forearm, visible even beneath the ink of his Heir Mark.

My eyes flicked up to meet his, and the sheen of desire gleaming in his stare made my breath catch.

His thumb slid quickly from my hand, and he looked away. I was happy to do the same. He would ignore it, and I was grateful for that. Psyche had hacked into our subconscious like a butcher.

It didn't mean anything.

It couldn't mean anything. I was loyal to the sun. I wouldn't betray him, not even in my mind. Not when he would be able to see the black marks piling up on my soul and punish me for them appropriately.

Instead I pushed my mind to more pressing thoughts.

Asar's hands were now folded in his lap. The deep red ink of his Heir Mark swirled over them, delicate strokes that followed the bones of his hands. He followed my stare and stretched them out before him, one open eye and one closed staring back at us.

"A part of me thought it was part of Psyche's tricks," he said grimly. "Too simple, apparently."

"I'm sorry about your father," I said.

"I'm not. He was a bastard."

"I'm sorry that your sister tried to kill you."

Sometimes there was no delicate way to say it.

He scoffed. "I should have seen it coming. Egrette wants nothing more than she wants that throne. She chose the perfect time to move. She could have tolerated being second when Malach was alive. But for the bastard, exiled half brother to get the crown over her . . ." He shook his head. "But I can't fault her for how she turned out. She was the spare daughter to the cruelest king the House of Shadow has ever seen. You've been a vampire for long enough to understand what that had meant for her."

I nodded. Vampire lifespans made their offspring their greatest liabilities. They typically groomed a single heir, and any other children were either killed or maimed—unnecessary risks when succession nearly always came at the price of blood. The House of Night was the most notorious for this practice, but vampires of the House of Shadow were no less ruthless about protecting themselves. They just valued appearances more. Maybe the Shadowborn king hadn't hacked off Egrette's legs or stripped her of her magic, but I had no doubt that he'd been shackling her for years in other, less obvious ways.

Maybe she, too, had spent the last century thinking that she could pay her dues, earn her keep, and finally, finally, be given the acceptance she so craved.

"It's only the start," he went on. "She won't settle for being a queen. She wants to be an empress. If what Elias said about the House of Blood is true, if they did indeed conquer a human nation . . . that sets a precedent that I know Egrette will want to seize." His jaw tightened, and I followed his stare to the coffee table. I hadn't noticed when I woke up, but items had been neatly lined up atop it—the relics. The branch, the ring, and—

My brow furrowed.

Four red petals.

Four. Not five.

"Shit," I whispered. "When did he—"

"I don't know." The words were a frustrated growl. "Elias was— he's more competent than I gave him credit for. We used to work together. I should have known." His throat bobbed. "I let my personal . . . issues with him cloud my judgment."

Issues.

I thought of what I had seen in Asar's memories. His tears on Ophelia's mutilated body. The work, surely, of more than one man.

Then his words to Elias after we'd returned from the Sanctum of Breath: *You can't handle witnessing the results of your actions.*

The pieces snapped into a sickening picture.

Asar let out a dry, humorless laugh. "Your face keeps no secrets, Iliae."

"Was he—did he—" I didn't mean to ask.

"Malach gave him orders then, and he followed them. Just as he followed Egrette's now. He wasn't the one who tortured Ophelia or killed her, but he was there. I was blindsided by them because I thought we were friends. But this time I was blindsided because I let myself think he was an idiot." He shook his head sharply. "A bastard, maybe. But not an idiot."

Elias had a relic of Alarus in his possession—albeit a small one. The thought made me nauseous.

"I can still conduct the resurrection with what we have," Asar said. "Elias wasn't so stupid as to strip me of my ability to do that, just in case Nyaxia did come knocking. But if he makes it back to the surface and offers that power to Egrette . . ."

"What can they do with it?"

A muscle twitched in Asar's jaw in a way that, I knew by now, meant he was trying to avoid saying *I don't know.*

"Use it for its own power. Or offer it as a consolation prize to win Nyaxia's favor if I fail. Countless other terrible things. Probably better that we don't find out."

And yet, I felt like I already knew. It would be bad if Egrette used the relic as a source of power in itself. It would be even worse if she used it as leverage to become Nyaxia's new chosen champion if Asar failed. My head swam with the visions Atroxus had showed me. I felt as if the air had curdled with a rapidly shifting fate. As if all those bloody futures had just swung sharply closer to reality.

"But she can't do anything yet," I said. "Because you're the Heir, not her."

Asar didn't answer for too long.

He pulled up his sleeves to reveal the full, glorious expanse of his Marks. My brow furrowed. I'd missed it before, but under the light . . .

"Why are they doing that?" I asked.

The tattoos flickered ever so slightly, as if the ink strokes were shadows from a shifting lantern.

"Because right now, I'm closer to dead than alive," Asar said, "and a dead Heir isn't much of a king."

"Does that mean Egrette is up there with half an Heir Mark?"

Again, that long pause, the one I knew meant *I don't know.*

At last, he said quietly, "You should go back."

My brows lurched. "I should *what?*"

Even Luce lifted her head, as if this shocked her, too.

"I can help you back to the nearest roots of Morthryn. Elias will be moving slowly. You're better at navigating these halls than he is. You can catch up to him. Tell him whatever bullshit he wants to hear. Say that you escaped me. He'll give you whatever you want. Or leave him to rot, and go free yourself."

I couldn't believe what I was hearing. "Why would I—"

"We're getting very close to the underworld now. Morthryn has collapsed down here. Even I can barely get to the next two Sanctums, Secrets and Soul. They'll be more dangerous than anything we've faced so far, and with Ophelia—"

He bit down hard on her name. He stood and turned away, tucking his hands into his pockets, as if to physically raise a shield between us. I understood the impulse. But there was no escaping what we'd seen in each other. The weight of his memories hung heavy between us.

"She's stronger than she was the last time I—the last time I saw her," he said. "And she will keep following me until the end."

"Can you do the—" I actually didn't have the word for it. "The thing? Can you help her like you helped Eomin?"

I knew Asar was serious, because he didn't even seize upon that perfect opening for an arrogant correction. Instead, he flinched, like the answer to this question was viscerally painful.

"No. I can't. I've tried. I've tried so many times."

One more time, he had said to her, the first time we encountered her. Opening his arms to her.

"She isn't fully dead," he said. "She isn't fully alive. And she isn't what she used to be. She's . . . Perhaps if I can resurrect Alarus, he can . . ." He swallowed thickly, like he was afraid to even give voice to this hope. But understanding fell over me.

"It's her," I murmured. "You're trying to help her."

He was quiet for a long moment, a muscle flexing in his jaw. "You saw. That night. It was wrong from the start, and I was too selfish to care. The Descent is crumbling with neglect, and I dealt a blow to it that night. Ophelia is not the only lost soul trapped here. The others just don't know enough to blame me."

"What's happening to the Descent isn't your fault, Asar. Even I know that."

He shook his head. "No. But I feel a responsibility for it all the same. And yes. For her, too."

I heard the echo of what he'd said to me the first time I helped him close a gate:

The world is built atop the invisible, abandoned souls. They needed someone.

A pang twisted in my heart. Sadness for him. Maybe something else I didn't want to examine too closely, because I felt it too deep.

I thought of Atroxus and the secrets I kept carefully tucked away behind my mental walls. Uncertainty spilled through me because I could stop it. For a moment, the outrageous thought of telling Asar the truth flitted through my mind. Of course, I couldn't—for Asar's sake and mine. I couldn't back away from my task now, not when the terrible fate Atroxus warned of was swinging closer than ever, and not when my redemption was so precarious.

And yet, I found myself so easily stepping into Asar's dream with him.

"All right," I said. "So we continue, and we resurrect Alarus, and—"

"I deserve this," Asar cut in, "but you don't."

I couldn't help it. I rolled my eyes.

He scowled, getting to his feet so he loomed over me. "I'm serious, Mische—"

I'm serious, Mische. I couldn't count how many times protective men had said that to me.

I threw out my hands, gesturing to the room around us. "I've already made it halfway through purgatory, you self-sacrificing idiot."

"*I'm* the self-sacrificing one?"

My smile disappeared under the scalpel of his tone. I didn't know why it hurt a little to have that little jagged shard of my past—something I had entrusted to no one else—wielded against me.

A second later, the smile was back.

"You're being ridiculous."

He took a step forward. He was now so close to me that I could feel the warmth of his body.

"I appreciate your boundless optimism," he said, voice low. "But some things are serious, Iliae. Some things are dark. It isn't all jokes and games and smiles. And I don't want to watch this destroy you."

My anger caught me off guard.

"Do you think that I don't know what darkness is?" I said. "Why? Because I smile too much? Because I talk too much? It's my choice to be the way that I am. A choice that I make even when it's hard. That doesn't make me weak, Asar."

"That's not what I—"

"I *know* what you meant." I drew in a deep breath and let it out, my anger fading. "You meant that you care about me."

I half surprised myself by even saying it that way. Asar's brows twitched, like he was surprised to hear it. And maybe both of us were equally surprised to realize how true it was.

I gave him a weak smile. "You have a good heart, Asar. Thank you for trying to protect me. But just because I talk a lot and smile a lot doesn't mean I'm stupid. I know what I'm asking for. You can't do the rest of this alone."

"You don't deserve to die for this," he said.

"You were the one who told me that everyone in Morthryn deserved to be here."

He winced. "I didn't—"

"You were right. It wasn't an accident that I ended up here. You saw—" I swallowed thickly. I wasn't ready to acknowledge aloud what Asar had seen of my past. One step at a time.

His gaze softened, like he knew this, too.

"I'm here because I'm meant to be," I said. "And I know you won't admit it, but you can't finish this without me. So stop being such a stubborn oaf and just let me help you."

"A stubborn oaf?"

"I stand by it."

He was quiet for a long time. Then his gaze flicked up, a smirk tightening at one corner of his mouth. "Does that make me your latest project, Dawndrinker?"

Was he? For a while there, I'd thought that was what I felt toward him—that familiar euphoria of a wound to heal. But that had always been so comforting. Safe. Simple.

Nothing felt safe about the way he looked at me just then.

But I just grinned slyly at him. "That's the trick, Asar. You've been my project from the start."

He snorted. The tension broke as he leaned back, shaking his head.

"If anyone can melt a stone heart."

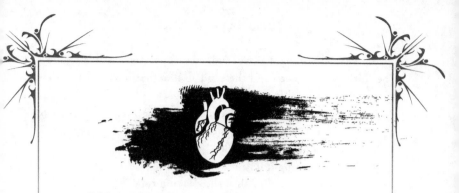

CHAPTER TWENTY-SEVEN

Morthryn no longer offered us hallways to travel between, not even the broken ones we'd used to get to Psyche. We had no choice but to travel on foot through the barren deserts of the Descent. Asar directed us on winding, convoluted paths to avoid the worst of the souleaters and wraiths. I was expecting that the journey would be difficult, and it was. But the harsh terrain and cold air were the least of our problems. The greatest challenge of being a vampire journeying to the underworld was that vampires required live prey, and there wasn't much alive down here at all. Our injuries healed slowly. Asar had managed to salvage just one bottle of blood, the stash he'd personally been carrying, in the wake of Elias's attack. We carefully rationed it, drinking what we needed to survive and not a drop more.

It was enough to keep us moving—for now—but not enough to keep the hunger away. The scent of Asar's blood was torturous.

I grabbed onto whatever distractions I could. My favorite of these activities was asking Asar unrelenting questions—what's your favorite color, what's the prettiest place you've ever been, who was your first best friend, what's your biggest petty annoyance? Asar must have really been suffering, too, or maybe he took pity on me, because he was shockingly tolerant of them (the answers being "Green," "Morthryn at sunset," "Luce, *obviously*," and, with a petty smirk, "This conversation," respectively).

"What's something you've always wanted to learn but never

have?" I asked one night as we trudged through rolling, dusty dunes. The hills were so steep and the sand so fine that we moved in slow motion, each step falling out from under us.

Asar, to his credit, always took my questions seriously. He thought for a moment, then answered, "The cello."

My nose scrunched. "The cello?"

"Is there something funny about that?"

"You just don't seem like the cello-playing type."

I'd seen instruments in his various chambers in Morthryn—several pianos, and a violin, once—but for some reason it had never occurred to me that they were there because he actually played them. I thought they were just artifacts from the prison's mysterious, ancient past, like so much else in its halls.

Asar gave me a flat stare over his shoulder. It was so cold that his exhale puffed from his nose like cigarillo smoke, emphasizing his indignation. "What type do I seem like?"

"You seem like the type who likes . . . books. And rules."

"I do like those things." He turned back, but sounded like he was trying not to smile. "But I also appreciate music, Iliae. Like all sophisticated people should. Is that really so surprising?"

I considered this.

No, I decided. It actually wasn't surprising at all.

The version of Asar who regretted he hadn't yet learned the cello might not fit with the image of the Wraith Warden, blood-soaked exiled son of the cruelest Shadowborn king. But I'd come to know a different version of him since he dragged me out of that party. And maybe that man—the man who loved his home with his whole stone heart, who considered his dog his best friend in the world, who devoted his life to fixing broken things—would love to learn how to play the cello.

I smiled, cheeks stinging against the cold. "When we get back, I'll personally go find you a cello."

When we get back.

I said those words so simply, because I had to believe them to be true. I pretended not to notice how Asar's expression changed at the sound of them. I just as dutifully ignored the twist in my own heart, too.

We no longer had visibility into the world above, but we were very aware of what Elias held and what he could do with it if he had managed to make it back to the surface. And though we'd managed to avoid Ophelia, we knew she was definitely still following us. Even Asar wasn't sure what we'd encounter once we reached the Secrets, but he seemed confident that whatever it was, it wouldn't be pleasant. To make things worse, both Asar and I were feeling the weight of weeks of both physical and magical exhaustion.

Still, that didn't stop Asar from constantly barking instruction at me, pushing me to practice my Shadowborn gifts. If this was how Oraya had felt under my instruction, I made a mental note to give her an apology. It was much more fun to be the teacher instead of the student. I liked coming up with my own ridiculous exercises more than I liked being given someone else's, especially since boredom made Asar's especially creative. Witnessing me use my Shadowborn magic in the Sanctum of Psyche had reinvigorated him. He had that air of petty victory about him, like I'd confirmed a suspicion of his.

And maybe he was right—I wasn't sure if it was because of what had happened in Psyche or our descent closer to the underworld, but the shadows called to me louder than ever. I felt the pull of Asar's magic constantly. The darkness offered a constant well of power, its beckoning temptation even stronger than my starving draw to Asar's blood.

It terrified me.

I have always been loyal, I had told Atroxus. I'd offered the sun my life, my body, my soul. I'd already challenged the limits of Atroxus's forgiveness by becoming the creation of his worst enemy. During our sparse moments of rest, when I listened to Asar's steady breath beside me, I curled around myself and cradled the sour knot of guilt in my stomach.

I don't want it, I told myself.

I belong to the sun, I told myself.

But what would Atroxus say if he knew what I had done? I'd done it to survive—to fulfill the mission he'd given me. I could tell him that, and it would be true. But I had also enjoyed it. That was the sin.

My fingers would trace the tattoo on my arm, fighting back tears. How much did Atroxus see of me, down here?

Did he already know?

What were the consequences of a bride of the sun betraying the god she had given herself to?

Sometimes, I would roll over in the darkness and watch Asar sleep. Even then, he was so serious—like some other version of him was still trekking to the underworld, never to truly rest. No wonder he always looked so exhausted.

In these moments, my mind would riffle through a thousand terrible answers to a terrible question: if I completed my mission, what would happen to Asar?

Would Atroxus see him as just another tainted son of his traitorous cousin? Another scourge to be purged?

Doubt was a disease. The harder I tried to wipe it out, the hotter the fever blazed.

I would save Asar, I told myself. I could earn back Atroxus's love, and with it, convince him to spare Asar. It was my greatest weapon. My only currency.

I had saved countless souls before. What was one more?

"WHERE ARE WE going?"

It was the fifteenth time I had asked that question. I wasn't sure why I thought Asar was going to give an answer now.

When we'd woken up, Asar had taken one look at Luce and me and said, "This is unacceptable."

"I don't look that bad," I'd grumbled—though I probably did look that bad. The exhaustion and the hunger were starting to get to me. Even poor Luce was beginning to seem a little worse for wear, the shine of her skull dulled and angle of her tail a little lower. She'd taken to curling up with me at dawn, which had dented my prayer time, but it was so sweet I couldn't bring myself to care. Asar had touched his chest when he'd seen it. "The betrayal wounds, Luce," he'd said, but he'd scratched her behind the ears in a way that seemed to say, *Good girl.*

Now, we trudged along a rocky, narrow path. We'd been traveling mostly through wide-open plains, avoiding the packs of souleaters who wandered in the distance, but today, Asar had taken us on a complex, treacherous side path. We walked until he found a gap in the cliffs so narrow that I laughed when he'd pointed it out—it seemed *that* ridiculous that we could squeeze through it. I wasn't sure how we managed. Maybe it was good we were starving because if any of us had as much as an extra pound, I didn't think we would've fit.

"Almost there," Asar said when Luce let out a disgruntled whine. "Stop complaining."

"Almost where?" I asked, exasperated.

My patience for Asar's secretiveness was wearing thin. But just when I thought I couldn't stand a single second more, the path opened up.

"Here," Asar said, triumphantly.

We emerged from the cliffs into a field—an actual field, with actual grass, not the dusty bone deserts we'd been trekking across. Fine, the grass wasn't exactly green—more of a luminescent gray—but it still was a welcome sight. It shivered under the breeze, rippling like a silver sea. Ahead, a house perched atop of the hill.

I blinked at it, confused.

It looked far too normal to be real. This was not one of the ethereal temples that dotted the Descent. It was a stone building, with two crooked spires rising from it. Smoke rolled from a lopsided chimney. It looked like it had been plucked from some farm out in the land of the living and dropped here, out of place in every way, right down to the warm browns of its stone and the distinctly mortal imperfections of its slightly askew wooden door.

Luce perked up immediately, and Asar gave her a smile and a scratch on the head.

"This is why you trust me," he said, and the two of them started down the path to the house.

"What is why we trust you?" I asked, half running to keep up.

I decided that maybe I didn't trust Asar.

We reached the door and he lifted his hand, but it swung open before he could knock.

A woman with dark ash-brown hair piled atop her head, streaks of white swirling in it like cream in tea, leaned against the frame. She wore an elegant dress in the classic Shadowborn style, tight, dark velvet following the shape of her body.

"Well, well," she purred, with a fanged smile. "A visit from the warden. What a special surprise."

I stopped short, my eyes widening. My hand went to the sword at my hip.

Because she was a wraith—semi-transparent, the other side of the room barely visible through her abdomen. A brutal wound cut straight through that admirable cleavage, dripping black down the center of her dress.

"Asar—" I squeaked.

But Asar actually smiled. A real, full smile.

"It's good to see you, Esme," he said. "It's been too long."

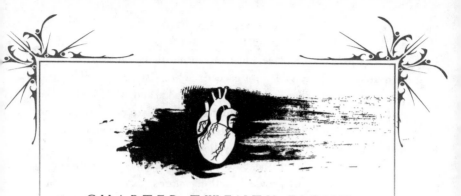

CHAPTER TWENTY-EIGHT

I'd seen plenty of supposed impossibilities in my lifetime. But as I sat at the ghost's table, watching her command a small legion of little formless shadows about her kitchen, I still had to take a moment to adjust to the situation. When I first left the Citadel in the hopes of seeing the world, I couldn't have imagined this. Apparently I'd made it further than even my fifteen-year-old self could ever have imagined.

Still, somehow the thing that seemed strangest of all was how at ease Asar looked. He was in an armchair, one foot propped up on the coffee table.

Lounging.

I never thought I'd see Asar *lounge*. It was like witnessing a dog sing.

He caught my gaze and narrowed his eyes.

"What?"

I looked down at my drink. "Nothing."

I wasn't sure why I didn't tease him about it. It just didn't feel right.

Esme sat across from Asar, back straight, glass of blood—*ghost blood?*—perched in long, slender fingers. Once one got past the gaping wound in her chest, she reeked of sophistication. Everything about her exuded the grace of vampire nobility, save, maybe, for the fact that Asar seemed to actually like her. Even the styling of the decor could have been lifted from any Shadowborn noble's apartment—all lush velvets and rich colors. An arrangement of fine furniture circled

a majestic black fireplace, blue translucent flame burning within. I
sat at a mahogany table in a brocade chair. Esme's servants—or at
least, that's what they seemed to be—floated in and out of the kitchen,
their nebulous bodies rearranging to carry platters of drinks and
food. When one of them set a plate of sliced steak in front of me, the
strips of meat wrapped in flaky yellow pastry, I gasped.

The smell—gods help me. Food hadn't smelled like this in decades.

"I'm sorry I can't provide anything more . . . substantial," Esme
said.

"Substantial?" I had to remind myself to use my fork instead of
my hands. The pastry melted over my tongue. The meat was perfectly cooked. I couldn't remember the last time anything had tasted
this good. I had this thought and then silently apologized to Raihn
for it. "This is amazing. It's—"

"A particular favorite? I know. Or rather, the Descent knows."
Esme gestured above us. "This is Psyche, after all. Your mind is no
secret."

"The food isn't real," Asar said. "The blood, either, unfortunately.
It tastes good, but that's all."

"I don't care," I said—and I really didn't. Another puff of shadow
set down a plate of cake beside me, and my eyes went round.

Sweet tastes had been the first to go. I couldn't even remember
what human buttercream had tasted like. Gods above. I was in
heaven.

Asar gave a low chuckle, and I glared at him.

"Don't judge me, Lord Joyless Warden, for enjoying a few mortal
pleasures. Even if they're false ones."

He touched his chest. "I would never deny you a mortal pleasure,
Iliae."

Something about the way he said it made another memory float
through my mind: *Until you were so exhausted with pleasure you begged me
to stop.* Asar's smile flickered, like he was having this thought, too. I
looked back to my plate.

A much simpler temptation.

I cleared my throat, gaze darting up to Esme, who watched me
with a curious stare. "So . . . how do you know Asar?"

It seemed like a much more polite way to word it than, *Who are you and what are you and why are you dead?*

Esme laughed. "I appreciate your attempt at tact, my lady."

"Oh, I'm not a lady," I said around a full mouth.

"No, definitely not," Asar agreed, and I gave him a scowl.

"I am Asar's predecessor," Esme said. "I was the warden of Morthryn for nearly three hundred years. Until I displeased the great Shadowborn king." Venom dripped from the title. She gestured to her chest. "I suppose even in death, I cannot escape my charge."

Asar raised his glass. "We're fortunate to have you."

Esme lowered her head in a demure, flattered bow. "How sweet of you."

"It's the truth." Then, to me, "Esme's soul remained in Morthryn when I was banished. She helped me learn how to take up the post. I wouldn't have survived it without her."

She let out a *psh*. "I always have been a fool for a pretty face. Gets me into trouble time and time again. And yet, do I learn?"

"I like to think I've repaid you, Esme."

She picked lint from her velvet armchair. "I suppose one cannot complain. The underworld sounds terribly dreary."

"And then you ended up . . . here?" I still wasn't exactly sure where "here" was.

"I tried to help Esme pass," Asar said. "But she is . . . an unusually stubborn soul."

"What a kind way of putting it," Esme said.

"It may be because of the ties she had to Morthryn. Or perhaps even the ties Morthryn had to her. Maybe her exile bound her even in death. But this is the farthest I was able to get her."

"Such woe." Esme sighed dramatically.

"But what is this?" I asked. "The house?"

"I learned quickly that there are a few benefits to death," she said. "Perhaps because of my knowledge of the Descent in life, I was able to use the illusion of Psyche to build the life I wanted for myself." She gave Asar a knowing smile. "With some help, of course."

Asar shook his head dismissively.

"It was a benefit for us both. Even with the pathways I've built over the years, it's difficult to venture beyond this point. Esme helps keep things in order where I can't."

She waved her hand. "It passes the time. But . . . I will say, it is a pleasure to see two beautiful faces after so long in solitude." Her gaze slipped between us, her tongue darting out against the point of one of her teeth.

I had no doubt that Esme had been a woman of appetite in life.

"Still, I must ask, what brings you here? I sense this is not a routine visit. The path here is no simple stroll. And the only reason I didn't think the two of you were wraiths when I saw you was because of the smell."

"I thought we were beautiful faces," Asar said.

"Faces, perhaps. The rest of you . . ." She shrugged. "Eh."

Ouch.

I couldn't bring myself to be too offended as I started in on the cake.

"We are on our way to resurrect Alarus," Asar said.

I stopped mid-bite. I was not expecting him to be so forthcoming.

Esme's flirtatious joking disappeared. She sat upright. "I hope, Asar, that these dead ears of mine misheard you."

"Nyaxia gave me the task," he said, and her sculpted brows hitched higher.

"That is . . ." Her mouth opened, then closed. Then she looked to me. "And this one?"

"Mische is a former Dawndrinker. I was fortunate enough to have her placed under Morthryn's care."

Placed under Morthryn's care. What a kind way to say, *sentenced to execution.*

He gave Esme a pointed look and added, "She killed Malach."

He said it like he was bragging about one of my accomplishments, which set an interesting mix of emotions fluttering in my stomach.

"Did she?" Esme's face broke into a vicious smile. "I like her, Asar. Be sure to bring her more cake." She turned to me, eyes sparkling. "Tell me, lovely, how did you do it?"

I swallowed. "I stabbed him."

She touched the wound in her chest with a soft chuckle. "Excellent. I hope he died slow."

I thought of my hands around that sword's hilt, slick with his blood, pushing and pushing and pushing until there was no more flesh to cut. I thought of the look on his face, staring right into my eyes as the life left them.

I took another mouthful of cake. "Slow enough," I said.

She let out a low laugh. "Excellent. Excellent." Then, to Asar, "And is she so very impressive that she is the only one you and Luce have trusted to come on this . . . mission?"

Asar's amusement faded. "There were others, but it didn't go well. Trouble at home."

He pulled up one sleeve, revealing his Heir Mark.

Esme's eyes went wide. She set down her glass.

"I see."

There was a long silence. Esme was no longer in a joking mood.

Asar said, "How are Secrets and Soul these days?"

"Even I can't make it far. You two have quite a journey ahead." Her gaze went far off, her fingers toying at the gold chain around her neck. Then she blinked, shaking herself from her reverie, and returned to that easy smirk.

"Good, then, that you came here to rest."

"Only for one day," Asar said, and she waved her hand.

"Even so. But I must insist you take a bath before we can truly enjoy each other's company."

I nearly dropped my fork. "A *bath*?" I gasped.

There was a *bath*?

"Well yes, of course. I'm not a barbarian," Esme said. "Upstairs."

I didn't care if it was an imaginary bath with imaginary soap and imaginary hot water. At least it would get the imaginary Descent grime off me.

I had already started rising when Asar said, "You can go first."

It hadn't even occurred to me to offer him the first one, and I didn't feel guilty about it at all.

I started to go upstairs, following Esme's direction, but halfway up the steps I heard lowered voices below.

I should keep walking, I told myself.

But maybe I was too nosy. Because my legs didn't move.

"You cannot be serious about this," she said in a grim hush.

"You've known me for a long time, Esme. I am always serious. Some call it a flaw."

"I am not joking." Her whisper came in a vicious hiss. "What use does Nyaxia have for this? The gods are restless, Asar. I can feel it here, closer to death. Even the wraiths can sense it. You know as well as I that Egrette cannot be queen. Turn back while you still can make it back to the surface. Be king. Live happily ever after."

"And deny Nyaxia? How would she take that?"

"Even she can barely see what happens down here. Tell her you failed. Offer her the consolation prize of what you have collected so far. She'll be grateful to have that much more of her husband. And you will still be alive."

I was holding my breath. Why did a part of myself agree with her? I needed Asar to complete his mission in order for me to complete my own. Yet . . .

You don't deserve to die here, Asar had told me.

He didn't deserve to die here, either. I was a dreamer. And right now, the dream of Asar, returning to the House of Shadow, becoming the king to lead it into a new age, seemed like such a wonderful one. The kind of dream that I, as a missionary of the light, would once have helped him fulfill.

"Somehow, I doubt Nyaxia will accept my failure so easily," Asar said.

"You must tell me, Asar, that this is not because of Ophelia."

Silence.

A pang twisted in my heart.

"I need to right my wrongs," he said at last. "You know what this place has become. It will just keep getting worse."

Esme scoffed. "We all have our regrets. Don't follow yours to the grave."

"It isn't about regret. It's . . ."

His voice trailed off. He couldn't explain it. But I knew what he meant. I knew what it felt like for your past to mark your flesh, a wound that would never heal, a wrong that you could never right.

I knew what it felt like to want more than anything, anything, anything in the world that redemption. To be clean again.

"I am not going back, Esme," he said at last. "I can't."

"And her?"

Me.

My cheeks heated.

"What about her?" Asar said coolly.

"I'm no fool. Try to keep her alive, at least. I like her."

"You're just saying that because she killed Malach."

"Perhaps. But you must admit, it is quite a selling point."

He let out a low laugh. "Yes. It is. Though . . ."

His voice lowered conspiratorially. I inched closer to the doorframe.

"She does have some flaws."

I stopped breathing in favor of listening.

"Oh?" Esme said.

"Yes. She's . . . well." A scraping sound—it sounded like he was dragging his chair closer. "She's nosy, and a terrible spy. No shame about eavesdropping."

My shocked laugh sputtered through my lips, though I quickly clapped my hand over my mouth.

"At least be good enough not to get caught, Iliae," Asar called from the next room. "The Shadowborn are supposed to be masters of espionage."

"I don't know what you're talking about," I called back. "I'm just taking a bath."

CHAPTER TWENTY-NINE

The bath was incredible. I did not care even a tiny bit that it was imaginary water. It was hot and clear and full of bubbles that smelled like roses. I felt like a princess, and not the murderous vampire kind, the kind from the human story-books Saescha read to me as a child.

By the time I sauntered downstairs again, I was practically glow-ing with happiness.

Esme set down her glass, looking me up and down, one brow arched. "Ah. I see my shadow friends have offered you one of my nightgowns."

I stopped mid-movement. "Is that all right?"

"Yes, of course. You could not put that atrocity back on. Besides, this suits you. Better color on you than me."

I was secretly grateful that I didn't have to change. The night-gown had been waiting for me, laid out on the bed, when I got out of the bath. It was gold silk, trimmed with black lace. The neckline hung low in a deep V, thin straps crossing across my back. It was shorter than the dresses I typically wore, but then again, I rarely had the opportunity to wear dresses at all, let alone ones like this. The fabric was light and luxurious as a caress. The way it slid over my skin reminded me of how sunlight used to feel.

I adored it. I unabashedly adored it. I liked pretty things, and I'd missed them.

Still, I'd stared at myself in the mirror for too long before coming down. The nightgown revealed the full, terrible expanse of my scars. It had been some time since I'd looked at myself, and it struck me with a terrible knot of shame just how *many* of them there were. Not too long ago, they only covered my arms, elbow to wrist. Now, they had crawled all the way up to my shoulders and all the way down my hands. My tattoo languished, barely visible, beneath the mottled distortion of scar tissue.

I'd searched the room for something to cover myself with and found a flowing robe of equally luxurious silk. It was blue with white flowers—not exactly matching the brilliant gold of the nightgown, but who was I here to impress?

"I hope you don't mind," I said, touching the robe. "I was, uh, a little cold."

Esme waved dismissively. "Of course. Though what a shame to cover up that magnificent décolletage. Don't you agree, Asar?"

I wasn't sure why I had avoided looking at Asar. He, certainly, was avoiding looking at me. But when his gaze at last rose, it hung there for a breathless moment, and I felt it on every inch of my bare skin. When he finally looked down at the book on his lap again, it was like he had to pry his eyes away.

"I don't comment on décolletage unless invited," he said coolly.

"Men today!" Esme sighed, then shooed him away to go bathe. He took awkwardly long to stand up, spending an inordinate amount of time rearranging the pages of the book on his lap, before at last closing it and excusing himself.

Esme and I sat together alone, watching the fire. I continued to munch on the seemingly never-ending supply of pastries. I supposed the upside of the food having no nutritional value was that I could eat as much of it as I wanted without getting full. One had to find joy in the little things.

Esme did not hide that she was watching me very, very closely, and I probably wasn't any more subtle, either. I wanted to ask her so many questions. Asar not only liked her, but actually *trusted* her. I felt like I was being presented with a treasure trove of information about him, unsupervised, where he couldn't *tsk* me for rummaging through it.

But Esme was the one to break the silence first. "The burns will not get better."

I froze mid-chew.

"Excuse me?"

She gave me a cryptic smile. "This is my house. I see all things."

I swallowed and self-consciously adjusted the sleeve on my robe. "I know I can't heal them. I don't try."

"That is not what I said. I said they will not stop."

I wasn't sure what to say to that. Luce had curled herself around my legs, and I reached down to scratch the top of her head, finding comfort in her little sigh of pleasure.

"Just a price I have to pay," I said lightly. "Nothing is ever free, right?" I held up a pastry. "What is this? It's—"

"Asar likes you very much," Esme said nonchalantly. "I can tell. He doesn't trust many, that boy, and goddess knows no one can blame him for that. But you." She tapped a long, manicured finger in my direction. "You, I think, he does."

Unexpected warmth suffused my heart.

I shrugged. Smiled. "We've become friends."

Friends. That was the first time I had even used that word aloud to describe Asar. It didn't quite fit right.

Esme scoffed and rolled her eyes. "In the name of the Mother, girl, he could not stand up after he saw you in that nightgown. *Friends,* she says."

Now my face was burning, and I was certain that Esme could see it. "I really don't think he—"

She raised a hand. "Spare me. I don't care if you admit it. You are both welcome to skip along in your pretty ignorance. I only say this so you know the gravity of your decisions. Do you, girl? Do you understand what you have been entrusted with?"

My smile disappeared.

I thought of Asar, hunched over his desk, scribbling his notes. Asar, lazily stroking Luce's ears while she curled up at his feet. Asar, using every bit of his strength to pull another gate closed, and another, and another.

Asar, the way he looked at me when he cradled me into darkness at the Psyche temple.

"Yes," I said. "I do."

"My cold soul cares for little in this life or the next, but it cares deeply for Asar. And perhaps I could tell you that you should be careful about how much of yourself you sacrifice to your sun god, because once that man decides that he cares for you, he will never stop. Not ever. Your sacrifice will become his, and I fear that fractured stone heart of his cannot bear another blow."

She took a long sip from her glass, then set it down and shrugged. "I *could* say this because it is true. But I will not."

She leaned across the table, eyes sharp.

"I will tell you that you should be careful how much you sacrifice to your sun god," she said, pointedly, "not because of Asar, but because of *you*. Because *you* did not make it this far just to let yourself burn up like some pretty little candle. You killed Malach of the fucking Shadowborn, Mother's sake. Have some self-respect."

I stared at her for a long moment. Her words hung between us.

And then I laughed.

She leaned back and crossed her arms. "So now I am funny."

"I'm just . . . so, *so* surprised that Asar likes you so much."

But even as I said it, I knew it wasn't quite true. I actually could see exactly why Asar, someone who had spent nearly his entire life in exile, would have so much affection for someone who seemed to have no regard for the conventions of the life that had rejected him.

Esme gave me a wry smirk. "I would say the same to you," she said, "but you have wonderful breasts, so I suppose I understand."

I sputtered an uncomfortable laugh. "Thank you, but it's just the nightgown."

She rolled her eyes.

And I was ready to let this conversation die, but instead, I said quietly, "I have my past, just like he has his. But I won't let it hurt him."

Even as the words left my lips, they tasted like impossibility. Asar and I walked a wire between two sides of a divine collision. How could I protect him from the wrath of gods? How could I protect him from the consequences of my betrayal?

But I was Mische Iliae. I never shied away from the impossible, and here, alone with a ghost, I swore I'd make that vow true.

Esme's mouth curled with a sad smile. She looked at me as if she, too, knew I couldn't make such a promise, but that it meant something to her that I did, anyway.

"Every time he leaves," she said softly, "I hope that I will never see him again. But . . ."

But he always came back.

Because Asar was devoted.

My chest hurt. I no longer had an appetite. I took a sip of the not-blood and wished that the alcohol in it was real.

Footsteps padded down the stairs, and Asar appeared in the doorway again. His wet hair stuck to his temples and his neck. He wore a fresh shirt, a black cotton one, which clung to the still-damp skin of his shoulders. He actually looked refreshed for possibly the first time since I'd met him. Even the pulse of light in his left eye seemed calmer.

"Ah, at last." Esme clapped her hands together when he returned. "Now that you are fed and clean, I can put you to work."

Asar's eyes narrowed. They darted between Esme and me, like he suspected we had been talking about him but chose not to acknowledge it.

"Put me to work?"

She gestured to the corner—to a small piano. It was carved of gleaming black, ornate decoration lining its edges, ivory keys gleaming. A layer of dust coated its surface.

"Surely there must be new songs up there," she said. "Play me something. I miss music. My little pets are terrible musicians."

I gasped and leapt to my feet, hands together. "Oh, yes. *Yes*. Play for us."

I was absolutely dying to witness this.

He started to protest, but Esme let out a dramatic sigh.

"I let you and your friend here into my home, and I, a lonely dead woman without a friend in the world, ask for only *one* thing—"

"Oh, for fuck's sake." Asar rolled his eyes, but the corner of his mouth curled in amusement.

He shot me an apologetic look, then pushed aside the clutter to slide onto the piano bench. For a moment, his fingertips gently caressed the keys in a way that seemed nothing less than reverent.

And then he began to play.

Esme beamed in satisfaction. My mouth fell open.

Gods, he was incredible.

He launched into a dramatic, upbeat melody, the full layers of sound inflating to fill the room like a drawn breath. I crept closer, sliding into the armchair closest to the piano, my knees up against my chest.

I watched his fingers, long and deft, marked by ink and scars, dance over the keys.

"That's amazing," I whispered before I could help myself, and a barely there smile glinted in Asar's momentary glance my way.

Then, delicate whorls of his magic collected around his hands, supplementing his playing, the sound so rich and full it sounded like it didn't even belong in this mortal world.

"Wonderful, Asar. You still have it." Esme spun, her velvet skirt swirling around her, then extended a hand my way. "Dance with me, Mische. It's been too long since I've had a partner."

When was the last time I'd danced? I used to love it, a long time ago. A slow grin spread across my face. I took Esme's hand—which felt solid and not at the same time, somehow—and the two of us whirled around the living room. It was no practiced dance, no careful steps. But my body knew how to move to Asar's music, following a rhythm that felt as intrinsic as a heartbeat. The silk of my nightgown flared around my thighs, the robe wrapping my twirls in a smear of night. Esme laughed, lost in the mortal joy of it all. Even Luce's tail thumped against the rug in time to the music as it built faster and faster, like a bird taking flight.

I looked over my shoulder at Asar. And I almost stumbled at the sight of him—eyes shining, hands moving, a little dot of water that had dripped from his hair hanging onto the tip of his nose for dear life. And he was smiling in a way that made the entire world stop,

a smile that reminded me of the way the sun looked when it crested
the horizon the first time I saw it at the Citadel, and I had thought,
I am home.

I am home.

EVENTUALLY, WE WORE ourselves out. I lost track of how many
songs Asar played at Esme's demands. But she was the first to excuse
herself, stifling a yawn.

"You are a good enough musician to exhaust the dead, Asar. And I
suppose I should let the two of you get some rest, too, if you're to set
out again on your fool's mission tomorrow."

The mention of our mission sobered both of us, it seemed, though
neither of us acknowledged it. I wondered if wraiths actually did
need to sleep, or if Esme had just decided that it was time to let Asar
and me be alone, now that she had sufficiently stirred the pot.

The silence definitely felt heavy with her gone.

Asar and I remained in the living room. I would sleep on the
couch, and Asar insisted on taking the rug, though I'd offered many
times over. ("I can sleep anywhere!" I'd told him. "It's a very special
skill of mine.") But though my body was aching after weeks without comfortable rest, sleep was oddly unappealing. I had the strange
desire to cling to this moment before it slipped through my fingers. If
I closed my eyes, it would be gone when I opened them.

I curled up on the couch. Luce had fallen fast asleep by the fire,
lightly snoring—who knew spirit wolves could snore?—while Asar
still sat at the piano bench. We didn't speak. He had a glass of blood
wine beside him, which he sipped more and more frequently. I knew
the feeling. My hunger sat low in my stomach. The temporary relief
of the taste was doing less and less to quell it.

"You should get some rest," he said at last. "We have a difficult
journey ahead. Even this was probably too much of a detour."

"I'm glad we came here," I said. "Esme is nice."

He snorted. "That's not a word I typically hear used to describe her."

"I like her. I can tell she has a good heart."

"She has a wicked heart, which is why it ended up skewered. But a loyal one, for the select few she deems worthy."

"Sounds like someone else I know."

He let out a low laugh. "Perhaps so, Iliae. Perhaps so. I can hope."

I liked to watch Asar smile. It felt like a victory every time. I traced its path across his face now and wondered when I'd memorized the shape of it.

He was right that we needed the rest. But the thought of sleep seemed impossible. I was too jittery beneath my exhaustion.

"I can't sleep," I admitted.

"Nervous?"

I wondered if he was. Nervous didn't even seem the right word for it. Nervous was for exams at the Citadel. What I felt now was the future weighing down on me, possibilities closing in. I couldn't confront them yet.

I wasn't ready to let this night slip away.

"I think we need one more song," I said.

"Greedy of you. I've played you dozens of songs."

"Yes, but there's one thing you haven't done."

He raised a brow in a challenging, *Oh, is that so?*

I stood. "One more song, Warden."

"Because I'm at your beck and call."

I batted my lashes at him. "You can't deny me."

He stared at me for a moment too long. The joke landed awkwardly between us, heavy with all the ways we both realized it was true.

He cleared his throat and lowered his eyes to the keys. Another song poured forth from his fingers—a song that put all the others to shame. Mournful notes that sounded like hope after heartbreak, like the rise of the stars in the sky, like a flame warming a hearth.

Even after hearing his talents all evening, this one struck me straight to my soul.

His gaze flicked up at me. "Happy?"

I was toying with danger, I knew. I should go to bed and end this night now.

But I said, "Not yet. You've been watching Esme and me make fools of ourselves all night long. But I haven't seen you dance once."

He scoffed. "Nor will you, Iliae."

I couldn't imagine what Asar would look like dancing, and that was exactly why I was desperate to witness it. I pressed my hands together. "Please, great and terrible Wraith Warden, King of the Shadowborn. *Please*."

"You're right, I'm a king now. Kings don't dance."

I almost pointed out that actually, kings have to dance all the time— I'd seen Raihn dance many more times after his coronation than in the decades before, and always unwillingly. But I didn't need to say a word.

Asar held my stare. Maybe we both heard the echo of my joke: *You cannot deny me.*

"We don't even need music," I said, holding out my hand.

He made a face, offended. "That would be ridiculous." Writhing tentacles of his magic again worked from his hands, lying over his fingers. And when he stood, they kept playing in his place.

My smile brightened. "That's amazing."

I meant it. Of all the great feats I'd seen Asar perform, this music topped them all.

He held out his hand—the scarred one, with the closed white eye on his palm.

And even though I had asked for this, a momentary spike of fear bolted through me. I heard my sister's voice from so many years ago, crying, *It's dangerous, Mische!*

But I took his hand anyway.

This song wasn't one of the dramatic waltzes he'd played for Esme. It was slower, lighter, deeper. The melody still carried my body just as easily, but I was so painfully aware of how close it brought it to Asar's. His other hand settled at the small of my back. He swayed awkwardly with me.

I scowled. "You aren't trying. Your feet aren't even moving."

"I'm a musician, not a dancer."

I narrowed my eyes at him, scrunching my nose. "You. Aren't. Trying."

He met my gaze. The way the firelight flickered against the panes of his face, traveling along the texture of his scars like rivulets of liquid silver, struck me speechless. How could I ever have thought they ruined his beauty?

A spark of determination flashed in his eyes as an amused smile twisted his mouth.

And then suddenly, his arms tightened around me. He released me, spinning me into a twirl that I only barely managed to catch, and then he pulled me forcefully back to him, our stomachs pressed together, foreheads nearly touching. It happened so suddenly I couldn't prepare myself. The scent of him, the blood so close to the surface of his skin, briefly overwhelmed me. I wondered if he felt my breath hitch. Or if he knew that I noticed the way his did, too.

Danger, Mische, the voice in the back of my head warned again.

"Better," I said. "I guess."

He let out a *psh*. His mouth was so close that the sound skittered across my cheek.

The silk of this nightgown was so thin. I could feel the shape of his body against my stomach, my pelvis, my breasts. I liked it. I shouldn't like it.

I was so hungry.

We were both so hungry.

"I don't recognize this song," I said, trying, unsuccessfully, to defuse the tension. "It's different from the others you played."

"Nothing fancy. Just something I came up with."

My brows rose. "You wrote this?"

"Wrote is a strong word. I just . . ." I was too close to him to see him, but I felt his muscles shift as he shrugged.

And then he said, after a moment, "I just played the notes that sounded like you."

I stiffened. He spoke the words so softly, with such tender vulnerability. Like a confession to a priest.

So kind it hurt.

Danger, Mische. Danger. This is not what you're supposed to do.

But still, I didn't pull away.

I murmured, "It's beautiful."

And he whispered, "Yes."

Our movements had grown slower, more languid. We drifted closer, verging on embrace. I so fiercely wanted to melt into it, let my head fall against his shoulder, let my face bury into the soft flesh of his throat, where his pulse hammered. What would happen if I did?

Would he kiss me?

Would he lay me down on this bed of furs and stifle my cries of pleasure, just like he'd promised me?

Danger.

The thought dizzied me. It was so brazenly wrong. My hunger was twisting my thoughts. Making it hard to think.

I was a bride of the sun.

But maybe I was weak, because I just kept pushing, drinking up another second.

I pulled away slightly, enough to look into his face, and grinned. "You know, when I first met you, I never would have thought you were such a sensitive soul. The exiled prince of the Shadowborn, Wraith Warden, and skilled piano composer."

"I'm a lot of things. Just like you."

"No, I'm simple." The response, the smile, it all came so easily, a refrain I'd repeated countless times before: *Don't look at me. I'm not the one this story is about.*

He let out a low scoff. "Mische Iliae, you are full of secrets and surprises." The music swelled, and he twirled me again. When he caught me this time, he cradled me close.

Pull away, I told myself.

I didn't. I couldn't. My body begged for one second more, and another, and another.

"I should have known right away," he murmured. "What you were. A bride of the sun."

I stiffened. I missed the next step.

I knew he'd seen it in Psyche, just as I had experienced all his worst memories, too. But he hadn't acknowledged them these last weeks, for which I was deeply grateful.

"Why?" I said. "Because I seem that special?" The joke was strained and flat.

"Because I know what it looks like to be so desperate for redemption, you would sacrifice anything."

My stomach turned. "It isn't like that."

Asar pulled back just enough to look at me. I wasn't sure what I was expecting—judgment, or pity. But there was only compassion.

"How old were you when he picked you?"

The hunger muddied my thoughts, brought my emotions too close to the surface. I opened my mouth intending to change the subject.

But maybe that was the other great temptation. Maybe I wanted someone to carry those secrets beside me.

Before I could stop myself, I whispered, "Eight."

The sheer sadness in his face at that sliced my heart open.

"It was a gift," I added quickly. "It's what I was always meant to be. It's not Atroxus's fault that I—"

That I ruined it. That I ruined myself.

"What you were always meant to be?" Asar repeated. The words were low, but blade-sharp, sliding straight into my heart. "You were meant to be bound to a god from the time you were a child? You were meant to be one of hundreds of wives? You were meant to sacrifice yourself for him?"

The defensiveness jumped up like the tender hurt of an open wound. "Sometimes love requires sacrifice, Asar."

My voice came out weaker than I wished it was. A plea more than a declaration.

We had stopped moving. He stared at me for a long moment. And then, so slowly, his hand slipped from mine. His fingertips landed on my collarbone, just barely touching the edge of the robe.

His gaze pierced me, unblinking, asking permission for what came next.

Step away, I told myself.

Tell him to stop, I told myself.

Don't let him see, I told myself.

But I swallowed thickly as, with a feather-light touch, he pushed the silk from my shoulders. The fabric was so delicate. It slid down and pooled on the floor.

I was shaking.

I felt naked. So exposed. Asar's gaze held on mine for several long seconds, before finally breaking free, roving over my bare flesh.

My breath hitched as his fingertips traced my clavicle, my shoulder, the swells and dips of my bicep. And gods, that touch—it was like his hands over the piano keys. His scars against mine. Mistakes against mistakes.

I closed my eyes. Tears prickled at the back of my throat.

"It is an injustice, Mische, that this is what you got when you asked for love," he murmured. "This isn't what love should feel like."

It isn't? I almost said. Because this was what I was taught that love was—something you hurt for, something you bled for. You give your god your life, your blood, your virgin body. You give your charges your devotion and never accept theirs. You give and give and give until you have stripped your soul bare.

I should have told him, *That's faith. Don't you understand?*

But my tears slid down my cheeks. My hunger burned. Gluttony won out in the end.

I asked, "What should it feel like?"

Asar still held my wrist like a precious gift. He lowered his head, his dark lashes falling against those sculpted cheeks.

"Like this," he whispered, and brought his lips to my skin.

His kiss was so gentle, so tentative, that it was barely a brush against my flesh. Still, the touch sent a bolt of lightning through my body.

He lifted my arm a little more and kissed me again, higher, at the next cluster of scars. He lingered, the warm, soft stroke of his tongue making me draw in a shuddering breath.

Higher—my bicep. Then my shoulder.

"It should feel like this," he whispered against my skin.

Two tears slid down my cheeks.

I couldn't answer him. I couldn't pull away.

I had been hurting for so long that I had forgotten what it was like for something to feel good. And gods, it felt so good that it hurt. It reached past my scars, past my wounds, to the neglected version of myself that I'd long ago abandoned.

That version of me knew he was right.

It was what I would want for any of my friends. It was what I had wanted for Raihn, for Oraya.

I even secretly wanted it for myself.

I wanted to slip the straps of this nightgown from my shoulders and offer him more to worship. Let him kiss away all those scars, all that shame.

I wanted it like I wanted the sun. No—like I wanted blood.

But I cupped his cheek, lifting his head. I tried not to meet his eyes and failed.

His face changed, that pained want falling away in favor of concern. His thumb captured a tear over the curve of my cheek.

"Mische," he whispered.

When he said my first name, it felt like such an indecent intimacy. More sensual than his mouth on my skin.

"Don't do that," I rasped. "Don't."

The last of his glazed-over desire fell away. "I'm sorry. I—"

But then the blast cleaved us apart.

One moment, I was standing with Asar. The next, the world tilted. A deafening roar drowned out all sound.

I thought, *This all hurts a lot for a house that is supposedly not real.*

And my back slammed against the wall as smoke enveloped us.

CHAPTER THIRTY

G et up, Iliae."

Asar's voice was all sharp command, but his touch was gentle as he shook my shoulders. Almost pleading.

"Get up," he said again, with a note of fear in his voice that made me think foggily, *He really* does *like me, doesn't he?*

My cheek pressed against the bearskin carpet. Shades of gray danced across my vision. Distant screaming rang in my ears. I was dimly aware of pain pulsing through my left leg.

I lifted my head to see Asar leaning over me, letting out a breath of relief that he didn't even try to hide, and behind him . . .

Wraiths.

Countless wraiths.

It took me a moment to make sense of what I was seeing in the formless morass. A wall of the house had collapsed, smoke pouring through slabs of broken brick. The wraiths crawled through the wreckage like ants overtaking a discarded piece of rotten fruit. One of them emerged from the smoke behind Asar, mouth open.

"Watch it!" I shouted.

He whirled around just in time. He had no weapon—he pushed it back with his magic alone, shadow clashing against shadow. But the one wraith was followed by another, and another.

I staggered to my feet. Esme had come downstairs. Gods, she was a force—truly terrifying. The ghosts and monsters I dreamed of as a child looked just like her. She was floating, darkness swirling around her like the churning water of the sea, tentacles of it reaching out to snatch faceless wraiths from the air.

There were so many of them. I didn't even know where to look. Esme tossed us our weapons without looking our way. Asar snatched his from the air without even interrupting his fight. Mine, the clumsy steel sword, clattered uselessly to the ground several feet short of me. Luce grabbed it and dragged it to me while I wrestled with a faceless wraith.

"Good girl," I rasped as I used it to hack through the thing's mid-section. It let out a scream and withered away.

I fought my way to my feet in that brief reprieve. The wraiths were everywhere. The comforting solace of Esme's home had been de-stroyed. The two front windows were now shattered, globs of smoke and shadow pouring through them.

And from that smoke, Ophelia rose.

It was hard to believe that she had once been the pretty vampire woman I'd seen in Asar's memories. Every time I saw her, she grew more distorted, like a translation copied many times over. Now, she wasn't a person so much as an element, a living tempest of rage and pain and hunger.

"I have been looking for you," she purred, rising into the sky, hands out as if in supplication to some dark god. "You never come this far, Asar. You cannot imagine what Secrets has waiting for you."

Her eyes, empty and eternal, fell to me. Suddenly, I could feel Asar's lips on my skin, as if the remnants of his kisses were as visible as my scars.

"And you," she hissed. "Such enemies you have here. So many hungry souls search for you, Mische Iliae."

Asar fought toward her. I wanted to reach out and hold him back. I couldn't. Couldn't stop fighting long enough to even try.

"They've done nothing to you, Ophelia." His voice barely crested the rising buzz of the dead. "I deserve your anger. Let them go."

Even before she responded, I knew that it was useless. It was sweet, in a way, that he thought his sacrifice could be enough to stop her. Ophelia had been betrayed by her entire world. There was no more logic to her rage. She didn't want Asar anymore. She didn't want justice. She just wanted to destroy in the hopes that it might bring her peace.

It wouldn't. Maybe she even knew it. But that wouldn't stop her, either.

Her lips twisted into a sneer. "You were always so naive, Asar. I was so in love with you that I could not see it."

I cut down another faceless wraith. The hair prickled on the back of my neck, as if responding to an invisible breath. I had the eerie, unmistakable sensation that I was being watched.

I looked over my shoulder.

He stared back at me, a smile at that perfect mouth, his chest still open with my killing blow.

Malach, the Shadowborn prince, and my creator, stared back at me.

Fear paralyzed me as he stepped closer. "I have been waiting for you. I didn't think I'd see you here so soon."

Long, blackened fingers reached for me—

Move, Mische. Move.

I snapped myself out of my haze. I rose my blade and swiped at him, but the cut was clumsy. He laughed as I stumbled back.

"Dumb luck that you managed to kill me." His smile soured to a poison sneer. "I should have tied you down to that bed."

My heart banged against my ribs like a caged rabbit, frantic to escape. When I would have nightmares about the man who Turned me, I would remind myself that he couldn't hurt me anymore. But that wasn't true. I'd known it even then. He could always hurt me. Even now, even in death.

I wanted to run. I wanted to crawl under the bearskin and pray he never found me.

Instead, I swung my sword.

But Malach knocked my blow away like it was nothing. My back slammed against the wall. I thrashed, but he held me there, hand around my throat. His teeth glistened in the darkness. I couldn't look away from them—those fangs that had made me.

"You Turned bitch," he snarled. "How dare you."

He didn't need to elaborate. How dare I kill him, defy him, have the audacity to keep existing after he'd left me to die.

I wouldn't speak because I wouldn't let him hear the tremble in my voice. There was nothing I could say that he deserved to hear.

I killed him, I told myself. I already won this battle once before.

But his touch, the grip of death, sucked the breath from my lungs. He leaned close, eyelids fluttering with the allure of the living.

Across the room, Asar's head turned from the wraith he was holding off. His eyes met mine.

I swore that the entire world rearranged around his rage. The shadows at the corners of the room trembled and shivered, as if preparing to answer his call. Light poured from his left eye in a sudden burst.

He yanked his sword from the wraith and turned toward us.

He didn't need to say anything—no *get your hands off her,* no *don't you dare touch her.* No snarled stake of possession.

But the living and the dead, and all in between, felt it.

Malach felt it.

His head turned toward his brother, and I seized his distraction.

This time, when I struck, I seized every shred I could of the magic that cracked through the darkness.

Malach wasn't expecting that. The split second of shock on his face was a treasure. I wanted to put it in a locket to wear around my neck.

He released me, air flooding my lungs, as he stumbled back. But he regained his footing quickly. He'd set his sights on Asar now.

"Hello, little brother. It's been quite some time." His gaze fell to Asar's forearms and the Heir Mark that adorned them. His lip curled. His violent want rotted in the air. All that remained of him in death.

"Those belong to me," he snarled.

Asar did not dignify this with a response. He and his brother collided in a crash of darkness. I tried to jump in, tried to help, but the waves of wraiths were too much. Esme was trying fiercely to hold off the tide, but even in all her magnificence, she was failing.

Ophelia rose above it all like smoke into the sky, a smile on her face. But even that expression was joyless. None of this would bring her peace.

And then, the sound of glass shattering rang out from the back of the house. The force of it sent me back against the wall, and ripped Asar and Malach apart, sending Malach hurtling into the chaos. But the reprieve was a temporary gift.

Wide-eyed, I shot Asar a panicked glance. Esme whirled around, her hand still around a wraith's throat. Even Luce hesitated in dread.

I spun around to see countless more dead pouring into the cottage.

Too many. I knew it right away. We'd barely managed to hold off the first wave. This doubled—maybe tripled—their numbers.

We had to run.

But my eyes found a face in the crowd. A face I'd know anywhere. A face that made my heart stop, my lungs empty. I couldn't move.

Saescha looked just as she had in death, her throat torn open, blood smearing her face. And through a crowd of countless faces, I still knew she was looking for me. Her eyes speared straight through me.

Someone grabbed my shoulder and dragged me through the back door, the one corner of the house that had yet to be overrun. I found myself looking into Esme's face. Her other hand held Asar's wrist, tight.

"Go," she ground out. "Go. If you insist on taking on this ridiculous task, then go now. Quickly, before they notice. I'll create a distraction for you."

Asar scoffed. "Don't be ridiculous."

"We're not leaving you here," I said. "If we're running away, then you're coming with us."

Esme laughed. "I do not flee. Not from my own home. Besides . . ." Her eyes slipped over her shoulder, where Malach pushed his way through the dead. "There are some souls here I would not mind some time alone with."

"You're being foolish, Esme," Asar said. "Just because you've died once doesn't mean there isn't worse—"

"I am the only one here not being foolish," she snapped. "You are the one who insists you must do this. Then do it, Asar. Do it. Don't die here for me." Her gaze flicked pointedly to me, and Asar's followed. His mouth thinned.

And this time, when Esme pushed us again toward the back door, he took my hand and let her, even as I protested.

"Don't let them win," he said. "The Descent would be miserable without you."

She laughed. "They aren't as good at this game as I am. Of course they will not win." Her face softened. She touched Asar's cheek. "It was good to see you, my friend. I hope that if I don't again, it's because you are destined for better things."

That sounded far too much like a goodbye.

I shook my head, digging my heels into the dirt.

"No. We aren't leaving you alone."

But her face was resigned when she turned to me. "And you. I hope you watch them all burn."

"Esme—"

But she melted into the shadows as another shatter cut through the air, and then Asar was pulling me as we fled into the cold night air.

"Asar, you can't. We can't leave her alone."

His jaw was tight. The fleeting nightfire light caressed the feathering muscle in his jaw. I could feel his reluctance, too—more painful than his wounds.

"The best thing we can do for her is leave. She can hold them back. But it's not her that they want. If we're gone, they'll lose interest in her. And Esme is no delicate flower. She'll have her fun in the meantime."

It didn't feel right. And when Asar's stare lingered on me, I knew in my heart that if I were not here, he would've gone down fighting with Esme until the end.

We ran into the fields beyond the cottage. The sky was heavy with smoke, which undulated in unnatural swells. It blotted out the distant rivers of blood and the silvery remnants of the terrain above them. It was so thick that when I looked ahead, my eyes simply saw nothingness.

Two more steps, and I realized: it wasn't just the smoke.

It was because there was actually nothing ahead of us. The ground simply ended.

CARISSA BROADBENT

Oh gods. I hated heights. I didn't even like jumping off cliffs with Raihn, and he had actual wings.

I chanced one more look back—one more look at the burning cottage and the wave of lost souls that consumed it. And I could have sworn I saw her there, watching us go. She was a distant silhouette against the flames, but sometimes you know someone so well, you'd just recognize them anywhere.

Another plume of darkness, and she was gone.

"Hold on," Asar said, and looped his arm around my waist, clutching tight.

I cringed, squeezing my eyes shut.

And then we hurled ourselves into nothingness.

PART FIVE

SECRETS

INTERLUDE

It's a terrible thing to suffer even a glancing taste of divine rage.

One might think that removing a corpse is a harmless rebellion. The offering, after all, had already been made. But the act was not as important as the disrespect in the girl's intent. A god can sense dissent. A god can smell rebellion.

Atroxus rarely visited two days in a row. But that next morning, when the girl blinked away restless, nightmare-laden sleep, he was waiting at the foot of her bed.

"I am so very fond of you." His voice sounded like sparks on a drought-dead plain. "Perhaps my affection has made me blind."

The girl knew instantly that she had made a terrible mistake. She had long managed to pass off her imperfections as charming flaws. But in her moment of enraged recklessness, she had revealed too much. She had let her improper emotions reach the surface of her skin, where Atroxus could see them like pus-filled blemishes. Now, in the harsh light of morning, her actions seemed ridiculous. The sun had given her everything. She had seen the light bring comfort to countless souls, time and time again. Why would she question any of that over a vampire's corpse? Even for a moment?

She knew that she could not distract her god with anything as simple as charming chatter or physical offering. She fell to her knees. An avalanche of apologies fell from her lips, frantic as words of devotion tripped over each other.

Atroxus stood there and allowed her to shower him with devotion. And then, after what felt like an eternity, he raised his palm.

"*You have served me well all your short life, a'mara, and I can see in your heart your love for the light,*" he said. "*But I now have reason to doubt you.*"

"*I'll prove it to you.*" The words tumbled from her mouth. "*I'll—I'll go on a mission in your name.*"

"*You have gone on many missions for me.*"

"*Not like this. This will be greater than all of them. This will be the kind of mission that history remembers. Tell me what I can give you. Test me, and I'll prove myself.*"

She did not breathe as he surveyed her, silent.

Gods had killed wayward followers for lesser slights. But the girl did not fear death as much as she feared her lord's indifference. If Atroxus cast her out as one of his chosen, she would be forced to leave the Citadel. Perhaps she might still keep her magic, but she would no longer have the ability to spread the light to others as she had. And worst of all, the shame of her sin would spread to her sister, and perhaps even her closest friends, cutting them off from their home as well.

"*Please,*" she begged.

The sun god acquiesced, his face softening.

"*Perhaps,*" he said softly, "*there is one thing you can offer me.*"

The girl's heart leapt. She straightened, waiting for her command.

"*If you so believe that vampires can be saved, then who am I to tell you otherwise?*" Atroxus said. "*If what you claim is true, it would be a great tide turn in our blessed war against the darkness. It could change the world, a'mara. So this is my mission for you. Go. Go to Obitraes, the land of the damned. Give me a single vampire heart that can be shown the light.*"

Perhaps someone else—someone more cynical—might have seen this as an impossible mission. Perhaps someone else might have known that being handed this task was the same as being handed a death sentence.

But the girl was no cynic. Her face broke into a smile. She leapt to her feet. This was not an impossible mission. This was an opportunity. Because she did believe that vampires, like anyone else, could be saved. She did believe that there was goodness in all hearts, even ones that held black blood instead of red.

And so, that silly, naive girl didn't even hesitate as she said, "*Of course, my light. I accept.*"

CHAPTER THIRTY-ONE

I smelled salt and the sea.

A dream, I thought dimly.

It had been a long time since I'd had a dream like this—a dream of my home. The sand was soft against my skin, my cheek resting on my crossed arm, stomach to the dunes, just as I had napped countless times on the beaches south of the Citadel. The sea rolled in and out with the steady comfort of a mother's shush. The sun was so, so warm.

My lashes fluttered. Opened.

Closed.

Opened.

I saw sand. Smooth, white sand.

I blinked.

And still saw sand.

My brow furrowed. I let it run through my fingers. I realized I was still wearing Esme's silk nightgown, bloodstained and wet. I knew I was injured, but I didn't feel any pain.

"What the hell?" I whispered.

This was not a dream.

But it couldn't be reality, either.

I pushed myself up to my hands and knees. A breeze caught my hair as I blinked hard against the fine spray of sand. But gods, the scent—salt and lilies and damp soil. *Home.*

I lifted my head and froze.

Home. Yes, it was home. The white beach gave way to the forest line I knew so well that even now, decades later, I could have drawn the exact shape of it. The greenery was so unbelievably lush, framing the distant shape of the Citadel rising into the sky.

And there, standing at the brick pathway that led into the forest, was Eomin.

He looked exactly as I remembered him from those days. He wore the loose white pants from his Dawndrinker garb and no shirt, fair hair still plastered to his neck, like he'd just gotten out of the sea.

He waved at me and grinned.

I waved back, confused.

Was this Eomin's spirit? The one Asar had set free? He wasn't a wraith—he had no wounds, and he definitely didn't have the particular air of mournful discontent that the wraiths did. He also was solid, with no transparent shimmer.

He waved at me again, this time more frantically. He pointed out to the Citadel, then to the sun, then beckoned to me. I wasn't sure why he wasn't just calling to me—he was far away, but not too far to shout. Still, the message was clear: *Hurry up, Mische, we're going to be late.*

Late for what?

The answer dawned on me, blatantly obvious. Evening prayers. Of course. I wasn't supposed to be out here this time of afternoon. If we didn't make it back in time, my absence would definitely be noticed. I scampered to my feet, then frowned down at my dirty gold nightgown.

What was this? Why was I wearing this?

I blinked, and the silk slip shifted to the familiar drape of my Dawndrinker robes.

At the edge of the forest, Eomin waved at me again hurriedly—as if to say, *we are really, really, really going to be late.*

But I didn't move. Just kept staring down at myself. I touched my robes. I'd tied them up so the bottom wouldn't get wet, but they were slightly damp anyway.

No . . . I'd been wearing something else.

The gold slip.

The—

My head hurt.

I needed to look for someone. Who?

Saescha? Saescha was probably at the Citadel, ready to scold me for sneaking off. Or was she? Wasn't she somewhere else? I needed to find—

No, not Saescha.

Raihn? The name skewered my head, the pain unbearable. No. No, there was no one named Raihn with the Dawndrinkers. A brief memory of a rugged grin and a hug that felt like home flashed through my mind, then withered.

No, someone else. Someone important.

I touched my bare arms. I ran my fingers over unmarred skin.

I closed my eyes.

And just for a second, I thought I felt something else on my arms.

I felt warm breath, and soft lips. A voice whispering, *It should feel like this.*

And someone who had looked at me like I was the sun.

My eyes snapped open. Asar.

With a stab of pain, the memories burst through the fog.

Ahead, Eomin started toward me, face drawn into annoyance. I hesitated as he approached—was he real? Had I died? Was this my chosen afterlife?

I blinked, and suddenly Eomin was closer than it seemed like he should be in so little time. Up close, something just seemed *wrong* about his face. It was a little blurry, like his features were shifting between countless, minuscule variations.

No, this wasn't right.

I turned to the shore, looking for Asar—

Eomin grabbed me.

I screamed. I looked down at myself to see the warring realities clashing—scars and wounds flickering. Eomin's fingers dug into an open gash.

I tore myself away from him and ran down the beach. Now that the dream—was this a dream, or a hallucination?—had shattered, the pain of my broken body was unbearable. I could feel bones grinding, muscles straining, wounds tearing with every footfall. My gaze found a lump of black down the beach, lying motionless as the water washed over it.

Asar.

I had no weapon. The thought of calling my magic, either of light or shadow, seemed impossible. I was too weak. All I could do was run. Eomin followed, matching my steps. My breath came in choked gasps, but Eomin—no, he was not Eomin—was silent. I could feel him nipping at my heels, the scrape of his fingernails against my back.

I drew closer to Asar. He was face down. The lap of the ocean pulled his wet clothes against him. His fingers loosely wrapped around the hilt of his sword, which seemed to vibrate against the cream of the sand, as if the two realities refused to mesh.

I skidded to the ground and grabbed the hilt.

The swell of power that came with it disarmed me. Gods, was this how Asar felt every time he touched this thing? A sudden burst of energy coursed through me as I threw myself to the sand, practically tripping over Asar's unconscious body, and whirled around in a clumsy roll.

The thing that was not Eomin loomed over me, his mouth open a little too wide, his eyes slightly too far apart, nostrils flaring, teeth sharpening. He reached for me—

And with an animalistic cry, I swung Asar's sword straight through his face.

The creature drew back with an inhuman jolt and a high-pitched squeal.

I went in for another strike.

And this time, he simply collapsed around the blade. His body burst into countless formless shreds. The scent of ash filled my nostrils.

I was on my knees in the sand, blade still raised, panting.

Out of the corner of my eye, I saw Asar pushing himself up with a curse.

He lifted his head, then stilled. He didn't move for a long moment.

I collapsed back onto the beach.

Everything hurt. Badly. Very badly.

Asar ripped his stare away from the horizon with what seemed like great struggle. There was something odd about his gaze—glassed over. He seemed startled to see me.

He didn't speak.

"Thank the gods I found you." I rolled over and dragged myself closer, looking him up and down. "Are you alright?"

He blinked hard and shook his head. "I'm—yes."

"Are you hurt?"

We both looked like shit, and it was hard to tell what was aesthetic and what was structural.

"I'm f—" His eyes fell to my body. The glazed-over look vanished in an instant.

"What happened to you?"

I looked down at myself. Gods, there was more blood than I remembered.

"There was—" I actually didn't know how to describe what not-Eomin was. "I saw Eomin, but it definitely wasn't Eomin."

"It hurt you?"

"I'm *great*," I said cheerfully, even though I did not feel great.

Asar looked like he was struggling to focus. He rubbed his eyes.

"Careful with the sand," I said.

He gave me an odd look. "What?"

I grabbed a handful of sand and let it fall through my fingers. "Sand. Don't rub it in your eyes."

He blinked at me. Then looked around. Realization fell over his face.

"What do you see?" he asked.

"What do I—?"

"Where are we right now?"

"This is Vostis. Which, by the way, why are we in Vostis?"

"So this is a beach for you?"

It took me a moment to realize what he was asking.

"Are you telling me," I said, "that you don't see a beach right now?"

"No. I do not see a beach right now."

"What *do* you see?"

I wasn't sure why I expected a straightforward answer from Asar. He ignored me and stood, brushing himself off. He swayed halfway through the movement and frowned down at his wounds like they were a frustrating inconvenience.

The breeze blew, and I got a lungful of his scent, which made me dizzy. My gaze snapped to the patch of bare, bloody skin revealed between the hem of his shirt and the waistband of his trousers, and I had to suppress the overwhelming urge to lick it.

My stomach hurt. My *veins* hurt.

With great effort, I dragged my gaze back to the Citadel in the distance.

"So this is all . . . not real?" I asked.

"It's real. In a sense. I think the terrain is all the same, but the skin it wears is different." Despite his obvious weakness, Asar still seemed intrigued. "The Sanctum of Secrets is all about desire. Shame. The things mortals hide from themselves."

Great.

"Didn't we just do that?" I asked.

"Psyche primarily holds memories. Secrets holds emotions."

"There were plenty of emotions in Psyche, too."

Asar shot me an exasperated look. "Once we resurrect Alarus, you can let him know your critiques of his design of the Descent."

I wasn't sure why Asar's casual use of *we* hit me in a strange place.

"Sorry," I muttered.

"What you see here might change as we go deeper into the Sanctum. The souleaters get more intelligent the scarcer their prey becomes. They'll wear faces they pluck from your mind. It sounds like you witnessed that firsthand."

Eomin. Not a wraith. Just a souleater, luring in prey with kind bait.

Every time I closed my eyes, I saw Esme's house burning. And that silhouette emerging from the flames.

I'd recognize her anywhere.

"So what we saw at Esme's . . . those were just souleaters?"

I sounded hopeful, despite myself. But Asar shook his head.

"No. Those were wraiths. Souleaters can do mimicry, but not good ones."

Gods, I felt sick.

"So we might see them again?"

Asar misread my concern. "Malach? Likely. Esme could hold him off, but I doubt she'd be able to finish him. I never saw him in the chambers. I'd hoped it meant he just passed through. Or maybe I hoped a souleater got him." His face hardened. He touched my shoulder. "But he will not hurt you, Mische. I swear that."

My chest ached at the sincerity in those words. I couldn't bring myself to look at him. I knew he'd see the truth in my face.

Yes, I was terrified of Malach. He was the monster that haunted my nightmares. But he wasn't the regret that haunted my waking hours. That put my fear to shame.

"Right," I mumbled. I rubbed my temple. "So what now? We walk? Find the—the Secrets relic and be on our—"

I stood up and promptly tipped over. Asar caught my arm just in time. Luce jumped up and looped around my legs, as if to help support me.

I gave her a weak smile and a pat on the head. Good girl. The best girl.

I could feel Asar's eyes running over my body, taking inventory of my injuries. He was still touching my arm, and I didn't like it because it meant he was very close to me. The smell of his blood was intoxicatingly distracting.

I pulled away and managed to stand on my own. I was still holding his sword, which I offered back to him. He shook his head. "You keep it."

"I don't want it. It's yours."

"You need it more than me right now."

I wasn't sure that was true. I didn't like holding it. I felt like it was whispering to me in my mind, a caress against all the parts of myself that connected me to it—vampire, Shadowborn, Turned of the bloodline that had forged it. It felt too right, and I disliked that.

But I wanted to start walking before I keeled over again. The sooner we started moving, the sooner we could make it out of this chamber. Maybe if we moved fast enough, I wouldn't have to see Saescha's wraith at all.

"Fine," I sighed. "Let's just walk."

WE FOLLOWED THE brick path into the forest. It was incredible how realistic this hallucination was for something that was apparently not real. The plants were the same, the rough feeling of the bricks under my bare feet, the grit of the sand. The smell really got me—it brought me right back to my childhood, that perfect mix of the ocean and damp earth and the fresh flowers, even mixed with just a hint of the ceremonial smoke from the Citadel when the breeze blew the right way. It was everything that I thought of when I remembered Vostis. And yet, now that I knew it wasn't real, the glaring inaccuracies also jumped out at me. Asar was right—it was a skin, not even an actual memory. The path didn't go in the right direction, and the placement of the monastery above wasn't quite right. The terrain was different. All of this somehow seemed inconsequential, easy to dismiss, when held against that alluring familiarity that coated my thoughts in the saccharine comforts of an old home. But when I was looking for it, it seemed so obvious I couldn't believe I didn't spot it right away.

We were following the terrain of the chamber. "You see a big building up there?" Asar had said, pointing.

"The Citadel," I'd said.

He blinked, hesitating before nodding. I again had to wonder what he saw—was it something that he yearned for as much as I yearned for the monastery?

"I think we have to make it up there," he said. "It feels like the epicenter of this Sanctum."

So we started walking. Luce remained close to me, watching carefully. Nausea churned in my stomach. My headache was becoming unbearable. Sweat beaded on my skin.

I noticed Asar looking back at me more and more often. Eventually, he slowed so that he wasn't leading me, just walking alongside me at my clumsy, stumbling pace.

"We need to stop," he said.

Luce made a snort of agreement, as if to say, *Obviously.*

"I'm fine," I said.

I didn't want to look at him and see him notice the lie on my face. Every shred of my energy was going toward keeping my stitches together, putting one foot in front of the other. I couldn't sacrifice any to distraction.

"You—"

"Let's just get through this," I snapped, harsher than I meant to.

But what felt like an agonizing eternity later, when I tripped over a root because I was barely managing to drag my feet along, Asar's patience ran out. He spun around so abruptly that I nearly collided with him.

"This is ridiculous. We can't continue like this."

He was swaying, too. His blood had been leaving a trail on the bricks as we walked, despite his attempts to stop the bleeding. I knew because I paid terrible, involuntary attention to every single drop.

Asar reached for me, and I jerked away.

"I'm fine," I said, forcing a smile, which seemed to enrage him.

"You aren't helping anyone by doing this, Iliae," he snapped. "Enough with the self-sacrificing missionary role. It gets tiresome. Let me help you."

The self-sacrificing missionary role.

Here, in this place that smelled so much like the home I'd ruined myself for, with the image of my sister still burning in my eyes every time I blinked, that categorization stung like the barb of a whip.

My jaw snapped down so tight it trembled. My brain was so fuzzy I couldn't think of an appropriately venomous comeback—though, even in the best of times, that had never been my forte. Instead, I yanked my arm away from him with as much force as I could muster.

"You want to get through this," I said. "So do—"

And I promptly fell backward into the trees.

My vision sputtered in and out. Everything was blurry. For a moment I thought I saw a gray, lightning-dotted sky and bloody mist, before I blinked and was back in the forest, Asar leaning over me.

He no longer looked annoyed.

He looks beautiful, actually. This thought was the only one that emerged through a sea of gummy sludge.

"Get up, Mische," he murmured. "Come on."

Dimly, I noticed Luce dart off into the trees.

I gave Asar a weak smile. "You only say my name when you're worried about me," I tried to say. "It's sweet."

But the darkness took me before I could get the words out.

CHAPTER THIRTY-TWO

The next moments—*minutes? hours? days?*—ran together like the beach sands through my fingers. Asar helping me walk, even though soon he, too, struggled to put a foot in front of the other. Luce barking at us, running through the lush greenery of the jungle. She looked like a deer, or a forest spirit, as she dove through the leaves—*good girl.* Asar letting out a hiss of pain as he tore one of his wounds open on a branch, the ensuing burst of blood so agonizingly potent that my fangs bit into my lip. I remembered, too, the way he stared at my mouth—the blood trickling down my chin.

"Quickly, Luce," I heard him say. "Quickly."

The next time I forced my eyes open, I was lying on the ground. I stared up at a ceiling of broken stone, the blue peeking through like a beak through an eggshell. Vines covered the rafters, and moss blanketed the floor—part tile, part stone—beneath my body. Despite the broken roof, it was oddly dark in here, as if the light from the hallucination of Vostis's sun-drenched sky couldn't pass into this room. When I lifted my head, I immediately recognized Morthryn; it had the same bronze, rib-like rafters, the same ancient stained glass windows, the frozen ivy winding up its walls. But it was a shell of the version I'd spent the last months in, the ceiling shattered, one wall partially collapsed. The furniture in here—a single couch, a broken coffee table—was rotted, sinking into the ground, as if the Descent was reclaiming it by force. I was lying on a rug that was now half-consumed by a bed of fluffy greenery.

I tried to push myself up and mostly failed.

Asar was saying something, but it took a moment for my mind to decipher his words.

"—safe here for now," he said. "Luce is guarding us. But I don't think souleaters would come in here."

I wasn't sure if my mind was slurring his words, or if he was having a hard time speaking, too.

"Where are we?" I forced out. I managed to push myself up just enough to rest my back against the ivy-covered wall. My head protested being upright, but I preferred to see.

Asar was doing something at the doorway, which was little more than a crooked board of rotting wood over a broken stone arch. My skin reacted to his magic, which sparked darkness at the frame. Protection spells.

When he looked over his shoulder, he seemed surprised to see me upright. And I noticed how he carefully avoided my gaze as he dragged himself back to me, practically collapsing at my side.

Drip, drip, drip, taunted his blood.

Pop, as my fang reopened the cut in my lower lip.

Asar's gaze, heavy lidded, lingered on it. "You need to drink."

"I'm—"

"You're not fine."

He pulled up his sleeve, revealing a slice across the open eye of his Heir Mark, and my entire body had such an intense reaction to it that I nearly bashed the back of my head against the wall in my frantic attempt to look away.

Gods, *why* did he smell like that? No vampire should smell like that.

"An animal," I forced out. "I'll get an animal."

"There are no animals here."

My lashes fluttered. *That's not true,* I wanted to say. *I saw a bird. A firefinch.* But I couldn't make my mouth work.

"None of that is real," he said. "Nothing down here is alive but us. You need blood. I'm the only one here who has it."

I wasn't sure if the twist in my stomach was hunger or revulsion.

"I don't do that."

I'd never drunk from live prey. Certainly not human or vampire prey. I'd managed that even when it was hard—even when it felt impossible. Clung to it. That one shred of humanity.

"You are a vampire," Asar said, annoyed. "Next you'll tell me you don't breathe."

He threw that statement at me so casually. And why shouldn't he? It was simple fact. Still, I so rarely thought of myself that way.

Everything hurt. My eyes stung.

"I can't."

"You will die if you don't do this."

I'd already survived so many would-be deaths. I should have died a child of starvation or illness, like countless other children just like me. I should have died when I came to Obitraes's shores, shredded by the teeth of vampires or beasts, like Saescha and Eomin were. I should have died in the Kejari, when my god damned me.

Maybe I was already on borrowed time.

I looked up at the sky through the cracks of the ceiling. The blue sky, drenched in the perfect warm sun of my memories, that I would never feel again.

"Iliae." Asar sounded furious. "Look at me."

I shouldn't, I told myself.

But I did anyway.

He didn't look angry. He looked terrified.

I touched my scars.

"He'll hate me," I whispered.

I was a bride of the sun. I knew that Atroxus would smell that corruption on my soul. Not the blood—I could justify that, if I had to. But just how much I'd wanted it.

Already, my loyalty was a dirty, cracked thing, barely worth keeping.

Could I still call myself loyal, if I put my lips to Asar's throat?

Understanding fell over Asar's face. Not pity, but sympathy. When he looked at me that way, it made me feel like I was letting him see too much.

"I won't let you die here because you're too ashamed to live, Mische," he said. "You are so much more than this. And it would be a waste to throw all that magnificence away—for what? Because the sun told you to hate yourself? No. I won't allow that."

I won't allow that. So simple.

I appreciated that about Asar. He liked to set wrong things right.

Before I could answer him, I felt the world tilt. My head lolled. Asar cursed, and then he was pulling me onto his lap. He held my head against his shoulder so that my face was against his throat—the right side, unscarred. The scent of his blood beckoned my consciousness back to me.

"It's all right," he whispered. One hand stroked the back of my head. The other settled between my shoulder blades, holding me to him, chest to chest.

It felt right. Smelled right. I was so tired. I wanted so much. I swallowed. My lips brushed the tender skin of his throat, and I felt his muscles flex against the touch.

Still, I clung to the edge of that cliff.

"Five," I whispered.

"Hm?"

"Five drinks."

Just five. I could handle that.

It took him a moment to understand what I meant.

"Ten," he countered. Then, before I could argue, "Don't even say it, Iliae. You need strength. The sin only starts at eleven. I promise."

My laugh was a pitiful, pathetic sound. I couldn't argue with him, especially not when I inhaled and the scent of him filled my lungs like smoke.

He guided my head closer, and that nudge was all I needed. I bit down hard.

His blood, thick and sweet, flowed over my tongue.

Oh, gods.

Gods, gods, gods.

A lifetime wielding the magic of the sun, and yet, I had never felt so aflame as I did in this moment. Goosebumps broke over my flesh at the first taste of him, rich and dark. The moan dragged out of me without my permission. I felt his heartbeat quicken the flow of his blood, like he wanted to offer me more in response to my pleasure.

Instantly, strength flowed through me.

No, I thought. *It isn't supposed to be like this.* A vampire shouldn't taste this good. Feel this good.

But all logical thought and protest drowned in the next taste, the next breath, the next beat of his heart. My fingers clutched fistfuls of his shirt, even though I wanted skin.

"Good girl," Asar whispered. The words vibrated against my lips, serrated with a hunger sharp as mine.

In my blind want, I barely remembered to count each swallow. His blood dribbled down my chin and I would have stopped to lick it off, rescue every magnificent drop, except that I couldn't tear myself away. The flimsy nightgown had been made flimsier by the journey, and my skin was hot and sensitive. Asar's hold had gotten firmer, pulling me tight against him, his fingers tangled in my hair.

After five gulps, I forced myself to slow.

"Take what you need," he said, misreading my hesitation.

It was an offer, but it was also a command. The dark edge to his voice sent a shiver over my tongue, up my spine, between my thighs.

I slowed myself, my next drink long and deep.

He let out a low groan.

His pants, still the light clothing from Esme's, did nothing to disguise the rigid length of his erection beneath me. It jumped against me, rubbing against my hip. It wasn't where I wanted to feel it.

Venom, I told myself. It subdued vampire prey. Often, that could manifest as sexual desire.

But did venom have such a strong effect on other vampires? And why was I feeling it so intensely, even though I was the one feeding? I was drunk with it, logic drowning under mindless desire. My hands clutched blindly at him. Somewhere between my sixth and seventh gulps, one of my hands decided that his shirt wasn't enough, reaching beneath it to the bare flesh of his shoulder. And gods, I loved the sound he made at that.

"Dangerous, Iliae," he murmured.

Yes. All of this was so, so dangerous.

Dangerous like the way he'd kissed my scars in Esme's living room.

Dangerous like the way his hand had slid up my skirt in Psyche.

Dangerous from that very first night, when I saw him with his wet shirt clinging to him and couldn't get the image out of my mind.

Eight.

My bare skin was covered in goosebumps, desperate to be touched. His hand traveled down to my bare thigh. One fingertip traced the crease of my backside, and I let out a sigh against him that made his fingernails dig into my flesh.

What are you doing, Mische?

Nine.

My fingers slid down, relishing the topography of his body, until I felt his length—hard and straining, a bead of moisture soaking through the painfully thin fabric separating us.

His muscles strained, trembled. Like it was taking that much effort to keep himself from pulling me on top of him.

Ten.

I swallowed. I breathed heavily against him, my teeth still buried in his throat, my fingers still lightly, so lightly, touching his tip.

Still hungry.

Ten. You said ten.

I forced myself to open my mouth, teeth sliding from his vein.

Our breath mingled between us in rough pants. His left eye was darker than I'd ever seen it, the clouds roiling within. I felt that way, too. Like a storm was raging inside me, ready to rip down the walls that contained it. It felt intrinsic, natural, and that terrified me.

"I like how your pleasure looks." His thumb traced circles against my thigh. I wanted to open it, let him inside. Let us find out what real pleasure was.

Instead, I did something else nearly as risky.

I lifted my chin. "Your turn."

I felt—actually *felt*—his all-consuming desire then. Perhaps our magic, linked as it was, had left ourselves raw to each other. Perhaps I could just sense it in the way his fingernails dug into my thigh, or the way his cock strained against my hip, or the ragged groan that shuddered, barely audible, from the back of his throat.

"May not be a good idea." It sounded as if it took all his effort to get out those six words.

No, it was not a good idea.

I had not let anyone drink from me since Malach. It shocked me just how much I wanted it now. My vows to Atroxus held on by a single thread, and my body was begging me to sever it. Once Asar's mouth was on my throat, his venom in my veins—

Allowing that was more dangerous than any trial in the Kejari. Than any Sanctum of the Descent. A beautiful blade hanging right over the throat of my eternal soul.

But Asar had been starving for as long as I was. He needed the strength, too, and he would just continue to weaken if he kept on going without blood. We wouldn't make it through whatever was ahead without him at his best.

All rational reasons. All true.

But they were not the things I was thinking about.

"You need it," I whispered.

"I'll be fine."

"We don't have to lie to each other right now."

I held his stare as I slowly slid off his lap and lay back against the dilapidated remains of the couch. His blood cooled on my chin, mixing with mine from the wounds my fangs had left on my lower lip. Some of it had dripped down onto my chest, beads rolling down to my breast.

Asar watched me, eyes sharp. This, I thought, was what he must have looked like at the height of his power—every predator's instinct pressed right up against the surface.

He lowered his body over mine. One hand cupped my face. The other fell to my hip.

But he paused a few inches away from me. And that touch was still so gentle, so tentative, despite what I knew was overwhelming desire.

"I will be fine," he said again.

He meant, *Are you sure?*

But I had already decided. I turned my head slightly, offering my neck. My chest rose and fell a little too quickly, nipples beaded against silk.

Dangerous, I warned myself.

"Do it," I said.

He let out a breath, and he lowered himself over me like a beast untethered. I braced for him, ready for his teeth in my throat.

Instead, I felt a soft, wet touch on my breast.

I drew in a sharp inhale. Asar's tongue licked our mingling blood up, to my collarbone, then my chin. He paused there, breath shaking. I carefully did not move my head; if I did, I would be kissing him. And gods, I wanted to. I wanted to taste our blood together.

"Just five," he whispered. "Don't argue. You're too weak for more."

I didn't. He was right that I was weak. But the shameful truth was that my vows, I knew, could not handle ten. So I just nodded.

He brought his lips to my throat and bit.

The pain was exquisite. The rush was instantaneous. The weight, the warmth, of Asar's body over mine became all-consuming. His hand tangled in my hair, cupping my face, thumb at the corner of my open mouth.

Like mine, his first few gulps were frantic. He groaned a wordless curse, the vibration running down my body and settling between my legs. My back arched, though he held himself up over me. Probably good. If he lowered himself, I would have wound around him like ivy, pressing all my aching wants to his.

But gods—gods, those aching wants *ached*. It was painful, to feel so good, to want so much.

I whispered, "Slow."

He stopped immediately. He started to pull away, but I put my hand at the back of his head.

I understood his question: *Am I hurting you?*

And I was glad he didn't speak it aloud because I would be too ashamed to say the truth: *No. Make it last. Let me live in this pleasure a little longer.*

As the understanding fell over him, he let out another long, shaky breath. "Mische," he growled against my skin. He licked my throat, slow and languid, before drinking again.

I squirmed against him. My nightgown bunched up around my hips, his palm now flat against bare flesh. My legs opened in an attempt to feel his length where I wanted it most.

Four.

The sensations surrounded me. He still held himself above me, but somehow, I felt his touch everywhere, sliding up the inside of my thighs, swirling around the sensitive peaks of my breasts. I opened my eyes to see clusters of smoke surrounding us. Magic. Whose? Mine? His? Both, whipped into a frenzy together? I didn't care. I just wanted more, harder, firm sensation.

I wanted release.

Your vows, a voice—Saescha's voice—in the back of my head reminded me. *You are a bride of the sun. You must not betray him.*

But gods, I wanted more. I needed more.

"Asar," I choked out. I wasn't sure what I was trying to tell him—that it was too much or not enough.

I could feel how much he wanted me. How much he wanted to push up my slip and sink between my legs. How much he wanted to taste my lust with his mouth or strum it free with his fingers. All lines I desperately wanted to cross. All lines that led to damnation.

But instead, he pulled my arm from his shoulder and guided my hand down—guided it between my thighs, leaving it to me to close the distance.

Five.

And I did, sliding my fingers inside myself as his teeth speared me deep, as his tongue coaxed forth that last devastating drink from my veins, as my maddening desire reached an impossible apex.

I cried out, back arching, as my orgasm consumed me. His self-control collapsed. He pressed himself against me at last, cock grinding against me through our clothes. He drank my pleasure as if it were wine.

When the final aftershocks of my climax faded, he pulled away, leaving my throat cold with the ghost of his lips. He sat back on his heels as I panted, exhausted, my torn dress hiked around my waist, blood trickling into my cleavage.

I had done the impossible.

He had unraveled.

His hair was messy where my hands had run through it. His mouth was smeared with my blood, which he wiped with a thumb at the corner of his lips. His shoulders rose and fell heavily. I knew that he was imagining what it would be like to tear this scrap of fabric off me and sink into me. I knew it because I was imagining it, too.

To be a vampire was to be only a few steps away from an animal, driven by carnal hungers. I'd let mine out of the cage tonight.

I should be ashamed. But maybe his venom still held me, because instead, I just felt a giddy delight in the way he looked at me. Like witnessing my pleasure had driven him to the brink of his sanity.

"That's enough," he said quietly, as if to himself.

It didn't feel like enough. Not even close.

I liked seeing Asar disheveled. I wanted to see how much it would take to see him obliterated.

But my eyelids were sagging. The blood I had taken and the blood I had given both weighed heavily on my body. I tried to sit up, but Asar's lust fell away, leaving behind concern.

"You have to heal. Rest."

"Luce—"

"Luce is fine."

"We need to walk."

"Not yet."

Asar settled beside me. He looked exhausted, too—the circles dark beneath his eyes, the storm in his left one calm.

I frowned. "I took too much."

"You didn't take enough." He pushed a stray curl out of my face. "You're beautiful when you take, Mische."

He was wrong. I was a giver, not a taker. But I didn't have the energy to argue with him.

He started to sit up, but I pulled him back.

"Stay," I murmured.

He hesitated.

"Do you want me to?"

It was strange that we were both thinking the same thing. I'd drunk his blood and he'd drunk mine. He had held me as I came. And yet, it was offering him a place to rest beside me that felt like the great temptation, the closest I'd ventured to breaking my vows.

My stomach was full, but I still felt so hungry. So sinfully selfish.

"Yes," I whispered. "Stay with me."

Once he decides he cares about you, Esme had said, *he will never stop.*

He settled beside me. "As you wish, Dawndrinker." His eyes were already closing. As we both faded away, the words echoed like a vow.

CHAPTER THIRTY-THREE

Warmth surrounded me. I was curled up, my head tucked against Asar's chest, which rose and fell in peaceful breaths. Another body was pressed against my back— Luce? I was still half-asleep, too far away from coherent thought to make sense of the logistics and too happy to question it. I'd always been a touchy person, thriving on those brushes of affection. It wasn't sexual or romantic. Sometimes, you just need a hug. Vampires, unfortunately, were not a very huggy bunch.

Asar's arms wrapped around me, the two of us intertwined like the light and shadow of the moon. Luce must have come in once she was confident there were no threats to us, and she curled around my back, completing the circle.

I didn't want to move, lest I disturb this perfect equilibrium.

I opened my eyes. Asar was still fast asleep. I didn't fully realize until this moment just how well I had memorized his face over these last few months. I knew the arrangement of his scars, all the hidden meanings of all the minuscule twitches of muscle he didn't know he made, the full delightful array of his expressions. Yet, this one—utter peace—struck me because I had never seen it before. His brow was smooth, his mouth full and relaxed. He looked so young, like the little boy I had seen in his memories.

How long had it been since Asar had truly been at peace?

He was always handsome—I'd given up on denying to myself that

I thought so. But now, watching him, a bittersweet longing tightened in my heart.

In another life, I might have liked to see this tranquility across this perfect face every night.

In another life.

I touched his cheek before I could stop myself, fingers tracing the harsh lines over soft angles.

And gods, I wanted.

His eyes fluttered open. The right one was an endless sea of deep brown darkness. The left was calm, the abyss within gently pulsing like clouds in a summer sky.

His smile bloomed easily over his face, as if seeing me was a delightful surprise.

"Hello, Warden," I whispered.

"Hello, Dawndrinker."

That term pierced the haze of my comfort, letting the uncomfortable reality flood back in.

The memory of Asar's blood on my tongue, his mouth on my neck—gods, my hand between my legs—came back to me with a rising tide of shame.

I'd drunk blood. I'd given blood. I'd let Asar hold me as I indulged in the pleasure of it. All while bound to a god giving me a chance I didn't deserve.

But the real sin of it all was that I'd wanted it. I'd wanted more.

Even now, I wanted more.

That was what we had always been warned of, back in the Order. Desire begot desire. Sin begot sin. Selfishness begot selfishness.

I sat up, suddenly nauseous. The movement was too abrupt and startled Luce, who didn't seem to appreciate the rude awakening.

"Sorry," I muttered, scratching the top of her head in an offering of penance, which she reluctantly accepted.

I could feel Asar's stare as he sat up, too. It swept over my injuries one by one. I had no doubt that he was comparing them against a meticulous inventory, making sure that I was healing to his satisfaction.

Again, that pang in my heart.

"I take it you're feeling better?" he said.

I nodded. I felt a lot better, actually. The wounds on my abdomen had even closed while we rested, my vampire healing restored.

"What about you?" I asked. He looked much better, too. He actually didn't look tired for maybe the first time since I'd met him. Though that typical weariness of his now seeped back in, like he was remembering all the reasons he had to be irritated with the state of the world.

"Better," he conceded.

"Good. That's good."

It was good. At least it reinforced my mental narrative that there were only logical, practical reasons for why I had offered him my blood.

Logical. Practical. Completely in service to the mission given to us by our gods.

Asar frowned. "Are you all right?"

I smiled brightly. "Yes. I am wonderful."

His frown deepened.

Luce looked between us, as if sensing the tension, and let out a low yip.

"She's right," I said. "We should be going, shouldn't we? Before a bunch of angry wraiths find this place?"

I stood up, and a rush of cool air had me conscious all over again of exactly how undressed I was. I crossed my arms over my chest, avoiding Asar's gaze.

"Clothes first. Then we go."

I WAS REALLY, really grateful that I wouldn't have to go conquer the Sanctum of Secrets while practically naked. I'd grown surprisingly affectionate toward Morthryn these last few months—more affectionate than I ever thought I'd be toward a magical death prison— but when we went through the few remaining functional drawers and happened to find a shirt and trousers that, miraculously, fit me, I actually hugged the doorframe.

"Thank you, Morthryn. Thank you, thank you, thank you."

"It was probably a coincidence," Asar said, amused.

A coincidence? What were the chances? "I choose to believe it's a gift." I patted the cracked wall. "And I think Morthryn should be thanked for her efforts."

"Her?"

"Morthryn has feminine energy."

Luce barked in agreement, and Asar, wisely, didn't argue.

Now, we ventured back out into the forest—forest for me, at least. Asar was presumably seeing something else entirely, a fact that I was reminded of when he stepped out and blinked in surprise, like he was startled by it all over again. I knew the feeling. Our little ruin of Morthryn was removed from the illusions of the Sanctum, so the moment we stepped from its door, the sheer presence of Vostis overwhelmed me all over again—the scent, the sun, the steamy heat. It brought me straight back to my past.

The sensation clashed violently with the still-fresh memories of what had happened the night before. I found myself touching my neck. Asar's bite had healed immediately, but I could still feel it. I suspected I always would.

A knot pulled tighter and tighter in my stomach.

Outside, I squinted up at the Citadel looming over us. Odd—at a casual glance, everything inside me recognized it as the Citadel. But when I forced myself to stare at it carefully, I realized that so much about it was different from my old home—spires misplaced, the layout wrong, its shape in the skyline off. Asar was right—what I saw was just an illusion draped over the terrain of the circle, like a skeleton skinned with the flesh of my past.

"The relic must be somewhere in that castle," Asar said. "It's too central. Fortified. He must have kept it in there."

Castle. I gave Asar a sidelong glance as he stared up at the Citadel. What did he see, I wondered?

"The Shadowborn castle?" I guessed.

Was that where he was right now? In the capital of the House of Shadow, about to enter the castle that, if we survived this, would become his when we returned?

He blinked, momentarily confused. "Oh. The—yes. The Shadow-born castle."

For someone so committed to being mysterious, he was such a horrific liar. But I still had a hard time wrangling the emotions that bubbled up in me when I looked at Asar for too long, so I decided to let it lie.

We'd come a good ways from the beach the night before, but we still had a long walk up to the Citadel. Despite the conflict that roiled in my gut when I thought about Asar's blood on my tongue, I wouldn't have been able to make the journey without it. We tramped up the winding brick path through the forest. The scent of it was so overpowering that it started to give me a headache, the flowering musk sticky-sweet. Patches of sun filtered through the leaves, painting bright gold on the deep ashy brown of Asar's hair and the rich hue of his skin. It seemed to pass right through Luce's shadowy body entirely. When we reached a clearing in the trees, I paused and tilted my face up. I stared at the sky, blue and clear as a firefinch egg, then closed my eyes.

"What are you doing?" Asar asked from ahead.

I breathed in. Breathed out.

In Vostis, the sun had felt like home. I could close my eyes and slide into it, let it roll over my skin like honey.

But right now, there was no warmth, no embrace. Just a false imitation of the real thing. Convincing, but falling short in all the ways that mattered.

It shouldn't have been a disappointment.

"Nothing," I murmured, and turned away.

CHAPTER THIRTY-FOUR

You're terribly quiet, Iliae." Asar spoke only as we ventured closer to the entrance of the Citadel. "I don't think I've ever heard you go this long without talking. No mundane observations? No pestering about my second cousin's favorite pet or some equally mind-numbing question?"

He had been glancing back at me every few minutes the entire journey, and every time, the wrinkle between his brows etched deeper. He was concerned about me, and he was doing a bad job of pretending he wasn't.

The thought hit me with a shockingly powerful pang of affection.

I gave him a cheerful smile, summoned only to the surface of my skin. "I thought you'd enjoy the break."

His brow furrowed again. I looked away before I spent too much time tracing the angle of it.

"I don't," he said.

I stuffed my hands into my pockets and kept walking.

"Eva," Asar said, a few steps later. "She was a parrot."

"Hm?"

"My second cousin's favorite pet."

"Oh." I let out a weak, very fake-sounding laugh. Asar stopped so abruptly that I almost walked into him. He turned on his heel, jaw set, left eye pulsing silver.

"Is this because of last night?" he said.

"Is what because of last night?"

"I'm not good at dancing around things." He sounded a little help-less beneath his frustration, and again, I felt a pang of hurt on his behalf.

He'd been kinder to me than I deserved. And it wasn't his fault that this place dug its fingers into all my freshest wounds. Most of all, the ones that he'd left on my throat, the ones that had felt so good it burned.

I tried harder for the next smile. Tried to make myself believe it, too. "I'm just a little tired."

Asar didn't look like he believed me. Even Luce eyed me suspi-ciously, tail thumping against the dirt. But my gaze fell behind him, to a glint of gold through the trees, and my eyes widened.

He followed my stare. The three of us pushed through the last thicket of vegetation. The soil and brick beneath my feet gave way to smooth, polished marble.

I let out a shaky breath.

The entrance of the Citadel of the Destined Dawn looked exactly as it had in decades of memories. Gleaming white stairs led to a set of golden double doors, brilliant beneath the unforgiving sun. Grand columns framed the entryway, each bearing a sculpture of another of Atroxus's symbols—the wings of a phoenix, the disk of the rising sun, torch bearing the flame that never died. Above the entryway was the marble visage of Atroxus himself. He stood with arms open in invitation over the doorframe, long hair falling over his shoulders and crown polished upon his serious brow.

Those white stone eyes felt like they were staring directly at me.

The resemblance was stronger than I remembered, too—the first time I met Atroxus, when I was only eight, I'd been struck by how little he looked like the statue I knew so well. He'd seemed amused when I told him so, too young to know any better.

"Am I such a disappointment?" he had said, and I had shaken my head.

"No," I'd answered. "You are the most beautiful thing I have ever seen, my light."

I had meant it then. I was, after all, in the presence of a being that rearranged the fabric of the world simply by existing. He was divine perfection, and he had smiled at me—*me*, Mische, little beggar girl with dirty feet and freckles—like I brought him genuine joy.

But I was just an innocent child then. Nothing but potential.

How did you manage to get so dirty? a jeering voice whispered in the back of my mind.

Asar was staring at the entrance, too, jaw set. His expression was a mask, but I could sense a fear that felt just like mine.

I touched his arm.

"Just a memory," I said softly.

His mouth twisted into a wry smile—like he appreciated the attempt at consolation but didn't quite find it comforting. I understood that. Memories were still dangerous. Especially here, where they blurred into reality.

This was the Sanctum of Secrets. Shame and desire. With the ghost of Asar's lips still on my throat, a powerful fear lurched in my stomach at the thought of what could be waiting for us beyond these doors.

I drew in a deep breath and stepped forward first. The doors opened before I even touched them, the grand atrium spilling out before me. A mosaic of the sun sprawled over the floor in thousands—tens of thousands—of brilliant ceramic pieces, gleaming beneath flecks of light from the glass ceiling. Tapestries covered the walls, depicting Atroxus's greatest feats—his conquering of the land of the gods, his coronation as king, and the largest, a grand tableau of him ruling over the other eleven gods of the White Pantheon.

In reality, there had been many hallways branching from this central room. Here, there was only one.

Luce's stance lowered, smoke unfurling from her spine as if her fur raised in anticipation. Asar nudged my arm, jutting his chin toward his sword at my hip.

"Draw that," he said.

I did. But holding it called to something within myself that I didn't want to acknowledge here in my holy homeland, real or no. A pulse of shadow swirled around its edge, sliding up and hovering near my fingertips.

"Maybe you should wield it," I said. As I knew he would, Asar dismissed me without hesitation.

"I'll be fine without," he said. "You need a weapon."

I didn't like swords in the best of times, but I especially hated this one—not because it felt clumsy and uncomfortable, like most blades did, but because it didn't.

Our footsteps echoed in a way that seemed like it didn't quite fit with the size of the room, as if we were actually in a much bigger space. It was so uncomfortably silent. In every other Sanctum, the temple had been a magnet for wraiths and souleaters, drawn by the call of Alarus's magic.

Here?

Nothing.

The halls stretched before us and behind us. Finally, I chanced, "Is it strange that there's nothing here?"

The silence swallowed my words like drops of blood in the ocean.

"Maybe," Asar said quietly, sounding a bit frustrated by his own uncertainty. We were deeper in purgatory than most mortals ever made it. Who knew what was strange?

We kept walking. Soon, more paths veered off from the main stretch. Sometimes, the hall would split, forcing us to choose a direction. Asar would hesitate for a long moment at each of these branches, weighing our options, before nodding in one direction or the other with no explanation.

Though the layout of the building was far from that of the real Citadel, it still captured my memories with such eerie accuracy. Tapestries lined the walls, a perfect representation of those in my old home. I remembered some specifically, which illustrated Atroxus's most well-known stories—like the ones of him lifting the sun over a field of livestock or healing Ix after a cursed lion nearly killed her.

But the longer we walked, the more gruesome the artwork became. What began as images of Atroxus's benevolence became depictions of brutality. Atroxus, hovering over a sea of flame at the beginning of the world, when he purged it to ashes to promote new life. Atroxus, kneeling over Alarus's body, hacking his head off with Srana's blade while Ix held him down. Atroxus, standing over Nyaxia, holding her chains as she wept over her husband's decapitated corpse.

Blood ran into blood, violence into violence.

I stopped at a tapestry that did not seem to depict Atroxus at all. A figure stood silhouetted against an orb of gold thread. Broken bodies, some missing limbs or heads, cluttered the ground around them. A crack split the sun in two.

My brow knitted.

Ahead, Asar turned to me expectantly, Luce at his heels.

I was about to follow him, but then I noticed something odd out of the corner of my eye. A strange, unnatural movement in the shadows where the ceiling met the wall.

I stared at it.

It was hard to tell if it was a trick of the light. The darkness seemed to be writhing. Then it twisted, running down the wall in slow drips.

No . . . those were . . .

I jumped as a wail split the air.

It was distant at first, and so abrupt that I wondered if I'd imagined it—was certain I had, because it held an uncanny resemblance to Chandra's final scream for help as the wraiths dragged her away. A mocking reminder of what had become many betrayals to my faith.

I froze. My eyes leapt to Asar. He heard it, too. Beside him, Luce's body coiled, a growl rising from her throat.

This was no mind trick.

The sound came again, horrific and twisted.

"Let's go," Asar said urgently, reaching for me as I dove to close the distance between us. Together, we ran. Black now dripped from the ceiling, from underneath the tapestries. I soon realized what had seemed so naggingly odd about those streaks.

They were hands.

They reached from the corners where the ceiling met the wall. From up between the tiles of the floor. From beneath the tapestries, which now immortalized my greatest sins. I couldn't stop to look at them, and yet, even as they blurred by, I recognized the images. Myself sawing a vampire corpse from a noose. Sitting in the garden with a handsome vampire prince. Denying Chandra her final plea.

Asar and I, tangled up in each other, our blood rendered in gleaming black thread.

It wasn't real. It wasn't real.

"Did you think that I wouldn't find you?"

Ophelia's features formed one by one—icy eyes, smiling lips, that long, blood-red scarf around her throat.

Asar and I skidded to a clumsy stop. He threw himself in front of me, his hand tightening around my arm. Luce snarled, ready for a fight.

"Let us pass, Ophelia."

She solidified, though only barely. It was difficult to make out where her body ended and the shadows began. The bounds of her mortal form had deteriorated, as if she sacrificed more and more of what she used to be the farther we journeyed. "Let you pass," she repeated slowly. "Such irony, my love. Why should I give you what you have denied me?"

My palm was sweaty around the hilt of his blade. It called to my magic in great pulses now, like a heartbeat racing in preparation for the inevitable.

"I can help you," he said. "If you let us through. If you let me—"

But Ophelia dissolved, re-formed, floated closer. Her fingertips brushed my cheek. I drew in a sharp breath—in that one touch, her soul flashed through me. I saw a young woman with the world ahead of her and the will to take a bite out of it. I saw her fall in love with a quiet young prince and that love come crashing to the ground.

Ophelia went suddenly still.

"She smells like you, Asar."

Her voice wavered. I felt sadness, then anger.

Inky tendrils moved to my throat, lingering right over the invisible mark that Asar's teeth had left.

"Do you think it will end any differently?" she hissed. "You are a regret to every person who ever loved you. I know this better than any other."

Asar's eyes met mine. His magic rose beneath the fabric of the world like a surging tide ready to crash to the shore.

I raised his sword.

But Ophelia's touch evaporated. Her rage strangled the life from the air.

"I do not even need to haunt you, lover," her voice echoed. "I am the least of your ghosts. Let them consume you."

The last thing I heard was Asar's shout.

The last thing I saw was Ophelia's face, tear-streaked, as she dragged me down.

CHAPTER THIRTY-FIVE

It was dark. So dark. Panic climbed up my throat.

Light the candle.

I called to the sun. But there was no answer.

I tried again, again, again—

"Let me help you."

A gentle hand offered a blossom of flame. It caught the wick, and the room ignited into the light of a summer day.

I stood in my chambers in the Citadel. My knees were weak, my thoughts mushy. I'd just been so afraid, but I wasn't sure why. I stood in front of a mirror, wearing a golden dress.

"Let me help you," my sister said, buttoning up the clasps in the back.

My sister.

Saescha.

A wave of emotion struck me, even though I wasn't sure why. I watched her in the mirror, unable to tear my eyes away. She had our father's elegance—the high cheekbones, the slightly deeper skin, the rich black hair. Even at eighteen years old, when she had led us to the Order of the Destined Dawn, she'd had the grace of someone twice her age. It was impossible to be scared when Saescha was around.

She smiled at me, pushing a lock of curly hair behind my ear before adjusting the fit of my offering dress over my bust.

"You look beautiful, Mi." Her eyes shone. "I am so proud of you."

I strove for Saescha's pride more than I strove for anything. Secretly, sometimes I wondered if I treasured that more than the love of Atroxus.

"I'm nervous." I spoke like it was a shameful confession. And it was, wasn't it? This was the greatest honor that anyone in the Order had been gifted in centuries. I felt like I shouldn't be feeling anything other than unfettered elation.

"Why?" Saescha said. "To be chosen by him is the greatest gift. He saved us because of you. And now, because of you, you will always be cared for."

You, she said. But I knew it really meant *we.* The Order might have sent us away if Atroxus hadn't chosen me that day. Saescha had risked everything to find us both a life of abundance and safety. As one of Atroxus's chosen, I would never have to worry about either again, and by extension, neither would she. I could repay her for everything she did for me.

Eternal fealty didn't seem like such a high price for that.

"It won't hurt too much," she said. "If that's what you're nervous about. I'm sure he'll be gentle with you. Just follow his lead. He will be happy."

Even that instruction now felt so intimidating. *Follow his lead. He will be happy.* He was a god. He had so many chosen, and surely had bedded countless others beyond them. I was a sixteen-year-old girl. I couldn't imagine my virginity being all that captivating.

Saescha was experienced. She had worked as a prostitute for a while, to earn enough money to help us travel to the Citadel. She didn't talk about it, but I knew. And what right did I have to complain about offering myself to one man—one god—in exchange for a lifetime of prosperity, when she'd had no choice but to offer herself to many just to help us survive?

I stared at my sister—my gorgeous, wise, kind sister. She was the better priestess, the better magic user, the better heart. I often wondered why Atroxus hadn't chosen her that day. She deserved it more.

She cradled my face between both hands. "This is your highest calling, Mische. The rest will fall into place."

The corners of the room wavered, but I thought I'd imagined it.

My eyes fell over her shoulder, where other acolytes prepared offerings for Atroxus's arrival. One priest held a firefinch, carefully affixing a jeweled collar around its throat.

The bird stared at me.

Something nagged at the back of my neck. I grabbed that fraying thread.

Pulled.

Saescha.

Gods, *Saescha.*

Reality crashed over me. The weight of all these years. The knife of my grief over Saescha's death. My eyes widened. I clapped my hands over hers, squeezing them tight.

We were in the Sanctum of Secrets. In the Descent. Was this a vision? Or . . . ?

"Saescha," I gasped. "Is it—are you—"

Are you real? I didn't want to ask because I didn't want to know. I touched her face, her hair, her shoulders. She felt real. She smelled real. That smile was real, serene and endlessly wise, the greatest stabilizing force of my world.

She blinked, as if awakening from a haze.

"Mische?" she whispered. She touched my face, too, tentatively. The smile broadened. "Light bless us, it *is* you."

Tears stung my eyes. A lump rose in my throat. I threw myself against her in the fiercest hug. Gods, she *smelled* the same. Like childhood safety. Like home. Like innocence.

"I missed you. I missed you so much, Saescha."

For a moment she didn't move, startled. But then her arms tightened around me. "I missed you, too, Mische. You can't imagine how much."

Oh, I could imagine. I could really, really imagine.

Saescha's hug grew tighter. Tighter.

Words bubbled out of me like a broken fountain. "I'm sorry. I love you. I missed you so much. I never meant it. I thought of you every day. I—I—"

It was getting difficult to speak. Saescha's grip was unrelenting. I gasped a laugh, patting her back. "I really missed you, Sae."

Tighter.

"I gave you so much, Mische." She spoke low in my ear. "You don't even know all the things I did for you."

A prickle at the back of my neck.

"Saescha—"

Tighter.

I opened my eyes. It had gotten so dark. Across the room, I watched the priest holding that little firefinch. The collar constricted and constricted, until—

Snap.

I gasped at a jolt of pain.

The gruesome truth of this reality hit me.

If Saescha was here, she had not passed on to the underworld.

If Saescha was here, she was a wraith.

The tapestries on the wall smoked, flame nibbling at their edges.

"Saescha," I pleaded. I was fighting her now as she clung to me.

"Why did you let this happen to me?"

Her voice cracked. Her pain was a serrated blade, gutting me like hunted game. I wrenched free, stumbling back against the wall as I gasped for breath. Saescha was transparent, bleeding into the ghost of our old home. Her serene composure had shattered. Blood smeared her throat, which was torn open, crimson soaking the white of her Dawndrinker robes. For a moment, the sight of her like this—how she had looked in death—paralyzed me with horror.

The edge of a terrible memory brushed past me.

"Look at me, Mische." Her elegant face twisted in agony. "Look at what has become of me. Years and years and years I wait. I pray and I pray. But no one answers. Why doesn't he answer?"

Saescha's despair spilled through me. I knew it so innately. What it felt like to be abandoned by the one you had devoted your very soul to.

"I did everything," she ground out. "I gave him my life. I followed the rules. Why am I here?"

The flames consumed the tapestries, the visage of the Citadel now a blazing inferno. Heat clawed at my flesh. Smoke burned my tear-filled eyes.

She was right. None of it was fair. She was the better acolyte. The better sister.

"I will help you, Saescha," I said. "I'll find a way. You'll pass on and I'll—"

But she dove at me. My head smacked against stone. When my blurred vision cleared, all I could see was her face. Her hunger surrounded me. "I was so proud of you. My sweet sister, my good sister. Bride of Atroxus. You had everything. Why did you have to ruin it?"

She was right. She was right. She was right.

How many times had she said that to me? *Count your blessings, Mische. Appreciate what's under your two feet, Mische.* She had known that I never should have climbed up to that vampire corpse that day.

But I was so fucking stupid. So impulsive. So reckless.

Tears streamed down her cheeks. When was the last time I had seen Saescha weep?

"And now, *look at you*. I raised you. I protected you. You were my child, not just my sister." Her mouth twisted, a sob, a sneer, a hiss. "And look at what you've done to that innocent baby I raised. I was a baby, too, once. Who protected me?"

She inched closer. I couldn't think. I couldn't breathe. My fingers were tight around the hilt of Asar's sword, but though its magic called to me, I refused to use it. This was no souleater—this was my sister.

I would help her. Asar would help her. She could pass, like Eomin. I just had to get her to him. I had to—I had to—

She lunged for me, and in my clumsy attempt to evade, I crashed through a half-ajar door. My back slammed against the floor, shadows and flame filling my vision. Someone called my name. I looked up to see Asar through the fire, barely holding off another figure. Though the smoke obscured his opponent's features, I still recognized Malach immediately. You don't forget the man who Turned you.

Asar's eyes widened, looking over my shoulder, and he raised his hand, magic flaring—

"No!" I threw myself in front of Saescha before he could let his strike fly. It was a rash, stupid move. Saescha's poison grip nicked my arm as I sent myself sliding into the wall. My head banged against stone, pain exploding with the impact as I threw out my hands to steady myself.

I had only a split second to feel the carvings beneath my hand. I frowned down at it, sliding my palm away to see swirling marks carved into the wall—

Saescha lunged for me again, and I barely managed to evade her this time. Her touch singed the edge of my sleeve. She would have grabbed me had Luce not leapt between us, snarling. It bought me precious seconds to steal another glance at Asar. He wasn't *just* fighting, I realized. He kept going back to that inner wall, lips moving in silent spells as he pressed his hands against it.

Glyphs.

This was a door, I realized. The hallway here was curved, running in, I suspected, a circle. The glyphs were designed to gate off whatever sat within, and Asar was pulling it closed.

His gaze met mine. He extended his magic to me, a thread for the needle of my wielding. When I accepted it, my breath shuddered. The intensity made my steps falter—so much more powerful than it had felt in Morthryn's halls.

Saescha finally managed to throw Luce, grabbing her by the scruff of the neck and tossing her aside like a discarded doll. By then, I was already running, hands dragging along the wall, searching for that next glyph. The first two, I could sense, had already been connected. If the construction was the same as the gates, there would be five total.

My fingers brushed indents in the wall. I grabbed Asar's magic, infused it with my own, poured it through.

Three.

The wraiths crawled from the floor, the ceiling, beneath the tapestries. These were faceless, formless, like they'd been here so long they had lost even the basest remnants of their mortality. They reached blindly for me as I pushed through them. Behind me, Saescha gained ground.

Another glyph. Four.

"Look at me, Mische," Saescha begged behind me, and coward that I was, I couldn't. She sounded sad now, not angry.

Storm clouds brewed overhead, the false sun of my memories of Vostis devoured by hungry darkness. My body was so innately attuned to the magic around me that I felt suspended in it, like a spider by her web. I rounded the next curve and saw Asar on the other end of the hall, weaving his half of the gate with Luce at his side.

Gods, he looked like more than a man. His scarred eye was bright white against the eternal black that surrounded him, wisps of lightning dancing in its midst. I could feel the power tugging at the connection we shared, stronger than I'd ever felt it before, barely tethered.

A door sat halfway between us, closed, though light pulsed at its edges. The apex of the gate, maybe? It flickered as a rumble of thunder shook the ground. Wind swirled through the halls, sweeping my hair behind me.

"You can't leave me again," Saescha pleaded as I dragged myself toward the final glyph.

Six steps.

"I won't," I whispered, even though I knew she couldn't hear me— knew she wasn't listening at all.

Three steps.

My bloody hand trailed black over the marble. My eyes settled on Asar, pulling himself toward me as Malach's wraith bore down on him. He extended his hand, reaching for the final set of glyphs.

Saescha barreled into me, her touch burning around my wrists.

I pressed my bloody hand to the final mark.

A flare of power surged through me. Saescha let out a horrific, animalistic scream. The door sprang, and Asar barreled into me at the exact moment that it did, hauling me inside.

The last thing I saw was Saescha's wide eyes as she reached for me. "Don't leave me—"

Asar thrust his hand out, and the door slammed shut.

The magic drained away in a sudden exhale. A heavy blanket of quiet fell over us. The screams of the dead sounded like they were miles away. Thunder trembled in the rafters, the tempest raging against the glass ceiling far above.

Asar, Luce, and I ended up in a pile on a tile floor. Luce was splayed out oddly, letting out a high whine. I rolled to my back and stared up at the ceiling—a gold-lined glass dome—and the storm beyond it, a sea of billowing silver that reminded me eerily of Asar's left eye.

I couldn't get Saescha's face out of my head. Her voice. Her touch.

The screams on the other side of the door sounded as if they were miles away. But I could hear them still.

I could hear her.

Don't leave me.

Asar lifted himself slowly. He assessed me first, but then, when his gaze fell to Luce, his face paled.

She tried to get up and promptly collapsed again.

Asar dropped to his knees beside her as I crawled closer.

"Luce?" I said.

She let out a rattling whine, as if to weakly—and unconvincingly—reassure us. Asar cradled her head.

But then, when he lifted his eyes, he whispered a curse and stood. I followed him.

We were in a temple. This room no longer wore the skin of the Citadel. This was all the Descent—bone pillars, ice-dusted ivy, roses frozen in a forever-dead bloom. The room was circular, with nested steps leading up to a platform at its center.

Asar approached, then fell to his knees before it.

I followed, then sank down beside him.

No. No, no, no.

At the center of the circle was a grand marble box covered in markings of the language of the gods.

It was open. It was broken.

"Fuck," Asar whispered as he sagged over the shattered stone.

It was empty.

There was nothing here at all.

CHAPTER THIRTY-SIX

The storm raged on outside. The dead pounded at the door. They sounded far away, yet I still was certain I could hear Saescha's voice wherever we went. There was only one way in or out. We had barricaded ourselves in our own cage, with no relic to show for it.

It had clearly once been here, Asar insisted.

The lid had been laid alongside the box as if placed there by someone who knew and respected this place. This was no sloppy grave robber. Five massive stone crocodiles wearing bone faces, like the guardians we encountered in Breath, lay arranged in a perfect circle around the dais. The marble was so immaculately detailed that it looked as if they had once been living beings who had simply laid down to rest one day and never gotten up again.

Perhaps Elias had chosen to push forward alone and had managed to claim it before us—Asar scoffed at this idea. Or perhaps someone else had claimed it long before. All that mattered now was that it was gone, and we were trapped.

There was nothing to do but wait. If we were lucky, the storm would pass and the crowd of dead beyond the door would thin. Then we could figure out how we were going to make it out of here in one piece. We were in no condition to fight our way out now. Luce needed time to heal.

"She has a higher tolerance for the dead than we do, but it still takes a toll," Asar said as he ran his hands over her limp body, clusters of shadow trailing them. She whimpered as he patched one of her worst wounds, and he patted her on the head.

"She's survived worse," he murmured. "She'll be all right." But his voice was low with worry.

I put my hand over his. "She already came back from the dead for you. I don't think she'd leave so easily even if you wanted to get rid of her."

A humorless smile twitched over his lips. "Likely so."

Later, while Asar watched over Luce, I paced the temple. Stairs spiraled along the edges of the room, leading to two upper levels. The first was mostly empty, save for a few more crocodile sculptures and some discarded, overturned chairs. The second housed what appeared to have once been a place of worship. A marble altar sat upon a dais. Behind it, a statue stood watch. The head was broken off above the chin, leaving only half a set of pensive lips and a partially clothed body with palms outstretched.

It had once been Alarus, if I had to guess—the only option that made sense. But still, the scene looked as if it could've been ripped from the Citadel or any of the other countless monasteries I had visited over the years. It was all the same. The statues, the carved altar, the tapestries so bleached by time I couldn't even begin to make out what they'd once depicted. Even the smell, that smooth hint of incense.

I could so vividly imagine this balcony full of kneeling acolytes.

I could so vividly imagine myself among them.

The glass ceiling and the large window behind the statue let in the swirling shadows of the storm beyond, striking and unsettling, another reminder that we were not in the mortal world.

I crossed the room and knelt before the altar. My hands folded before me, palms up, position so instinctual it came like breathing. I stared up at the faceless statue. I had seen so many of these depictions of Atroxus. It was easy to fill in the missing pieces with his visage.

The first time I had knelt before an altar like this, I had been given a second chance. From that moment on, I was tethered to him. The arrow in my heart, forever leading me to the sunrise.

"See, Mische?" Saescha had told me, all those years ago. "Whenever we're lost, all we have to do is pray, and we will hear the light call to us."

I closed my eyes.

But there was no light down here. And the only call I heard was Saescha's.

Asar's footsteps were so light they barely whispered across the floor. But in the silence, I heard them anyway. How had I gotten this far without realizing that I'd memorized the way they moved? The thought unnerved me, because it made me wonder how much of me he had memorized, too.

I felt so terrifyingly exposed. I had no defenses right now. And even if I did, Asar, it seemed, could always slip right past them.

I didn't turn around.

"Luce is resting," he said. "She's feeling better. A little time, and she'll be fine."

I let out a breath of relief. "That's good."

I wished I could cling to that piece of good news. Instead, it felt like one little drop of hope in a sea of despair.

Silence.

I could feel him staring at me. He approached slowly, every step of the distance closed between us agonizing. I was waiting for the searching questions. They didn't come. Instead, he settled beside me.

I finally allowed myself to look at him. He knelt at the altar next to me.

"What are you doing?" I asked.

"Praying with you," he said. As if it were obvious.

"I thought you didn't believe in prayer."

"I don't," he said. "But you do."

Strange how it was this small gesture of kindness that shattered me.

I closed my eyes. I leaned forward until my forehead pressed against cold marble. My chest tightened, tightened, tightened. When I finally had to force myself to breathe, my inhale was a horrific sob.

"Mische," he whispered. His fingers brushed my back. Too much of a reminder, now, of everything I shouldn't want. I pulled away, jumping to my feet as I wiped my tears with the back of my hand.

"How do you do it? Help them pass?"

A wrinkle formed between Asar's brows as he rose. "What?"

"The wraiths. How do you help them pass through to the under-world?"

Understanding fell over his face.

"Who was she?" he asked. Because of course he saw. Of course he knew.

"There has to be a way to help her through. Like you helped Eomin."

I sounded manic, and I knew it. I'd already started drifting toward the stairs, ready to escape complicated questions in favor of a painful solution.

"I've never been able to do it here. It gets harder the longer they've been here, and the deeper we go." His throat bobbed. I knew how painful it was for him to admit this—defeat. "I've never succeeded."

"But you have to keep trying," I pressed. "You can't just give up because it's too hard."

He flinched, like I had slapped him. Even as I said the words, I regretted them. I knew their cruelty to someone who had spent his entire life trying to fix something that couldn't be fixed.

"I need to try," I corrected myself. "I need to right my wrongs."

I didn't even realize the echo in my words until they were coming out of my mouth. What Asar had said to Esme—*I need to right my wrongs.*

Asar took another step closer, and I stepped back. I didn't deserve the way he was looking at me.

"Whatever she said to you isn't true," he said softly. "Souls here have languished for a long time. Their hunger has festered. They're angry at the world because their anger is all they have left."

"She meant it. She—"

"She can mean it and it can still be untrue."

I wondered how many times he had told himself that about the things Ophelia said to him.

"She's here because of me. This is my fault. I can't leave her that way."

"We won't, Mische. We won't." It was a vow. "But hating yourself won't help her. Sacrificing yourself won't help her. You were so young. You can't bear that weight forever."

He didn't understand. I was shaking, my fingers curled tight at my sides. "Yes, I can. I have to."

Another step closer. A gentle touch to my chin as he tilted it up, forcing me to look into his eyes. They were so soft, so searching. How could I ever have thought that Asar was cold?

"Why?" he whispered.

Something cracked inside me, and the ugly truth poured free, scalding hot, burning me up.

"Because who will I hate instead? If it's not my fault, whose is it? She's not supposed to be here. She was the best priestess in the Citadel. The most pious, the most devoted. She was always the better one. She gave him everything. She gave him—" My voice cracked. "She gave him *me*."

I was sixteen years old again, hugging my sister goodbye as she sent me off into that bedchamber.

I was eight years old again, bathing in the light of the god who was supposed to save us all.

I drew in a ragged, painful breath. "He was supposed to protect her. And I understand if he rejects me. Because I'm—I'm the monster. I'm the tainted one. I'm the one who destroyed myself. But *Saescha*. Saescha was perfect. And the only piece of her I have came from him. The only good thing I can offer the world." I wasn't crying anymore. The poison that had broken free in my veins was hotter than sadness, colder than grief. Strange licks of darkness curled at the edges of my vision, and dimly, I realized that it was my magic, peeling from me like there was just too much of it to be contained beneath my skin.

"So then what?" I choked out. "What will I have left, if I don't have the light anymore? Nothing. I'll have nothing."

Asar had been listening in silence, his jaw tightening with every word, the shadows in his scarred eye roiling in slowly mounting fury.

"Is that what you think of yourself? That everything good about you came from a fucking church? Atroxus didn't make you special by choosing you. He chose you because you already were, and even when you were eight Mother-damned years old, he knew that. You owe him nothing. *Nothing*."

His fingers tightened, hand sliding to the back of my head, as if to keep me from retreating from his words.

"I'll tell you what you'll have if you lose the sun, Mische. You'll have a soul gentler than any vampire's I've ever known. You'll have an incredible magic and the skill to wield it better than the bastard who gave it to you. You'll have a soft heart and a sharp wit and the wisdom to know when to use one or the other. You'll have countless inane questions and horrible taste in food and a penchant for making lost souls love you."

I couldn't breathe. Couldn't speak. He leaned closer until his forehead touched mine.

"And if you'll take it, Mische Iliae, you will have me, too." This whisper was an exhale, like he didn't mean to say it aloud—like the words surprised even himself.

Only a few inches separated our bodies. My magic, beyond my control, coiled around him in desperate caresses. I stared into his eyes, one the brown of the earth and one the silver of the stars, belonging to a soul who bridged two worlds just as I did.

The space between us was an executioner's blade—thin as a hair's breadth, and yet, the difference of an eternal soul.

The lush curve of Asar's mouth twisted. The muscles of his throat flexed. He started to pull away.

But my hands fell to his shoulders. I traced the muscular lines of them, to his throat, his chin.

I was so sick of wanting.

This isn't what love should feel like.

"Show me what it should feel like," I whispered.

The blade fell. My sentence was written.

We crashed together into beautiful damnation.

CHAPTER THIRTY-SEVEN

Asar's mouth tasted as good as his blood. His arms folded around me like he'd been waiting for this for days, weeks, months. His kiss was vicious. The hand that had been tangled in my hair now tilted my head to deepen it, like he was desperate to savor as much of me as he could.

My hands ran down his back, tracing the hard lines of his body through the fabric of his shirt—gods, I wanted that gone. My fang opened a small cut in his lip, and the taste of his blood awakened a maddening rush in my veins.

But he broke the kiss, pushing me away. His eyes kept going back to my mouth, the smear of blood at its corner. His lust was etched into every line of his form. His cock was already hard between us, thick and ready. But he blinked away that haze of desire, and when his hand slid to my cheek, brushing a strand of hair from it, it was all gentle concern.

I didn't want gentle right now.

"You're upset," he said.

"I want this."

I wanted to seize it while I could. I wanted to find something right in all these broken pieces. And gods above, I wanted him. I wanted him while I could still have him—here, in this moment where it all aligned, fleeting as an eclipse.

The muscles in his throat worked.

"I don't want to be something you regret, Mische."

THE SONGBIRD & THE HEART OF STONE 337

I knew it was a confession that came from the most vulnerable parts of himself. The echo of Ophelia's words hung between us: *You're nothing but a regret to everyone you ever loved.*

My heart hurt for him.

I cupped his cheek, thumb caressing the elegant threads of his scar. "I'll never regret you."

An easy truth. My soul had been marked by a litany of shames. I'd carry them forever, and I'd likely carry more, too—I knew that. But Asar, I knew certain as the nightfall, would never be one of them.

He leaned his forehead against mine, swallowing thickly. I wondered if perhaps no one had ever said that to him before. The thought made me so overwhelmingly sad.

I kissed his cheek, drawing a deep inhale of his scent of ice and ivy. Then his throat, right where I'd drank, the pulse beneath his skin intoxicating. Lower—his collarbone, half-covered by the collar of his shirt. My fingers went to his buttons, undoing the first one, but his hand fell over mine.

When I peered up at him, he looked back at me with an unspoken fear.

"I want to see you," I said softly.

Had anyone ever said that to him, either?

He hesitated, then released my hand and took over the buttons, avoiding my gaze. His shirt fell open, and I slid it from his shoulders.

The shifting light from the storm outside highlighted the swells of his lean muscles, silver light dripping down the ridges of his abdomen, where a line of dark hair led into his trousers. It was the body befitting of a vampire prince—a vampire king.

And then, there were the scars.

They trailed down his throat and over his shoulder, extending across his left pectoral and all the way down his arm. Black swirling lines crawled along his ribs, then down the muscles of his stomach, falling off into little fractures near his hipbone and barely brushing the edge of his waistband. They looked like cracks of lightning. Like ivy caressing stone.

I flattened my hand against his chest. His flesh twitched beneath my touch.

CARISSA BROADBENT

"They're beautiful," I said.

I meant it. It now seemed ridiculous that when I first saw him, the scars seemed like a mar on an otherwise perfect face. But I'd now seen what he'd looked like before them—like a boy trying hard to be something he wasn't.

He flinched, giving me a look that said, *You don't have to lie to me.* But I kissed the knot of black at his shoulder, his pectoral, his bicep, his throat, and then his mouth again, dizzy all over again with the want of it.

"Really," I murmured against his lips, and with the length of my body pressed against his, he didn't seem to have it in him to argue.

He tilted my head up as my lips opened for him, our tongues sliding against each other like silk. My hands roamed his bare skin, and his tightened around the fabric of my shirt, as if offended by its existence.

He let out a low sound deep in his throat as my fingertips slid beneath the waistband of his trousers, feeling the hard curve of his backside.

"You're challenging my self-control, Dawndrinker," he growled.

My lips curled beneath his kiss.

"Good. You're too restrained."

Let him unravel. Let me see what he looked like in the ruins of all that self-control. Let him drown my grief and my sadness beneath the exquisite sin of his touch.

He loosened a rough breath against my lips, and suddenly, he spun us around. My back hit something hard—the edge of the altar. One of Asar's large hands braced my hips against it, holding me still. The other worked at my shirt. Halfway down, I muttered, "Gods help us," and ripped it off myself, sending buttons raining to the marble floor.

What was wrong with me, that I was so eager to expose myself to him when I'd spent years now hiding my body as my greatest shame? The self-consciousness hit me when the cool air did. He pulled back to look at me. He drank me in inch by inch, a line of concentration over his brow—like witnessing me was a task that required his total attention.

When I had lain with Atroxus, I'd thought that the way he had looked at me was lust. Like I was an attractive item to be coveted, all my value in the surface appearance of my beauty.

But Asar looked at me like he wanted to *see* me, layer by layer. It was uncomfortable. I wished he'd return to the harsh desire, too furious to allow for thought. Tenderness was painful. And yet, I couldn't bring myself to stop him as he lowered his mouth to my throat. My collarbone. The swell of my breast, brown nipples peaked with anticipation. His tongue darted out to taste one, gently swirling its peak, while his thumb rolled over the other.

His hand flattened around my waist, fingers tracing the curves of my hips. I resisted the urge to shy away as they encroached on my scars, the newer ones that had extended over my shoulder blade and down my side. But he touched them so gently, so lovingly.

It had been a long time since I had let anyone touch my bare skin at all, for fear of showing them all those shameful marks.

Stop, I wanted to tell him. *I don't deserve that.*

But I couldn't make myself.

His mouth kissed down my body as those deft fingers moved to the clasp of my trousers. They were a little too big for me. With the button undone, they slid right down, pooling around my ankles.

Asar straightened, eyes starting at the floor, moving up, up. I wondered if he could smell the desire at the apex of my thighs, the slick already starting. I could smell his, heady and sweet, clouding my thoughts in a tantalizing haze.

His eyes darkened. The light of his left eye smoldered like a flaring flame. His nostrils flared, ever slightly, as I forced my thighs to loosen, the cool air startling against my core.

It was too much, the way he was looking at me. Too real. I gave him a lopsided smile that probably looked as weak as I felt.

"I thought I was challenging your self-control," I said. "You're being awfully slow for someone who—"

His hands slid beneath my backside, quick but firm. The next thing I knew, I was lying upon the altar, my back against cool stone, looking up at the raging storm clouds through the glass ceiling. Asar leaned over me, a curl at the corner of his mouth.

"Slow," he scoffed. "You've seen how I work now, Dawndrinker. I'm thorough. I'm patient."

"You're uptight."

"I have impeccable attention to detail."

His teeth grazed a spot on my breast that made my breath hitch. He paused there, smiling.

"Like that." His tongue slid out, soft and wet, giving that sensitive skin a long, sweet caress. My self-consciousness fell away. A small, wordless sound escaped my throat.

"Noted." One hand slid up to my shoulder, gently pushing me back to the slab, while his mouth lazily worked over the underside of my breast.

"One learns a lot about bodies in my line of work. Every one is different. But yours—"

His tongue pressed over a spot on my abdomen, and a deeply unseductive giggle escaped my lips. My knees jerked up, and I would have hit Asar squarely in the jaw if he hadn't dipped out of the way.

"Sorry!" I sputtered, pushing myself to my elbows. "That just— that tickled."

Asar's smile, the amusement dancing in his eyes, reminded me of the dawn.

He gently replaced my wayward knee. "It's nice to find your weaknesses. Even if that wasn't the one I was looking for."

Nice to find my weaknesses. What a ridiculous thing to say. I felt like I was all weaknesses.

"You'll tickle the dead back to life?"

I was still giggling a little, struggling to compose myself. I felt lightheaded. The sight of Asar's bare skin struck me all over again. The cocktail of nervousness and overwhelming, carnal desire was scrambling my thoughts. I felt like my human self and my Dawndrinker self and my vampire self were at war with each other.

A wrinkle formed between Asar's brows. He touched my cheek in a way that I knew was an unspoken question—*Are you all right?*

The affection in his gaze sobered me immediately. The sensation it stirred in my heart was more complicated than lust.

I coaxed him toward me, giving him a kiss that started tentative and quickly deepened, my vampire desire rising in my veins again. When he broke away, I let out a small sound of protest. He gave me a *tsk*.

"Typical of you. Always rushing."

His mouth suckled at my throat. Moved down to my nipple, then my waist—carefully avoiding the spot that had nearly gotten him kicked in the face.

My hipbone.

Oh, gods.

I stared at the clouds. Asar's hands fell to my knees.

Pushed them open, as he lowered himself to kneel at the altar.

"You asked me what love should feel like," he murmured. I tensed as his lips brushed my inner thigh.

"It should make you think of nothing else."

Higher, where the skin was so sensitive that I jolted when he dragged his teeth over it.

"It should make you see stars."

Gentle force on my inner knee. My legs widened for him at that lightest touch. My heartbeat thrummed in my veins, and I knew he could smell the rush of my want, now overtaking all other thought.

With Atroxus, he had taken what he wanted hard and quickly. Maybe some part of me had been expecting the same from Asar, not this torturous wait.

I could feel his breath on the heat of my desire. The faintest brush of his lips when he said, "This was what I wanted to do that night."

His kiss, long and slow, wrung a languid moan out of me. His tongue slipped between my folds and ran up, lingering at my bud.

My back arched against the altar.

Holy gods. I had never felt anything like that.

My legs had opened in a request for more. But he'd already withdrawn, his kisses retreating to my inner thighs.

I didn't intend to make the needy sound of disappointment aloud. He chuckled against my skin.

"I'm patient," he murmured. "A man can't rush worship."

And gods, that was what he was doing. Worshipping. He moved

over me like his hands had moved over the piano keys, as if my every
sigh or moan of pleasure was a symphony to be composed. He kissed
and nipped at my flesh, moving to my breasts until he felt my muscles
go taut, before returning between my legs to offer another agonizing
indulgence. Heat built. My hips rolled against him without my permission. When his tongue pushed inside me, sucking greedily, I cried out
so sharply my voice echoed against the glass ceiling.

"Mm." He hummed his approval as he withdrew again. Now he
kissed my throat, his face close enough that I could scent my own
pleasure on him.

I couldn't think of anything but the proximity of his body. My
hips lifted, but he kept himself carefully suspended over me, never
touching. When my hand slid between us to curl around his length
through his trousers—gods, it was incredible, so thick I couldn't curl
my hand around it—he sucked in a breath and roughly pushed my
arms back against the altar.

He lifted his head to look into my eyes. They were dark with
want, the deadly edge of his desire exposed. I liked it. I wanted to
let it rip me open.

"Not yet, Dawndrinker. I want to taste you as you come the first
time. There will be plenty more."

He continued his work, giving equal attention to every inch of my
flesh, dropping back between my legs to lick and suckle until I was
crying out for release, only to leave me there on the precipice again.
Slowly, heat rose across my entire body. Every flick of his tongue on
my hip or my breast or even the rough skin of my scars threatened to
throw me over the edge.

"Asar," I begged, the next time he pulled away from me. I tried to
pull him closer, tried to sit up to take control myself, but he pushed
me back to the altar and held me there, firm.

I could see now how Asar had once been a master at torture. He
was so cruelly attentive, so aware of every unwilling tell of the flesh.
He knew exactly how to bring my body to the brink of collapse,
and how to pull away right before it happened. And yet, my agony
translated to such unbelievable euphoria. Every inch of my body had
turned so sensitive, the pleasure burning me up.

"I'm being slow now, because I want to remember this. Exactly how you sound." His tongue flitted out against my nipple, and I gasped. "I like that one."

"You're such an asshole," I ground out. It wasn't a very inspired response, but it was all I could get out.

He laughed, low and cruel.

"And I'm being slow now, because I won't be able to later."

And then, at last, his mouth pressed to the soft skin of my inner thigh.

"I was so jealous of your hand that night. I wanted to taste you come even more than I wanted to taste your blood."

His breath, hot with desire, tortured me.

"You make me so greedy, Dawndrinker," he murmured. "I can't deny myself around you."

And then he held my thighs apart, and slid his tongue inside me, long, slow, hard, vicious.

The pleasure he had been wringing out of me for a slow eternity crashed over me all at once. My eyes squeezed shut. My muscles spasmed. I clutched for him, anything, for an anchor as he ripped me apart at the edge of his blade.

When awareness slowly filtered back to me, my hands were tangled in his hair. He was breathing heavily, quickly. He was still kneeling before me, licking the sweat off my inner thighs.

"Exquisite." The word was barely audible, like he didn't mean to say it aloud. His eyes rose slowly, trailing up my shaking body, until they met mine.

Did I look like he did? So shattered? Like all his defenses had broken apart, leaving the tender vulnerability of our want exposed and raw. I'd never known it could feel so good, to let yourself be unmade.

And holy gods, he was perfect. The storm beyond roiled, the eerie dark light falling over his body like streaks of paint.

I pushed myself up. I kissed him, tasting myself on his lips, and gently urged him to stand. He did, our kiss deepening, never breaking, as my hands slid over his body. Slid down, to the cut V running into his trousers. His tongue slipped into my mouth as I undid the button—I nicked it with my fangs as it came free, relishing his hiss as an intoxicating drop of his blood hit my tongue.

And then his trousers were on the ground, and his cock, hard and wanting, was in my hands. I stroked it as I kissed him, enjoying the way he tensed when my thumb ran over the bead of moisture at its tip.

I'm being slow now because I won't be able to later.

I pumped him once, and I was barely able to complete the movement before he let out a growl and pushed me back against the altar.

That one challenge, and the self-control of the eternally thorough, eternally patient, eternally uptight warden of Morthryn shattered, releasing the monster.

We crashed together. He lifted me, my backside against the edge of the altar, the height perfect to align our bodies. My thighs opened for him—I was so wet, so ready. His cock notched at my entrance, and he buried his face against my shoulder as he pushed.

But partway through the movement, he paused. One arm cradled me, the other leaning against the altar, palm splayed. We both were panting, our bodies twitching in protest at the pause here, right at the precipice of finally, finally being brought together.

I looked down to see us combined, him barely inside me, the tip gleaming with my slick.

Two sinners on the edge of something we both knew would change everything, here upon an altar of all that had destroyed us.

I raised my eyes to meet his.

And that was all it took. One glance at each other, at all our wants.

He plunged into me.

I gasped and clutched him, my fingernails digging into his back. From that first thrust, I knew that the time for patience was over. This was raw and frantic and brutal. This was pleasure and pain and desperation, faith and destruction, fire and ash.

He drove into me like I was the only thing tethering him to life, and I clutched him and rode against every violent clash of our bodies. I reshaped around him, his length searing every part of me.

The pleasure he'd given me had been unbearable before—but this, to experience it with him, feeling every muscle respond to me, was devastating. Some part of me had known that this would change me.

I didn't realize the extent of it until this moment. Before, sex had been an offering, something to be taken from me.

But here, as my body and Asar's writhed together, moving in time with our heartbeats, the innate connection terrified me. I had opened myself up for him, and now, he was offering me his guts, too.

I knew it when he was getting close to his own release, his muscles coiling, his hands clawing at my thighs. He pulled back, forehead pressed against mine, his eyes bearing into me as his body did. He pushed deep, pausing there as our bodies strained against each other. A moan, almost a sob, escaped my lips. He captured it in his.

"Ignite, Mische." He was commanding me. He was begging me.

I shifted my hips, urging him into another thrust as my hands tangled in his hair, eyes staring unblinking into his. I wanted to watch him as we both fell apart.

"Fall with me," I whispered. Because I was oddly terrified to lose control—terrified to do it alone.

He exhaled against me, our pace rising to a desperate crescendo.

"I'd burn with you till the end of it all, Dawndrinker."

I fell back against the altar as he drove into me, the two of us collapsing against the stone in a swell of pleasure. I cried out as he slammed into me, and I felt him spill within me as my climax wrung his from him. I watched his pupils dilate, watched the pleasure of my body destroy him. Watched him watch me through it, too.

And then I wrapped my limbs around him and held him through the aftershocks as the fire subsided. His lips pressed against my temple, my cheek, like he wanted to make sure I was still here, with him.

I would always be with him, I knew in this moment. I would never be able to leave.

I kissed him, tasting the remnants of our pleasure. He was still inside me, and I was still so conscious of his presence. I wasn't ready to let it go. I was selfish. Sinful.

My mouth moved to his throat. I ran my fangs against his pulse in a silent question. He stilled, his cock twitching inside me, then lifted his chin for me. One bite, and his blood flowed over my tongue, sweet and thick and wonderful, too good to be wrong.

He exhaled, his presence inside me hardening unmistakably now.

I drank deep, then released him and offered my throat to him in return. The stab of his teeth made me gasp. His near-silent groan of pleasure as he took my blood was dizzying. I slipped free and urged him down to the altar. Then I crawled astride him and slid his again-ready cock back inside me, filling an emptiness that now felt meant only for him.

We took each other slowly this time, smoldering and sweet, pausing to drink each other's blood—relishing in skin against skin. I came again on him as he whispered sweet urges against my flesh. Then I let him roll over me and we found one last euphoria with each other, our limbs so entwined that we became a single being. He kissed me through my last climax as he came for me one more time, his fingers locked with mine as if he would never let me go.

He slipped from me, but our bodies still folded around each other, peaceful in the darkness.

"Exhausted with pleasure," he murmured. "I keep my promises."

I laughed. My heart felt heavy and full. My palm flattened over his chest as my lashes fluttered. I traced the lines of his scars, painting affection over pain. And as exhaustion fell over me, I watched our blood, ruby black, drip over the edge of the altar.

I didn't regret any of it.

I hoped our blood would stain this stone forever.

"YOU HAVE ALWAYS been such a foolish, impulsive little creature, a'mara."

My bare body was cold—alarmingly cold. Asar's absence struck me like an icy blow. Without him, I felt like I was missing a limb.

A dream.

I opened my eyes to blinding sunlight.

This was a dream.

"But this," the voice said, inevitable as the dawn, "is an *affront*."

The rage of a god is impossible to describe. It reshapes the world. You feel it in the air. It seeps into your soul and burns from the inside out. Gods wear the faces of mortals, but they're closer to a storm or the sea than a human—forces capable of crushing a mortal life out of nothing but fickle whim.

I had loved Atroxus my entire life. I'd showed him my childish gifts. I'd let him into my body. Sometimes, even I forgot the true nature of what he was.

This was a dream, I prayed.

But dread fell over me as Atroxus's rage rose like smoke from a pyre.

It was not a dream.

I lifted my head. Atroxus stood before me, sun scorching in his eyes, flames licking from his flesh, his fury so hot it warped the air.

"Do you still wish to tell me," he breathed, eyes burning, "that you have been *loyal*?"

CHAPTER THIRTY-EIGHT

My breath caught in my throat. Fear paralyzed me. I had basked in Atroxus's love for so long that I had thought nothing could hurt as much as his abandonment.

I was wrong. His hatred was obliterating.

"Get up," he commanded. His voice boomed through the room, and my body rushed to obey before my mind told it to. I stumbled off the slab of marble and dropped to my knees. I was naked, still. But this place wasn't the room where Asar and I had fallen asleep—at least, it wasn't completely. Some of it seemed the same—the arrangement of the altar, the white stone, the glass window and ceiling. But while that place had been dark and broken, here everything was blindingly bright and clean. The world beyond the glass was cloudy nothingness. There were no statues, Atroxus standing instead where the broken idol had loomed.

Where was I?

Where was Asar?

How could Atroxus be here? I thought gods couldn't see into the in-between realm of the Descent. The gravity of my miscalculation rolled over me with the slow, steady rise of my panic.

"My light—" I started.

"I sent you here with a purpose you have squandered. How weak of me to believe that you could still be deserving of the sun, even as your heart rotted with Nyaxia's disease." A hand grabbed my chin and wrenched it up. Pain shot through me at his touch. The scent of burning flesh surrounded me. But I forced my eyes to meet his—stars of utter rage.

"And this is how I find you? Naked and reeking of death, covered in its desecration? You spilled blood upon an altar. Did you think I would not see you?"

I cursed myself. The altar. Blood over an altar could thin the veil between the mortal and god realms. We were getting close to the end of the Descent. The boundaries must have been just thin enough . . .

Atroxus's nose wrinkled in disgust. "I have been too fond of you for too long, a'mara. I did not see you as the animal that you are." He released me, sending me stumbling backward. "Cover yourself. I don't wish to look at you."

He thrust his hand to a pile in the corner. My panic choked me as I slipped on the white shirt and pants. The fresh burns on my face throbbed.

The first time I had disappointed my god, I had spent hours self-flagellating at the feet of his altar, begging for his forgiveness. And maybe in my heart I was still that little priestess girl, because that was my immediate urge now—to let him hurt me. Add more scars on top of scars to show him just how much I loved him: *Look how much I suffer for you. Don't you enjoy my pain?*

But something was different in me now. This time, beneath the wave of shame, something dangerous sparked.

Anger.

"What do you have to say for yourself?" he hissed. "Tell me why I should not burn you like the monster that you are."

I heard my sister's voice: *Why am I here with the monsters?*

"You're right." I turned to him. I was shaking with fear, but it didn't show in my voice. "I am a monster. You have every right to burn me. But Saescha—why did you allow Saescha to come here?"

A pause.

"Saescha," he repeated.

He didn't know who she was.

I didn't know why that would surprise me. He was a god. He had countless worshippers. He never even used my name, and I was one of his chosen, his special brides. Did he, I wondered for the first time, even know what it was?

Does one memorize the name of every exotic fish in a tank? Every golden bird in their cage?

"She was one of your most devoted followers." My voice wavered as I lifted my head to face him, his brilliance staggering and terrifying. Once I started talking, I couldn't stop. The words poured out. "A member of the highest echelons of the Order of the Destined Dawn. She gave her life to you. And she was promised peace in the life that came after in exchange for her loyalty. But instead, she is here, trapped between worlds. Why did you let this happen to her?"

He stared at me for a long moment.

And then his fury exploded.

Flames tore over the tile, surrounding us both. The sun of his eyes flared searing white. His lips curled in rage.

"How *dare* you speak to me with such insolence. You allow death to defile you. You let an acolyte of the sun die with hate in your heart. You desecrate yourself with the base impulses of your tainted flesh. You spit upon your vows. And *now*." He grabbed me, pushing me to the wall. I couldn't struggle—I didn't even try. "And now, you immoral wretch, you cast blame upon *me* for the fate of your kin?"

He leaned closer, his breath fanning over my face. Once, that breath had felt like the kiss of dawn. Now, it was the promise of damnation.

"No," he hissed. "No, that is not mine to bear. Do you wish to know the truth of your sister's end?"

My momentary reckless bravery had burned away.

A tear slid down my cheek.

I didn't want to know.

But Atroxus was not in the business of sharing information. He was in the business of punishment, and punishment did not wait for permission. He shoved my face against the stone, turning it to the fire.

I wanted to fight it. But the past, like the dawn, was inevitable.

I am so sick. Fever rages in my veins. My vision is garbled, too sharp and too blurry all at once. I do not know how long it's been since the vampire left me. One moment, he was shoving his wrist against my mouth, forcing hot blood down my throat. The next, I am here, crawling down the dusty desert street, death at my heels.

I am so hungry—

No. I tried to look away, but Atroxus's grip held me, forcing me to the past.

I am so hungry. I have stuffed my mouth with bread and plants. I have gulped water. All of it does nothing.

I collapse sometime in the night, and when I close my eyes, I'm certain I won't open them again.

But then I hear her.

"Mische."

Tears prickled my eyes. I wanted to close them as the image of my sister's face appeared. But I couldn't. The door had been shredded. The memory crawled out like a starved beast. I couldn't lock it up again.

Saescha is my savior. I am so grateful to see her that I start to cry. I am eight years old again. My sister always comes when I need her. She always makes it safe when I am frightened. And right now, I am so, so frightened.

She falls to her knees before me, cradling my face. "What happened to you, Mische?" she weeps. "Holy gods, what did he do to you?"

I cling to her, and I keep saying the only thing I can think:

"I want to go home. I want to go home. I want to go home."

She strokes my hair like she has a thousand times since I was a child.

"I know, my love. I know. I'll take you home."

And for one beautiful moment, I believe her.

I couldn't. I couldn't see this.

"Look," Atroxus spat. "Look at what you are."

But then, there is the smell.

The smell changes me. It makes my pupils dilate, my nostrils flare. It makes my muscles go rigid.

I am so, so hungry.

I do not know what is happening to me.

I turn my head against Saescha's neck, breathing deep.

"Stop," I begged. "I understand. I'm sorry. I—"

"You will look at what you are!"

And I had no choice.

I watched.

I watched myself become the monster.

Saescha doesn't realize what's happening at first, when my teeth first sink into her throat. She does not yet know what I have become. I do not know, either. Already, the world is blurring again, my thoughts disappearing beneath blind, mad hunger, drowning in the fever of my Turning sickness.

She tries to pull away, confused. But at that first taste of blood, my impulses take over. I fall back into darkness.

My teeth sink into Saescha's throat, again, and again, and again.

I do not get to go home.

I squeezed my eyes shut, but it did nothing to stop the images. It wasn't Atroxus showing me Saescha's final moments anymore. The memory ravaged me.

I never thought I could envy the traumatized girl Raihn had rescued, so terrified of all the things she couldn't remember. But gods, I wished I was her again. I wanted to hug her and tell her, *Just let the fever burn it all away. Never look back.*

But it had always been there, hadn't it? A shadow that I ignored. Easy enough to look away when I could bury myself in everyone else's problems and tell myself that it was my calling, instead of just another word for selfishness.

My last words to my sister were, *I want to go home.*

This isn't my home, I had said to Raihn, the night I told him I was leaving, and he'd looked at me with that devastating sad puppy face. He had so wanted to give me a home, and I had so badly wanted to let him. Even then, I wasn't quite sure why it didn't feel right, why I couldn't just accept it.

Now I knew. Because I'd lost my home years ago. I had ripped it apart with my own cursed teeth.

I didn't even feel it when Atroxus released me. The next thing I knew, I was on my hands and knees, retching.

Atroxus's flames ebbed, as if he found some minor satisfaction in my punishment. He stared at me, chin raised, lip still curled in disgust. I was only dimly aware of how pathetic I must look, on the floor in a puddle of my own sick.

"Such terrible final moments," he said softly. "To die at the hands of a monster wearing her beloved sister's face."

The thought made bile rise in my throat again. Now I understood her wraith's fury.

Whatever she said wasn't true, Asar had told me, looking at me with such affection.

He'd been wrong. It was all true. Every word of it.

"Do you understand how fortunate you are that I have given you this chance?" Atroxus said.

"Yes." My voice was so small.

"Rise," he commanded. I did, mildly surprised that I could support my own weight.

"You understand more than any the consequences of Nyaxia's actions," he said. "You will finish your task."

I couldn't speak. I could barely keep myself standing.

"Answer me," Atroxus spat.

"Yes," I whispered. "Yes."

I lifted my gaze—not to Atroxus, but to the clouds beyond him. They reminded me of the storm that had raged beyond the temple windows in Secrets.

"What will happen to this place?" I shouldn't be speaking. But I couldn't help myself. The words were sticky and rough. "To the Sanctums? It could—it could be healed. So many souls are lost here and—"

"There is nothing but suffering here. The world is better off without it."

Nothing but suffering? That wasn't true. I shook my head without meaning to, and again, Atroxus's eyes flashed.

"You disagree?"

I shut my mouth. Shook my head.

But Atroxus snarled, *"Speak."*

His command dragged the words from me.

"It's just—Alarus fueled this place with his love. It isn't all bad. It couldn't be."

"His *love*," he sneered. "You speak as if Alarus was so very pure. As if he, too, did not have his share of mortal lovers in the years before her. As if his interest in Nyaxia was so sweetly selfless. If Alarus had done what was asked of him from the beginning, what a better world this would be."

I didn't understand. But I couldn't question him further. With the memories of Saescha's last moments lodged behind my eyes, I didn't care to, anyway.

Atroxus tilted his head, observing me. The fire of his rage dimmed, tempered with a hint—just a hint—of pity. "To think that despite all you are, you still have that sweet human naivete. You cannot help your nature. You will not question this, a'mara. You will complete the task you are so fortunate to have been given. And you will not speak of it until the deed is done."

"The relic is gone," I said. "Someone else already took it."

Atroxus scoffed. "The Sanctum of Secrets is where souls go to hide their shame. Alarus, coward that he was, hid his, too. I helped him build this temple, once, long ago. Look beneath the surface. You will find what you need."

His eyes slid back to me. Whatever he saw made the disgust fresh in his expression all over again.

Once, Atroxus had looked at all my mortal imperfections with such amused affection. Now, they weren't charming anymore. A lifetime of training made my supplication an immediate impulse. I wanted to fall to my knees, beg for his forgiveness, lay my undying loyalty at his feet.

But instead, I remained standing.

Through my tears, I chanced a demand.

"And my sister?"

"What of her?"

My voice was shaking. "She was so loyal to you. A better acolyte than I ever was, my light. She deserves so much more than I do. She would serve you forever, if you let her."

Once, my sister had offered me up to her god to save me. It seemed like a twisted fate that now, years later, I would do the same to her.

He watched me, considering. I fell to my knees, pressing my forehead to the floor. "Please, my light. I know—I know I can't ask my own salvation from you." Maybe once I could have earned it back.

Not anymore. "But you are so benevolent. So kind to those who give you their devotion. Saescha was the most devoted of all."

Silence.

And then: "You speak truth that you are beyond saving. But perhaps I can offer your kin the redemption that you have squandered. Should you complete your task, I will offer her life once again—the life she should have had, if you had not cut it short."

My breath of relief was fractured with a sob. "Thank you. Thank you."

In this moment, I loved him all over again. At least I could right this one wrong.

But then another face unfurled in my mind.

Atroxus now gazed out the window to the brilliant white beyond, content to be reassured of his generosity.

"I must ask you for one more thing," I said.

He turned his head slightly, his sculpted profile silhouetted against the light. A dare, a challenge. But I had to ask.

"I know that this is . . . that this is a big request." I swallowed thickly. "But you are so benevolent, my light."

He faced me, hands clasped behind his back.

"Asar." The name made my heart ache. "I can't complete this task without him, even if he doesn't know it. When this is done, I ask you . . . spare him. Please."

Atroxus's fury rose in an immediate wave. Heat scalded my face. My arms flew up to cover myself.

"I give you so much more than you deserve, and yet you ask me now for mercy for the vampire lover who defiled you? I do not take kindly to those who sully what is mine—"

I knew it. And that was why I needed to ensure Asar's safety—because regardless of what would happen to me when this was done, or what Atroxus's plans were, I knew he would smite Asar for the sin he'd committed by touching me at all the moment he no longer needed him. And I wouldn't let that happen.

I'd never been a very good schemer. I was better at fixing straightforward wounds, whether in bodies or hearts. But I thought of the gods and what was most important to them.

Atroxus hated Nyaxia, and even more than that, he hated the world she had built.

"Asar is the Heir of the House of Shadow," I said. "He's the rightful king of one of Nyaxia's kingdoms. If he owes a favor to the White Pantheon, that could be valuable."

Asar would never be loyal to Atroxus. I knew this in my bones—not because of Nyaxia, but because of the scars on my skin and the fresh burns on my face. But the gods could be petty. Simply undermining the loyalty of each other might be appealing enough to him. Atroxus paused, and I leapt on that opening. "Nyaxia will be angry that you interfered with her followers, of course, but—"

And just as I hoped, that dangling bait pushed him over the edge.

He waved a hand to silence me. "Very well. Because I am kinder than I should be, I will make you a deal. I will not smite your lover."

Another tear slid down my cheek. "Thank you," I whispered. "Thank—"

"But you will speak nothing of this to him. And you will do exactly as I command until your end."

"Yes, my light. I will."

I meant it. I'd do anything. Everything. For this.

Atroxus's expression softened. He touched my face, bloody burns trailing his fingertips. I thought of my offering night, when I had believed that being looked at that way by a god was the greatest thing that would ever happen to me.

"Such a shame," he said softly. "You were so lovely once."

His grip tightened, tightened, tightened, fingers digging into the back of my neck.

"Remember just how merciful I am."

CHAPTER THIRTY-NINE

ears streaked my face when I awoke. I didn't stop to question, even in the hazy half second between sleep and waking, whether it was a dream. That was no dream. The fresh burns throbbed, stinging under the salt of my tears. I was wearing the clothes Atroxus had thrown at my feet. And I was alone.

I sat up, disoriented. I was no longer on the altar, but I recognized this place as part of the temple right away—the same white stone and big glass windows, overlooking thick, misty fog. No more storm. No more wraiths banging at the door.

The room was empty, save for a single set of stairs that curved up.

I stood, knees trembling.

"Asar?" I called.

Fear pooled in my stomach. I went to the stairs and climbed.

In the distance, I heard a distinctive *yip*, and my heart leapt.

"Luce!"

Another *yip*, this one hopeful. A moment later, Luce bounded around the corner. I dropped to my knees and wrapped her up in a hug.

"You're feeling better!"

She nuzzled my cheek with her snout, wriggling against the hug. But gods, I'd missed her. Maybe she sensed something was wrong, because she momentarily stopped squirming and curled around me when I buried my face against her neck.

But then I heard another voice:

"Mische?"

The note of panic in it made my heart skip a beat.

Luce barked and broke free, as if to say, *Found her, found her!* I got to my feet, climbing up the rest of the stairs, and—

Just as I turned the corner, the scent of ice and ivy was all around me, and a wall of warmth surrounded me, and Asar was clutching me like I was a gift returned to him.

I fell into his hug like it was a natural state. My arms wound around his neck, face against his chest. He was solid and safe and gods, how had I missed him so much in so little time? I wanted to fall apart here, melt into his love, let him take care of me as I spilled out every ugly truth.

I couldn't, of course. But it meant something that I wanted to.

I was so grateful for his embrace that it took me a moment to realize that he was shaking. He clutched me fiercely, face pressed to my hair like he was breathing me in. He held me and held me and didn't move for a very, very long time.

I flattened my hand over his back, brow furrowing. Something was wrong.

His blood had spilled over that altar, too. Had he gotten a visitor, like I had?

"Asar," I whispered. "What happened?"

"I just—I'm glad to see you."

His hand touched my face, right over the burn that Atroxus's touch had left. I flinched, hissing with the pain.

Asar's eyes snapped open. Fell to that wound. His entire demeanor changed.

"What happened?" He tilted my head, examining the burns. Did they look as bad as they felt?

I could have sworn I felt the shadows in the room tremble. "Is this a *handprint*?" he growled.

Every word sounded like a death sentence.

I pulled away. "It's not bad."

"There is a handprint on your throat—"

"I saw the past," I said. "That's all. It's . . . not happy."

Asar's face softened. "Who?"

I hesitated. I hated lying. Especially to Asar, when he was looking at me like I was the most precious thing in the world.

"My sister," I said.

A partial truth.

My gaze swept over Asar's face. He looked unhurt, though something about him looked different in a way I couldn't place. And he was shaken. I didn't have to see that on his body—I could feel it. Even now, he touched my hand, like he was afraid to let me go.

"Did you . . . see something?" I asked.

"Secrets manipulates your mind. We should have known that even in the temple, we wouldn't be safe from that."

"Is that a yes?"

A hesitation. A wince flitted over his face.

"Malach?" I said.

He paused. And then, like it pained him, he nodded. "Yes."

It wasn't the truth.

At least, it wasn't the whole truth.

But I could let him lie to me. I didn't care. I just wanted him here. I wanted to drink up every second I had with him until the end.

For the first time, I took in our surroundings. We stood at a landing between two staircases, the one I'd come up and an identical one behind Asar. Another, grander set of stairs spiraled up to our right, while a smaller door led down to our left.

"I woke up down there," he said, jerking his chin back toward the stairs behind him. "Luce was with me."

He rubbed her head affectionately, and I scratched her chin as her tail thumped in satisfaction. Of course Luce would have found Asar the moment she could. Of course she would have guarded him until he woke up. She was the very best girl.

"I'm glad you're feeling better, Luce," I said.

She gave a disinterested snort, as if to chide me for worrying about her at all. Still, she leaned into those head scratches, willing to accept the praise regardless.

I looked up. The ceiling was high above us. It looked like layers and layers of stained glass, all in conflicting designs, built on top of each other.

"Are we still in the temple?"

"I think so."

I stared up at that design. Why did it look so familiar?

And then it hit me.

"We're under the floor." I pointed up. "Those are the mosaics. The underside of them."

Look beneath, Atroxus had said.

Asar turned to the staircase leading down.

"There's a relic here," he said. "We were wrong. It wasn't missing."

His voice sounded off in a way I couldn't place. Oddly certain.

He took my hand in his, and together, we went down the stairs. As we walked, the opulence fell away. There were no more columns, no more carved decorations, no more tapestries on the walls. The hall grew narrower, the steps uneven. By the time we reached the bottom, this was no longer a shrine at all. This was an unmarked tomb, meant to hide something away.

A door stood before us. It was stone, the surface smooth and polished. A bird was carved upon its center, wings spread, flames rising from it.

"A firefinch," I said.

"A phoenix," Asar corrected.

I touched the tattoo burning beneath my shirt sleeve, buried beneath years of scars.

"Atroxus's contribution, I take it," Asar said. He shot me a glance. "Now it's worth it that I saved your life. I was beginning to wonder."

He often sounded a little awkward when he joked, but this one was downright flat. His hand touched my back as I approached the door.

For a moment, I doubted whether I would have the magic to open it. My skin was covered in the marks of my god's disappointment. But I had a purpose to fulfill. He wouldn't abandon me completely until I'd finished it.

I laid my hand over the phoenix's chest and called upon the sun.

It burned. But it obeyed my command, molten light flooding the carvings, igniting the bird in flame.

The door opened.

The room within was small—barely big enough for all three of us to fit. An empty black arch sat on the opposite side. Two skull-faced marble alligators curled around a cracked, circular hole in the floor.

Luce approached and sniffed them.

"Cousins of yours, Luce?" I asked.

Maybe Luce was a guardian. She was loyal enough.

We stepped through the door and knelt beside the hole. And when we leaned over it, the past—Alarus's past—collided with us once again.

The Sanctum of Secrets is the Sanctum of shame, of desire, of everything you do not wish the world to see. This is true of all beings. Mortal, or god.

I kneel at the circle, holding my greatest regret. I hate those who put this in my hands. I hate myself more for accepting it. I could have destroyed it. I could, still, in this moment.

I do not.

Instead, I lower it down, down, down, far beneath the ground. It will be buried here for millennia. It will remain here, where my beloved wife may never find it.

She will never know what was once intended for her heart.

The images faded, leaving Asar and me breathless.

I peered into the crevice.

I expected darkness. Instead, light bathed my face. I reached down, my fingers closing around Alarus's secret relic.

A golden arrow.

God-crafted—that was obvious. The divine light pulsed through my bones. It was long and slender, the tip death-sharp. Yellow feathers curled at its end. I recognized them immediately: firefinch feathers.

The nature of what I was holding settled over me.

This was a weapon. A weapon crafted by the gods to kill a god.

If Alarus had done what was asked of him from the beginning, Atroxus had said, *what a better world this would be.*

Asar met my eyes. Understanding fell over us both.

This was a weapon that had been intended for Nyaxia. Alarus had been meant to kill her all along.

And now, this was the weapon that I would use to kill the god of death.

CHAPTER FORTY

S oul will be next." Asar's voice was distant. We were both un-characteristically quiet as we entered the dark arch leading us out of the temple and into the shadowy world beyond. It was warm and silent out here, the ground dusty gray sand, the sky dark, the path before us surrounded by what appeared to be great tree trunks—except where one would expect branches or leaves, they just extended up into the mist forever. There were no wraiths, no souleaters. If I listened very carefully, I thought I could hear their mournful cries in the distance, but even that might have been a trick of the wind.

Asar still insisted that I hold his sword, which banged against my hip. He had carefully wrapped the arrow and placed it in his pack along with the other relics—three monuments of love and one of betrayal. The golden light seeped between the stitches of the pack.

"How long until we get there?" I asked.

It felt like such an inane question, all things considered.

"I'm not sure. A week or two, on foot." A pause, then, "Less, maybe. Secrets and Soul are closely intertwined. The boundary between them is very thin."

"So the wraiths—"

"If something wants to follow us badly enough, it likely can."

He answered quickly enough that I knew this was on his mind, too. Ophelia, Malach. Saescha.

A muscle feathered in Asar's jaw. He barely looked at me. Something was wrong. Whatever he had seen in that temple had shaken him as much as my encounter had shaken me.

"It doesn't matter," he said, as if reassuring himself. "We only have to get in long enough to perform the rite."

"Isn't there one more relic?"

A pause. Then, "The Sanctum of Soul is more a doorway than anything. The passage itself will act as the fifth relic."

I supposed that by now, I should have stopped trying to apply logic to any of this. It was magic. None of it made sense. I'd relished that for most of my life—that my magic was driven by the emotions in my heart, unbound by the rigid rules that I'd chafed against in the Citadel.

I could use some rules now. A loophole to slip through.

We walked a few steps in silence. Asar was serious, a line of concentration between his brows. Even the light of his scarred eye was dimmed. Yet, he reached for me like it was second nature, long fingers twining around mine.

I couldn't make myself pull away.

My gaze fell to the pack at his hip and the light pulsing from within, even through the fabric and leather.

"Do you think that was really intended for her? The arrow?"

Even as I asked it, I knew the answer. I just wanted to rail against it. Nyaxia had always struck me as so lonely. I didn't want to think that her one love had been tainted by this hidden betrayal.

"Some believe that the gods' power is communal," Asar said. "Perhaps they were afraid that the addition of a thirteenth major god would dilute their strength. Or maybe they were just threatened by her because she wouldn't do what she was told. She was a runaway, after all."

That was an uncomfortably familiar story.

"So they . . . sent Alarus to kill her? Was that what he was supposed to do when he found her?"

The stories always made it sound so fortuitous. That Alarus had rescued Nyaxia when she stumbled, starving and injured, into his territory. She had wandered for weeks in the lands between the mortal and immortal worlds. Maybe she'd even wandered here, on the path we now walked.

"Perhaps," Asar said. "Alarus had always been looked down upon by the rest of the White Pantheon. Maybe he saw Nyaxia as an opportunity. Leverage against his fellow gods."

"But he decided not to do it."

"He still kept the weapon."

My heart hurt.

I shook my head. "No. He loved her."

Asar's mouth twisted into a wry, sad smile. "People hurt the ones they love all the time. It might be the one thing we have in common with the gods."

I knew he was thinking of Ophelia and how he had damned her. Saescha's face flashed through my mind, too. Eomin's. All the others.

I stopped walking. My hands curled at my sides.

"*No.* Not always. Sometimes people just love each other and do right by each other and always make up for it when they make mistakes. Sometimes people are just happy together for the rest of their lives. Sometimes—sometimes it all *works.*"

I needed to believe that. I thought of the last time I saw Oraya and Raihn, standing on that balcony together, nose to nose. That was love. I believed that with my whole heart. And I needed to believe it could last for them. That good things could exist in this world for good people.

I had lost so much of my faith. But I couldn't lose that.

"I need to believe that it all can be worth it," I said.

Looking at Asar's face was like staring into a mirror. He was so much more expressive than I'd realized when I first met him. I just hadn't known how to see it then. Right now, I could see all the conflict beneath the surface. Because he wanted to believe it just as much as I did. His heart was just as tender as mine. That was why he had devoted his life to fixing broken things, just as I had.

He approached me slowly, footsteps silent in the dust. His fingertips brushed my cheek and tilted my face toward him. He kissed my forehead.

"It will be worth it, Iliae," he murmured.

I so wanted to believe him.

I really, really did.

WE WALKED FOR a long time before we stopped to rest. Neither of us seemed eager to confront the things that would catch up to us once we stopped moving—things that were, somehow, so much more frightening than wraiths. Asar and I lay beside each other in the sand, staring at the sky. At first, I'd thought nothing was visible up there but the mist, but staring into it long enough, I realized that I could actually see our entire journey if I looked hard enough—the distant rivers of blood, the silver ghosts of the mortal world above, the deserts and the ice and pools of crimson. The hazy silhouettes of souleaters drifted in and out of the clouds, so far away that they looked like lazy shooting stars.

I felt the warmth of Asar's body beside me, and I was painfully conscious that the last time we had lain down, it had been intertwined with each other, naked and spent. It felt like a lifetime ago.

"You're quiet, Dawndrinker," Asar murmured.

"You're quiet, Warden."

I turned my head. He was propped up on one side, watching me, a wrinkle between his brows.

He paused before speaking again, like he had to summon the courage to do it.

"Regrets?" he asked.

Gods, did I have regrets. I regretted the pain I'd brought to so many people I'd loved and who had loved me in return, even when I didn't deserve it. I thought of my sister's final moments, Raihn's hurt face at my goodbye, the way he might look when he learned of my death. Because surely, I was going to die when this was done. I tried not to think about that, but it didn't make it any less true.

I had regrets.

But I knew what Asar was asking with that searching, tentative stare. *I don't want to be something you regret.*

I folded my hand over his, scars against scars.

"I told you I'll never regret you," I said. "I meant it."

He said nothing at that, the wrinkle of concern still not fading. But he held my hand as he slept, and I traced my thumb over the shape of his—raised scars, knobby knuckles, elegant fingers.

No, I would never regret Asar.

But I knew that one day, he would regret me.

CHAPTER FORTY-ONE

We traveled in a death march to the end, hours blending together. The terrain slowly shifted around us, the trees eventually giving way to dunes of white sand, which in turn soon shifted to rippling fields of grass—all of it rendered in mournful shades of silver, a ghost version of the mortal world. It was impossible to tell how long we walked. There was no moon to rise or fall, no markers to gauge the passing of time save for the bounds of our own exhaustion. We slept when we were too tired to go on, and continued walking the moment we woke.

There were no more kisses, no more trysts, even though every time we lay down, our awareness of each other was agonizing. I could feel Asar's eyes on me constantly, and when he slept, I traced the lines of his body, too. But I couldn't let those walls down for him again. Not with Atroxus watching, his hand over Asar's throat.

This wasn't like the other legs of our journey. Something had shifted in a way that neither of us could—or would—name.

In every spare moment we had, Asar pushed me to practice my magic. It was constant, and he was an even tougher instructor than usual, his patience stretched thin.

"I know you know how to do this," he snapped one night, after I fumbled a thread of shadow that he kept passing me as we walked, asking me to manipulate it into more and more intricate arrangements. "I've seen you do far more. Stop stifling yourself."

I let my hands drop to my sides, staring hard at the gray ground as we walked. "I'm not stifling myself."

I just couldn't focus. My Shadowborn magic felt wrong in all the ways it felt right. Every time I let it slide under my skin, I heard Atroxus's voice—damning me, and worse, damning Asar.

I didn't want to tempt that fate.

Asar stopped short, turning so fast I almost went stumbling into him. His scarred eye flared.

"I know you too well for that now, Mische," he said. "Yes, you are."

A flare of frustration rose up in me, quickly tamped down beneath my hopelessness.

I gave him a weak, painfully fake smile. "I'll just have to try harder." I tried to push past him, but he angled himself in front of me, forcing me to look at him.

"We are about to attempt one of the greatest feats of Shadowborn magic ever to be recorded," he said. "It will be dangerous. You need to be able to do this."

The note of desperation in his voice made me pause. Not frustration. Not the chiding of a teacher with a student who wasn't applying herself.

Desperation.

I stared hard at him.

"You're the necromancer. This is your ceremony."

He said nothing.

"Can you please just tell me what the ominous silence is for?" I said.

The corner of his mouth twitched, but there was no joy in the expression.

"I wasn't going to say anything unless I knew you could do it."

Dread rose in my stomach. "You weren't going to say anything about what?"

"I'll need your help. To conduct the ritual."

I blinked. My eyes went wide.

Necromancy was taboo, yes, but it was also notoriously difficult. Even when I'd watched Asar set up his ceremony for Chandra what felt like a lifetime ago, I'd been able to feel the complexity of it.

"You want *me* to help you do the resurrection? I'm—" I rasped an awkward laugh. "I've only been wielding Shadowborn magic for what, a few months?"

"But you're talented. And more valuable than that, you've spent your entire life studying magic. Your technique is perfect. It's obvious every time I see you work. You just . . . understand it." The curl to his lips had returned. If I wasn't too busy trying not to keel over at the thought of performing necromancy, I might have felt something warm in my heart that Asar was talking about me with such admiration. I knew by now that nothing meant more to Asar than someone who was truly committed to their art, and it was nice to know that he thought I fit that description.

"But why?" I asked.

Asar took a long moment to answer. "This journey has taken more of a toll on me than I wanted to admit. You saw how I struggled to even close the gates in Morthryn alone. I needed your help then. I'll need it for this, too."

I was silent.

My limbs felt heavy, exhaustion weighing on me. The glow from the arrow still pulsed bright enough to seep through the seams of Asar's pack.

I'd help drag Alarus back to life, only to kill him. And I'd have to do all of it while connected to Asar, our magic shared, our souls intertwined in that uncomfortable intimacy. I'd have to feel his reaction as I betrayed him.

I could handle impossible magical feats. But this almost brought me to my knees.

For a moment, the desire to tell Asar everything overwhelmed me. The worst part was, I didn't even think he would blame for me for any of it. I could imagine his sigh of exasperation, his clenched jaw of concern on my behalf. And then he would set his sights to righting these wrongs, just as he did in the halls of Morthryn.

But I could now feel Atroxus's eyes on me in perpetual watch. The walls I'd constructed to protect Asar from the consequences of my actions were so feeble that a strong gust of wind could destroy them. If I blatantly disobeyed Atroxus's only stipulation, Asar would be the one to pay for it, and I would not allow that to happen.

So I drew in a breath and let it out.

"When I boarded that ship to Obitraes," I said, "I never thought that eventually, I'd be doing gods-damned necromancy."

Asar's mouth curved in a smile that, despite everything, made every wrong in the world feel manageable.

"I thought you liked adventures. This is the greatest one you'll ever take. Besides." He brushed a stray hair behind my ear. "Can't think of anyone better suited to master both the sun and the stars, Iliae."

THE AIR GREW so unbearably still, as if the Descent itself was holding its breath in wait for what was to come. We didn't encounter a single other being—not Ophelia, not wraiths, not souleaters. Even Luce was now always quiet, the wisps of shadow at the back of her neck wiggling as if her hackles were perpetually raised.

"We're getting close," Asar said one day as we paused our drills to stop and look out over the distant horizon. "I can feel it."

I could feel it, too. Fate creeping up behind us.

Sure enough, the next day we reached the door.

We were hiking through rocky bluffs, exhausted after hours of travel, when we crested a hill and stopped short.

"Oh, gods," I whispered.

Asar let out a long breath of amazement.

A field of red poppies spread out before us, an endless blanket in all directions. They were searingly bright in a world of grays and silvers, so much so that it hurt my eyes after what felt like ages seeing no color at all. But gods, were they stunning—rippling against an invisible breeze, stretching off over the rolling hills, painting the entire landscape in blood.

A doorway stood in the center of that field.

The passage to the Sanctum of Soul.

The boundary between the Descent and the underworld.

The end of it all.

A lump rose in my throat. Funny that we'd spent gods knew how long traveling toward this spot and yet, now that we were here, it felt like an unpleasant surprise.

"That's it?" I said.

"That's it."

What else was there to say?

We started to make our way down the hill. The poppies were tall, nearly brushing my knees, and so soft. I held out my hand to touch them as I went.

Halfway across, Asar paused. He looked to the door. To the horizon. And then back to me. A gentle breeze rolled over the flower petals, sending his hair rustling and dousing me in the scent of flowers and him.

He offered me his hand.

"Let's sit here."

I frowned, gaze sweeping over him. "Why? Are you all right?"

"I'm all right. I just want to sit for a minute."

My frown deepened. "But we haven't been walking very long. And you don't usually like to rest. Or do anything fun."

"To think I actually thought you liked me, Dawndrinker."

"Well, Warden, I just speak the truth."

Asar settled down in the flowers, leaning back on his palms and gazing up at me. "Sit. You're too impatient."

I was impatient. The moment I saw that door, I felt like insects were crawling under my skin. On the other side, everything I knew would collapse. I just wanted to rush through it. Get it all over with.

And the way Asar was looking at me, that soft smile on his lips, was making this all too difficult.

"Sit with me," he said again.

The way he said it reminded me of how I had sounded as I asked him, *Stay with me*.

A lump in my throat, I obeyed. His shoulder brushed mine, the warmth of his body unbearable. Luce circled us, snapping at the silver butterflies rising through the flowers like smoke. In the sky, the faint ghost of the path we had traveled still hung over us, distant rivers of blood and mountains of stone and circling souleaters. Utter peace here, in the center of so much chaos.

It was one of the most beautiful things I'd ever seen.

"You know," Asar said softly, "it's very possible that no other living mortal has ever witnessed this sight."

And gods, what a sight it was.

"When I told Raihn that I was leaving the House of Night, I said it was because I wanted to see the world." I laughed. "I didn't mean the underworld. I meant the Lotus Islands, or something. But this . . . this is definitely more impressive."

"You'll have quite a story for him."

My smile faded. The thought of Raihn made my heart ache.

I was no fool. I knew I would probably never get the chance to tell him this wild tale. I hoped he never learned what happened to me. I hoped he would just go on forever thinking that I was off living my adventures, seeing all there was to see.

"Mhm," I said. "He'll love it."

Another breeze. The scent of ivy rolled over me. I drew it deep, holding it in my lungs.

"When you came to Obitraes," he said softly, "you came to preach the light to vampires."

I smiled weakly. "I'm not new to impossible missions."

It didn't feel right to joke about it, even after all these years.

But there was no joke in Asar's voice.

"I was born a vampire. I've never known the sunlight. What does it feel like?"

I closed my eyes. For a time, I'd feared I was forgetting what the sun had felt like. Now, for some reason, the recollection came to me so easily.

"It feels like waking up rested after a long nap. Or like going to sleep knowing you'll awaken safely. It feels warm and comforting. A fresh dawn makes you believe that the future can be better than the present."

Strange that when I closed my eyes, it wasn't the dawn that came to mind as I described these things.

"I imagine," Asar said, "that it feels the way music sounds. Like joy for the sake of it. Maybe it feels like hope."

"Yes," I whispered. "It's exactly like that."

"Hm." His touch, gentle as nightfall, fell over my hand. I wouldn't look at him, wouldn't turn to face him, but I felt his breath against my ear.

"You have given me all of that," he murmured. "So you have succeeded in your impossible mission, Dawndrinker. And I'm deeply honored that I had the opportunity to walk this path with you. Thank you."

I didn't like that he was talking this way. It all felt so damned close to a goodbye. I forced myself to meet his eyes, saw him drinking me in like his final sip of wine.

I drank him in, too—this man whom I'd come to see so much of myself in. This man who devoted himself eternally to righting wrongs and fixing the broken things that no one else cared about. This man who saw light in the darkness and heard music in the silence.

For a moment, I saw a glimpse of all that he could be, would be, once this was all over, and the thought that I would not get to see those things was devastating.

"I think you're going to be an incredible king," I said. "I think you make the world better."

And as we sat there in the field at the precipice of death, I kissed him, long and gentle and full of the truth I couldn't say. I didn't even care if the sun was watching.

We remained there, soaking up our final moments, for a long time.

And then we closed the chapter just as easily. We rose, we gathered our things. We straightened our scant armor and donned our weapons. Asar gave me one final kiss on the forehead and wound his fingers through mine.

And we passed through the doorway to the final Sanctum, sending our souls to hell.

PART SIX

SOUL

INTERLUDE

*L*et me tell you of the day that blessed girl—that chosen bride of the sun, that savior of the dawn, that missionary of the divine destiny—died.

As she promised her god, she made the journey to the land of the damned. Her sister and her friend came with her, even though she told them over and over again that they shouldn't risk their eternal souls for hers. They were perfect acolytes—devoted, obedient, in perfect standing with their god. Only she stood on the razor-thin wire between blessedness and damnation, and they should not have to walk it with her.

But they refused to let her go alone. Her friend insisted this with a dimpled smile, easy and clear as the sunrise. Of course he did. He had been in love with her for years, though she pretended not to know it. She was grateful for his companionship, but with every lingering stare he gave her, guilt speared her. His was the blind loyalty of teenage infatuation, sweet in its naiveté. It simply never occurred to him that she would fail.

It was not that way for her sister. She sat there and listened to it all, hands folded in her lap. When the story was done, she just stood, resolve steady. "I'll begin preparations," she said, and she wouldn't hear anything else of it.

No, her sister's loyalty was not that of a lover ready to follow their sun to a promised land.

It was that of a mother using her final moments to fling her body in front of her child.

They arrived in the land of vampires late midday, the sun still offering them scant protection from the teeth of their would-be sheep. They were received by the confused but curious occupants of the human districts, given lodging and food by people who shook their heads at them.

"Hell of a last meal," the innkeeper grumbled as he handed them their watery soup. It was not the first final meal he had served to acolytes like these, nor would it be his last.

The girl was anxious. The air smelled like change here. She was fascinated by the dark beauty of this world. Surely a place so stunning could not be all bad.

"You shouldn't go out," her sister told her, as the sun lowered. "Not tonight. It's not safe."

The girl nodded. It wasn't a lie then. She had meant to obey—she always did, in the moment. But when her sister and her friend both retired, exhausted by their travel, she lingered awake, staring out the window at the sunset-streaked horizon.

It's not safe, her sister had told her, and that had been right. But would there ever be a safe time to do what she came here to do? She cast a glance back at her sister and her friend, their faces soft and peaceful in sleep.

The girl had been called reckless many times in her short life. And that word would be hurled at her countless times in the years to come, too—most often by people who loved her.

Her recklessness was not borne of foolishness or stupidity. Always, it was borne of love.

She was careful not to wake those precious souls as she slipped out into the dusk, alone.

The humans who lived in the world of vampires did not try to stop her. She wandered past the bounds of the human districts, away from the tiny stone cottages to the open expanses of lush greenery beyond. She watched the sky turn dusky behind the silhouettes of ivy-wrapped spires in the distance and the sea thrashing beyond them. Everywhere she looked, she found a new amazement— bloody red blooms with emerald leaves, architecture crafted with such grand, deadly precision, rolling hills and obsidian cliffs. Eventually, she came to an empty garden of hedges and cascading flowers overlooking the ocean.

She didn't see the bench at first. Nor did she see the man sitting upon it. He was so still that he blended into the landscape. When she noticed him, she *froze mid-step. But her dull human senses, of course, were slower than his. He already knew she was there.*

He said something to her in a language she didn't understand. At her confused stare, he spoke again, this time in the common tongue of the human nations to the east.

"No need to be frightened," he said.

His voice was smooth as the dark green cape that fell down his back. He turned to peer at her over his shoulder, and the sight of his face made her already-quickening heartbeat stutter. Even that sliver of his profile was a thing of such devastating elegance. Vampires, after all, are predators. Their beauty is a spider's silk. His smile, a slow bloom over a perfect mouth, wound around her human heart thread by thread.

"Quite a view, isn't it?" He looked out to the horizon. "I enjoy the quiet. But I don't mind company." He shifted on the stone bench, offering her a seat.

He was beautiful, yes. But it was not his beauty that made the girl sit beside him that night.

She tentatively stepped closer and saw a flower in his hands.

This vampire looked nothing like the one she had befriended in the Citadel's captivity. That man had been so sickly, all the smooth polish of vampirism sanded away. But now, the sight of that flower reminded her of the dried petals lined up upon the cell floor. It reminded her what she had come here to prove: there was light in all hearts. Even those belonging to creatures of the dark.

She sat beside him. He smelled of roses, with just a hint of rot. His gaze roved over her in a way that made her very conscious of everything beneath her robes. The back of her neck prickled. But she smiled at him, anyway.

"Thank you. It's a gorgeous view."

"It has been a while since I've seen one of your kind around here."

"Humans?" she asked, confused. The first thing that came to mind, even though she knew that he surely saw humans often. It was difficult to think. Her mind felt as if it had been coated in syrup, like a honey cake left out in the sun.

A smirk curled his mouth as he glanced pointedly down at her robes. "No, lovely. Your kind." He brushed a stray strand of curly hair behind her ear. His touch skittered across the delicate skin of her cheek, brief before she pulled away. "You are very brave."

You might ask: why did she not run?

Didn't she know what he was? Didn't she know she was staring into the face of her own demise?

Later, the girl would not remember most of this night. But she would, too, ask herself this question. She would remember the thrill, low in her stomach, of standing upon the line between light and darkness. She would remember just how good its touch felt. So good she forgot about the claws.

"Why would I be scared?" she said, more carefree than she felt. "I only came to talk."

He laughed, charming and disarming. "Then we will talk. How I've longed for good conversation." He stood and extended a hand to her. "Come with me, and you can tell me all the ways I have sinned."

Why did she not run?

Was it her faith, so bright it blinded her? Was it her desperation, pushing her ever closer to the cliff? Was it his magic, drenching her in that honeyed haze?

Or perhaps the truth is simpler. Perhaps mortals, like gods, are mesmerized by their own damnation.

She took his hand.

CHAPTER FORTY-TWO

The Sanctum of Soul was cold. This was the first thought that returned to me.

Something smooth pressed against my cheek. I pushed myself up, and when my eyes opened, I startled.

I was on a sheet of ice-frosted glass, mirror smooth, Luce and Asar asleep beside me. My own face stared back at me. At first, I thought it was a reflection. But this version of myself was different—younger, hair longer, face rounder. She was transparent, like a reflection of a reflection of a reflection. This girl wore Dawndrinker robes. She seemed like she hadn't yet grown into her freckles.

I scrunched my nose. She scrunched her nose. I opened my mouth. She opened hers—revealing blunt human teeth.

My past self. The part of myself that died when I Turned.

Eerie.

I stood. My reflection did, too, standing upside down beneath me, her feet to mine. I wondered if she let out the same exhale of amazement that I did.

I thought after awhile all these tableaus of death would start to get mundane. But the Descent, it seemed, just kept surprising me.

The glass stretched out in all directions. The rocks and trees and vegetation of the terrain all sat atop it, creating little paths. Here, the leaves grew and turned and fell in a constant loop, caught in the endless passage of time. Their reflections were barren beneath the glass, leaves silver ghosts. Far ahead, a single tower rose up—a fountain, water running the wrong way, mirrored on all sides. The temple.

But none of this was as staggering as the sky. Above us, instead of darkness or sun or our past path through purgatory, was the mortal world, upside down, grayed out and cloudy. Cities and seas, plains and mountains. It floated by like clouds.

It was extraordinary.

Asar stirred. Luce had already gotten up, sniffing him. She had no reflection at all.

I shook him, and his eyes fluttered open. The sight of his left eye struck me for a moment—was it brighter than before?—but he was on his feet too quickly for me to discern why.

When he took in the scene around us, he, too, was speechless.

"The boundary between the mortal and immortal worlds," I said softly. I pointed to the sky. "Is that—"

"The land of the living," Asar finished. Then he gestured to the glass, and the shadowy reflection beneath it. "The underworld."

"That's—"

I stopped mid-sentence as my eyes lowered to Asar's reflection.

It was a blacked-out silhouette, smoke pouring from it, as if seen through the depths of nightfire. Like he was burning eternal. The only visible feature was one bright white eye—his right, the opposite side of his scars.

I gasped. "Why do you look like that?"

Asar hid his surprise well. But I knew him well enough by now to recognize it—those two quick blinks before he nonchalantly looked away.

"I have an interesting relationship to the underworld," he said dismissively. "I lost half of myself to it the night I tried to bring Ophelia back, and a little more with every night I spent warding over Morthryn."

I supposed that theory made as much sense as any, which was to say, none. Still, the stare of his silhouetted reflection was unsettling. It was both a perfect likeness and looked nothing like him, as if another visage had been transposed over his own.

But we didn't have time to sit around dissecting it, as much as the priestess in me would have loved to. We were more exposed here than in any Sanctum before. This close to death, the scent of our life would be overwhelming to the dead. Whatever was coming after us—and there would be things coming after us—would be here quick.

"That's the temple." Asar pointed to the tower in the distance. "It's the inflection point between purgatory and the underworld."

"That's where we do the ceremony?"

"That's where Alarus's presence will be closest. Yes."

The intersection between life and death and gods.

I'll be watching, Atroxus had told me.

Would he come? The veil between the mortal and immortal worlds would be so thin there that any tear, any foothold, would allow a god to pass through, even though it wasn't their territory. My presence would offer Atroxus his. And Asar's would call to Nyaxia.

It wasn't too far to walk. I drew my sword—Asar's sword—and Asar kept his magic at the ready. Shadows clustered in the reflection of the glass, barely resembling humanoid silhouettes—the dead, peering through to the living, but at least those spirits were safely on the other side of the veil. The ones I was more concerned about were the shadows I didn't quite see out of the corners of my eyes. I kept catching movement in the trees, only to find nothing when I turned my head. But as the trees grew thicker, I realized what I was seeing. The silhouette was faceless, near formless, at the very top of the tree. It stood on the highest branch, which seemed too thin to support the weight of a person, arms reaching up. Its limbs stretched too long, open hands dissolving into smoke.

"Don't look at it," Asar whispered. "Let it stay distracted. We don't need to rush being noticed."

I turned away quick. "What is it doing?"

"Reaching for life. It's been here a long time. That's why it looks like that."

Like it was barely clinging to what it once was.

The worst fate I could imagine. Never to rest in death. Never to find life again.

I shuddered.

I wouldn't let that fate befall Saescha. I wouldn't.

The silence stretched much longer than I'd expected it to. With every passing uneventful minute, the bowstring of our tension grew tighter. Asar's shadows poured from his hand now, and mine pulsed at the edge of the blade. Luce was low to the ground, reacting to every minute movement.

But I was the one who saw them first. The hands crawling down from the tops of the trees. Countless hands, all at once, like the blanket of nightfall.

I raised my blade and jabbed my arm into Asar's side. "Look—"

But Malach didn't come from the trees. He came from beneath.

He burst from the darkness. I saw his face only for a moment, handsome and smiling, fangs bared, as I had so often seen it in my nightmares.

I didn't have time to react before he grabbed me. My back was against the tree. Malach's face was inches from my own, smiling as he had the night he Turned me. His bodiless hands dug into me, reaching past flesh, as if to rip out my heart itself.

"We share taste in women, brother," he sneered. "But I got this one first."

For a moment, I was utterly petrified.

And then, I was angry.

"I already killed you," I snarled.

I poured all my power into that sword as I drove it into him, using the blade that was supposed to be his and the magic that he had never intended to give me. I struck right over the wound I'd given him the last time I'd skewered his heart.

He wore the same look of surprise as he had that night. It was just as satisfying the second time around.

He staggered backward. Over his shoulder, I saw Asar freeing himself from the wraiths as Luce held them back. He wore a proud smirk that made warmth rise in my chest. Darkness wrapped around him, flowing like water around his graceful movements. It was as if it thrived down here.

Malach regained his footing and whirled to Asar. When I'd known him, the prince had been elegant—cruel, yes, but beneath a veneer of discipline. All that was gone now, peeled away by death. He descended upon Asar like a rabid beast.

The two of them collided, stars in the night.

"This was mine." Malach's voice was a twisted distortion of what it once was. "Everything that you have. You're the bastard. The whore's son. Our father's dog, only suitable to lap up scraps. Crying over dead pets and dead lovers."

He clawed at Asar, his rage mindless. Through every strike, every blow, the words continued. He wanted Asar's reaction. He wanted to goad him into mistakes, just as he had in life.

But Asar's face was a mask. The thread of connection between us remained taut. I could feel his anger, hot but restrained; his control, careful in his grip. The two of us circled Malach. He landed his strikes, but we recovered quickly. Bit by bit, we chipped away at him.

In the end, he was only a wraith. Just like all the others.

I distracted him enough that Asar could get in a particularly devastating blow. With a burst of darkness, Malach's translucent form shuddered like a reflection in disrupted water.

When the smoke faded, Asar's fist was closed around Malach's throat, tentacles of darkness pinning him as he flailed.

"They'll never accept you," Malach growled. "You were never one of us, and everyone could always tell."

Asar held him there. The shadows took and took, serpents greedily consuming whatever remained of Malach's soul. It was horrifying. It was awe-inspiring.

Asar looked upon his half brother as he screamed and snarled, as the very essence of his being was consumed.

And he smiled like a man who was seeing something he had dreamed of for a very, very long time. Serene and calm and cruelly joyous.

He didn't dignify Malach's taunts with an acknowledgment. Instead, he looked at me, extending a silent offer.

Soul death was a horrifying fate. I wouldn't wish it on anyone.

Anyone, maybe, except for Malach.

Some souls, I thought as I drove the blade into Malach's heart, deserved to burn.

And burn Malach did. He let out a screech as his form exploded into lightning-hot spandrels. Asar jerked me out of the way, shielding me from the blowback. I jolted at his touch for a reason I couldn't identify—something felt odd about it, even within the connection we shared.

But I didn't have time to question it.

Because as Asar and I hit the ground, a low hiss slithered from above us.

I lifted my head.

Oh, gods.

The dead approached in a wave of darkness—wraiths upon wraiths upon wraiths, crawling down from the trees, up from the ground, from behind rocks and through grass and even unfurling from nothingness.

All drawn by an unmistakable call.

"So unfair, that she gets the justice that I never did."

Ophelia's voice reverberated in the veil that separated life and death. The power of it made goosebumps rise on my arms. More powerful than I'd ever heard it.

The hush of darkness fell over us, second by second, red dusk over the desert.

My back pressed to Asar's as the dead encroached. Luce circled our legs, growling and hissing.

"Why do you get to have this?" she moaned. "Another heart to break, when I am here, torn apart upon the pieces you left behind?"

Where was it coming from? She was so near, as if I'd see her when I turned my head, perpetually just out of view.

"Let me help you, Ophelia," Asar said.

I could feel his fear rising, quick as the tide. His fingernails bit into my wrist, grip trembling with force.

A cold touch brushed us, making my heart jump against my ribs.

"You hold on so tight, my love," she crooned.

"Ophelia—" Asar started.

"But nothing can stop her from slipping through your fingers."

I whirled to him, grabbing at his shoulders, panic spearing me.

But I saw his face only for a split second, eyes wide as he reached for me.

Before a great, terrible force wrapped around me, plunging my heart into cold water as Ophelia yanked me away.

CHAPTER FORTY-THREE

Ophelia's face was distilled devastation. She wrapped herself around me. Wind whipped around us as we hurtled through the air. She barely resembled a mortal form now, a face that flickered in and out of view, too many limbs that bent the wrong way and stretched too far. She tightened and tightened around me, prying my thoughts open and sliding inside.

I saw myself, a child kneeling at the altar of the Citadel.

Lying on the bed in my wedding gown.

Smiling with Saescha. Laughing with Eomin. Praying. Eating. Sleeping. Swimming. Faster and faster, as she tore through my memories like she was rifling through a drawer.

She drew back, thrusting me back to reality. We were on the ground again, my body aching and broken. The upside-down world of mortals spun above me. The underworld thrashed below. I looked up and glimpsed the tower looming over us. I tried to move my head to look for Asar, but she grabbed me and forced it back again. Her breath was cold, quick, a useless mimicry of life—one of the only ones she had left. I felt her pleasure, tangled hopelessly with pain, as she licked the remnants of my life off her lips.

I started to scream for Asar, but she lowered her mouth to mine, plunging back into my past.

I was in the temple of Secrets, weeping before an altar.

Asar's hands were on my skin. His mouth. His body. I was crying out his name as he pushed into me—

Ophelia recoiled. A shock of her pain and jealousy pulsed through me—but that paled compared to her yearning hunger. I had never felt more alive than I had in those moments, and she sensed that.

"He is such an attentive lover," she breathed. Her darkness reached deeper, again, into those memories—

I was on the altar, on top of Asar, his blood on my lips as we held each other—

She withdrew. I saw her face for a moment, taut with pain.

"He never held me like that."

For a moment, she sounded . . . confused. Sad. Not angry.

She sounded young. She sounded almost mortal.

My brow furrowed. My lips parted.

But then the sound of my name cut through the air. My gaze leapt beyond Ophelia—across the mirrored-glass plains, where Asar fought toward us.

The dead overwhelmed him, but he pushed through. His gaze, even from this distance, was fixed upon me, that one scarred eye shining star-bright against the dark, plumes of silver pouring from it. His mouth opened, and though the sounds of the death drowned him out, I knew he was calling my name.

He was too far away.

Ophelia watched him too. Her sadness reverberated between us.

"How he calls for you. He called for me that way, once."

Then the sadness shattered, her face snapping back to me.

"I called for him seventy-two times. Seventy-two unanswered calls. How many will you make before the end?"

She lunged for me again, invading me, splitting me open. The pain tore muscle from bone, soul from flesh. I didn't mean to scream, but my body had no other reaction to what was happening to me.

I was nineteen, on a boat to the land of vampires.

I was four, sitting on my father's lap.

I was twelve, watching Atroxus bite into an apricot.

I was here, body failing, head lolling, pain consuming, helpless as Ophelia killed me.

I'd dropped my sword, and even if I hadn't, it would do nothing to her. I lashed out blindly with my magic, but she absorbed it as if it were nothing.

Distantly, I heard Asar calling my name. Still too far. Too slow.

And what could he do, anyway, to stop this?

Ophelia was no wraith or souleater. She was—

She was—

I forced my head up. Forced my eyes open. She drew back, wiping my life from the corner of her mouth. For a moment, I saw her face— really *saw* her, as she had once been. Asar had remembered her as a flawless being. A representation of everything he had never been able to attain. Noble, respected, cruel, beautiful.

But that wasn't all she was.

Bloody tears streaked her cheeks. I reached out and touched her cheek. At first, I felt nothing—she had no solid body—but then . . .

There. Her fear. Her vulnerability.

Sometimes they just need someone to listen, Asar had once said of the dead.

How many times had I done that, as a missionary? I knew how to mend a broken soul. And Ophelia's was shattered.

I reached through the connection she'd forged between us. I let her anger and grief and agony flow through me. I let myself feel everything within her.

She had suffered so much for so long.

And just as she was about to descend upon me again, I murmured, "I'm sorry this happened to you."

I meant it.

She jerked back. Brief confusion overtook her face, only to drown beneath rage. Her mouth twisted. "You are sorry? How does your pity help me now?"

Her grip tightened, tearing a little more of my soul apart. The pain left me breathless.

But I managed to say, "Sometimes someone else just needs to feel it with you. Like when you're a child with a scraped knee. Do you remember that?"

She hesitated. Blinked. Her face came into view again, holding its form a little longer than before.

"You were little once," I whispered. "Do you remember what it was like to feel that way? Like someone else's affection could fix everything."

Her memory, weak and distant, flickered by. A tiny child with long dark hair, crying on a stone step. The safety of a brief, passing embrace.

Human or vampire. It was the same.

Ophelia, I knew, had not thought of her mortality for a long, long time. It shook her. Her sadness was overwhelming, grief for the life she'd once had, nearly powerful enough to break us both. But I held on through it, pulling that connection closer.

Quickly, her vulnerability hardened again. Pain wrenched through me as she grabbed me, claws biting my flesh.

"It was not supposed to end this way. It was such a—such a terrible, terrible end."

I felt it with her. Saw how Malach and his friends had drawn out her suffering. I felt every one of those seventy-two unanswered calls for help.

"No," I said. "It wasn't fair. It wasn't right."

"I live it every moment. Over and over again. I cannot escape it."

"I know."

Because of what she was. Because of Asar's butchered attempt to bring her back to life.

Her face was clear now, her nose nearly touching mine. She blinked, and the tears that slid down her cheeks were clear.

"He was supposed to love me. And yet, he did this to me."

Asar. I felt the pain of her attempted resurrection. From the start, it was wrong—I could see that now. She'd known it. She'd tried to resist it, but Asar had just kept pulling her back.

"He didn't mean to, Ophelia. He loved you."

She shook her head.

"He did not love me. He did not even see me."

"That can all be true at once."

She looked dismayed, like a frightened child.

"It shouldn't be that way," she wept.

"No," I murmured.

I reached further into her soul, and for a moment, she balked, preparing to push me away. I was so exposed that if she'd chosen to, she could have killed me. For a moment, I was sure that she was going to.

Out of the corner of my eye, I saw Asar getting closer. Almost close enough to reach me.

Don't, I wanted to tell him. Not yet.

Ophelia acquiesced, letting me see the true nature of her. Gods, no wonder she'd become so destructive. If the fate of the wraiths seemed horrible, this was torturous—half of her soul living, half of it dead, and all of it twisted and deformed beyond recognition. She fed on wraiths and emotion because she was starving for life, but she was also so tired. Utterly exhausted.

She looked it now, her icy eyes starting to flutter closed. She felt more solid against me. I could almost wrap my arms around her.

"I'm so tired. I'm so hungry." Her forehead leaned against my shoulder. I laid my hands over her back.

"Let yourself rest," I said softly. "It's all right. I promise."

"I'm afraid."

"You won't be alone."

I lifted my gaze over her shoulder. The waves of dead were thinning, scattering. She'd let go of her call. And Asar ran for me, Luce at his heels, sheer panic on his face.

I lifted one finger. *Wait.*

I understood now why Asar hadn't been able to explain to me how he helped souls pass. Even I wasn't sure what I was doing. I could see Ophelia's broken spirit, all the places where her wounds had been stitched together. I soothed them all, one by one. I saw all her darkest fears. All her shattered hopes. I saw her for everything that she was.

This was how Shadowborn magic could heal. Shadows were the negative space of a soul. I let myself spill through them.

"I want to go," she told me.

If I opened the door for her, she would step through. But here, I faltered. I didn't know how to pierce that veil for her, how to draw back the curtain—

Then, magic that mirrored mine enveloped us. Asar's thumb

swept over my back in a way that said, *Thank you and I'm proud of you and I'm so glad you're alive.*

But I didn't look at him, and he didn't look at me. Instead, he reached into that darkness with me, and he opened the door for her.

Ophelia lifted her gaze to him.

There was no more anger. No more hunger. No more heartbreak. Just sadness and exhaustion.

And, at last, relief.

"I'm sorry, Ophelia," he said softly.

He meant it. His regret had ruled him for so long. It seemed a little cruel that it was why he hadn't been able to help her all these years. He couldn't help her pass because he couldn't let go of everything that tethered him to her. Not love, but regret and shame.

She stared at him as the veil parted for her.

She didn't forgive him. That would be too tidy.

But she let go of her anger. Let go of her pain.

Her body disintegrated like ashes into the wind.

CHAPTER FORTY-FOUR

I sank to the ground, Asar beside me. I was trembling. No wonder Asar looked so drained after he'd helped Eomin. I was ready to keel over, and I'd had help.

Asar pulled me into a fierce embrace. I melted against it as Luce nuzzled my shoulder.

"I thought—" he said against my hair.

"Me too." I let out a shaky breath. "Me too."

It only hit me now exactly how close I'd just come to death, and exactly how much I wasn't ready for it. I clung to him and held his scent deep in my lungs.

This might be the last time. Enjoy it.

But he pulled away too soon, holding me by the shoulders and looking hard into my face.

"You are so foolish," he said, "and so extraordinary."

I smiled weakly. "I've been told that before. Mostly the first part."

It was easier to joke than to acknowledge the emotion in his voice. Or how much I enjoyed hearing him call me extraordinary—enough that it almost made me believe it.

But we didn't have time to bask. The dead had scattered when Ophelia had let go, perhaps put off by her embrace of death. But they still hovered around us, watching at a distance. Even if they hung back like cautious carrion birds for now, soon they would descend again.

My gaze skimmed the horizon. I couldn't count the wraiths. And yet, even among so many, I could've sworn I found Saescha in the crowd, watching me with hungry eyes, her hand to her torn-out throat.

Asar's eyes searched my face. He squeezed my shoulder, leaving the question unspoken: *Ready?*

No.

But I never would be.

Asar got to his feet and helped me to mine. We turned to the tower. It was taller than it had looked from a distance—an illusion, or had it grown? Now the waterfalls stretched so far into the sky that they seemed to puncture the boundary to the upside-down mortal world above. I stared at the sky, and with a bittersweet clench in my chest, I recognized the shores of Vostis drifting by—an endless ocean, a white sand shore, a lush forest, a great stone citadel. A part of me wanted to seize Asar's hand and point at it, tell him, *That's my home.*

But that word didn't feel right. My heart did not belong to Vostis anymore.

Hand in hand, Asar and I approached the tower. I let out a little gasp as my feet stepped through the glass, my underworld self shivering with the disruption. Asar didn't flinch. The silhouette of his reflection didn't, either. The raw emotion of our reunion was gone now. I watched his face, still and focused, as we continued into the water. Luce walked beside us, steps light on the surface, rippling but not sinking in. It was warm, and unnaturally still. I glanced behind us and still couldn't tell where the water ended and the shore began.

Asar stopped when we were waist-deep. His fingertips traced a circle on the surface, silver light trailing behind his touch. A thread of darkness followed his hand, grasping for me. My magic joined it before I had to ask it to.

I thought of all the times I had told Oraya that magic came from the heart. An impulse beyond thought or logic.

My magic reached for him. My heart reached for him.

He dug into his pack and withdrew the first relic. Body—the obsidian branch bearing Alarus's blood. Asar held it for a moment, then placed it in the spell.

I felt the power immediately. A gust of wind pulled strands of curly hair around my face. The wraiths let out a wordless moan, pushing forward. Something at the center of the world seemed to crack.

Asar, unfazed by it all, swept his hand over the circle. The branch quivered in its center as he murmured a hymn in a tongue I didn't understand—none of the countless ancient languages I'd studied at the Citadel. It was striking, and a little sad, like an artifact of a time long-ago past. Asar's voice rendered the syllables like music.

The magic started to pull at me, deep within. The surface of the water trembled, darkness swirling in the reflections. The weight of the spell shocked me at first, and my hold on it wavered. Asar's free hand brushed mine in a way that said, *You can do this.*

He was right. I could. The magic was heavy, but with his help, I could navigate it. A part of me even enjoyed it—it had been a long time since I'd challenged myself with a spell that actually felt right. And though so much of what we were doing went against everything I'd been taught, it felt like a key sliding into place.

We moved to the next phase, connecting Body to Breath. Asar drew another circle, and here he placed the next relic—the poppy petals. With them came the rush of breath of a first kiss.

A distant hum rose from the depths beneath us. The water had begun to churn. The tower loomed over us, black and red streaking the waterfalls running up its sides.

A shadow encroached beneath the surface of the water.

I looked down to see my own reflection curled up like a frightened child, eyes wide. And Asar's—I couldn't tell what was happening to his. His silhouette had gotten darker, the eye brighter, smoke now billowing off him and spiraling into the dark pit at the center of our ritual.

We moved to the next phase. Every step hurt now—the weight of the spell grew nearly unbearable. Asar drew another circle. Psyche. Here, he placed the ring. The memories of Nyaxia and Alarus on their wedding day, two ghostlike, silvery silhouettes rose, embraced, dissipated.

Death was so close. The sea churned. Luce paced beside us, her shadowy form shivering with the waves of magic. Out of the corner of my eye, I saw that wave of darkness approaching—the wraiths drawing closer to the shore, hands outstretched and heads bowed, like they couldn't tell whether they were eager or terrified. I couldn't tell, either. The dark power of what we were doing coursed through me in intoxicating waves. But the danger of it drew closer, too, undeniable.

I felt the veils to the underworld part. Felt our call extend to the world beyond, reaching out for just the right soul.

And I felt it reach back for us.

My heart was pounding. Sweat dripped into my eyes. Asar worked diligently. His scars glowed over straining muscles. His eye gleamed. His Heir Mark was stark in the darkness, even though we were closer to death than we'd ever been.

We moved to the next position. Drew the next circle.

He placed the arrow there. It hummed and shimmered, glistening with honeyed gold.

Something snapped into place. Pain careened through me.

Darkness roiled beneath the surface of the water. Something pressed to its underside, barely taking on the shape of a body.

The door to death creaked open slowly. Of the countless spirits within, one stepped closer.

I raised my gaze to Asar. He was staring at me now, not at the spell. Wind whipped his hair over his forehead.

No, this was wrong. I felt it in my bones.

I couldn't do this.

The truth of it struck me, immovable. I had made such a horrible mistake. What had I done?

"Asar—"

I wasn't sure what I intended to say—to tell him to stop, to tell him I was sorry, to tell him the truth of what I had done.

But he took my hands in his, clasping them around the symbol of Alarus's betrayal and mine.

"You'll need to do the rest, Iliae," he said.

My brows knitted. Dread flooded me.

This wasn't right.

Something wasn't right.

"That's ridiculous," I said.

But Asar had already started drawing the next line. Forming the next circle.

The surface of the water cracked like broken glass. The mouth of oblivion at the center of our spell opened.

I clutched Asar's hand, stopping him mid-movement.

"What are you doing?"

I could barely hear myself over the rising song of the underworld.

He cradled my hand in his, holding tenuous control of the spell between us.

"You can do it," he said. "Just focus. Keep the passageways clear, like I taught you."

I was slowly panicking, and he was here lecturing me about my technique.

"You're finishing this," I said, voice rising. "This is yours."

Asar finally—finally—looked at me. The sadness in his eyes split me apart.

"It's in my blood, Dawndrinker," he murmured. "In my bloodline. I can't finish it because I am a part of it. The offering of Soul."

The horrible realizations snapped into place.

I looked down at Asar's reflection again—that reflection that looked so familiar but I hadn't been able to place.

It looked familiar because I had seen it countless times, inked into scriptures and carved into church walls and woven into tapestries.

It was Alarus.

As if he had not had his fair share of mortal lovers, Atroxus had scoffed.

Soul. The most intrinsic piece of a spirit, and the hardest offering to satisfy. I felt so stupid for buying Asar's ridiculous excuse.

Soul demanded a sacrifice.

A descendant of a god, perhaps, might suffice.

"No," I bit out, but Asar just kept talking.

"Complete the ritual for Nyaxia. I made sure you'll be taken care of. It's not the sun, but she'll give you anything you ask of her. She'll give you your freedom."

I almost laughed as understanding dawned on me. He had, in-deed, had a visitor in Secrets. He'd learned of the sacrifice he could not avoid. And he had made a deal to save me as I had made one to save him. A cruel joke.

"Asar, I won't—"

"It's already done." He gripped my hand tight, knuckles white, gaze seizing mine in a way that made my words die. The only one I still had was *no, no, no*.

His throat bobbed. His brown eye gleamed.

"I never wanted anything so much as I wanted to show you that happy ending you so believe in, Mische," he murmured.

No.

His hand slipped from mine. Luce, forever loyal, came to his side.

No.

I reached for him—

But he stepped into the circle, the final offering to complete the ritual.

The spell opened for him, a gaping maw or a welcome embrace, swallowing him whole.

I screamed his name.

But death devoured the sound of my voice as the underworld split open like overripe fruit. The sky released a soundless scream.

The ritual completed.

And he was gone.

CHAPTER FORTY-FIVE

The spell ripped me apart. Consciousness slipped away, and when it returned, I was at the edge of the ritual circle. It burned silver, countless threads of light and darkness reaching into the hole at its center. A silhouette took blurry shape there, not yet defined, a ghost of what could be.

The sky shivered with the presence of the gods.

The earth quaked with the hunger of the dead.

I felt a spirit out in the ether, too powerful to be mortal, their head turning toward all these assembled pieces of their past.

But I still clung to Asar's soul. I couldn't see him anymore, but I could still feel him. The anchor at my chest, that stupid piece of magic he hadn't thought twice about, burned with his fading presence.

The ritual was trying to consume him.

I wouldn't let him go.

I couldn't let him go. That one thread of connection held my entire being.

I almost didn't even notice when the god of the sun appeared. Not until I felt the burning brilliance of his light scalding my back.

I still couldn't turn away from the thing at the center of the circle, grasping for life. That burning ember that remained of Asar.

"To think that he was once so great." Atroxus's voice was inevitable and cruel. "Look at how he fights for life. Nothing but a common mortal."

He was wrong. The blur at the center of the ritual wasn't Alarus. Not yet. I still held on to a piece of Asar, and I refused to let it go.

I turned. The sight of Atroxus nearly brought me to my knees. Golden light drenched him like honey, rays of sun pouring from behind his head, stark against the desolation of the Descent. This was not his territory, but we were closer to the world of the gods than we'd ever been before. His power leached through the veil—a force worthy of his crown.

He was more awe-inspiring than I had ever seen him.

And yet, in this moment, I hated him.

"You said you would spare him."

Atroxus laughed softly. Amusement sparkled in his eyes. He did always relish in the drama of his human followers.

"I kept my word. This is not my doing. Blame my brother for this. No one cares about a god's mortal love affairs. But it was sloppy of him to leave a drop of his bloodline in the mortal world. The rest of us take the appropriate measures against the unwanted byproducts of our human dealings." His smirk soured. "Apparently, Alarus could not even do that much. But why should I be surprised by that? For two thousand years, the world has been suffering the consequences of his mess. No longer. It ends today."

He lowered his gaze to me. It softened. The light of Atroxus's affection was so warm. It had been a long time since I'd felt it like this—like I had that morning when I first stood upon the steps of the Citadel.

"You have done so well," he murmured. "You have left your mark upon history today. Now make the final stroke of this tale."

Something searing hot was in my hand. I looked down to see the arrow there, glowing, the gold feathers quivering at its tail. Its power pulsed through me, the opposite of my Shadowborn magic in every way—dawn against dusk, fire against ice.

"Quickly," Atroxus said. "Nyaxia will come soon enough. But we will have raised a new dawn by then."

He spread his hands. Light spilled across the icy mirror of the boundary between the Descent and death, setting it aflame. The dead scattered away from it like rats fleeing a barn fire.

All but one. One priestess wraith, blood pouring from her throat, who looked at the sun like it was home.

I watched Saescha's eyes fall to me, the sadness in them infinite. She reached out.

My hand clenched around the arrow.

I still felt Asar's soul, clinging to life by my hold alone. The form at the center of the ritual let out a wordless scream, climbing to all fours. It wasn't anyone yet—neither Alarus nor Asar. With one more pull, I could bring Alarus back. But doing so would mean letting go of Asar forever.

And as I watched Atroxus, his arms lifted, chin tilted to the sun, a terrible realization fell over me.

This was not just about killing Alarus.

Atroxus was here because this was an inflection of power. A moment for him to seize more than had been given to him at the start of time. A surge that came with the true death of a god.

The power of the gods is communal. When one dies, another grows stronger.

No.

No, no, no.

I didn't say it aloud. But as if he heard it, Atroxus's rage exploded. White flames flared in his eyes.

"Do you understand what I am offering you?" he roared. Every word scorched my skin. "You swore yourself to me once. To the cause of bringing the light. I am offering you a sunrise."

The light kept growing, brighter and brighter. The wraiths now flattened against the ground, shielding themselves with arms or curling up into balls. Saescha had come closer still, staring at Atroxus with unfettered adoration.

I looked to the mortal world above, upside down in the sky, and with a start, I recognized it as Obitraes—the spires of the House of Shadow, and then, across the sea, the unmistakable rolling dunes of the House of Night.

"You understand better than most what Nyaxia created two thousand years ago." Atroxus's voice was inescapable. "An illness that would never stop spreading. Monsters that know nothing but hunger. They suffer, a'mara, as you have suffered. And it is not in their nature to stop. They will consume until there is nothing left. Unless we end it today."

I watched the sun, a great and terrible damnation, rise over the sky. I watched Atroxus's never-ending dawn flood across Obitraes.

Atroxus lowered himself to me and cradled my face.

"Think of what you are," he breathed. "Think of the gift you can give this world. There is no saving you, Mische Iliae. But after this, there will be no more monsters coming to devour children in the night." He showed me a little girl cowering in the human districts, screaming as a vampire sank his teeth into her throat. "There will be no more creatures coming to spread their plague to the human nations." He showed me a bloody shore, littered with bodies as an army of vampires fell upon the sands. "There will be no more end-less hungers for lives that should not exist." He showed me vam-pires starving in desert ruins, turning on each other in fruitless desperation.

He leaned closer. "And," he murmured, "there will be no more sisters dying at the hands of the one they loved most, nor any sisters who must carry the burden of that shame."

He showed me myself, falling upon Saescha as she screamed.

A sob escaped my lips. A tear slid down my cheek, rising to scald-ing steam under his caress. For a moment, he looked at me again the way he had on our wedding night. Back when I thought that this was love. "Do you not miss the sun, a'mara?"

I did miss the sun. I lifted my chin to that rising orb of light as it drenched me. The destined dawn. A horrible truth settled over me—that this was always intended to be the end. Salvation paid for with the blood of the unsalvageable souls. A dawn drenched in sin.

I remembered the sunlight feeling like hope. But this just felt like damnation.

My gaze settled on Saescha, her eyes wide with devotion, hands outstretched, and the love I felt for her dwarfed the warmth of Atrox-us's sunrise.

"I'm so sorry," I choked out.

And I drove the arrow into Atroxus's throat.

CHAPTER FORTY-SIX

Atroxus's eyes widened. He staggered backward, hand flying to his neck. Gold blood gushed from the wound, spattering my face.

He looked at me exactly as Malach had when I'd driven my sword through his chest. Like I had truly shocked him by existing beyond the bounds of what he thought I was. Sometimes they only see you for the first time when you force them to.

I rose to my feet as Atroxus, reeling with shock, drew himself up. Flames tore across the horizon as his fury rose. Whip cracks of lightning split across the sky.

He seized me by the shoulders, pulling me close. The fire consumed me, flooding my blood, my lungs, my eyes. I couldn't see anything but light. I couldn't feel anything but pain.

I was going to die, and it would be by the hand of the god I had sworn my soul to.

"I made you," he snarled. "You end with me."

"Then let me burn," I said.

And I yanked that arrow from his throat, and this time, I plunged it straight into his chest.

The two of us went up in flames together, god and traitor. It shakes the world when a god dies. It rearranges histories in mortal and immortal realms alike.

In his final moments, I watched the sun crack, shards spearing to earth like shooting stars.

Through it all, I clung to that thread of magic that connected me to what remained of Asar. The final steps of the resurrection spell came to me like a song someone had played for me once. All the notes sounded like him.

I reached for Asar's soul, the final sacrifice I could not make, as Atroxus roared his death cry.

As the sun shattered in the sky, falling into infinite pieces.

As my body, broken and charred, crumbled to the ground.

And the world plunged into eternal darkness.

CHAPTER FORTY-SEVEN

M ische."

He only said my name when he was worried about me. Now, it was fractured with almost-tears.

"Mische. Mische."

My eyes opened.

It was so dark. I was so cold. Asar leaned over me. Gods, he was beautiful—surely a dream. Smoke rolled off him. His left eye burned bright. Something looked different about him in a way I couldn't place.

Maybe it was because I was dreaming.

Yes. I was dreaming.

But what a nice dream it was.

"You foolish, magnificent woman," Asar was saying. "What have you done?"

Something cool and wet fell onto my cheek.

Rain.

No.

I tried to touch Asar's face. I frowned.

"Why are you crying?" I tried to say. But my tongue wouldn't form words.

Light and darkness swam through the sky like fish through a pond, circling ever tighter. The air was thick with immortality, restless with gods thrown into turmoil.

What a strange dream.

My vision faded.

"Where is he?"

My lashes fluttered. A stunning woman stood over us. Nyaxia was night and shadow and blood. She was a million shades of darkness. Her hair floated around her, a blanket of stormy night. Her eyes were bright with fury, bloody lips twisted in rage and grief.

She stood over the remnants of the ritual.

"This is not the task I gave you," she snarled.

She whirled to Asar. He cradled me close, as if to protect me. *Silly man,* I thought, through waning consciousness. *You can't protect me from a god's rage. It's already taken me.*

"You," she breathed, exhaling the word like an execution order. "I gave you the order to resurrect him. Instead, you have stolen his power. You think that because you have some pitiful drop of his blood in yours, you are worthy of what he was?" She approached us, darkness deepening with every step. "You are no god. You betrayed me."

"She killed Atroxus to save your people." Asar held me so tightly. "She—"

"What good does that do me?" Nyaxia roared. The dead shrank back. The sky quaked. The charred remains of Atroxus's body scattered across the icy ground. "I wanted my husband back. Instead, I have *you.*"

"You have vengeance. You have an endless night for your children. And you have Atroxus's head, if you want it."

Asar was trying so hard. I could see that, even as I slipped between layers of consciousness, in and out. But he did not understand Nyaxia the way I did. I fought for breath as I watched her go to what remained of Atroxus's body. She leaned down and picked up the arrow, still intact.

I sensed her pain as she observed it. Her betrayal. It had been her husband's weapon, after all, originally intended for her heart.

And it was a dangerous thing to offer a broken heart blood instead of love.

Nyaxia's tears fell, blood-red, to her enemy's ashes. She cradled the arrow to her chest. Then she looked up at the blackened sky, endless ink from which endless possibilities could be written.

I tried to reach for her, tried to say, *Wait, it doesn't have to be this way.* But I couldn't move.

And I saw it, the moment that Nyaxia decided to discard love in favor of power. The moment she decided that if she could not have her husband, she would have an empire.

She turned back to Asar, her gaze cold again.

"I suppose now you shall beg me to save her." Her voice dripped with bitterness.

Asar's thumb stroked back and forth, back and forth, on my charred arm. He was careful to keep his voice from wavering. "I failed you. But she didn't. She gave you this victory."

Nyaxia's lip curled. "You deny me my love but ask me to give you yours. It hardens a heart to lose what you love most. And you will need that steel for the war to come."

"Please—" Asar begged.

But Nyaxia had already turned away. She looked to the sky, churning with the attention of gods.

"The others are coming," she said. "I have no desire to see them tonight. You can come with me if you wish."

Asar didn't speak. He didn't move. He clutched me, as if he could hold me tight enough to keep death from taking me. Darkness rolled over me, then parted, and when I could see again, Nyaxia was watching us both.

She scoffed. "Very well, then. Let them take you. Perhaps they will let you hold her head as I held my lover's once."

Don't let her go, I wanted to tell Asar. *She can be saved.*

Like Ophelia could be saved. Like all the others. I could see it in her still, that rapidly closing wound of vulnerability. I looked at her and saw the young minor deity she had once been in Alarus's memories of her, full of possibility and love.

As she brushed past us, I tried to reach for her. My muscles, torn and burned, wouldn't work. I managed only a twitch of my fingers.

But maybe she saw it anyway, because she hesitated. Something indecipherable passed over her face.

She lowered herself to me, fingers of bloody night touching my cheek, as if in curiosity.

"She's one of yours," Asar said—still trying, to the end, for me. He'd fight to the very end for me. "She's the best of us. She—"

"She is a broken bird," Nyaxia said. She straightened. And maybe, just for a moment, she looked at Asar with genuine empathy.

"If you wish to be a god, then save her yourself."

"No—" Asar bit out.

But the sky had opened up, the veil to the world of the gods torn open. And Nyaxia was already gone.

MY BREATH RATTLED. My chest hurt. The pain was starting to set in now. The gods appeared, and I danced closer to death.

"She killed him. She killed him!"

Vitarus, the god of vitality and plague, was the first to arrive, crashing from the heavens in a cloud of rain and light. One of his arms was covered in green moss, flowers growing from his flesh— the other, blackened with decay. That was the hand he used to grab a fistful of Atroxus's ashes.

Ix was next, the goddess of fertility and sex—the most stunning being I had ever seen. Her gown wrapped around her body and floated back into the sky, the red of broken virginity and childbirth pains. Copper hair tumbled over her shoulders and pooled among Atroxus's remains as she fell to her knees.

Then Srana, the goddess of machinery and science, with skin of polished bronze and eyes of ticking clockwork. Zarux, the god of rain and sea, who walked upon a bed of storm clouds and waves. Shiket, the goddess of war and justice, six golden blades fanning from her back like steel wings. They surrounded us, taking in the ritual, the dead, Atroxus's corpse.

My lashes fluttered. Darkness took my hand. I fought it.

Not yet.

I couldn't die yet.

"They tried to resurrect a god and murdered another," Vitarus said. "This cannot go unpunished."

"Execute him," Shiket snarled, looming over Asar. "What else can be done?"

Asar shielded me, as if preparing to go down fighting the gods themselves. But another voice rang out above the others, quiet and deafening, ageless, smooth as time itself.

"He cannot be killed."

Acaeja, goddess of fate and sorcery, lowered from the sky. Her white eyes were wide open, as if taking in the rapid changes of fate set in motion by these events. Her six wings folded behind her, each offering a window into a different potential future. Every one of them now was shrouded in darkness.

"He may not be a god by birth," she said, "but he now carries the power of Alarus. It would be unwise to execute him yet, when he could still be of use."

I let out a rattling breath that was almost a laugh. It was just like when Asar had saved me. All of it was a circle, repeating over and over again.

Asar said something, but my consciousness faded.

Not yet, I begged.

"What of her?" someone asked.

I forced my eyes open. Glowing chains had appeared around Asar. He clung to me as they tried to drag him back. But he refused to let me go, even as those chains wrapped themselves around his throat, his wrists. Even as the gods themselves tried to tear him away.

I realized, as my fading vision took in his tear-streaked face, that Asar would never let me go. Not in life, and not in death. He would shatter it all for me.

"Let go," he rasped. "Let go, Mische, and I will find you. I will find you."

My lashes fluttered. Some god somewhere uttered a dismissive term. I was no god. The only thing that had ever made me special was the favor of a god who was now dead. I was not useful to anyone. I was not worth saving.

Shiket ripped me from Asar's grip and tossed me dismissively aside.

My neck snapped. My body broke. My chest tore open beneath her blade, black blood gushing free.

Somewhere very far away, Asar's voice echoed:

Stop! I need her.

I need her.

I need her.

A smile twitched at my bloody lips. I remembered those words. I remembered how he had used them to save my life, once, an age ago.

But they did not save me now.

There, in a broken heap of flesh, upon the discarded ashes of my god, I died alone.

PART SEVEN

DEATH

CHAPTER FORTY-EIGHT

The sun beat down hot on the back of my neck. The scent of flowers surrounded me, almost dizzying in its strength. I knelt in the garden, damp earth on my knees, staring at the pile of golden feathers.

"Ugh." Saescha's sound of disgust jerked me awake. "Get away from that, Mische. It's dirty, and it's already gone."

It didn't seem dirty. The firefinch's body lay among the roses as if it had all been arranged intentionally, an artful tableau of death. Its wings splayed among the ruby petals like it could, at any moment, leap into flight. The splashes of crimson echoed the blood on its chest.

A realization fell over me, like a word that had been on the tip of my tongue now springing to the front of my mind.

I looked up. Saescha was gone, and so was the sun.

"No," I said. "I don't think it is."

I reached down, and the bird ignited, golden feathers twisting into flames. It leapt up into the sky, burning against the velvet night.

I smiled up at it, touching an old tattoo on my arm. It was a phoenix after all, just as I thought.

Asar's voice was warm against my ear.

"Do not be afraid of death, Dawndrinker. Make death afraid of you."

I watched the bird burn, and I let myself rise.

I LAY IN a field of flowers. Dust filled my mouth. Mist shrouded my eyes. I closed them, opened them, closed them again. I wanted to let myself float away. Wanted to sink into the earth and let flowers sprout from my flesh.

No. Not yet.

Not yet.

I opened my eyes and stared up at the sky. Endless colors danced against the darkness—the green of fresh spring, the purple of night-fall, the red of blood.

I lifted my hand. There was no more blood on it. Just smooth brown skin.

Smooth brown skin, with a faint silver sheen to it, the sky peeking through the slightly translucent outline.

Footsteps approached. Someone knelt next to me.

I turned my head to see a man peering down, brow furrowed. He swept moon-silver eyes over me and pushed a strand of blond hair from his face.

"Get up," he said.

He didn't bother to introduce himself. But maybe he knew he didn't have to. I recognized him.

I took his hand, and he helped me stand.

"Welcome to the underworld," Vincent, dead King of the Night-born, said to me. "I hear we have some work to do."

EPILOGUE

Asar

I sit alone for a long time. I don't mind. Although I have many vices, impatience is not one of them. I can wait.

I'm not sure where they take me. The time after Mische's death runs together. I don't remember what I did after they dragged me away from her corpse. I don't remember what the gods said to me or to each other.

I do remember the sight of Shiket's blade driving through Mische's heart, though. I remember it vividly. I think of it over and over again.

The White Pantheon isn't sure what I am. I'm not sure what I am, either, so I cannot blame them for not knowing what to do with me. They chain me up and leave me in a room of black. I had never felt quite right among the living. But now, I'm more disconnected than ever from my mortality. I don't feel hunger, not even for blood. I don't sleep. Some part of me did not come back when Mische pulled me out of that ritual circle, and something new replaced it.

I wait.

The gods come to visit me sometimes, in what I think are attempts to understand just how much of Alarus I hold within me. Perhaps they're less concerned about the power than the memories. Ix was the one to lure Alarus to his ambush; Srana was the one to craft the blade that cut him up; Vitarus was the one to scatter his body. They watch me with wary stares, like I'm a snake that might strike at any moment—wondering if I'm really their betrayed brother in disguise, ready to punish them for their misdeeds.

I may hold Alarus's power, and I may hold a drop of his blood in my veins, but I do not hold his memories.

Still, they're right to be concerned.

Because while I don't remember their betrayal of Alarus, I do remember what they looked like standing over Mische's broken body.

I remember what she looked like going up in flames in the hands of the god of the sun, whom she had once loved more than anything.

I remember how the god of vitality had dismissed her like she was nothing more than a wounded animal.

I remember how the goddess of justice had inflicted the horrific injustice of her death.

I remember all of it, and I hate them more for that than any two-thousand-year-old betrayal. The death of one woman, one woman who was better than all of them, who had given everything until she had nothing left, was worth more than all of it.

But I'm patient. I'm determined. I have plenty of time to think about Mische and what I will offer her when—not if—I find her again.

If I were the god of the sun, I would have given her endless dawns and warm hearths.

If I were the god of the sea, I would have given her cool rains on hot nights and currents that always brought her home.

If I were the god of vitality, I would have given her sweet fruit and spring flowers.

I would have given her anything, everything, because that was what she deserved—every single thing she had loved, fully and completely, about mortality.

But I am not the god of any of those things. I have only one gift to lay at her feet.

And so, I wait.

END *of* BOOK III

Mische and Asar's story
will continue in book IV of
the Crowns of Nyaxia series.

AUTHOR'S NOTE

Thank you so much for reading *The Songbird & the Heart of Stone*! I hope that you loved it.

This was a challenging book to write because so much of my life changed as I was working on it (it was my first book since having my son!). But in some ways, it also feels appropriate that Mische's story, a tale of transformation, would be the one that guided me through this period of my life. Mische is so different from Oraya, but she is still just as messy and complicated (as we all are, I think!). I hope you connected with Mische and her journey of discovery as much as I did. As I type this, I'm so excited to dive into the next phase of her and Asar's story. It's going to be a wild ride, friends!

If you enjoyed the book, it would mean the world to me if you would consider leaving a review on your retailer of choice or on Goodreads.

If you'd like to be the first to know about new releases, new art, new swag, and all kinds of other fun stuff, consider signing up for my newsletter at carissabroadbentbooks.com, hanging out in my Facebook group (Carissa Broadbent's Lost Hearts), or joining my Discord server (invite at linktr.ee/carissanasyra).

Thank you for taking this journey with me! I hope you'll join me again for the next one.

GLOSSARY

ACAEJA—The goddess of spellcasting, fate, and lost things. Member of the White Pantheon.

ALARUS—The god of death and husband of Nyaxia. Exiled by the White Pantheon as punishment for his forbidden relationship with Nyaxia. Considered to be deceased.

ATROXUS—The god of the sun and leader of the White Pantheon.

BLOODBORN—Vampires of the House of Blood.

BORN—A term used to describe vampires who are born via biological procreation. This is the most common way that vampires are created.

DAWNDRINKERS—A term used to describe certain worshippers of the sun god, Atroxus.

THE DESCENT—The transitionary realm in between the mortal world and the underworld. It consists of five Sanctums that a soul must travel through to reach true death: Body, Breath, Psyche, Secrets, and Soul. The Descent was created by Alarus before his murder, and is now suffering the effects of many years of neglect.

HEIR MARK—A permanent mark that appears on the Heir of the Hiaj and Rishan clans when the previous Heir dies, marking their position and power.

THE HOUSE OF BLOOD—One of the three vampire kingdoms of Obi-traes. Two thousand years ago, when Nyaxia created vampires, the House of Blood was her favorite House. She thought long and hard about which gift to give them, while the Bloodborn watched their brothers to the west and north flaunt their powers. Eventually, the Bloodborn turned on Nyaxia, certain that she had abandoned them. In punishment, Nyaxia cursed them. The House of Blood is now looked down upon by the other two houses. Vampires of the House of Blood are called **BLOODBORN**.

THE HOUSE OF NIGHT—One of the three vampire kingdoms of Obi-traes. Known for their skill in battle and for their vicious natures, and wielders of magic derived from the night sky. There are two clans of Nightborn vampires, Hiaj and Rishan, who have fought for thousands of years over rule. Those of the House of Night are called **NIGHTBORN**.

THE HOUSE OF SHADOW—One of the three vampire kingdoms of Obitraes. Known for their commitment to knowledge; wielders of mind magic, shadow magic, and necromancy. Those of the House of Shadow are called **SHADOWBORN**.

IX—Goddess of sex, fertility, childbirth, and procreation. Member of the White Pantheon.

KAJMAR—God of art, seduction, beauty, and deceit. Member of the White Pantheon.

THE KEJARI—A legendary, once-per-century tournament to the death held in Nyaxia's honor. The winner receives a gift from Nyaxia her-self. The Kejari is open to all in Obitraes, but is hosted by the House of Night, as the Nightborn hold the greatest mastery over the art of battle of the three vampire kingdoms.

MOON PALACE—A palace in Sivrinaj, the capital of the House of Night, specifically there to house contestants of the once-in-a-century Kejari tournament held in Nyaxia's honor. Said to be enchanted and to exert the will of Nyaxia herself.

NIGHTBORN—Vampires of the House of Night.

NIGHTFIRE—A form of star-derived magic wielded by the vampires of the House of Night. Nightfire is commonly used in the House of Night but very difficult to wield masterfully.

NYAXIA—Exiled goddess, mother of vampires, and widow of the god of death. Nyaxia lords over the domain of night, shadow, and blood, as well as the domain of death inherited from her deceased husband. Formerly a lesser goddess, she fell in love with Alarus and married him despite the forbidden nature of their relationship. When Alarus was murdered by the White Pantheon as punishment for his marriage to her, Nyaxia broke free from the White Pantheon in a fit of rage, and offered her supporters the gift of immortality in the form of vampirism—founding Obitraes and the vampire kingdoms. *(Also referred to as: the Mother; the Goddess; Mother of the Ravenous Dark; Mother of Night, Shadow, and Blood)*

OBITRAES—The land of Nyaxia, consisting of three kingdoms: the House of Night, the House of Shadow, and the House of Blood.

ORAYA—Queen of the House of Night.

THE ORDER OF THE DESTINED DAWN—A major sect of worshippers of the god of the sun, Atroxus. They are known for their skill in wielding fire, as well as their occasionally violent crusading.

RAIHN—King of the House of Night.

RAOUL—King of the Shadowborn, known for being a ruthless master of torture and spycraft.

SANCTUM OF BODY—The first Sanctum in the Descent to the underworld, in which a soul loses their body.

SANCTUM OF BREATH—The second Sanctum in the Descent to the underworld, in which a soul abandons their life force.

SANCTUM OF PSYCHE—The third Sanctum in the Descent to the underworld, centering around a soul's memories.

SANCTUM OF SECRETS—The fourth Sanctum in the Descent to the underworld, in which souls must confront their hidden shames and desires.

SANCTUM OF SOUL—The fifth and final Sanctum in the Descent to the underworld, in which the dead undergo the transition of their soul from the mortal world to the underworld.

SHADOWBORN—Vampires of the House of Shadow.

SHIKET—Goddess of war and justice. She bears six swords in her back, each representing a different divine gift.

SIVRINAJ—The capital of the House of Night. Home to the Nightborn castle and the Moon Palace, and host to the Kejari once every hundred years.

TURNING—A process to make a human into a vampire, requiring a vampire to drink from a human and offer their blood to the human in return. Vampires who underwent this process are referred to as TURNED.

VINCENT—The former king of the House of Night. Father to Oraya, queen of the Nightborn.

WHITE PANTHEON—The twelve gods of the core canon, including Alarus, who is presumed deceased. The White Pantheon is worshipped by all humans, with certain regions potentially having favor toward specific gods within the Pantheon. Nyaxia is not a member of the White Pantheon and is actively hostile to them. The White

Pantheon imprisoned and later executed Alarus, the God of Death, as punishment for his unlawful marriage with Nyaxia, then a lesser goddess.

Zarux—The god of the sea, rain, weather, storms, and water. Member of the White Pantheon.

ACKNOWLEDGMENTS

I always write these things in a bit of a fugue state, and this time, it's doubly true because I'm typing it very, very late at night after a very, very long stretch of crunch time. I can't complain, because I love this job and I'm so happy I get to do it!

There are many wonderful people who helped me bring this book into the world. I owe a huge debt of gratitude to:

The wonderful team at Bramble for seeing the potential of this world and helping bring it to so many readers—including my editor, Monique Patterson; Mal Frazier for being an excellent editorial assistant; Caro Perny for publicity; Julia Bergen for marketing; and so many other amazingly talented folks.

My agent, Bibi Lewis, who is a force of nature, and without whom I definitely would not have made it through this book with my sanity (semi) intact. Thank you for excellent editorial feedback, for countless pep talks, and for getting this book into the world at all.

Story Wrappers, for absolutely incredible covers.

Clare Sager, Alicia MB, J. D. Evans, Krystle Matar, and Angela Boord, for being the most incredible friends I could ask for and highly tolerant of my complaining.

My assistant, Ariella Isabella, for keeping me sane and being awesome while she does it.

Alex Ogle, for keeping my online groups in order and for being a ray of sunshine.

My sister, Elizabeth, for constant book talk and occasional reassurance.

My parents, for being endlessly supportive.

Finally, above all, eternal thank you to my husband, Nate, for picking up so much childcare slack during my deadline phases, for being the best brainstorming buddy, for being the most supportive husband, and for being the love of my life. And Nico, I really hope you're not reading this, not even if it's twenty years in the future. But I love you, anyway.

ABOUT THE AUTHOR

Victoria Costello

CARISSA BROADBENT has been concerning teachers and parents with mercilessly grim tales since she was roughly nine years old. Subsequently, her stories have gotten (slightly) less depressing and (hopefully a lot?) more readable. Today, she writes novels that blend epic fantasy plots with a heaping dose of romance. She lives with her husband, her son, and one perpetually skeptical cat in Rhode Island.

carissabroadbentbooks.com
Facebook: CarissaBroadbentBooks
X: @CarissaNasyra
Instagram: @carissabroadbentbooks
TikTok: @carissabroadbent